Swimming to Catalina

Stuart Woods

Swimming to Catalina

WHEELER
PUBLISHING, INC.
ROCKLAND, MA

★ AN AMERICAN COMPANY ★

Published in Large Print by arrangement with Harper Collins Publishers, Inc. in the United States and Canada.

Wheeler Large Print Book Series.

Set in 16 pt Plantin.

Library of Congress Cataloging-in-Publication Data

Woods, Stuart.
   Swimming to Catalina / Stuart Woods.
      p. (large print) cm.(Wheeler large print book series)
   ISBN 1-56895-620-7 (hardcover)
   1. Barrington, Stone (Fictitious character)--Fiction. 2. Private investiga-
tors--New York (State)--New York--Fiction 3. Missing persons--California-
-Fiction. I. Title. II. Series
[PS3573.0642S93   1998b]
813'.54—dc21   98-29231
                                                                     CIP

*This book is for
Carolyn and David Klemm,
who have done so much
to make us at home in Litchfield County*

Mendy Menenzez:
"You got told, you better stay told."

Philip Marlowe:
"Oh, sure. I do something you don't like and I'm swimming to Catalina with a streetcar on my back."

—Raymond Chandler, *The Long Goodbye*

ACKNOWLEDGMENTS

I am grateful to my editor, HarperCollins vice president and associate publisher Gladys Justin Carr; her associate editor, Elissa Altman; and all the people at HarperCollins who worked so hard for the success of this book.

I am also grateful to my agent, Morton L. Janklow; his principal associate, Anne Sibbald; and their colleagues at Janklow & Nesbit for their continuing enthusiasm in the management of my career. I am in good hands.

PROLOGUE

The night was warm and lovely. To Stone Barrington's right, the bloom of smog over greater Los Angeles was lit from within like a dirty lampshade; to his left, the lights of Santa Catalina Island twinkled like the eyes of a merry whore. Only a couple of hundred yards from where he stood, the anchor lights of dozens of small craft winked as the wake from the sports fisherman on which Stone rode caught them and made them rock. Stone took a deep breath, which was difficult, since one nostril was clogged by an allergy to L.A. air, and his mouth was sealed shut with duct tape.

"Christ, Vinnie," the other one, whose name was Manny, said. "They're right there in the tool box."

"I'm looking, Manny," Vinnie replied.

"Any kind of pliers will do—short-nosed, long-nosed—anything."

"I said, I'm looking." There was the noise of metal against metal as Vinnie rummaged through the tool chest.

"Jesus," Manny said. "I'd like to get at a steak before the night is over."

"I'm *looking*, Manny," Vinnie said. Triumphantly, he held up the pliers. "I got them."

"Give them to me," Manny said. He accepted the pliers from Vinnie with one hand, while he held onto the length of three-eighths anchor

1

chain with the other. The chain was wrapped twice around Stone's waist. "Now hand me the shackle," Manny said.

"This one?" Vinnie asked, holding up a large stainless steel shackle.

"Isn't there a galvanized one in there?" Manny asked. "Stainless is real expensive; Oney will give us hell."

"Like this?" Vinnie asked, holding up another shackle.

"That will do nicely," Manny replied, accepting the shackle. "Come hold the chain for a minute."

Vinnie came and held the chain while Manny unscrewed the pin and slipped the shackle through two of the chain links. Then he inserted the pin, screwed it finger-tight, and tightened it further with the pliers. "There," he said, tossing the pliers at the toolbox and missing.

"Stone," Manny said, "I'm going to have to ask you to hop a few steps toward the transom thing."

Stone turned and looked at Manny as if he were an oversized, semiliterate troll, which he was. His ankles were taped together, and he had no intention of assisting Manny and Vinnie in their endeavor.

"Okay, okay," Manny said. "Vinnie, grab an arm. Stone, it really would help if you would hop just a little."

Stone sighed as well as he could through one nostril, then gave a hop and collapsed over the tool box, scattering its contents over the deck.

"Thanks a lot," Manny said acidly. "You were

a big help. Vinnie, hold him here for a minute." He moved to the port side of the boat and dragged a seventy-five-pound Danforth anchor over to Stone's feet. He rummaged among the tools scattered on the deck and came up with another shackle. "Where the hell did the pliers go?" he asked nobody in particular.

"There they are," Vinnie said, pointing.

"Hand them to me," Manny said. He took the pliers, shackled the anchor to the end of Stone's chain, and tightened the pin. "I think that'll do it," he said, picking up the anchor and handing it to Stone.

Stone cradled the anchor in his arms like an overgrown puppy.

"Any last words, Stone?" Manny asked, then he and Vinnie burst out laughing.

"Any last words," Vinnie chuckled. "That's a good one."

The two men muscled Stone over to the transom, which came up to his knees.

"Hold him right there, Vinnie," Manny said, leaving Stone's side and walking behind him. "I'll handle this." Manny grabbed a bolted-down fisherman's chair for support and placed his foot in the small of Stone's back. "Compliments of Onofrio Ippolito," he said, then kicked Stone over the stern.

Stone was not prepared for how cold the Pacific Ocean was, but then, he reflected, he hadn't been prepared for a lot of things. He let go of the anchor, then followed it quickly toward the floor of the sea, trying desperately to hold onto his final breath.

1

Elaine's, late. Stone Barrington sat at a very good table with his friend and former partner Dino Bacchetti, who ran the detective division at the NYPD's 19th Precinct, and with Elaine, who was Elaine.

The remnants of dinner were cleared away by Jack, the headwaiter, and brandy was brought for Stone and Dino. It was very special brandy; Dino had the bottle of his own stuff stashed behind the bar, and it annoyed Elaine to no end, because she couldn't charge him for it, not that she didn't find other ways to charge him for it.

"Okay, I want to know about Arrington," Elaine said.

"Elaine," Dino interrupted, "don't you know that Stone is still suffering a great deal of emotional pain over Arrington's dumping him?"

"Who gives a fuck?" Elaine asked, quite reasonably. "I want to know how he let her get away. She was something, that girl."

"There's a large body of opinion," Dino said, "that holds that she didn't want to be known as Arrington Barrington."

"And who could blame her?" Elaine asked. "Come on, Stone, spill it."

Stone took a deep breath and sighed. "I have to take a lot of shit from you two, you know?"

"I think you better cough it up," Dino said, "or we're going to start getting tables in Siberia."

4

"You bet your ass," Elaine confirmed.

Stone sighed again. "It was like this," he said, then stopped.

"Yeah?" Elaine encouraged.

"We were supposed to have ten days sailing in St. Marks in February."

"I never heard of St. Marks," Elaine said. "Where is that?"

"It's a nice little island, tucked between Antigua and Guadeloupe. Anyway, we were supposed to meet at Kennedy for our flight down, but she got tied up, and she was supposed to be on the next plane, but then the blizzard hit."

"I know about the blizzard," Elaine said, exasperated. "Tell me about the girl."

"While the blizzard was going on she got the *New Yorker* assignment to do a profile of Vance Calder."

"The new Cary Grant," Dino explained, as if Elaine had no idea who a major movie star was.

"Yeah, yeah," Elaine said.

"Apparently he hadn't given an in-depth interview for twenty years," Stone continued, "so it was quite a coup. Arrington had known Calder for a while—in fact, she was with him at the dinner party where we met."

"So much for social history," Elaine said.

"All right, I'm in St. Marks, sitting on the chartered boat, waiting for Arrington to show up, when this blonde sails in on a big beautiful boat, all by herself. But she had left the Canary Islands with a husband, who was no

5

longer present. So she gets charged with his murder, and I end up defending her."

"Like I don't read a newspaper?" Elaine interjected. "Like the western hemisphere didn't read about this trial?"

"All right, all right; I keep getting faxes from Arrington, saying she's all tied up with Calder, then I get a fax saying that she's going to L.A. with him for more research."

"'Research'; I like that," Elaine smirked.

"So I write her a letter, pouring out my heart, practically asking her to marry me..."

"'Practically'? What is that?" Elaine demanded.

"All right, not in so many words, but I think she would have gotten the idea."

"She didn't get the idea?"

"She didn't get the letter. I gave it to a lady headed for Florida to FedEx for me, and her plane crashed on takeoff."

"Wow, *that's* the best excuse I ever heard for not writing," Elaine said. "You sure your dog didn't eat it?"

"I swear, I wrote her the letter. Then, before I could write it again, I get a fax from Arrington saying that she and Calder were married in Needles, Arizona, the day before. What am I supposed to do?"

"You were supposed to do it a long time ago," Elaine said. "Why should this gorgeous girl wait around for you to get your ass in gear?"

"Maybe, but there was nothing I could do at this point, Elaine. I was going to trial in a couple of days; the woman's life depended on me."

"The woman might have been better off if you'd gone after Arrington," Dino said, "considering how the trial went."

"Thanks, Dino, I needed that."

"Any time."

"So now Arrington is married to the guy *People* says is the sexiest man in America, and I'm..." His voice trailed off.

"How long they been married?" Elaine asked.

"I don't know—two and a half, three months."

"It's probably too late," Elaine mused. "Unless it's going *really* badly."

"I've had a couple of letters from her telling me how *gloriously* it's going," Stone said glumly.

"Oh," Elaine said.

There followed a long silence.

Jack came over to the table. "Phone call for you, Stone," he said, pointing at one of the two pay phones on the wall nearby.

"Who is it?"

"I don't know," Jack replied, "but he's got a *beautiful* speaking voice on the telephone."

"Must be Vance Calder," Dino deadpanned.

Elaine burst out laughing.

Stone got up and trudged over to the phone. "Hello?" he said, sticking a finger in the other ear to blot out some of the noise.

"Stone?"

"Yeah? Who's this?"

"Stone, this is Vance Calder."

"Yeah, sure; Dino put you up to this?"

7

"What?"

"Who is this?"

"It's Vance, Stone."

Stone hung up the phone and went back to the table. "Nice," he said to Dino."

"Huh?"

"Guy on the phone says he's Vance Calder. Thanks a lot."

"Don't thank me," Dino said. "I never met the guy."

"You put whoever that was up to it, didn't you? It was a setup." He looked at Elaine. "You were probably in on it, too."

Elaine placed a hand on her ample bosom. "Stone, I swear."

Jack came back. "Same guy on the phone again; says you hung up on him. You know who it sounds like?"

"Vance Calder?" Dino suggested.

"Yeah!" Jack said. "Sounds just like him!"

After a glare at Dino and Elaine, Stone went back to the phone. "Hello?"

"Stone, we've met; don't you know my voice?"

"Vance?"

"Yes," Calder replied, sounding relieved.

"I'm sorry, I thought someone..."

"It's all right; it happens a lot."

"Hello, Vance; how'd you find me here?"

"There was no answer at your house, and I remembered that Arrington said you were at Elaine's a lot. I took a chance."

"How is Arrington, Vance?"

"That's what I'm calling about, Stone. Arrington has disappeared."

"What do you mean, disappeared?"

"Just that; she's vanished."

"When?"

"The day before yesterday."

"Have you been to the police?"

"I can't do that; the tabloids would be all over me. I need your help, Stone."

"Vance, you'd really be a lot better off going to the police; there's nothing *I* can do."

"Have you heard from her?"

"I had a letter about a month ago; she sounded very happy."

"She has been very happy, but all of a sudden she's gone, with no explanation."

"Vance, I don't know what I can do to help."

"You can find her, Stone; if anybody can, you can. I want you to come out here."

"Vance, really..."

"The Centurion Studios jet is at Teterboro Airport right now, at Atlantic Aviation, waiting for you. You can be here by morning."

"Vance, I appreciate your confidence in me, but..."

"Stone, Arrington is pregnant."

Stone felt as if he'd been struck in the chest. He could count.

"Stone?"

"I'll be at Teterboro in an hour, Vance."

"There'll be a car waiting for you at Santa Monica Airport."

"Write down everything you can think of, Vance; we'll have a lot to talk about."

"I will. And thank you."

"Don't thank me yet," Stone said, then hung up. He returned to the table. "You're buying dinner, Dino," he said. "I'm off to La-La Land."

"About what?" Dino asked.

"I'll tell you later," Stone said.

"Say hello to Arrington for me," Elaine said, looking at him over her glasses.

"You bet, Elaine." He pecked her on the cheek, walked out of the restaurant, and started looking for a cab.

2

Stone's taxi driver, a former resident of the Indian subcontinent who had recently arrived in the United States, well ahead of his English, got lost in New Jersey, and by the time Stone had redirected him to Teterboro Airport, using sign language, it had begun to rain hard. Finally at Atlantic Aviation, Stone paid the man, grabbed his luggage, and ran into the deserted terminal, waking up a young woman behind the service counter. "I'm looking for the Centurion Studios airplane," he said to her.

"It's the only one on the ramp," she replied, yawning and pointing at the rear doors.

Stone stopped at the doors, looked out onto the tarmac, and smiled. "A G-IV," he said aloud to himself. It was the biggest and best of the corporate jets, and he had never been aboard one. Its engines were already running. He ran through the rain to the airplane and clambered up the steps, hauling his luggage into the cabin.

A young woman in a pale Armani suit materialized before him. "Mr. Barrington?"

"Yes."

"Let me take your bags, and please have a seat; we're ready for takeoff." She disappeared aft with his two bags; he kept his briefcase and took the first available seat. In the rear of the airplane a distinguished-looking man was sitting on a sofa, talking on a small cellular phone. Stone buckled in as the airplane started to roll. He wanted to go forward and watch the takeoff, but the cockpit door was closed. Instead, he sat and watched the rain stream along his window.

The airplane never stopped rolling, but turned onto the runway and accelerated. Shortly they were airborne and climbing steeply. The attendant came forward again and hovered over his seat. She was pretty in a characterless sort of way, and she displayed some very expensive dental work. "Would you like something to drink?" she cooed.

Stone's heart was still pumping hard from his dash to the airport. "Yes, a brandy, please."

"We have some vintage cognac, a Hine '55, and some very old Armagnac."

"I'll try the Armagnac," he said. A moment later he was warming a tissue-thin crystal snifter between both hands.

"Mr. Regenstein would be pleased if you would join him aft when the seatbelt sign goes off," the woman said.

"Thank you," Stone replied. Regenstein: the name had a familiar ring, but he couldn't place it. He sipped his Armagnac, and presently the airplane leveled off and the seatbelt sign went out. He unbuckled and walked down the aisle toward where the other man sat.

As he approached, the man stood and offered his hand. "I'm Lou Regenstein," he said.

Stone shook his hand. "I'm Stone Barrington." The man was much older than he had looked from a distance; Stone reckoned he was in his mid- to late sixties.

"Oh, yes, Vance's friend. Please sit down, and thank you for joining me. It's nice to have some company on one of these flights."

Stone took a comfortable armchair facing the sofa. "I'm sorry to have kept you waiting; my cab driver got lost."

"Of course," Regenstein replied. "They always do. The trick is to order a car from Atlantic Aviation; that way you'll have a Jersey driver."

"I'll remember that," Stone said.

Regenstein wrinkled his nose. "You're drinking the Armagnac?" He extended his hand. "May I?"

Stone handed him the snifter, and Regenstein stuck his nose into it and inhaled deeply.

"Ahhhhhh," he sighed, handing back the glass. "I haven't had a drink in more than thirty years, but I still love the bouquet of something like that. It's just wonderful."

"It certainly is," Stone agreed.

"I believe I've come across your name recently," Regenstein said. "Something in the Caribbean?"

"St. Marks."

"Ah, yes; you defended that young woman accused of murdering her husband." He became conspiratorial. "Tell me, did she do it? Or would answering breach a confidence? I wouldn't want to do that."

"I can tell you with the greatest possible confidence that she didn't do it," Stone replied. "And no, answering doesn't breach a confidence."

"Keeping a confidence is a most important thing in life," Regenstein said gravely. "Especially in our business. The entertainment business."

"In any business, I should think."

"But especially in ours. There are so many gossips and liars, you see, that keeping a confidence and telling the truth are magnified in their importance. Although I have a very large contracts department whose task it is to set down every nuance of an agreement, I have always prided myself on keeping a deal sealed with a handshake."

"I suppose if everyone kept agreements sealed with handshakes, I and my colleagues would starve," Stone said.

"Yes, lawyers are necessary in our world. Tell me, are you proud to be a lawyer?"

Stone thought about that for a moment. "I was proud when I graduated from law school and proud when I passed the bar exam-

13

ination, because those milestones marked the acquisition of a lot of knowledge, but I can't say I'm proud of my profession as a whole; still, there are enough attorneys of sufficient integrity to keep me from being ashamed to describe myself as a lawyer."

"A lawyerly reply," Regenstein said, looking amused.

"I'll be more direct," Stone said. "I'm proud to be a good lawyer, the best I know how to be."

"I prefer the direct answer," Regenstein said. "I always have, and I so rarely hear it in our business."

Then the penny dropped. Louis Regenstein was the chairman of the board of Centurion Studios. Stone had seen articles about him in the entertainment news and the business pages but had never paid much attention to them. "Are you proud to be in the movie business, Mr. Regenstein?" he asked.

Regenstein smiled broadly. "You bet I am!" he said. "Like you, I'm proud of the way I do it!" He shook his head. "Of course, there are at least as many scoundrels in our business as in the legal profession, and there are no boards of ethics or bar associations to even attempt to judge and regulate their conduct."

"What do you love most about your position in the industry?"

Regenstein smiled again. "The power to say yes," he replied emphatically. "There are hundreds of people in our business who have the power to say no, but only a few who can say yes." He leaned forward and rested his elbows on his knees. "Of course, like all power, it must be wielded with the greatest possible discretion. Used indiscriminately, such power can destroy the wielder, and more quickly than you might imagine." Regenstein narrowed his eyes. "Tell me, Mr. Barrington, have you ever done any acting?"

"Only in front of a jury," Stone said. "No, I'm wrong. I played a lead once—in my high school drama club's production of *Stalag 17*."

"Were you any good?" Regenstein asked.

"I... well, the cast got a standing ovation, three nights running."

"I'll bet you were *very* good," Regenstein said. "I'm a very good judge of actors, and I think you're a natural. You're good looking, you have a resonant voice, and you project a very positive presence."

Stone was nonplussed. "Why, thank you, Mr. Regenstein; coming from you, that's high praise."

"Please call me Lou," he said.

"Thank you, and I'm Stone."

"Stone, if you should ever wish to leave the legal profession, let me know, and I'll put you into a movie. Not a lead, of course, but a good supporting part. It would give me pleasure to see you do it well, and I know you would. Leads might not ever come—you're what, in your early forties?"

"That's right."

"That's a bit long in the tooth for becoming a star, but you would be in great demand for featured roles."

Stone laughed. "I doubt it."

"Oh, I'm not just flattering you; you'd be very good. You have only one fault that would work against you."

"What's that?"

"You're not insecure enough. Oh, we all have our little chinks in our armor, but actors, the best ones, thrive on insecurity, and you don't have it at a high enough level to make you malleable. Our business would find you *difficult*."

"Well, Lou, if I decide to give up lawyering, you'll be among the first to know."

Regenstein stood up, took off his jacket, and kicked off his shoes. "If you'll forgive me, I think I'll get a little sleep," he said. "You'd be well advised to do the same. It will be very early when we get into L.A." He stretched out on the sofa and, without another word, closed his eyes and appeared to sleep. The flight attendant appeared and spread a light blanket over him.

Stone went back to his seat, took off his jacket and shoes, accepted a blanket, which turned out to be cashmere, and pushed his seat as far back as it would go. The cabin lights dimmed, and he looked out the window at the stars and tried not to think of Arrington. He had done too much of that already.

3

Stone was gently wakened by the flight attendant, and he brought his seatback forward. He looked at his watch, then out the window; dawn was on its way.

"Mr. Regenstein asked if you would join him for breakfast," the young woman said.

"Of course."

"If you'd like to freshen up first, you can go just there," she said, pointing to a door.

Stone went into the washroom, which was bigger than any he had ever seen on an airplane. There was even a shower. He chose a tooth-brush from a selection and scrubbed his teeth, then combed his hair, slipped on his jacket, and walked down the aisle to where Louis Regenstein was already consuming a large breakfast of scrambled eggs and lox.

"Good morning," Regenstein said with some gusto. "Did you sleep well?"

"I got a few winks," Stone replied.

The attendant appeared. "What would you like, Mr. Barrington?"

"Just orange juice and coffee," he replied. "I had a late dinner." Moments later, both beverages were on the table.

Regenstein glanced at his watch. "We should be on the ground in half an hour," he said. "Where are you staying? May I offer you a lift?"

"At the Bel-Air, and thank you, but Vance said I would be met."

"How long have you known Vance Calder?" Regenstein asked.

"A year or so, I guess; actually, I've met him only once, at a dinner party in New York."

"So that would be when you met Arrington?" Stone was surprised. "Yes."

"You and Arrington were close for a time." More surprise. "Yes."

Regenstein seemed to take a cue from Stone's reticence. "Vance is a most remarkable man, for an actor," he said. "I've never known a movie star so in control of his career. That would drive many studio executives crazy, but I prefer dealing with people who know what they want and insist on having it. Vance always has a keen perception of what is available in a deal and what isn't—of what's reasonable, you might say."

"That's a rare attribute in any field," Stone said.

"I suppose it is." Regenstein put down his fork and napkin. "Well, if you will excuse me, I want to get in a quick shower before we land; that way, I can go directly to the studio." He left Stone to finish his coffee.

The big Gulfstream landed at Santa Monica Airport and taxied to a Fixed Base Operator called Supermarine. As the door opened, Stone saw two cars waiting on the ramp—a limousine-sized Mercedes and a little convertible, a Mercedes SL 600. He followed Regenstein from the airplane, and they shook hands.

"I expect I'll see you at Vance's tomorrow evening," the studio head said.

"I hope so."

"I'll look forward to seeing you again."

"Thank you, so will I."

Regenstein got into the limousine and was driven away, then a young man handed Stone a sealed envelope. He tore it open.

My dear Stone,

Rather than having a driver, I thought you might like the freedom of driving yourself. I'll call you later in the day, when you've had some rest.

> *Regards,*
> *Vance*

There followed typed directions to the Bel-Air Hotel. Stone put his bags in the open trunk and settled behind the wheel. He adjusted his seat and started the twelve-cylinder engine. He had been thinking of buying a Mercedes, but this was out of his reach—something like a hundred and thirty-seven thousand dollars, he remembered. He drove out the gate, made a couple of turns, and found himself on the freeway. At that early hour traffic was busy, but not heavy, and he drove quickly, enjoying the open car, which made a pleasant noise, like a distant Ferrari, he thought. He turned off the freeway onto Sunset Boulevard and followed the winding road toward the hotel, looking around him at Beverly Hills. He had been to L.A. only once before, when he and Dino had retrieved an extradited felon, and that had been a brief trip. He turned left on Stone Canyon Road and drove another mile to the hotel. Even at this early hour there was someone to unload his luggage and park the car.

The bellman didn't stop at the front desk, but led him through the small lobby and down a walkway. The hotel was set in a garden, and the cool morning air was scented with tropical blossoms. Shortly the bellman let him into a handsome suite overlooking the hotel's pool, accepted a tip, and left him alone. Stone walked around the place; it seemed more like the apartment of a friend than a hotel suite. He liked it. He could get used to it, he thought. He ordered breakfast, had a shower, then stretched out on the bed for a moment.

He was awakened by the phone. A glance at the bedside clock showed that it was half past two in the afternoon. He grabbed the phone. "Hello?"

"Stone, it's Vance; I hope your flight out was pleasant."

"Yes, Vance, thank you."

"Are your rooms all right?"

"Better than that; thank you."

"Not at all. Why don't you relax this afternoon, and we'll have dinner this evening."

"All right."

"I'll pick you up out front at seven; that all right?"

"That's fine, Vance. And thank you for the car."

"It's a wonderful car, isn't it?"

"Yes, it is."

"Drive it anywhere you like while you're here. See you at seven. Goodbye."

"Goodbye." Stone hung up and sat on the bed, trying to wake up. Could he possibly have jet lag with only a three-hour time difference? Possibly. He had to do something to wake up. He called the desk and asked if they could provide him with a swimsuit.

Fifteen minutes later he sat down at a table by the pool and ordered a club sandwich and a Heineken. Perhaps half the available lounges were occupied, a dozen of them by quite striking women. *It's Hollywood,* he thought. He shucked off his robe, dove into the pool, swam a couple of laps, then walked back to his table. Moments later, his sandwich arrived, and he ate hungrily. Then he found a lounge and fell asleep in the afternoon sun.

It was nearly six when he woke, feeling refreshed. Maybe he'd finally adjusted to the time difference, he thought. He went back to his suite, showered, and dressed in a tropical-weight blazer and gray slacks. After a moment's debate with himself, he put on a knitted necktie.

Stone was standing under the awning at the entrance to the hotel when, precisely at seven, a dark green Bentley swung in and stopped before him. The parking lot attendant ran around the car and opened the driver's door. "Good evening, Mr. Calder," he said.

"Thanks, Jerry, but I'm just picking up a friend," Vance Calder replied.

21

Another attendant opened the door for Stone. He got in, and received a warm handshake from his host.

"Ever been to Spago?" Calder asked.

"No."

"Let's go there, then."

"Sounds good. Have you heard anything from Arrington?"

"No. We'll talk about it over dinner." Calder drove out of the parking lot and into Stone Canyon.

Stone leaned back in his seat. He was on his way to Spago in a Bentley with a major movie star. He liked it.

4

Vance Calder drove the Bentley smoothly down Sunset Boulevard, chatting amiably about the California weather and flying on a corporate jet, then turned left, went up a steep hill for a short distance, and turned right into a parking lot. Before the car stopped, it was surrounded by photographers.

Calder took it well. "Good evening, fellows," he said to them, waving and smiling.

Stone followed along in his wake, marveling at his aplomb in the circumstances. The doors closed behind them, and the photographers were gone. Stone noticed two heavy-set young men enter after him.

Calder was greeted effusively by the young woman at the desk, who hardly gave Stone a glance before escorting them to a corner table at the window. Along the way, Stone had an experience he had previously had only in the company of a beautiful woman: he was ignored by everyone in the restaurant; they were all looking at Vance Calder.

They stopped at a few tables so that Vance could say hello to a few people—Billy Wilder, Tony Curtis, and Milton Berle. Stone shook their hands, marveling at the facts of Wilder's youthful looks, Curtis's age, and that Berle was alive at all. Finally they were settled in the corner, with Stone in the gunfighter's seat, facing the room, and Vance with his back to the crowd.

"I hope you don't mind sitting there," Calder said, shaking out his napkin. "My back will discourage unwelcome callers."

"Not at all," Stone replied. "It must be difficult for you to go out in public like this." Stone noticed that the two men who seemed together when they had followed him into the restaurant were now sitting in different places, one at the bar, the other at a small table.

"One learns to handle it," Calder said, gazing at the menu. "Fame is a two-edged sword; it gets one lots of things, like this table, but it exacts a price, the photographers. I reconciled the two sides of the blade long ago. By the way, don't order a starter; that will be taken care of."

As if by magic, a waiter appeared with a small pizza decorated with smoked salmon, capers, and onions. "Compliments of Wolfgang,"

23

the waiter said. "May I get you a drink, Mr. Calder?"

"Stone?" Calder asked.

"I'll have a Beefeater's and tonic, please."

"Bring me a very dry Tanqueray martini," Calder said pleasantly. "A twist, no olive."

The waiter vanished, then reappeared faster than Stone had ever seen a waiter move.

They ordered, then sipped their drinks.

"I met Louis Regenstein on the airplane," Stone said. "A charming man."

"That he is," Calder agreed, "and one of the three smartest men I've ever dealt with."

"Who are the other two?"

"David Sturmack and Hyman Greenbaum."

"I've heard of Greenbaum, I think; an agent, isn't he?"

"Was; he died nearly ten years ago."

"Who is... ?"

"David Sturmack? Of course, you've never heard of him—that would have pleased him—but along with Lou Regenstein and Lew Wasserman at MCA, he has more personal influence in this town than anyone else. You'll meet him tomorrow night."

Stone wondered why Calder was entertaining while his wife was missing, but before he could ask, Calder began talking again.

"Hyman Greenbaum was my first agent—in fact, my only one—and he gave me the best advice a young actor could ask for."

"What was that?"

"He taught me the relationship between money and good work."

"You mean, if you're paid better, you do better work?"

"No, no. When Hyman signed me, he sat me down over a good lunch and talked to me like a Jewish Dutch uncle. He said, 'Vance, you've got everything going for you in this town, but there is something you have to do.' What's that, I asked. He said, 'Pretty soon you're going to begin to make some real money; what you have to do is not spend it, at least, not at first.' He went on to explain. He said, 'I've watched talented young actors come to this town for a long time, and this is what they do: they get a good part that pays pretty good money, and the first thing they do is move out of the fleabag where they've been living, take a nice apartment and buy a convertible. They make a couple more pictures, getting even more money, and they buy a house in the Hollywood Hills, then, after a couple more pictures, in Beverly Hills, and they buy a *Mercedes* convertible. Then there's a pause, and nothing good comes along. Then a script comes in that's not good, but there's a good co-star, and it's being shot in the south of France, so what the hell—there's a mortgage on the house and a loan on the car, and expenses have to be met, so they take it. The picture bombs, and after a couple like that, they're overlooked for the best scripts. After that, it's a TV series and some movies of the week, and once they start doing those, it's almost impossible to get a good feature part again. Don't behave that way.'"

"And you didn't?"

"I certainly didn't. I was sharing an apartment with two other actors, and I stayed right where I was. I drove a motor scooter to and from the studio, and I let Hyman invest my money. After two years of this, I was getting first-class supporting parts and learning my trade, and the money was good, too. I moved into a nicer apartment, but small and cheap, and I bought a used car. After five years I was hitting my stride, and when I bought my first house it was in Beverly Hills, and I paid *cash* for it, and when the bad scripts shot in nice places came along, I was able to turn them down and wait for the good stuff. I learned never to do a movie for money alone, or because it was being shot in Tahiti or some other paradise. You have no idea how many actors have made those mistakes and how much it cost them."

"I see your point," Stone said. "Vance, what have you heard about Arrington?"

Vance glanced to either side of him. "Is anyone listening to us?"

Stone looked around. "Everyone seems to be trying to."

"Let's not talk here."

"I take it you're entertaining tomorrow night?"

Calder lowered his voice. "I am. It's been planned for nearly a month, and if I cancel, people will start to talk. When people start to talk, somebody tells somebody in the gutter press, and the next thing I know, I'm all over the tabloids, and I have a battalion of paparazzi camped at my front gate. It's important that I behave as I normally do, no matter what's happening in my personal life, and it's important that you understand this."

"I understand."

"One other thing: I expect all our conversations on that subject to be conducted under the attorney-client privilege."

"As you wish."

"Good, now here's our dinner; let's enjoy it, then we'll talk on the way home."

Back in the Bentley, Calder finally opened up. "It's been three days now, and I haven't heard anything from her."

"What precipitated this?" Stone asked.

"I don't know. I came home from the studio, and her car was gone. It was seven in the evening, and it was unusual for her not to be waiting for me. She hadn't given any instructions to the cook for dinner, and the houseman, who usually has a nap in the afternoon, hadn't seen her leave the house."

"Did she take anything with her?"

"I'm not sure. I suppose she could have taken a few clothes—I couldn't look at her closet and say for sure. She may have taken a suitcase, but there's a room full of luggage, and I can't know if one or two pieces are missing."

"Had you quarreled? Was she angry about anything?"

Calder pulled into the Bel-Air parking lot, stopped, and waved away the attendant. "No, not angry, but she was... different. I don't know how else to explain it."

"How was she different?"

"The night before, she had told me about the baby. I was overjoyed; I've always wanted a child, and I thought she did, too. She... was not overjoyed."

"What did she say?"

"It's not so much what she said as the way she behaved. Then I did some thinking, and it occurred to me that the child... might not be mine."

Stone said nothing.

"Stone, you and I both know that Arrington and I married after the briefest of courtships and that she was living with you up until a week or ten days before we married."

Stone still said nothing.

"She didn't come right out and say that the child was yours, but she was very subdued."

"Did you ask her?"

"No, but she knew I was thinking that."

"What about the following morning?"

"She said nothing. I had to be at the studio at seven—I'm in the middle of a picture—and she wasn't up when I left, so we had no opportunity to talk. I went to work, and I thought about nothing else all day, and I came home prepared to tell her that I didn't care who the biological father was, I wanted to be the father who brought up the child. But she was gone."

"She didn't leave a note?"

"No. Nothing."

"And you still haven't called the police?"

"Stone, I just can't do that; I think I've already explained why not."

"The tabloids."

"Yes. That, and the fact that I don't really feel that she's in any danger."

"What do you expect me to do, then?"

"I've told you about the dinner party tomorrow night."

"Yes."

"I've done something unusual; I've invited a reporter. The following day, there'll be a story recounting the evening and the guest list. Your name will be mentioned."

"And you think she might read it?"

"Almost certainly; she follows the trade papers closely."

"And you think she might try to get in touch with me?"

"I'll see to it that it's mentioned that you're staying at the Bel-Air."

"And if she doesn't call me?"

"Then I'll take your advice on how to proceed. I promise I will."

Stone shrugged. "It's your decision, I guess."

Calder handed him a card. "Here's my address and all my private numbers. Wear a tie, dinner's at seven, and people are usually on time. I'm five minutes from the Bel-Air."

Stone took the card. "I'll be there."

"Oh, if you're not busy tomorrow and you'd like to visit the studio, call my secretary—her number is on the card—and she'll arrange it."

"Thanks, I might do that. By the way, Vance, are you aware that two men have been following you all evening?"

"*What?*"

"They're in a car parked about thirty yards behind us. They followed us into Spago, too."

Calder glanced over his shoulder and smiled, revealing astonishingly white and even teeth. "Oh, those are my boys; they watch my back." He held out his hand. "Thank you for coming out here, Stone. I hope you don't think I'm too much of a fool for handling it this way."

"I hope it's the right way," Stone said. He got out of the car and watched the Bentley disappear into the scented night, followed by Calder's backwatchers. He wondered if somebody had been watching Arrington's back.

5

After breakfast the following morning, Stone called Betty Southard, whose name and number were on Calder's card, said he'd like to see the studio, and was given the address and was told to be at the main gate at ten-thirty. He was on time.

He gave his name to a guard at the gate and was directed to a parking lot just inside. As he got out of the car a golf cart pulled up, and a tall, slender woman got out and came toward him. She seemed to be in her late thirties and was comfortably but elegantly dressed in a pale Italian suit; her hair was a deep auburn and fell around her shoulders "Mr. Barrington?" she asked. "I'm Betty Southard."

"I'm Stone," he replied, shaking her hand.

"Welcome to Centurion Studios; hop in and we'll get going."

Stone got into the golf cart and Betty pulled out of the lot and soon turned left. Stone was suddenly submerged in a wave of déjà vu; the street was overwhelmingly familiar, as if out of some long-recurring dream. "It's... I mean, it's..."

Betty laughed. "A lot of people have that reaction," she said. "I suppose a couple of hundred movies have featured this street in one or another of its guises. Have you spent much time in L.A.?"

"No, I was out here a few years ago for a couple of days, but the company was not nearly so nice."

"Why, thank you," she said, smiling.

"I wasn't flattering you all that much; I was a cop at the time, and my partner and I came out here to extradite a small-time Mafia hitman. He weighed about three hundred and fifty pounds, and the three of us sat in adjacent seats, in steerage, all the way back to New York."

She laughed aloud, a pleasing, unexpected reaction. "I'm glad there's more room on my cart seat," she said.

He smiled. "I'm not."

She laughed again and turned down a street with a large office building on one side and a row of nondescript smaller buildings on the other. "This is executive row, more or less," she said. "Mr. Regenstein's office and those of most of the studio executives are in the big

31

building; the smaller ones are occupied by producers with production deals, small businesses who work with the studio, and, of course, writers and actors."

"Actors have offices?"

She nodded. "Wait until you see Vance's. We're on the way to Stage Ten right now, though. Vance is shooting a big scene, and he thought you might find it interesting."

"I'm sure I will."

She turned down a side street and drove between a series of immense hangar-like buildings, each with a huge number painted on the front. They stopped in front of number 10, Betty parked the cart, and they entered through a small door, past a guard. As soon as they were inside, a loud bell rang, several people shouted, "QUIET!!!," and Betty held a finger to her lips. She pulled him around a pile of equipment, and Stone was astonished to find an entire New England farmhouse sitting in the middle of the soundstage, surrounded by about a foot of fresh snow. As he watched, a series of commands was shouted by someone somewhere, ending in "ACTION!"; a car drove up to the front of the house, and Vance Calder got out, carrying half a dozen brightly wrapped packages, walked up the front walk, opened the door, and walked inside the house, closing the door behind him.

"CUT!" somebody yelled. "Print that! Next setup, Scene Eleven, back yard!"

"I've seen that house somewhere," Stone said.

"Probably; it's a pretty close copy of one in Litchfield County, Connecticut."

"Why don't they just shoot it there? Wouldn't it be cheaper than building it here?"

"Absolutely not. Here, the director has total control of everything—weather, light, snow. He doesn't have to wait for all the variables to be just right, and when he's ready for interiors, the walls come off, exposing the living room, kitchen, et cetera, and the camera can roll right in. They're getting their money's worth out of that house, believe me."

"I'll take your word for it."

"They're setting up in the back yard; would you like to go inside?"

"Sure."

She led the way up the front path and through the front door. They walked into an entrance hall, then into a large, comfortably furnished living room. There were books and pictures, magazines on the coffee table, and a fire glowing cheerfully in the fireplace. "Notice that the doors are all a bit wider than usual," Betty said. "That's so a camera can follow the actors around the house."

"It's amazing," Stone said, looking around. "It feels as though you could move right in."

"You could. The bathroom works, and your toothbrush is probably in the medicine cabinet." She led the way into the kitchen and opened the refrigerator. It was full of food, some of it half-eaten. They walked to the back door and looked out into the yard. Three small children were sitting on the "snow" next to a large snowman. Vance Calder sat a few yards away in a folding chair, reading his script. Somebody yelled out an order, and Calder got up and came into the house.

"Hello, Stone," he said, offering his hand. "I'm glad you could come. You and Betty had better go into the living room, or you'll be in the shot."

Stone followed Betty out of the kitchen, and they sat on the living room sofa. He pointed to a butler's tray with an array of liquor bottles. "If it weren't so early, I'd expect you to offer me a drink," he said.

"You wouldn't like it," she replied. "It's all tea or water." She looked at him frankly. "So, what brings you out here? You've missed Arrington. I suppose you know she's back East, visiting her family."

"I didn't have anything else to do," Stone replied. "I'd just wrapped up a case, and I was at loose ends."

"A case? You're still a police officer, then?"

"No, I'm a lawyer these days."

"What kind of a lawyer?"

"A very good one."

"I mean, do you have a specialty?"

"My specialty is whatever my clients need."

"I didn't know law was practiced that way anymore."

"It isn't, very often."

"Are you with a firm, or on your own?"

"Both. I'm of counsel to a large firm, Woodman and Weld, but I mostly work out of an office in my house."

She cocked her head and frowned a little. "I've heard of Woodman and Weld, of course, but what does 'of counsel' mean?"

"It's a catchall phrase, usually applied to an elderly lawyer who doesn't practice full-time anymore, but who the firm calls on from time to time for advice."

"You're not exactly elderly."

"Not yet."

"What does 'of counsel' mean in *your* case, *exactly*?" she persisted.

"It means that I'm not quite respectable enough to be a partner at Woodman and Weld. I'm at arm's length, but they can reel me in whenever the need arises."

"What sort of need?"

"Let's say a valued client is arrested for drunk driving, in a car with a woman who is not his wife; let's say the daughter of a client is beaten up by her boyfriend, but the family doesn't want to prosecute; let's say the son of a client rapes a nun. That sort of thing."

"Sounds pretty sordid."

"Sometimes it is. All sorts of people need all sorts of legal representation, and not everything a client needs can be directly provided by a prestigious firm. The firm, in fact, is as concerned about its own good name as the client's. They want these cases to go away in the quietest and most expeditious manner possible."

"I suppose it must be interesting at times."

"It's interesting *all* the time," Stone said. "And it beats estate planning any day."

She laughed again, and he enjoyed it.

"Vance is tied up for lunch," she said, "so you'll have to make do with me at the studio commissary."

"Making do with you sounds good; you're a lot more interesting than Vance and nearly as beautiful."

She threw back her head and laughed until someone in the distance screamed "QUIET!"

6

Back in the golf cart, they drove down the street past more soundstages and made a couple of turns, finishing up in front of a low building with a well-kept front lawn. A patio was filled with tables, and people in all sorts of dress—period, Western, and just jeans—were having lunch.

"Let's walk through the main room and I'll ask the maitre d' if he has a table outside; it's such a nice day."

Stone followed her through a handsome dining room, and as they were approaching the doors to the patio, Stone heard someone call his name. He stopped and turned toward the voice. Louis Regenstein was at a booth in the corner of the room, standing, waving him over. Stone touched Betty's arm and motioned for her to follow him.

"Stone, it's good to see you," Regenstein said, offering his hand. He gestured toward his companion. "This is Mario Ciano; Mario, this is a new acquaintance of mine, Stone Barrington." The two men shook hands. "Stone, will you join us for lunch?"

"Thank you, but..."

"You go ahead, Stone," Betty interrupted. "I have some work to do back at the office." She leaned closer. "I'll see you at Vance's house tonight." She vanished.

Stone took a seat facing the two men, with his back to the room.

"Would you like something to drink?" Regenstein asked.

"Some ice tea would be good," Stone replied.

Regenstein waved a hand and the ice tea and a menu appeared. When Stone had ordered, Regenstein turned to Ciano. "You see what I mean?" he asked, nodding at Stone.

"You're right, Lou," Ciano replied. "He's perfect." Ciano turned to Stone. "Have you ever done any acting?"

"Not since high school," Stone said.

"Except in front of juries," Regenstein chuckled. "That's what he told me."

"You're actually a lawyer?" Ciano asked.

"Yes."

"A trial lawyer?"

"From time to time."

"What was your most recent trial?"

"I defended an American woman on a Caribbean island against a murder charge," Stone replied.

"And what was the outcome?"

"She was hanged."

Ciano burst out laughing. "He's typecasting, Lou; our guy loses the case, too."

"May I ask what you gentlemen are talking about?" Stone said.

"The voice is good," Ciano said, ignoring him, talking about him as if he weren't there.

"Good for what?" Stone asked.

"He wouldn't have to join the Screen Actors Guild, would he?" Regenstein asked.

"Nah, he gets one freebie, then he has to join."

Regenstein turned to Stone. "You're planning to be out here for a few days, aren't you?"

"Yes, but Vance..."

"How would you like to appear in this picture with him?"

"With Vance?"

"Of course, with Vance; Mario is the director."

"Oh."

"Well?"

"Are you perfectly serious, Lou?"

"Perfectly. We'll pay you, let's see, twenty-five thousand dollars for a week's work."

Stone turned to Ciano. "You look like a perfectly sane person, Mario," he said. "What the hell is Lou talking about?"

Ciano leaned forward. "We have this scene to shoot this week, a courtroom scene, and the actor who was to play the lawyer got a better offer and wants out. Lou and I would like you to test for the part."

Stone shook his head. "Gentlemen, you'll have to forgive me, but I come from New York, where things like this don't happen. I mean, I've heard about Schwab's Drugstore and the casting couch and all that, but..."

"Schwab's is long gone," Ciano said, "and don't worry, neither Lou nor I wants to fuck you; we just want you to stand in front of a camera and read a few lines. If you do it well, you'll play a prosecuting attorney who is trying to put the client of a lawyer played by Vance Calder in jail. You'll lose, of course, but you'll look good doing it."

"I can't believe there aren't a hundred real actors who could do it better," Stone said.

"That remains to be seen," Ciano said. "Don't worry, if you're lousy, we'll hire an actor."

"Actually, you'd be doing us a big favor if you'd do this, Stone," Regenstein said. "Mario is due to start shooting the scene tomorrow morning, and he doesn't really want to spend the afternoon casting instead of shooting."

"It's settled, then," Ciano said. "My first assistant director will direct your test this afternoon. We can do it in a corner of Stage Ten while we're between setups."

"I'd really need to talk to Vance about this," Stone said.

Regenstein produced his tiny cellular telephone and dialed a number. "Betty, this is Lou; find Vance for me, will you?" He looked at Stone. "This'll just take a moment. Hello, Vance? We've solved the casting on the prosecutor; how about Stone Barrington for the part? I'm sitting here with him right now, and Mario thinks he'd be great; we'd do a test this afternoon. Great! See you tonight." He hung up. "Vance is all for it, Stone, so you're out of excuses."

Ciano produced his own phone, called his assistant, and ordered preparations for the test. He hung up. "Welcome to Hollywood," he said, grinning.

Stone stood in the dining room of the Connecticut farmhouse on Stage Ten and listened to the young man who was directing him.

"Okay, you've had a few minutes with the lines," the director said. "You okay with them?"

"Seems almost as if I've said them before," Stone said.

"That's the way! Now, you pretend that the dining table there is the railing in front of the jury. I want you to deliver the lines across the table as if the jury were there, but *don't* look directly into the video camera, just to either side. Got it?"

"I guess so," Stone replied, putting his script on the table.

"You can hang onto the script," the young man said.

"I think I can do it without it," Stone replied.

"All right, here we go."

A man stepped in front of Stone and held up a slate. "Barrington test, take one."

The director spoke up. "Camera?"

"Rolling," the cameraman said.

"Action."

Stone waited for a moment, then pointed behind him to an imaginary defense table. "That young man sitting over there in his nice blue suit looks like a very nice fellow, doesn't he?" He stopped. "Can I move back and forth along the table?"

"Cut!" the young man said. "Sure, whatever; we'll follow you. Ready, here we go again."

"Barrington test, take two," the slate man said.

"Camera?"

"Rolling."

"Action."

Stone began again, but this time he leaned on the table and looked directly at his imaginary jury. "That young man over there in his nice blue suit with the neat haircut looks like a very nice fellow, doesn't he? Well, if you'd seen him a month ago, his hair was in dreadlocks, and under that suit he's covered in prison tattoos. This, ladies and gentlemen, is not his first time around the block." Stone straightened and began pacing back and forth along the dining table. "That nice-looking young man kidnapped a fourteen-year-old girl, took her out into the woods, tortured her, raped her a few times over the course of an afternoon, and then strangled her to death. You've heard the evidence; it doesn't leave any room for doubt. Your choices are simple: you can send him up to the state prison to be put to death, or you can put him back on the street. Next time, maybe it'll be *your* daughter."

"Cut!" the director yelled. "That was good for me; good for you, Bob?"

"Good for me," the cameraman said.

"Good for you, Mr. Barrington?"

"Whatever you say."

"Okay, rack it up in Screening Room One for Mario and Mr. Regenstein to see. I'll let them know."

Everyone grabbed his gear and walked away. Stone sat down at the dining table and wondered what he'd gotten himself into.

Half an hour later, Stone sat in a tiny movie theater with Louis Regenstein, Mario Ciano, and Vance Calder.

"Roll it," Ciano said into a phone.

Stone stared at himself on the screen. As the lines came out he slunk lower and lower into his seat; the scene seemed to go on forever, and it was very clear to him that he was no actor. Then it was over, and the lights went up. Stone sat up straight and started looking for the door.

"Jesus, that was damn good," Ciano said, sounding surprised.

"I wish I'd looked that good in my first movie," Calder said. Both he and the director turned and looked at Regenstein.

"Stone, you're hired," the studio head said.

"Be in makeup at eleven tomorrow," Ciano said, rising. "We start shooting at one."

Stone, stunned, stood up and shook the men's hands. But he had been terrible, he

42

thought. Couldn't these people see that? He had never been so embarrassed. These people were crazy.

7

Stone pulled up at the gate to Vance Calder's house and rolled down the window. An armed, uniformed security guard approached.

"Good evening, sir," he said. "Your name?"

"Barrington."

"Go right in, Mr. Barrington." The gate slid open.

Stone drove some distance up a winding drive, and it was not until he had crested a little hill that he saw the house. It was of white stucco, in the Spanish style, with a tiled roof. A valet took charge of the car, and Stone walked through the open double doors into a broad tiled hallway that ran straight through the house. A man who looked Filipino, dressed in a white jacket, approached.

"Mr. Barrington?"

"Yes."

"I thought so; I know all the other guests. Will you come this way, please?"

Stone followed him into a very large living room where at least a dozen couples were chatting. He had worn a tan tropical suit and a necktie, and he was glad, because everyone he saw was, for L.A., very dressed. Vance came toward him from the other end of the room, wearing a white linen suit. Stone had always wanted such a suit, but he didn't have the nerve to wear one in New York.

"Good evening, Stone," Calder said, grasping his hand warmly, "and welcome to the cast of *Out of Court.*"

"Is that what the picture is called?"

"That's right; everyone is talking about your test. Come on and meet some people."

Stone followed Vance around the room, greeting other guests. Half of them looked or sounded familiar from the papers and television—some were actors, others were producers or directors. He spotted Betty Southard at the other end of the room, talking to another woman.

"Stone," Vance said, "I'd particularly like you to meet my good friend David Sturmack."

"How do you do?" Stone asked. He remembered that Vance had said that Sturmack was one of the most powerful men in L.A.

"I'm very pleased to meet you, Stone," Sturmack said. "I've heard a great deal about you from Vance and Lou." He was a tall man in his mid-sixties, slim, dressed in beautifully cut but conservative clothes. He turned to an elegant blonde woman next to him who was a good twenty years younger. "This is my wife, Barbara. Barbara, this is Stone Barrington."

"Oh, hello," she nearly gushed. "You're Vance's and Arrington's friend from New York. I read about your Caribbean case in the papers. I'm so sorry about the way it turned out."

"Thank you," Stone replied, "I'm glad to meet you, Barbara."

Louis Regenstein joined the group. "Everyone's talking about your test this afternoon, Stone," he said.

"Oh," Stone said, uncomfortable. Why the hell was everyone talking about it? A waiter took Stone's order for a drink, and everyone chatted amiably for a few minutes. Stone wanted very much to get Vance alone for a moment to ask him why he wanted him in his picture, but his host was busy with his guests. Someone gently took hold of Stone's elbow and turned him a hundred and eighty degrees. He was faced with a deeply suntanned man of forty who took his hand, squeezed it, and began shaking it, slowly, as he talked.

"Stone, I'm Fred Swims of the SBC Agency. You need an agent, and I'd like very much to be the man."

"An agent?" Stone asked, nonplussed.

"I saw your test, and I understand why everyone is so excited about it. It's the best test, bar none, I've ever seen."

"Excuse me, but I'm baffled. It's only been what, four hours, since we did that thing."

"Good news travels fast in this town," Swims said. "Let me tell you a little about us: we're made up of a group of younger agents who left CAA and ICM to form our own shop, and we've got a very hot list of clients. I'd like very much to make you one of them."

"Mr. Swims..."

"Fred."

"Fred, I'm not an actor, really I'm not. I'm a lawyer, and I don't even live out here."

"You will soon, Stone, trust me. Can I ask—I hope I'm not prying—what is your real name, the one you were born with?"

"The one I'm still using."

"Are you serious? That's amazing! I couldn't have come up with a better one myself, and I'm *very* good at bankable names. You know what Vance's name was, don't you?"

"No."

"Herbert Willis." He held up three fingers, Boy Scout–style. "I swear to God."

"That's fascinating," Stone said, trying not to offend the man.

Swims stopped shaking his hand, took him by the arm, and steered him a few feet away from anyone else. "I've got to tell you what a test like this and a role like this can mean. We're talking the biggest bucks here, and I'm not kidding."

Stone laughed. "Lou Regenstein tells me I'm too old to be a star."

"God forbid I should contradict Lou, but the mature leading man is *in* right now—look at Harrison Ford—Christ, look at Clint Eastwood! The man is in his late sixties! And you're what, thirty-eight?"

"I'm forty-two."

Swims leaned forward and spoke conspiratorially. "Promise me that number will never pass your lips until you're fifty," he said. "That number will be between you and me;

46

you're thirty... well, in your late... in your *early* late thirties."

"I promise," Stone said gravely.

Swims slipped a card into Stone's jacket pocket. "I want you to call me tomorrow morning, early, and we'll do lunch and talk about what the future holds for you. Believe me, it's very bright, but I don't want to impose on my host's good nature by talking business in his house." He gave a Boy Scout salute and wandered off in pursuit of a waiter.

Stone was finally able to find Betty Southard, who was still talking with the only other unaccompanied woman in the room.

"Hello," Betty said warmly. "Stone, this is Arlene Michaels of the *Hollywood Reporter.*"

"So you're the new *actor* in town," the woman said, shaking hands. "I've heard about your test."

Stone shook his head. "I think that test is going to turn out to be a great embarrassment," he said.

"My dear, whyever would it be embarrassing? I saw Fred Swims buttonhole you. He's tops, you know; you couldn't do better for an agent. Your dreams are about to come true."

"I'm afraid my dreams don't run in that direction," Stone said. "I'm a lawyer, and I like to confine my acting to the courtroom."

"Well," Betty said, "that *is* where you'll be doing your acting. They're working overtime tonight to build the set; the scene wasn't scheduled for another three weeks, but I guess Lou Regenstein really wanted to get you into that part while you're here."

Stone was surprised. Regenstein had told him that the scene had already been scheduled for the next day. "I'm baffled by the whole experience," Stone said.

Arlene Michaels suddenly produced a notebook. "It's two r's, is it?"

"That's right."

"And you're a New York lawyer?"

"Right again."

"You used to live with Arrington, didn't you?"

"I live in my own house," he replied. "Arrington and I are good friends."

"Well, 'good friends' can mean *anything* in this town," she said, scribbling away. "This your first movie part?"

"Oh, yes."

"You sure?"

"I think I'd remember if I'd been in a movie."

"Tell me, how does Vance feel about having Arrington's old beau in town?"

"You should ask Vance; I'm here at his invitation."

"A little male bonding while the wife is out of town, huh?"

"I hadn't thought of it that way," Stone said.

"Really, Arlene," Betty broke in. "You're grilling Stone."

"It's what I do, honey," Michaels said. "What are your first impressions of L.A., Stone?"

"I'm very favorably impressed," Stone said, looking around the room.

"Well, it's not all like this," she said. "My first time in this house, I can tell you. Vance isn't known for inviting the press into his home."

Betty spoke up. "Arlene, you know Vance is a very private person."

"Shy, you could say."

"You could say. I'd think you'd be pleased to be the first reporter in this house for years."

"Well, there was the *Architectural Digest* piece last year, wasn't there?"

"It's hardly the same thing."

Stone took Betty's arm and guided her away. "Arlene, would you excuse us for just a moment? There's something I have to discuss with Betty."

"Sure," Michaels replied.

Stone made sure his back was to the woman. "I understand that L.A. parties end early."

"Always," Betty said. "It's an early town; everybody is at work at the crack of dawn."

"Do you think you and I could have a drink somewhere later?"

"All right, but I have to be at work early, too. Let's meet at the bar in the Bel-Air Hotel," she said.

"Fine."

"Now, we'd better rejoin Arlene; we don't want her to go away miffed."

They turned back to the woman and found her gone. She'd cornered Vance, and he was saved only by the tinkling of a silver bell.

"Dinner is served," the Filipino butler called out.

The crowd, which had grown since Stone had arrived, moved out of the rear doors to a wide terrace, where tables of eight had been set. Stone looked at the place cards and found his seat, between Barbara Sturmack and a man who appeared, like Stone, to be alone. He helped Mrs. Sturmack with her chair, then turned to meet the man next to him.

"I'm Onofrio Ippolito," the man said. He was shorter than Stone, heavily built without being fat, with thick, short salt-and-pepper hair.

"I'm Stone Barrington." They shook hands.

"What brings you out here, Mr. Barrington?" the man asked.

"Just visiting friends," Stone replied.

"That's not what I heard," Ippolito said.

Stone was about to ask what he'd heard when Barbara Sturmack tugged at his sleeve and began introducing him to others seated at the table. Stone never did resume his conversation with Ippolito.

When dinner was finished, they rose to go into the house for coffee, and Stone found David Sturmack walking alongside him. "Could I have a word with you alone?" he asked.

"Of course," Stone replied and allowed himself to be steered into what he thought must be Vance's study, a medium-sized room paneled in antique pine, with many fine pictures on the walls. When they were comfortably seated, Sturmack began.

"Stone, I do a great deal of business on

50

the West Coast and some business in New York. I'm considering changing my legal representation in the city, and I wondered if you might be interested in representing me?"

"That's very flattering, Mr. Sturmack..."

"David, please."

"David. What sort of business do you do in New York?"

"Some real estate; I have interests in a couple of restaurants, and I may want to develop more with some friends; I invest in businesses; I buy, I sell; occasionally I litigate something. I'm a lawyer myself by training, but I haven't practiced in years."

"I should tell you that I don't have any extensive experience in real estate and none at all in restaurants."

"I'm aware of that; I spoke at some length with a Mr. William Eggers at Woodman and Weld this afternoon. He says that since you're of counsel to his firm, they'd be willing to lend backup support and expertise in various specialties as needed."

Stone was off balance; he hadn't expected this. "Who represents you at the moment?"

"My principal attorneys are Hyde, Tyson, McElhenny and Wade, but I've been contemplating a move for some time."

"What sort of billing have they experienced with you?"

"In excess of a million dollars a year. Of course, you'd have to take care of Woodman and Weld, but all the billing would be through you, and I imagine you'd be able to hang on

51

to most of the fees. Also, there would be opportunities to invest some of your fees in various ventures, at an extremely good rate of return."

"Mr. Sturmack, may I be frank?"

"I'd appreciate that."

"You and I have met only this evening; you know little about me or my skills; why do you want me to represent you?"

"Stone, I know a great deal more about you than you think: I know about your record with the NYPD, I know about the major cases you've handled, and I know about how you handle yourself."

"You must understand that Woodman and Weld make some demands on my time, and it's an association I value; I couldn't undertake to represent you as my only client."

"Of course I understand that, Stone. I'm not making this offer off the top of my head."

"You don't seem the sort of man who would do that," Stone said.

"You're right. Understand, a great deal of what I want from a lawyer is his personal skills—the way he handles himself in a situation. I like to avoid litigation when possible, but I like to get my way, too."

Stone smiled. "All clients do. David, I really don't think I can give you an answer immediately. Of course, your proposal is extremely attractive, but I think I'd have to talk with Bill Eggers about it, preferably in person, and I expect to be here for another week, maybe longer."

"Of course. Tell you what: I'm jammed up for the next few days, but I expect to be in New York late next week. Why don't you and I sit down and talk about it then. I'll gather some specifics on my current situation, and we can discuss the workload."

"That sounds very good." They exchanged cards, shook hands, and rejoined the other guests.

Over coffee, Stone exchanged a glance with Betty Southard and nodded toward the door. She smiled and nodded, and after a moment, he said his goodbyes to his host and left, a minute behind her.

8

Stone pulled into the Bel-Air parking lot and surrendered the car. In the lobby, he had to ask where the bar was. The room surprised him; it was more English than Californian, darkly paneled, with a blazing fire in a handsome fireplace. He found Betty already seated on a small sofa near the fireplace, a waiter hovering nearby; it was only a little after ten, but there were few people in the room.

He sat down beside her and ordered a brandy. "Thanks for coming; I'm sorry we didn't get to talk more at the party."

"Oh, it was my job to shepherd Arlene, the journalist, around the place; Vance didn't want her talking to any one person for too long. He was very nervous about having her there at all; I still can't figure out why he wanted her, and he wouldn't tell me when I asked."

"I'm sure he had his reasons," Stone said, a little uncomfortable with knowing something she didn't. "Does he confide in you about everything?"

"Not necessarily; it's just that I work so closely with him that it's hard to hide anything." She smiled. "Say, you were quite a hit at the party."

Stone squirmed in his seat. "Aren't they that nice to everybody?"

She shook her head. "Normally, an out-of-town lawyer at a party like that would find himself talking to the wallpaper."

"So how come I'm so popular?"

"You're a handsome man they've read about in the papers, you're younger than most of the other men there, and you're the personal guest in town of their host, who is a major movie star."

"And what was all that about the screen test?"

"Have you *seen* the test?"

"Yes. I found it excruciating."

She laughed. "I saw it in a room with a dozen secretaries who'd heard about it, and there was a heavy scent of vaginal juices in the air."

"Stop it!" he groaned.

"I believe you really are embarrassed," she said, surprised.

"The whole thing is humiliating."

"Forgive me; I'm accustomed to actors, any one of whom would have understood immediately what that test meant to his future in this town."

"I don't have a future in this town."

"You do if you want it."

"That's what Fred Swims said," Stone replied disconsolately.

"Come on, Stone, cheer up! It's not as though you're being tarred and feathered and ridden out of town on a rail. You're having a moment in the limelight; enjoy it! Most men would be jumping up and down with glee!"

Stone laughed. "I suppose you're right, but it's a lot more than I'm accustomed to. I'm a bit at sea."

She put a hand on his cheek. "What is it, baby?" she asked as if talking to a small child.

"Well, the test is pretty strange," he said. "Then there's the party tonight."

"What about the party?"

"Look, I'm in town for hardly more than twenty-four hours, and I get a screen test and a part in a movie for very nice money. Then an agent—apparently a top one—wants to represent me, and then..." He stopped himself.

"Go on."

"Here we get into a confidential area."

"Most of my job is keeping Vance's secrets; I suppose I can keep yours, too."

"What do you know about David Sturmack?"

She shrugged. "He's very important in these parts—behind the scenes, mostly."

"How do you mean?"

"Well, you never see anything in the trades about how Sturmack made this deal or even made a movie, but you hear stories..."

"What sort of stories?"

"Did you see Vance's movie *Parting Time*?"

"Yes, a long time ago."

"Vance wasn't supposed to be in that movie; he was under contract to another big studio, and they wouldn't release him. Story is, Sturmack made one phone call and ten minutes later, Vance was in *Parting Time*. It got him his first Academy Award, and the picture did half a billion dollars worldwide. A lot of informed opinion says that the picture would have tanked without Vance. So you see the kind of power that Sturmack can wield in a single phone call."

"How did he come by all this power?"

"He had something to do with the unions."

"What unions?"

"The craft unions, the ones that have all the technicians in the business as members. He got a reputation early on for solving the most difficult contract negotiations—he represented at least two of the unions, I forget which ones. That's really about all I know about him, except that he and Vance are very close. I can tell better than anybody who Vance is really close to by the way he responds to their telephone calls. He drops *everything* when Dave Sturmack calls. The only other person who gets that kind of attention from Vance is Lou Regenstein. And right now, you."

"Me?"

"You're on the hot list right now."

"You mean, for the moment."

"Nobody stays on Vance's hot list forever, but right now, you're up there." She frowned. "Why is that, Stone?"

"Beats me," Stone replied.

"Yeah, sure. I know it's something to do with Arrington, but I can't figure out what."

"I haven't spoken to Arrington for months." Not many months, he thought, but months.

"You're not going to tell me, huh?"

He shrugged. "I'm a lawyer, Betty; some things have to remain..."

She patted his hand. "I understand. I operate under pretty much the same strictures. When you work for somebody like Vance, confidentiality is currency. If Vance suddenly clutched his chest and turned blue, half the town would be trying to hire me before the paramedics arrived. But if I talked out of turn about Vance..."

"I understand," he said.

"Then we both understand." She smiled. It was something she did well.

"Will you give me some advice?" he asked.

"Sure."

"Should I actually do this part in the movie?"

She placed a hand on her chest. "Good God! If you don't, Lou Regenstein will have a stroke. Mind you, he strokes very quietly: he'll lift an eyebrow and you won't ever get a dinner table in this town again."

"So I'm stuck?"

She put her hand back on his cheek. "Don't

take it so hard, baby; it's only fame and fortune. Most men would jump at the chance."
She lowered her voice. "And most men would
have propositioned me by now."

"You are bold, miss."

"By this time tomorrow, any woman on
the Centurion lot can be yours; I figure I'd better hurry."

"I live near here."

"Show me."

Stone signed the check, and they left the bar
and walked through the cool evening toward
his suite. She put her hand in his, but neither
of them said anything. Along with the scent
of frangipani, there was anticipation in the air.

The suite was softly lighted, and she went
straight to the bedroom, dropping articles of
clothing along the way. A message envelope
had been pushed under the door; Stone could-
n't think about that now. He dropped it on the
bedside table and started working on his own
buttons.

She was naked first. "Leave the lights on,"
she said, stripping the bedcover and top sheet
off the bed.

He followed instructions.

She stretched out on the bare bed and
clasped her hands behind her neck. Her tan
ran from top to bottom without interruption,
something he wasn't accustomed to seeing in
New York.

"Me first," she said.

He started with her breasts and worked his
way down. She kept her hands clasped behind

her neck until he hit bottom, then her fingers were in his hair, pulling, while she made little noises.

After a while, it was his turn. It was worth the wait.

9

Stone woke slowly, at first disoriented in the strange room. The bed was a wreck, with covers everywhere, and he was alone. He stretched and thought about the night before, which was indeed a pleasant memory, then jumped as the phone rang. The bedside clock said six-thirty. He grabbed the phone.

"Hello?"

"It's Bill Eggers; why didn't you call me last night? I was up half the night waiting."

"Why Bill, I didn't know you cared."

"Didn't you get my message?"

"Oh," Stone said, ripping open the little envelope. It read: "Call me tonight, no matter how late." "Sorry, Bill, I was preoccupied, I guess, and I didn't even read it."

"How the hell did you get to know David Sturmack?"

"I met him at a dinner party last night, at Vance Calder's house."

"Only last night? He called me about you yesterday afternoon; that was before you even met him?"

"That's right."

"Jesus, what are you doing in Hollywood,

59

having dinner with movie stars and fixers?"

"Fixers?"

"Don't you even know who David Sturmack is?"

"I know he has a lot of influence in the movie business; that's about it. Who else is he?"

"Stone, if it doesn't happen on the Upper East Side between Forty-second and Eighty-sixth Street, you don't have a clue, do you?"

"Am I *supposed* to know who Sturmack is?"

"Well, maybe not. Only a handful of people really know, and I happen to be one of them."

"Why is he so little known for such a powerful fellow?"

"Because he wants it that way. Things usually get to be the way Sturmack wants them."

"Oh."

"You bet your ass. That was some conversation I had with him yesterday; he called me right out of the blue. I'm glad I was in."

"Bill, you were telling me who Sturmack is."

"He's the prince of fucking darkness, that's who he is."

"You copped that line from a movie."

"That doesn't make it any less true," Eggers said defensively.

"I guess not; now explain yourself."

"It started like this: Sturmack's old man, whose name was Morris, or Moe, was Meyer Lansky's right-hand man for thirty years."

"No kidding?"

"Absolutely no fucking kidding. Word is, he

sent son David to law school both to make him respectable and to make him useful."

"And he was useful?"

"You better believe he was. His specialty was the mob connection to the unions; he was very tight with Hoffa and Tony Scotto and a dozen other big-time labor guys. In the late fifties he went west and became a conduit between the Hollywood unions and the mob. He was always very discreet; he didn't even practice law out there, so nobody could go running to the bar association if they didn't like his methods. Over the years, he's sunk more and more out of sight until he's practically invisible, but at the same time he's gotten a better and better grip on the town."

"How do you know all this, Bill?"

"I know everything about everybody; didn't you know that?"

"Come on, tell me how you know."

"I once had a client who was in business with him, who murmured a word about him from time to time. He enjoyed telling stories about the old days. The guy died earlier this year, but apparently he had mentioned me to Sturmack. That's how he knew who to call about you. Now I've got a question for you."

"Okay, shoot."

"How the hell did you impress Sturmack so much in so short a time? I mean, I know you a lot better than he does, and *I'm* not all that impressed."

"Thanks. The whole thing is a mystery to

me. The only person Sturmack and I have in common is Vance Calder, and Calder and I have never had any dealings."

"Maybe not, but Calder probably heard a lot about you on the pillow."

"He did say that Arrington had told him a lot about me, but still..."

"Well, I think you ought to grab the opportunity, pal, and we'll back you up over here, but the name of Woodman and Weld is never going to appear on any piece of paper that goes from here to you to Sturmack. Do we understand each other?"

"Yeah, but I haven't taken him on yet. He seems like the kind of guy who might tend to monopolize my time; right now I have a lot of independence, but if I find myself working full time for him, then I'm no longer self-employed."

"I get your drift, and you're smart to think that way."

"Something else that bothers me: he says he does some, not a lot, of business in New York—some real estate, a couple of restaurants—but he also says his present lawyers billed over a million a year from him. That doesn't quite add up, does it?"

"No, it doesn't; if he's spending a million a year on lawyers, he's either doing a *lot* of business in the city, or he's in a lot of trouble here. I'd raise the question, if I were you."

"I will. He also says that I'll have investment opportunities in my dealings with him."

"I'd be real careful about that, boy; you're liable to end up in front of a grand jury or a congressional committee. Whatever the investment is, make *sure* it's squeaky clean."

"Well, I don't know yet if I'm even going to take him on. What kind of name is Sturmack, anyway?"

"He's a Swedish Jew, if you can believe that."

"I guess there are Jews everywhere. Why not Swedish?"

"Why not indeed. The way I hear it, Sturmack's grandfather was a big wholesale fish dealer in Stockholm, and his son, Moe, got into big trouble, maybe even killed somebody, and had to flee the country. He ended up in New York, and through some family connection met Meyer Lansky; it was apparently love at first sight."

"By the way, there was another guy at dinner who struck me as a little odd, name of Onofrio Ippolito. That ring any bells?"

"He's a banker, that's all I know; straight arrow, I'm told."

"Funny, he looked more like a mob guy."

"Stone, you were a cop too long. Not everybody with an Italian name is mobbed up."

"Yeah, I know."

"Now tell me, what are you doing in L.A.?"

"Oh, I'm doing a part in a movie."

"You're *what*?"

"I had a screen test yesterday, and I passed. I'm apparently the town's hottest new discovery."

"Okay, you're obviously not going to tell me what's going on, so I'll go now."

"I kid you not, Bill," Stone said, but Eggers had already hung up.

Stone had a shower and ordered some breakfast, and when the waiter arrived, Stone noticed a fat envelope on the living room coffee table. He opened it and found a script. Well, he had some work to do, he thought.

He went over his lines for the next hour, then the phone rang.

"Hello?"

"Stone Barrington?"

"Yes."

"I'm Bobby Routon; I'm doing the costumes for *Out of Court*."

"Right; how are you?"

"Harried. Listen, the wardrobe department at Centurion isn't up to dressing this lawyer you're playing—not on short notice, anyway, so we've got to get you some duds."

"Okay."

"Whose suits and shirts do you normally wear?"

"Ralph Lauren's suits, Purple Label, when I can afford them, and Turnbull and Asser shirts."

"Yeah, they've got the shirts at Neiman's. What about size?"

"I'm a perfect 42 long in a suit; they only have to fix the trouser bottoms."

"What size shirt?"

"16. The T and A sleeve lengths are all the same."

"Shoe size?"

"10 D."

"Got it. I'll have some stuff for a fitting when you get to the studio at eleven. You're furnishing your own underwear, and remember, you might get hit by a streetcar, so don't embarrass your mother."

Stone laughed. "See you at eleven." He hung up. "Jesus," he said aloud, "I guess I'm not in Kansas anymore."

10

Stone arrived at Centurion Studios, and this time the guard at the gate had his name. He was given a parking pass marked "VIP" and directed to Stage Twelve. Following his route of the day before, he found his way to the huge building and slipped the Mercedes convertible into a VIP-reserved spot. A young man in his early twenties was standing at the stage door.

"Stone Barrington?"

"That's me."

"I'm Tim Corbin, assistant production manager; I'll get you oriented, then I'll take you to wardrobe and makeup. Follow me." He led the way around a corner into a street between soundstages, dug a key out of his pocket, and unlocked a medium-sized recreational vehicle. "This is number twenty-one; it's yours for the duration."

Stone followed Corbin inside. There was a living room, a bedroom, a kitchenette, a toilet, and a small room with a desk, a phone, and a fax machine. The refrigerator was stocked with mineral water, juices, and fruit. "Very nice," he said.

"It's a cut above what a featured player usually gets," Corbin said. "You been sleeping with the director?"

"He's not my type."

"This is where you'll hang out when they're not using you. Unless you're told different, you're expected to be on the lot from eight A.M. until six P.M., and if you haven't been told to be on the set, this is where they'll always look for you. You've got a phone line and a fax machine with its own line. By the way, the keys are in the ignition, but don't ever *ever* crank it up and move it; that's a Teamster's job, and we don't want to annoy the Teamsters, do we?"

"Certainly not."

"You're going to find that a lot of stuff on the set gets done by union guys, so don't ever move any furniture, or even a prop, unless it's called for in a scene, okay?"

"Okay."

"When in doubt, ask me."

"Okay, Tim."

"Now let's get you to wardrobe." He led Stone to a golf cart and drove quickly to another building.

Bobby Routon greeted him, sticking out a hand. He was short, plump, and gay. "Hey, Stone," he said. "I think we got you togged out." He grabbed a suit off a rack, and Stone slipped into the trousers and coat. "You were right, a perfect forty-two long." He pinned up the trousers, and Stone tried on three more suits while a woman hemmed the trousers of the first. "All actors should be so easy to fit," Routon said. "Okay, get into suit number one, and I'll find you a tie." He handed Stone a lovely ivory-colored Sea Island cotton shirt. "You've got a dozen of these, in case you sweat or spill something. For Christ's sake, don't eat lunch in any of the suits; if you spill catsup on it, we don't have a backup, and it could cost an hour's shooting while it's cleaned, and an hour's shooting is more bucks than either of us can imagine."

"I'll be neat, I promise."

"A dream actor," Routon sighed. Stone got into a shirt, and Routon got a tie around his neck. "Let me tie it, I can do it better than you; it's my job to make you look good."

Stone checked himself in a mirror while Routon folded and stuck a silk pocket square into his breast pocket.

"Shoes," Routon said, holding up a pair of Italian-looking captoes. He helped Stone into them and tied the laces. "Comfy?"

"Comfy," Stone said, walking around.

"You're ready to be famous," Routon said. "All the suits will be put in your dressing room, and you'll be told which one to wear on which day of the trial you're shooting, but I think you'll be in this suit all day. When you have as much as half an hour to yourself, go to your RV and take the suit off; a wardrobe lady will press it. Get used to being seen in your underwear by strange women." He waved goodbye.

"That was easy," Stone said as he and Corbin left.

"Bobby's the best in the business," Corbin said. "Now makeup." He drove a couple of buildings down.

Inside, Stone was greeted by a pretty young woman in jeans who relieved him of his jacket and sat him down in a barber's chair. "I'm Sally Dunn," she said, "and I'm going to make you even more beautiful."

"What, exactly, are you going to do to me?"

"Not much," she said, unbuttoning his shirt collar and lining it with tissues. "Your problem is you're the world's whitest white man." She ran her fingers through his hair. "Can't tell you how long it's been since I saw a real blond, male or female. You have fairly blond skin, too, although I see you've picked up a little sun since you've been in town. You're going to have a lot of light dumped on you on the set, and without makeup, you'd look like a corpse, especially next to Vance, who's so tan he doesn't need makeup. My job is to make you look like a living person under those lights." She tilted his head back onto the headrest and went to work.

When she had finished Stone opened his eyes and looked into the mirror. "I'm orange," he said.

"You won't be under light. I'll be on the set to touch you up between takes. Try not to get

too hot and start sweating; it just makes everything hotter. I'll have a fan for you. At the end
of the day, you can come back here for cleanup,
or there's cold cream in your trailer. Use that
before you shower."

Corbin drove Stone back to Stage Twelve,
and escorted him inside.

It was as cavernous as the first stage Stone
had visited, but instead of the farmhouse, there
was a warren of sets—offices, a conference room,
a jury room, a bedroom, and, finally, a courtroom.

There was a lot of action in the courtroom—technicians of every sort swarmed
over the set, adjusting lights and props. Gradually, actors arrived, dressed as lawyers, cops,
jurors, and spectators, then Mario Ciano
made his appearance.

"Good morning, Stone," he said. "We're
going to shoot Scene 14A, where you question
your first witness, the junkie."

"Right," Stone said, finding the right page.

"We're not going strictly in chronological
order; I don't want you to have to shoot your
opening statement to the jury first time out of
the stall. We'll get you warmed up with a
rehearsal, then your little scene, then we'll shoot
Vance's cross-examination, then we'll get
reaction shots from both of you. You'll have
to be on the set most of the day, because you
can be seen in backgrounds."

Stone was introduced to the actor playing
his second chair, then rehearsals began. Stone
learned to stop on a mark and ignore the
camera, then they began shooting. It was

more difficult than he had imagined it would be, but he got it done.

He had a sandwich in his RV dressing room at lunch; his suit was pressed, and Sally Dunn came and redid his makeup. "I hear it's going well," she said.

After lunch, Vance Calder did his scenes, then Stone sat and did reaction shots while Vance read his lines off-camera, then Stone read while Vance reacted. By the end of the day they had finished five pages of script, about five minutes on film, which Stone was told was a good day. When shooting was done, he removed his own makeup, showered, and surrendered his new suit to wardrobe, which would press and, if necessary, clean it overnight. By the time he arrived back at the Bel-Air, he was exhausted.

He opened the door to his room and found two little envelopes on the floor containing his day's messages. The first was from Bill Eggers.

"So how's the movie star?"

"Exhausted. You wouldn't believe how hard actors work."

"Yeah, sure."

"What's up?"

"I made a few calls about Onofrio Ippolito."

"What did you find out?"

"It was really weird; *nobody* would say anything about him, good or bad."

"What do you mean?"

"I mean, every time I asked somebody about Ippolito he'd say, 'Oh, he's a banker, I think,' and then he'd get Alzheimer's. And these are people who should know stuff about him, people who know stuff about *everybody*."

"So they're protecting him?"

"More likely, they're scared shitless of him."

"Maybe I should have been nicer to him at dinner."

"I hope you didn't spill anything on him."

"I hope so, too."

"It worries me, Stone. I've never run into anything quite like this before. Usually I can find out anything about anybody with three or four calls."

"Well, there's nothing to be worried about. I sat next to him at dinner, and that's it. There's no reason why I should have any further contact with him."

"I'd keep it that way, if I were you."

"I'll try; thanks for your help." Stone said goodbye and hung up.

He opened the second little envelope and the message froze him in his tracks.

"Sorry I missed you," it read. "I'll try later, if I can." It was signed "A."

11

Stone immediately called the hotel operator. "I got a message signed 'A.,'" he said. "What time did the call come in?"

"It should be written on the message, Mr. Barrington," the woman replied.

"Oh, yes; less than half an hour ago."

"I'm double-checking... yes, that's right."

71

"She didn't leave a number?"

"No, sir, just said she'd try and call later."

"Do you have caller ID on your phone system?"

"Yes, sir, but we rarely use it."

"Would you please make a note that on all the calls I receive to make a note of the caller ID number?"

"All right, I'll do that; and I'll let the other shifts know."

"Thank you." Stone hung up. Vance had been right; getting his name into the trade papers had produced results. If only he'd been at home when she called. He fixed himself a drink from the bar, switched on the television news, and watched it blankly, absorbing none of it. When his glass was empty, he got into the shower and stood under the very hot water, letting his muscles relax. Then, as he turned off the water, he heard the phone ringing. Grabbing a towel, he raced into the bedroom, but just as he reached for the instrument, it stopped ringing; all he heard was a dial tone. "Dammit!" he yelled at nobody in particular. He called the operator. "You just rang my suite, but I was in the shower. Who called?"

"Yes, Mr. Barrington, it was the young lady again; she wouldn't leave a number, but I got it on the caller ID." She read out the number, and he wrote it down. "The name that came up on the screen was Grimaldi's; I think it's a restaurant. The concierge would know."

"Please switch me to the concierge."

"Concierge desk."

"This is Stone Barrington; do you know a restaurant in L.A. called Grimaldi's?" He gave her the number.

"Yes, sir; it's on Santa Monica Boulevard, I think, though I haven't booked a table there for anyone in a long time. It's sort of an old-fashioned place, not exactly chic."

"Could you book me a table there at eight?"

"Of course, sir; for how many?"

"Ah, two."

"I'll book it and call you back if there's any problem."

"Thanks; I'll stop by the desk on the way out and pick up the address." He hung up, thought for a moment, then dug in his pocket for a number and dialed it.

"Hello?"

"Betty? It's Stone."

"Hi there; I was just thinking of you."

"Telepathy at work. You free for dinner this evening?"

"Sure."

"Where do you live?"

"In Beverly Hills; why don't I meet you at the Bel-Air?"

"Seven forty-five?"

"Perfect. I'll meet you in the car park. You want me to book something for us? I can always use Vance's name."

"Not necessary; I'll see you at seven forty-five." He hung up and started to get dressed.

• • •

Betty climbed into the passenger seat and gave him a wet peck on the cheek. "Where are we going?"

"A place on Santa Monica called Grimaldi's."

"Don't think I've ever heard of it," she said, "and I didn't think there was a restaurant in L.A. I'd never heard of." She looked at the address on the card in his hand. "That'll be somewhere down near the beach; let's take the freeway."

Stone followed her directions, and they found the restaurant, its entrance tucked in a side street off Santa Monica.

"How'd you hear about this place?" Betty asked as they approached a glass door, which was covered with credit card stickers.

"I'll tell you later," he said, opening the door for her.

They descended a staircase which emerged into a large basement dining room, half full of diners, with low ceilings and elaborate decor—textured wallpaper and heavy brocade drapes much in evidence. Stone gave his name to the headwaiter, and they were shown to a banquette table in the middle of the room, where they sat beside each other with their backs to the wall.

"The decor is right out of the fifties," Betty said, looking around her. "It looks like a set from an old black-and-white Warner Brothers movie." A waiter appeared, took their drinks order, and left them a heavy velvet-bound menu. "This thing must weigh ten pounds," she said.

Stone opened the menu and was astonished at the range of dishes, which were from every region of Italy. "I don't think I've ever seen anything quite like this," he said. The waiter came with their drinks. "Give us a few minutes," Stone told him. "It's such a big menu."

"Would you like some recommendations?" the waiter asked.

"Please."

"The specialty of the house is the rabbit in a cream sauce, and any of the pastas are excellent."

"Thanks," Stone said. "I'll try the rabbit."

"I'll try the pasta," Betty said, grimacing. "Which one?"

"The bolognese is good," the waiter replied.

"Fine."

"Shall I leave you the wine list?"

"Suggest something," Stone said. "A big wine."

"Try the Masi Amerone, the '91."

"Sold."

"Something to start?"

"A Caesar salad," Stone said.

"Make it two," Betty echoed.

The waiter departed, leaving them with their drinks.

"Okay, so how did you come up with this place?" Betty asked.

"Arrington called me from here earlier this evening."

"But she's still in Virginia," Betty said. "I made her flight reservations."

"I'm going to have to trust your discretion."

"Sure."

"She's not in Virginia; she disappeared nearly a week ago."

"*What?*"

"Vance called me and asked me to come out here and find her."

"Disappeared?"

"That's right; he doesn't know where she is."

"I can't believe this could have happened and I wouldn't know about it."

"He's keeping it very quiet, because he doesn't know what's going on."

"She just ran out on him?"

"He doesn't know; she hasn't been in touch with him."

"And she called you?"

"Arrington must have read the piece in the trade paper; that's why Vance invited the reporter to the party."

"Well, I must say, I thought there was something weird about that; it was very unlike Vance. What did Arrington say to you?"

"I was in the shower; the hotel operator got the calling number from caller ID."

"Well, this is very mysterious, isn't it?"

"It certainly is." Stone looked around the restaurant at the other diners. "Wait a minute," he said, half to himself.

"What?"

"You notice anything about the other customers?"

Betty looked slowly around the restaurant. "I guess a lot of them look Italian. That speaks well of the restaurant, I suppose."

"It's a wiseguy joint," Stone said, keeping his voice low.

"You mean *Mafia*?"

"Not so loud. That's exactly what I mean. It's just like a New York wiseguy joint; just *look* at these people."

"Well, the women are a little flashy."

"Yes, they are."

"And I don't think I've ever seen so many Italian suits outside of Rome."

"Right."

"Does this make me a racist pig or something?"

"No, it just makes you observant. I'll bet half the faces in this place are in the mug books down at the LAPD."

"But what could Arrington possibly have to do with the Mafia?"

"I don't know, but there's got to be some kind of connection." As he spoke, Stone looked up and saw four men coming down the stairs into the dining room. "Look who's here," he whispered.

She followed his gaze. "You know those guys?"

"One of them," Stone said. "I met him at Vance's."

12

Stone pretended to consult the wine list, covering his face. "Don't look at him," he said. "I don't want him to see me."

"Look at who?" Betty asked. "I can't see a thing." She leaned back and looked behind him. "One of those backs looks familiar," she said.

"His name is Ippolito."

"I remember his name on the invitation list, but he was the only one I didn't know."

"Stop craning your neck."

"It's okay, he's sitting at the round corner table with his back to us."

Stone peeked over the wine list. "Do you know any of the other three?"

"Nope; they don't even look familiar. A lot of beef on the hoof, though."

The waiter arrived with their salad, and they tucked into it.

"This is the best Caesar I ever had," Betty said.

"If the goombahs can't make a Caesar salad, who can?"

"It isn't an Italian dish, you know."

"I thought it was."

"Nope, it was invented by a Mexican at some famous restaurant in Acapulco, or someplace like that. I can't remember his name."

"Caesar, maybe?"

"Nobody likes a smartass, Stone."

Their main courses came, and Stone tasted

the wine. "Absolutely perfect," he said to the waiter.

"Of course," the waiter replied, pouring the wine.

Stone tasted the rabbit. "Words fail me," he said.

"Me, too," Betty said, tasting her pasta. "Why does nobody know about this place?"

"We like it that way," the waiter said, then he left them alone.

"I think everybody knows about this place that they want to know about it," Stone said.

"God, the wine is good!"

Stone made a note of it. "I want some for home," he said.

"I want the chef for home," Betty cried, stuffing more pasta into her mouth. "I could make him very happy."

"Heads up," Stone said. "One of them is coming this way." He addressed his rabbit as the man walked past and entered a hallway at the rear of the restaurant. "He was looking right at me; do you think he recognized me?"

"Really, Stone," she replied, "he was looking at *me*."

"Oh. I wonder what's in the rear hallway."

"The men's room. See the sign?"

"Oh."

Stone watched as the man returned to his table. "You're right, he was looking at you."

"I'm accustomed to that," she said, twirling the last of the pasta on her fork. "That is the first time in ten years I have finished a whole meal in a restaurant," she said, swallowing. "If you bring me here again I'll be able to audition for Roseanne's replacement."

The waiter appeared and began gathering their dishes. "How about some of our cheesecake?" he asked.

"Don't say that," Betty said, throwing up a hand. "I could gain weight just listening."

"A double espresso for me," Stone said.

"I'll have a cappuccino," she said.

The waiter left.

"I want to have a look around the back," Stone said, rising.

She caught his sleeve. "Are you nuts?"

"I'm just going to the men's room; I'll be back in a minute." He walked into the rear hallway, looking to the right and left. He passed the kitchen and came to the men's room door, looked inside, found it empty, and continued down the hall, where he found a door marked STAFF ONLY. He looked over his shoulder, then walked in.

It was a good-sized storeroom, with refrigerators lining one wall and steel shelving lining the other. In the middle of the floor were empty crates with the remnants of vegetables stuck to them. Stone walked to the rear of the room and found a toilet and, across from that, a small office.

"Hey!" a deep voice yelled.

Stone spun around. A large man in kitchen whites was standing a few feet behind him. "I was looking for the men's room," he said, and he caught sight of something familiar on the floor between him and the man.

"You walked right past it," the man said. "Come on, I'll show you." He turned and walked toward the door.

Quickly, Stone stooped and picked up the small object, tucking it into a pocket.

"It's right here," the man said.

"Thanks, sorry for the trouble," Stone replied, turning into the men's room.

"No trouble."

Stone opened the men's room door and found another of Ippolito's party standing at one of the two urinals; he took his position at the other one. The man ignored him, in the way of strangers standing at urinals. Stone washed his hands and went back to his table.

"So?"

"I got caught in a storeroom," he said.

"Drink your coffee, and let's get out of here," Betty said under her breath.

Stone sipped his espresso, then dug into his jacket pocket. "I found something, though." He held it up for her to see.

"A matchbook? Congratulations, you've won the California lottery."

"But look where it's from."

She didn't look. "Tell me."

"It's a matchbook from Elaine's," he said.

"Can we get out of here now?"

They were driving back to the Bel-Air with the top down, enjoying the desert air.

"Elaine's in New York?" she asked.

"Right. Arrington and I spent a lot of time there; she used to steal matches by the handful."

"I guess finding one at Grimaldi's is a little too much of a coincidence, then?"

"Yes, especially since we know that Arrington called from the restaurant."

"No, we don't," she said.

"Why not?"

"Did you speak to her?"

"Well, no."

"Did she tell the hotel operator who she was?"

"No."

"Then all we know is that a woman called and left a message and said to put the initial 'A.' on it."

"You should have been a lawyer."

"You should be a better one."

"All right, all right."

"You know any other women whose names start with an 'A' and who've been to Elaine's?"

"Possibly; I can't think of any at the moment." He could think of two.

"What kind of food does Elaine's serve?"

"Italian."

"Any wiseguys ever go there?"

"All the time."

"So we don't know but that one of *them* dropped the matchbook in the storeroom."

"You'd make a fine lawyer but a lousy detective. Didn't you ever hear of a hunch?"

"I'm a woman."

"Oh yeah, I forgot."

Her hand wandered onto his thigh. "I guess I'm going to have to reimpress you with the fact." She began unzipping his fly.

"Uh, Betty, can we wait a few minutes?" They were on the freeway now.

"I'm an impatient woman," she said, freeing him.

"Jesus," he breathed as she arranged herself with her head in his lap.

I'm driving up the freeway, he thought, *and...* he made a noise... *and I hope the cops don't pull us over.* He kept to the speed limit as best he could, under the circumstances.

13

Stone got to the studio on time the following morning, but he was tired; between Betty's attentions and thinking about the events of the night before, he hadn't gotten a lot of sleep. He was in the makeup chair when the assistant director came in.

"Morning, Stone; good news: so you've only one more scene to shoot."

"I thought I was working for four days," Stone said, surprised.

"They've done some doctoring for time on the script, so you've just got one scene left—your closing statement to the jury, then a quick pickup to get your reaction when the verdict comes in."

"Whatever you say," Stone said, picking up his script. He thought he knew the speech, but he hadn't expected to give it today; by the time he was dressed and on the set, though, he felt ready. Vance was nowhere to be seen, but since the scene was Stone's alone he was not surprised. He rehearsed the scene once, then did a take.

"Cut, print," the director said. "That was great, Stone, now let's get your reaction to the verdict."

Surprised, Stone sat down at the prosecution table and tried to look pissed off when the bailiff read the verdict.

"That's a wrap for Stone," the director said. He came over, shook Stone's hand, and thanked him for his work. "I'll send you a videotape when we're done. Take care."

Stone stood up; it was not yet ten o'clock. Vance came onto the set and strode toward him, smiling, his hand out. "I hear you were great," he said, then, still holding Stone's hand, he pulled him to a corner of the court set. "Great news," he said. "Arrington called last night."

"What did she have to say?" Stone asked.

"Everything is all right. She had been worried about my reaction to having a child, and she just needed a few days alone."

"Where has she been?"

"Staying with a friend out in the Valley."

"So she's home?"

"She will be in a day or two. She's helping her friend with some personal problem."

"Well, I'm relieved to hear that, Vance. She apparently tried to call me last night, but I wasn't in at the time."

"Yes, she mentioned that; she was embarrassed that you'd made a trip out here for nothing, and she wanted to apologize. She sends her love." He clapped Stone on the shoulder. "Well, old man, thanks for everything; we'll call you when we're in New York. Oh, Betty will take you to the airport." He clapped Stone on the shoulder again and went to take his place on the set.

Stone stood there, puzzled. Betty walked up.

"Your plane leaves in an hour and a half," she said, handing him a ticket. "I'm afraid the Centurion jet wasn't available; you'll have to make do with first class."

"I guess I can stand that," Stone replied.

"And here," she said, handing him an envelope, "is your paycheck; don't spend it all in one place. Oh, and Mr. Regenstein said to keep the clothes—a personal gift from him."

"That's very kind of him."

"Come on, let's get to your dressing room and get that makeup off."

As they left the set he saw a man standing at the rear wearing a suit identical to his own. He hadn't been aware that he'd had a stand-in. He followed Betty to his RV, where he found the wardrobe lady packing the suits and shirts he had worn in the film into a handsome, old-fashioned leather suitcase. He gave her the suit he was wearing and started rubbing on cold cream. Ten minutes later, they were on the way to the airport, with Betty at the wheel of Stone's temporary car, Vance's Mercedes SL600. Stone turned in his studio pass at the front gate, and soon they were on the freeway.

"I have to pick up my clothes at the Bel-Air," he said.

"They're in the trunk; the hotel packed for you," she said. "You know, I think the very least you could do would be to return the favor of last night. Loving and leaving a girl, as you are."

Stone laughed. "I'd be delighted, but not on the freeway. You have no idea how close we came to death last night. You'll have to come and see me in New York."

"Maybe," she said.

They were quiet for a while as they zipped along in moderate traffic. "Betty," he said as they neared the airport, "what's going on?"

"Going on?" she asked innocently. "I can't imagine what you mean."

"I mean why am I being rushed out of L.A.?"

"Rushed?"

"Rushed. And after the big push to get me to act in Vance's movie, why was there an actor on the set wearing the same suit as mine?"

She glanced at him. "You're very observant."

He thought he noticed a hint of a blush. "So?"

She pulled up at the airport setdown. "So, I don't know *what's* going on. I honestly don't."

"Vance said Arrington called him last night, and that she's fine."

"I have no reason not to believe that," she said.

"Let's rewind for a moment. What time did you leave me this morning? I was dead asleep."

"Around five."

"And what time did you speak to Vance?"

"Not until I got to the office."

"Did you speak to anybody else?"

"Is this a cross-examination?"

"Yes. Did you speak to anyone else?"

She looked at her lap. "I got a call," she said.

"From whom?"

"All right, it was Vance."

"What was the substance of your conversation?"

"It doesn't matter."

"Did he ask you why we were at Grimaldi's last night?"

"Yes," she said with reluctance.

"Did you tell him?"

"Yes." She looked at him. "Stone, I've told you that my loyalty to Vance is complete."

"I believe that. Do you really believe you're acting in his best interests?"

"Do you think I'm not?"

"I think that something is terribly wrong here, and that I might be able to help, if I'm allowed to."

"Vance doesn't seem to want any help."

"Don't you think he needs it?"

She shrugged. "Maybe, but..."

"I know you're in a tough spot, but you've got a decision to make. I wouldn't want either Arrington or Vance to get hurt because you make a mistake."

She reached over, took hold of his necktie,

and pulled him toward her. "I would *kill* to help that man."

"I don't think that will be necessary," Stone said, disentangling his tie from her grip, "but could you act against his wishes if you thought it would help him?"

She thought about that. "Probably," she said.

"Then let's get out of here."

"I'm supposed to call after I've seen you get on the airplane."

"So, call."

She reached into her purse and produced a card and a key. "Here's my home address and the key; the alarm code is four-one-one-four. Repeat that."

"Four-one-one-four," he said.

"Go into the terminal, rent a car, and go to my house. I'll be home around seven, and we can talk."

Stone smiled and kissed her. "You're doing the right thing," he said.

"I hope to God I am," she replied, "or I'm going to be in a lot of trouble."

14

Stone was feeling flush, what with a check for twenty-five thousand dollars in his pocket, so he asked the rental car agent for a Mercedes. After half an hour's wait, he was picked up and driven to the agency's Beverly Hills location, where he was given a choice of a dozen luxury cars, including a Rolls-Royce.

He chose a Mercedes SL500, which had a smaller engine than he had grown accustomed to but would do in a pinch.

Using the supplied map, he found his way to Betty's house, which was on a quiet street south of Wilshire Boulevard in Beverly Hills, near Neiman-Marcus. He let himself into the house, tapped in the alarm code, and left his luggage, including his elegant new suitcase, by the stairs. He thought the house probably dated from the thirties, but it had been renovated in striking fashion and was handsomely furnished. Apparently there was good money in working for movie stars.

He checked the refrigerator and found the makings of a sandwich, along with a lot more food, and had some lunch, then he found his way upstairs, hung up his clothes, and collapsed on Betty's king-sized bed. It was after six when he awoke.

He went back downstairs, checked the fridge again, and looked through the cabinets, then started making dinner. At a quarter past seven he heard the front door open, and Betty walked into the kitchen.

"Jesus, it smells good in here," she said. "What are you making?"

"Just some pasta; would you like a glass of your wine?"

"Thank you, yessir."

He poured her a glass of chardonnay. "So how was the rest of your day?"

"Weird. I'm unaccustomed to keeping things from Vance."

"I appreciate your helping me."

"As long as I'm helping Vance, too."

He got dinner onto the kitchen table, and they sat down.

"This is delicious!" she said. "I don't know why I would have wanted the chef from Grimaldi's, when I could have you."

"Anytime," Stone said, raising his glass.

"I'll drink to that."

"Why don't you bring me up to date on what you know so far? Start when Arrington disappeared."

"I didn't know she had disappeared," Betty said. "Vance came into the office and said she had to go back to Virginia to see her folks about some family matter. I got her a round-trip ticket to Dulles and sent it over to the house. I assumed she made the plane."

"Was there anything in Vance's behavior that was different from the way he usually is?"

"He seemed preoccupied, I suppose, starting that day. I had to tell him things two or three times before he'd remember them. That was about it."

"Had he ever been that way before?"

"Yes, I suppose he had, when he'd had something on his mind. Vance tells me a lot, but he doesn't tell me everything, and usually I don't ask."

"Did he get any unusual phone calls around that time?"

"What do you mean by 'unusual'?"

"Any calls that frightened him or made him angry?"

"Vance is an actor, and like most actors he's always acting. He doesn't give away much."

"Not even to you?"

"Sometimes, not often."

"Did he repeatedly get calls from the same person?"

She thought about that. "I remember, the day after Arrington left, Lou Regenstein called him several times over the afternoon, but that's not really unusual. They do a lot of business together, and they're very close."

"Any calls from David Sturmack?"

"Not that I recall, but that wouldn't have been unusual, either."

"Any from Onofrio Ippolito?"

"That's a name I had never even heard until Vance gave me an invitation list for the dinner party with his name on it. Although I noticed him at the party, I didn't put a face to the name until we saw him at Grimaldi's."

"So Vance and Ippolito aren't friends and haven't done business?"

"Not that I'm aware of, and there isn't much in Vance's life that I'm not aware of."

"Let me ask you something else: from my perspective, Vance seems to have a seamlessly successful life—he's handsome, rich, at the top of his career, married to a wonderful woman, and has the esteem of everyone he knows and millions that he doesn't."

"That's a pretty fair assessment, I guess."

"What are his weaknesses?"

"Personal? Business?"

"Both."

"Well, on a personal level, he's not as good a lover as you are."

Stone laughed. "I'm flattered. So, you've had an affair with Vance?"

"I wouldn't go so far as to call it that. Vance has probably slept with very nearly every woman he knows, at least once."

"So how often did you sleep with him?"

"Now you're straying into my personal life."

"You're right; I'm sorry."

"An even dozen times," she said. "I counted."

"Why did you stop?"

"He stopped. It was his call."

"Why his call?"

"Because he's a movie star."

"And that's more than just a man?"

"In this town, it is. You don't know anything about movie stars, do you?"

"No; Vance is the only one I've ever had a conversation with."

"Let me tell you about movie stars."

"Shoot."

"There are several kinds of power in this town: the most important is the power to get a movie made. After that, there's personal influence, wealth, beauty, sexual magnetism, and, finally, the power to tell anybody in town to go fuck himself and that person has to go fuck himself. Vance is one of the very few people in town who has every one of those powers—in spades. Not even men like Lou Regenstein and David Sturmack have every one of those.

92

"Movie stars are centered on themselves in a way that ordinary mortals can't begin to grasp. Friends, wives, children—all those people come second to The Career, which means the movie star. The star can feel that way about himself without a trace of guilt or doubt, because he knows that everything depends on The Career—which friends he has, the support and protection of the wife and children. Therefore, any decision that must be made is made on that basis—'Will this action react to my benefit?' I'm not speaking of momentous decisions, I'm speaking of any decision. 'Where shall I have dinner tonight,' for instance, translates into 'Where will I be seen, be shown off to the maximum benefit for me?'"

"You're perfectly serious?" Stone asked.

"Perfectly. And if small decisions are made this way—the relative warmth of a greeting, where to park the car, when to go to the men's room—then you can imagine how much effort goes into a major decision, such as which movie to appear in. A movie star's first question to himself when he's presented with a script is 'How will this script advance my career?'"

"That's not unreasonable, I suppose."

"Of course not. Anything is reasonable that promotes the career. That's why, when a movie star gets a script, strange things happen to it: scenes written for other actors are suddenly rewritten for the star; a single word the star likes is taken from another actor and given to him; producers and directors are hired or fired; some supporting actors get closeups, others don't; his whole wardrobe for a film disappears into his closet. By the way, you've already gotten that one down pat."

Stone laughed.

"Are you beginning to hear what I'm telling you?"

"I think so. If a movie star's wife disappears, his first reaction is to worry about the tabloids finding out."

"You're a quick study, buddy."

"And every other action he takes with regard to her disappearance is predicated on protecting himself."

"You've just earned your Ph.D. in Hollywood, pal."

15

Stone woke without a left arm. The bed was dappled by the sun, his chest was covered in long red hair, and his left arm was gone. It took him a moment to realize that Betty was lying on it. Gently, he disengaged the arm, flexing his fingers to get the blood going.

"What time is it?" she asked without moving.

Stone lifted his head and spotted a bedside clock. "Ten minutes past six."

"Oh, God, I don't even have time to molest you," she moaned.

"You sure?"

She struggled out of bed, sweeping her hair out of her face. "I should be on the way to the studio in twenty minutes!" She disappeared into the bathroom, and Stone heard the shower running. He lay on his back, staring at the shadows on the ceiling. He felt remarkably well, considering. This girl was awfully nice, and he liked her no-nonsense attitude about sex. He got out of bed, slipped into a pair of shorts, went down to the kitchen, and started making coffee. When she came down the stairs, dressed, he handed her a cup. "Can I make you some breakfast?"

"Ooooh," she breathed, "every girl's dream, and I have to go to work!" She poured her coffee into a Thermos cup. "Listen, don't call me at any number but this one." She scribbled it on the back of her card. "That one doesn't ring anywhere but on my desk, and if anybody but me answers, hang up. Where are you going to be today?"

"I still have to figure that out." He took her pen and another card. "This is my cell phone number; it's a New York exchange, but you can still call me on it. Maybe I'll get an L.A. number, just to make things simpler."

"Don't park your car in my driveway; I don't want it noticed. Find a spot on the street; it won't be hard."

"Okay."

"What do you need from me today?"

"For the moment, just assume that there's something very wrong about Arrington's absence, and keep an ear out for anything that might confirm that or give us any other information we can use."

"My beeper number is on the card; if you can't reach me in the office, use that, and I'll get right back to you."

"Good idea."

She gave him a lascivious kiss and ran for the door, pausing on the front steps to toss two newspapers at him, then she was gone.

Stone toasted a muffin, had some juice and coffee, and read both the *New York Times* and the *L.A. Times*. That ritual behind him, he went upstairs, showered and shaved, got dressed, then went into Betty's study, sat down at her desk and began to think. Finally, he called Dino.

"Lieutenant Bacchetti."

"Hi, it's Stone."

"Hi, buddy; are you back?"

"Nope, I'm going to be here for a while longer."

"What's going on?"

"It's a very long story, and you wouldn't believe some of it."

"Try me."

Stone gave him a rundown on his activities since arriving in L.A.

"Very weird," Dino said. "What was that Italian name again?"

"Ippolito?"

"Yeah, that sounds familiar. There was a guy by that name a long time ago that was with Luciano, I think."

"Couldn't be the same guy; maybe a relative?"

"Let me see what I can find out."

"Okay, but before you do that, I need some local help on the ground here. You remember when we extradited the fat wiseguy from L.A. a few years back?"

"I'll never forget the plane ride back."

"What was the L.A. cop's name who turned him over to us? He was something to do with an organized crime unit or something."

"Yeah, you're right. It was... wait a minute... ah, some whitebread name... Grant?"

"Richard Grant, that's it."

"Yeah, he seemed okay."

"I'll call him."

"What hotel are you at? I'll call you when I get something on Ippolito."

"I'm at the nicest hotel you ever saw, and with the best maid service."

"Already? You're disgusting."

Stone gave him the number. "If there's no answer, don't leave a message; call me on my pocket phone."

"It works out there?"

"We'll find out."

"See you."

Stone hung up and called LAPD headquarters. "Hello, I'm trying to reach a detective named Richard Grant; can you tell me where he's stationed?"

"He's here at headquarters, sir; I'll connect you."

The phone rang. "Detective Grant."

"Rick? This is Stone Barrington, late of the NYPD; my partner, Dino Bacchetti, and I took a bad guy off your hands a few years ago."

"Yeah, Stone, I remember. You said 'late'?"

"I retired a couple of years back."

"What's up in the Big Apple?"

"Actually, I'm in L.A., and I wondered if you'd like to do a little moonlighting?"

"I'm afraid that sort of thing is not done these days, but you can buy me lunch."

"Tell me where and when."

"You remember the old Bistro Garden, on Canon Drive?"

"Nope; I'm a stranger here."

Grant gave him the address. "It's called Spago Beverly Hills now. See you there at twelve-thirty; I'll book the table."

"You're on, and I'm buying."

"Right. Bye."

Stone hung up and called Betty's office number.

"Hello?"

"It's your guest; can you talk?"

"Make it fast."

"What kind of car does Arrington drive?"

"A twin to Vance's Mercedes—the one you were driving—except it's white."

"What year?"

"Brand new."

"You wouldn't happen to know the license number?"

"It's a vanity plate." She spelled it for him: "ARINGTN."

"Thanks, that's it."

"Bye."

"What time tonight?"

"Around seven; I'll call if I'm going to be later." She hung up.

Stone called Bill Eggers.

"You still in L.A.?"

"Yeah. You said you knew an old-timer with mob connections who liked to talk?"

"Right."

"Call him and ask if he ever knew a guy named Ippolito who worked for Charlie Luciano."

"You're still hung up on this Ippolito guy?"

"Yep."

"Okay."

"Ask him if the guy had a son in the family business, too."

"Okay; where can I reach you?"

"Try my cell phone; I'll be moving around."

"It'll be after lunch, my time."

"That's fine."

Stone hung up, then checked in with his secretary. He left for lunch with precious little to go on and no cooperation from the injured party, the husband. Unless one of his phone calls paid off, he was back to square one.

16

Stone gave his car to the valet and strolled into Spago Beverly Hills. He was shown to a table in the garden, where he ordered a mineral water. The place was already full, and he spotted a number of familiar faces from films and television, then he saw Rick Grant coming toward him. The cop was grayer and heavier but otherwise much the same as Stone remembered.

"How are you, Stone?" Grant said, extending a hand.

"Not bad, Rick; you?"

"Getting by."

"You're at headquarters now?"

"Yeah, I've got soft duty as a deputy to the chief of detectives."

"Administrative stuff?"

"More like consulting on various cases. Right now I'm writing a long report on the state of organized crime in L.A., that being my old specialty."

"That's very interesting," Stone said. "Why don't we order?"

They chatted amiably while their food was served.

"What was that about moonlighting?" Grant finally asked.

"I need some local knowledge and, maybe, influence on something I'm working on. I'm sorry you're not available."

"I didn't say that; I said that the department

frowns on it. It didn't seem like a good idea to talk about it on the phone. What's involved?"

"Five hundred a day; I'm not sure for how long, but it's cash, and I'm not going to issue a 1099 to the IRS at the end of the year."

"That's nice, but I meant, what is it, exactly, you need?"

"Advice; intelligence; absolute discretion; maybe an occasional flash of the badge."

"Tell me about the problem."

"A friend of mine has disappeared; her husband called me a few days ago and asked me to come out here and find her."

"Domestic thing?"

"I thought so at first; I don't now."

"What changed your mind?"

"As soon as I got here everybody, and I mean *everybody*, the husband knows went to a great deal of trouble to distract me from the problem. Then the husband told me he had heard from his wife, that she was fine, and I was hustled out of town."

"But you're still here."

"I didn't like being hustled. Also, I had two phone messages from the lady, and my hotel's caller ID made them from a restaurant called Grimaldi's."

Grant's eyebrows shot up. "I know that place, or used to."

"I thought you might." Stone told Grant about his visit to the restaurant and finding the matchbook in the storeroom.

"Sounds like the lady's leaving a trail of crumbs."

"It does, doesn't it? I can't go any farther with this without telling you who these people are, so I need to know if you're in."

"Tell me who they are, and I'll tell you if I'm in."

"The husband is Vance Calder."

Grant put down his fork and leaned back in his chair. "Holy shit," he said.

"That about sums it up. His wife and I used to be... close, in New York. She went off to do a magazine piece on Calder and ended up marrying him."

"So why didn't Calder call us?"

"He's terrified of the publicity, especially the tabloids. I think he's led pretty much of a charmed existence with the press, and he doesn't want that to change."

"But it's his *wife*."

"Yeah."

Grant shook his head. "I haven't had all that much contact with the showbiz community," he said, "but these people never cease to amaze me. They think they're operating on a nearby planet of their own, where they call all the shots and nobody else matters."

"From what I've heard, that's how it was in the twenties and thirties, when the studios were big."

"I guess so, and maybe it's still like that a little, but it rubs me the wrong way."

"I can understand that, but it's not my purpose here to drag these people and their friends down to earth; I just want to find the lady and talk to her."

"Talk to her? Not reunite her with her husband?"

Stone shrugged. "If absolutely necessary."

"You still want her?"

Stone looked at his plate. This was the question he had been avoiding asking himself. "I want to know if *she* still wants *me*, after... all that's happened."

"But you don't *know* what's happened."

"That's right, and I want to find out."

"Well, on the face of it—I mean if Calder walked into the cop shop and I caught it—I'd read it as a purely domestic matter."

"It may be, but I doubt it."

"You could be right; it's the Grimaldi's connection that intrigues me. I doubt if that joint is even in the phone book; it's not the sort of place a movie star's wife would wander into."

"That's how it struck me; it looked like half a dozen New York wiseguy hangouts I've seen."

"Is there anything else about this that smells like mob?"

"There's a guy named David Sturmack."

Grant blinked. "He's the mayor's favorite golf partner. Once I had to deliver an envelope to hizzoner at the Bel-Air Country Club, and he introduced me to Sturmack."

"What else do you know about him?" Stone asked.

"That he's a big-time fixer. There were rumors a while back about mob connections, through the unions, I think. He seemed to have an in with the Teamsters."

"You know any more details about that?"

"No. By the time I was on that particular job, Sturmack had faded into some pretty expensive woodwork. His name used to come up in subtle ways, but I never knew of any hard connection between him and anybody who was mobbed up. I'd say he's at the pinnacle of respectability now, or the mayor wouldn't be seen with him. The mayor's a squeaky-clean guy."

"I'll tell you what I know: Sturmack's old man was with Meyer Lansky way back when. Young David grew up amongst the boys, knew them all, apparently."

Grant smiled. "No kidding? The family business, huh? Now you mention it, I seem to remember a rumor of a connection between Sturmack and the Teamsters pension fund, which bankrolled half the construction in Vegas when the boys were in charge."

"Sounds right."

"But I can't think why Sturmack would have somebody's wife disappeared; even if the rumors are true, that wouldn't be his style, not at all."

"Time to tell me if you're in, Rick."

Grant smiled. "Sure, I'm in; what's more, I'm intrigued. What do you want me to do?"

"Can you get the lady's car on the patrol sheet without listing it as stolen?"

"Probably."

"It's a new white Mercedes SL600, California vanity plate, ARINGTN." He spelled it, and

104

Grant wrote it down. "The lady's name is Arrington Carter Calder; it'll be registered either to her or her husband, I guess."

"Maybe not; a lot of these people drive cars registered to their production companies. Why don't you want it listed as stolen?"

"I don't want it pulled over; I just want to know where it is, if it's anywhere, and I'd like a description of whoever's driving it."

"Okay, I'll specify position reports and descriptions only, and directly to me."

They ordered coffee, and Stone asked for a check. "There's another name; see if it rings a bell."

"Who's that?"

"Onofrio Ippolito."

Grant laughed. "Jesus, Stone, you're really in high cotton here, you know?"

"Am I?"

"Ippolito is the CEO of the Safe Harbor Bank."

"Big outfit?"

"Dozens of branches, all over, ads on television, lots of charity sponsorship, the works."

"No mob connections?"

Grant shook his head. "Ippolito is the mayor's personal banker."

"Yeah? Well, I saw him at Grimaldi's with some guys who didn't look like branch managers."

Rick Grant sat like stone, his face without expression.

"Rick?"

Grant moved. "Huh?"

"You still in?"

Grant shrugged. "What the hell."

17

While they waited for the valet to bring their cars, Stone pressed five hundred-dollar bills into Rick Grant's hand. "It's all I've got on me at the moment."

Grant pocketed the money without looking at it. "Arrington's car will be on the patrol list in an hour; how do I get in touch with you?"

Stone gave him a business card, writing the portable number on the back. "Is it safe for me to call you at the office?"

"As long as you're careful. If I say I can't talk, call back in an hour, or leave a message, and I'll call you back. Use the name Jack Smith." Grant's car arrived, and he got in and drove away.

After the payment to Grant, Stone was low on cash. "Where's the nearest bank?" he asked the valet.

"Right across the street," the man said.

Stone looked up and saw a lighthouse painted on the window. "Safe Harbor Bank," the sign read. He took his Centurion paycheck from his pocket and looked at it; it was drawn on Safe Harbor.

"Hold my car for a few minutes, will you?" he asked.

"Sure."

Dodging traffic, Stone walked across the street and entered the bank. There was another lighthouse high on a wall, and a nautical motif. A large ship's clock behind the tellers chimed the hour. He walked to a teller's window and presented the check. "I'd like to cash this, please."

The teller looked at the check and handed it back to him. "For a check of this size you'll have to get Mr. Marshall's approval," she said, pointing to an office behind a row of desks. "See his secretary, there," she said, pointing to a woman.

"Thank you." Stone walked to the secretary's desk. "I'd like to see Mr. Marshall, please, about getting approval to cash a check."

"Your name?"

"Barrington."

"Just a moment." She dialed a number, spoke briefly, and hung up. "Go in, please," she said, pointing at the office door, which was open.

Stone rapped lightly on the door and entered. "Mr. Marshall?"

"Mr. Barrington," the man said, rising and offering his hand. "Please have a seat; what can I do for you?"

Stone handed him the check and sat down. "I'd like to cash this," he said.

Marshall examined the check. "Do you have some identification?" he asked.

Stone handed over his New York driver's license.

Marshall looked at Stone's photograph,

compared it with the original face, wrote the license number on the back of the check and handed it back. "May I ask how you happen to have a check on the account of Centurion Studios for twenty-five thousand dollars?"

"It's a paycheck; I had a role in a Centurion film this week."

"Ah, an actor."

Stone didn't disabuse him of the notion. "I live in New York, you see; I'm just out here for the job."

"Can we open an account for you? That's a lot of cash to be walking around with."

"No, I'm going back to New York shortly, but you're right, it is a lot of money. Why don't you give me a cashier's check for fifteen thousand, and the rest in hundreds?"

"As you wish." He buzzed for his secretary, then signed a form and handed it to her. "Have a cashier's check drawn in that amount, please, payable to Mr. Stone Barrington, and bring me that and ten thousand dollars in hundreds." He turned the check over. "You'll need to endorse it," he said to Stone.

Stone signed the check and sat back to wait for his money. "You've a handsome bank here," he said.

"Thank you; all of our offices are designed with something of the nautical in them. Mr. Ippolito is something of a yachtsman."

"Mr. Ippolito?"

"Our chairman," Marshall replied.

"What does he sail?"

"He has a small armada," the bank manager

said. "A large sailing yacht, a large motor yacht, a sports fisherman, and several run-abouts."

"Business must be good," Stone said.

"Oh, yes; we're the fastest-growing bank in Southern California. We've got fourteen offices in the greater L.A. and San Diego areas, and by this time next year we'll have closer to twenty. We're expanding into San Francisco."

"Might you have a copy of your most recent annual report?" Stone asked. "I'm going to need to invest some of this paycheck."

"Of course," Marshall replied. He reached into a cabinet next to his desk and produced a thick, handsomely designed brochure.

"Thank you," Stone said. "I'll read myself to sleep tonight."

"I think you'll find us a good investment; our stock has doubled in the past two years."

"Sounds interesting," Stone said.

The secretary returned with the cashier's check and Stone's cash. Marshall signed the check with a flourish and handed it over, along with a thick stack of hundreds, held together with a paper band. "Better count it," he said.

Stone stood up and tucked the check and the cash into his inside pockets. "I trust you, Mr. Marshall," he said. "Thanks very much for your help."

They shook hands, and Stone left the building. He didn't know a hell of a lot about banking, he thought as he crossed the street to his waiting car, but Safe Harbor seemed to be growing by leaps and bounds. He wondered what was fueling the growth.

Once in the car, he opened the annual report and flipped through it, stopping at a list of the bank's officers. Ippolito was indeed chairman, and Louis Regenstein and David Sturmack were listed as directors. His portable phone rang.

He dug the little Motorola StarTac from an inside pocket and flipped it open. "Stone Barrington."

"It's Rick Grant. I've got a report on Arrington's car."

"That was fast. Where was it spotted?"

"Driving away from Spago Beverly Hills less than five minutes ago."

"Jesus!" Stone said. "I'll get back to you." He closed the phone, hopped out of the car, and ran to the valet. "Did a white Mercedes SL600 just leave here?"

"Yessir," the man said, "just a minute ago."

"Can you describe the driver?"

"You bet I can: she was tall, dark hair, late twenties or early thirties; a real looker."

"Did you see which way she went?"

"She turned left at the corner, toward Rodeo Drive."

"Thanks," Stone said, then jumped into his car. He gunned it, then made a left turn across two lanes of traffic, the sound of horns following him. A block ahead, the traffic light was turning green, and the white Mercedes was turning right on Rodeo.

Then there was the sound of a siren in his left ear, and a cop on a motorcycle pulled in front of him, lights flashing, and stopped. The cop got off and sauntered toward him, while Stone dug for his ID.

"Afternoon," the cop said, producing a ticket book. "In a terrible hurry, are we? License and registration, please."

Stone opened the small wallet and flashed his NYPD badge.

The cop took it and read the ID thoroughly. "Retired, huh? You look a little young for retirement."

"A bullet in the knee did the job."

"Now *that's* a lucky break, you still being alive and all. Makes for a nice pension, huh? Let's see your license and registration."

"Listen, I've *got* to catch up with a lady in a white SL600 that just turned into Rodeo Drive."

"You listen, ah..." he glanced at the ID, "...Detective Barrington. Did you happen to see the Rodney King videotape?"

Stone sighed. "Two or three hundred times," he said.

"Well, I heard that Mr. King was reluctant to show *his* license and registration, too."

Stone produced his driver's license and dug into the armrest compartment for his rental contract. "All right, all right," he said, handing them over.

The cop glanced at the license. "You take a very nice picture, Detective Barrington," he said.

"Could you just write me the ticket and let me be on my way?"

"Oh, it's a rental," he said, reading the contract. "Well, seeing how you're a brother officer and all, sort of, I'm going to let you go with a warning. Here's the warning; this is *not* New York City, and we frown on high-speed left turns."

"Thanks; in New York, the average speed is four miles an hour, and you can't turn left, ever."

The cop smiled appreciatively. "You'll have to go faster than that out here; we like our traffic to move, but not quite as fast as you were moving, okay?"

"Okay, and thanks," Stone said.

"Have a really nice day," the cop replied. He got on his motorcycle and moved out, stopping at the traffic light, which had just turned red.

Stone couldn't turn right with him sitting there, so he just sat and tapped his fingers on the wheel. When he finally turned onto Rodeo Drive, the SL600 was nowhere in sight, and fifteen minutes of searching the adjoining streets didn't turn it up, either. Stone drove disconsolately back to Betty's house.

18

Stone was wakened by a finger running lightly down his cheek. He tried to sit up, but a hand on his chest pressed him back down. He blinked and looked at the face above him.

"Don't get up; I like you in a horizontal position," Betty said.

"Oh, hi; I guess I fell asleep."

"Waiting anxiously for me to come home, huh?"

"What time is it?"

"A little after eight. I take it you're not cooking for me this evening."

"Why don't I take you out? You book us a table somewhere you like."

"Good idea; I'd like to change out of my working togs, too."

Stone went into the bathroom, threw some cold water on his face, and combed his hair, then got into one of his new Ralph Lauren Purple Label suits and went downstairs.

Betty came down in a little white dress, very short, and slipped a hand into his. "We've got a table at Maple Drive," she said. "That's a restaurant, as well as a street. Let's take your car; I hope you like jazz."

"You bet."

They had a table near the piano player, who was very good. "Dudley Moore and Tony Bill own this place," she said, sipping her drink. "Dudley comes and plays sometimes."

"Sorry I missed him; I like his piano. How was your day?"

"Long; they're still shooting on Stage Twelve, redoing your scenes, so we can be sure Vance won't turn up here. It's a favorite of his."

"I must have been pretty bad, huh?"

"Not in the least; I saw all your dailies, and you were very good indeed. I told you about the female reaction."

"So why would they go to all the trouble to get me to do that, then hire somebody to do it over?"

"The word on the lot is, the actor they wanted was unavailable, then suddenly he was available."

"Do you buy that?"

"It's not the first time it's happened."

"*I* don't buy it."

"Okay," she said, downing the rest of her martini, "what's your theory?"

"I think they were trying to keep me busy so I wouldn't be looking for Arrington."

"So they tie up a whole company and a soundstage filming you, just to keep you off the streets? That's not how the movie business works, Stone; they don't waste that kind of money."

"Are you kidding? From what I read in the papers, they waste a lot more than that on a lot of films, and for less reason."

"All right, I'll grant you that; I've just never seen Lou Regenstein do it. I think he *really* wanted the other actor. Can I have another martini?"

Stone signaled a waiter for another round; he brought the drinks, and they ordered dinner.

"Did Vance say anything about Arrington today?"

"He said she was still visiting her family in Virginia."

"Funny, he told me she was staying with a friend in the Valley."

"This is all so weird," she said.

"Did you pick up on anything helpful today?"

"He talked with both Lou Regenstein and David Sturmack this morning."

"Did you overhear any of it?"

"No."

"Hear anything about Ippolito?"

"Nothing."

"Don't mention that name to Vance."

"Okay. What did you find out today?"

"Well, I came within about a minute of seeing Arrington."

"Come again?"

"I had lunch with a cop friend, and he put out a bulletin on her car for me."

"Jesus, I hope Vance never finds out you went to the cops."

"This was all very informal, just a favor. Turns out Arrington was at the same restaurant—Spago Beverly Hills."

"And you didn't see her?"

"Nope; I went to a bank across the street to cash a check, and when I came back, I got a call from my cop friend that she had just left the restaurant. I tried to catch up, but a motorcycle cop pulled me over for a bad turn."

"So she's not in Virginia with her family, and she's not in the Valley, either?"

"Right. And she's not in the storeroom at Grimaldi's or at a table at Spago."

115

Betty shook her head. "This is all too much for me, after a martini and a half."

Dinner came, and they ate slowly, enjoying the very good food.

"Where are you from, originally?" Stone asked.

"A small town in Georgia called Delano," she replied.

"What brought you out here?"

"Fame and fortune; I wanted to be an actress. I even was an actress, for a while."

"Why didn't you keep at it?"

"I wasn't good enough, and I knew it. There were an awful lot of girls who were better than I who were out of work. If I'd kept it up I'd have ended up giving producers blow jobs for work, and I wanted to keep my private pleasures private."

Stone smiled. "How did you meet Vance?"

"I had a little part in one of his pictures; it wasn't much, but it kept me on the set for a month. Vance and I had our little fling, and I started helping him on the set—answering the phone, that sort of thing. He didn't like his secretary, so he offered me her job."

"Did you find it easy to give up acting?"

"Vance sat me down and talked to me like a Dutch uncle," she said. "He told me that I didn't have any sort of real career ahead of me, and when I thought about it, I realized he wasn't being cruel, he was right. I took the job and never looked back."

"You never married?"

"Nope. It doesn't appeal, really. I mean, I

couldn't get married and keep the job with Vance; he'd drive any husband to the wildest kind of jealousy; I'd be dead in a month."

Stone laughed. "I guess I'm a little jealous myself."

"Oh, no, you're not," she said. "You're just like me; you like your independence and take your sex where you find it. And you'd make a lousy husband."

"I would not!" Stone said. "I'd be a very good husband."

"Oh, come on, Stone; you're still in love with Arrington, but you're fucking me." She smiled. "Not that I'm complaining."

"What makes you think I'm still in love with Arrington?"

"A woman's intuition."

"Let's just say that Arrington and I never had the kind of closure we should have had. I'd have felt better if we'd had a fight and she'd walked out. And there are other reasons I'm..." He stopped himself.

"Not to pry, but what other reasons?"

"Don't pry."

"Oh, all right. I'll find out eventually anyway."

"Probably."

"Well," she said, putting down her fork, "that was an excellent dinner. Now would you take me home and do lascivious things to me?"

"Love to." Stone signaled for the check.

They pulled away from the restaurant, which was in a residential neighborhood, and as they did, Stone caught sight of another car pulling in behind them, halfway down the dark block. He thought nothing of it until after a couple of turns, when it was still there.

"I don't think we should go directly to your house," he said.

"Why not?"

"Not to get all dramatic, but I think we're being followed. Don't look back."

"Who would be following us?"

"I don't know, but I'd rather not have them follow us to your place." They crossed Santa Monica Boulevard and drove up Beverly Drive. "Is there such a thing as a cab stand in this town?" he asked.

"The Beverly Hills Hotel is a few blocks ahead."

"That'll do. Why don't you take the scarf you're wearing and put it on your head, just to hide the red hair."

She did as instructed.

They crossed Sunset Boulevard and turned into the driveway of the hotel. "Okay, here's what we do; there's only one car and they can't follow us both. I'm going to drop you at the entrance to the hotel. You go inside, use the ladies' room, then get a cab and go straight home. I think the car will stick with me; I'll lose him and turn up at your place later."

"Whatever you say," she said as they pulled under the hotel's portico. "I'm off." She jumped out of the car and ran inside the lobby.

Stone drove straight through the hotel drive, and his tail picked him up again on

118

Sunset. He caught a glimpse of the car under a street light; it was a Lincoln town car. He devoted himself to losing it.

19

It was late now, and there wasn't a lot of traffic on Sunset. Stone drove quickly along the winding road, up and down hills. When he reached the freeway he turned south toward the Pacific; the Lincoln stuck with him, a discreet distance back. Stone turned onto the Santa Monica Freeway, then onto Santa Monica Boulevard, driving right down to the beach. He turned left and, glancing at the rental agency's map, saw he was headed for Venice. The Lincoln had closed to within half a dozen car lengths, which bothered him. Apparently his pursuers didn't care if he knew they were following him.

He was on a broad street that was nearly empty of traffic, and he began to get annoyed, so he decided to do something he'd been taught years before in a police driving school. He checked his mirrors for traffic, then stomped on the emergency brake, locking the rear wheels, and spun the steering wheel to the left. The car traded ends, then he released the emergency brake and stood on the accelerator. The car behaved impeccably, its three-hundred-plus horses rocketing its small mass back down the street.

The Lincoln blew past in the opposite direction and, simultaneously, the two men in the front seat raised their left hands, blocking his view of their faces, as if they were accustomed to doing it. A moment later, Stone checked his rearview mirror; the Lincoln was behind him again. Still, the driver made no effort to overtake him or close the distance between them.

Using his map, Stone worked his way back toward Beverly Hills, taking care to keep to wide, brightly lit streets. He was *not* going to lead his tail down any dark alleys. He found himself on Wilshire Boulevard, now only a dozen blocks from Betty's house, and he saw something ahead that looked very inviting. A block short of the Beverly Wilshire Hotel, a cop car had pulled over a driver, his patrol car parked behind the car he had stopped, the lights flashing, and he was now leaning on the car, talking to the driver. Stone pulled up next to the cop. "Excuse me, officer, can you direct me to the Beverly Wilshire Hotel?" he asked. The Lincoln drove past him, not slowing down.

"Just up ahead, sir," the cop said politely.

Stone reflected that a New York City cop would have responded differently to a stupid question. "Thanks very much," he said, then drove on. He took his next right, figuring that the Lincoln was going around the block, and then he saw the Beverly Wilshire's garage. He whipped into the entrance, took a ticket from the machine, made two quick rights and parked the car. He took the elevator to the lobby, walked to the front door, and looked outside. A single cab was waiting out front. He checked up and down Wilshire, then ran to the cab and hopped in, waking the driver.

"What?" the man said, sitting up.

"Sorry to disturb you." He gave the man Betty's address, then hunkered down in the seat.

"That's only a few blocks from here," the driver said wearily.

"Let's call it an airport run," Stone replied.

The cab pulled away from the curb and Stone watched as the Lincoln drove past in the opposite direction. This time he got a better look at the driver. He had last seen him standing at a neighboring urinal, he remembered.

The cab was on Betty's street in two minutes. "Drive slowly down to the next corner," Stone said.

"The address you gave me is in the middle of the block," the driver said.

"Just do it, okay?"

"Yeah, yeah, sure." He muttered something under his breath.

"All right, stop here." Stone looked up and down the street, gave the man twenty dollars, got out of the cab, and looked around again. He had the block to himself. He walked quickly to Betty's house, half expecting the Lincoln to beat him there, let himself in, and went upstairs.

"Stone?" Betty called from the bedroom.

"Yeah, it's me." He walked down the hall, shucking his jacket, and into the bedroom. Betty was sitting up in bed, naked.

"Where have you been?"

"It took me longer than I thought to shake the other car." He got out of his clothes and into bed.

"You sure you don't have another girl stashed someplace?"

"Positive," he said, kissing her.

"I've been waiting up for you," she said, running a finger up the inside of his thigh.

"Why, whatever for?" he asked.

She showed him.

Betty was already dressed for work when Stone woke up. "Now," she said, sitting on the edge of the bed. "What was all that about last night?"

"Don't you remember doing it?"

"Not *that*. I mean, that thing with the car following us."

"I don't know, but I recognized the driver; he was with Ippolito at Grimaldi's. I saw him up close, in the men's room."

"Are you and I in any kind of trouble?" she asked.

"What kind of trouble could we be in?"

"Do you think the car followed us from here to the restaurant?"

"No, it was still daylight then; I'd have noticed. They picked us up at the restaurant."

"How'd they know we were there?"

"Did you see anybody you knew at dinner?"

She shook her head. "No."

"Somebody saw us there."

"Somebody who knows Ippolito?"

"Yeah."

"This is very creepy, Stone."

"I know. Look, we have to assume that if Ippolito knows, then probably Regenstein and Sturmack know, too."

"And that means that Vance knows."

"Maybe. I think you have to be ready for that."

"What can I say to him?"

"Say that you dropped me at the airport, and that you thought I left. Then I turned up at your door last night and took you to dinner. It's the only time we've been out together since I was supposed to have left town. Grimaldi's was before that. And we never discussed Arrington."

"Then what, after dinner?"

"That I dropped you at the Beverly Hills Hotel and told you to get a cab home, and you haven't seen me since. I think you can be pissed off at having been treated that way."

"Okay."

"In fact, why don't you spill that to Vance at the first opportunity; don't wait for him to hear about it from somebody else. There's no reason why you shouldn't have gone out with me, after all."

"I guess not. So why didn't you leave for New York when I thought you did? I'd better have a reason."

"Say that I said I had some personal business to take care of, and I said I was leaving L.A. today."

"Suppose he calls you in New York, and you're not there?"

"That won't be your fault. I think I'd better move into a hotel today; it can't be good for you to have me staying here, now that we've been seen together. Can you recommend someplace quiet?"

"There's a place in West Hollywood called Le Parc, a suite hotel. It's the kind of place where the studio puts visiting writers. Neither Vance nor any of his friends would ever be seen there." She looked up the address in the phone book and wrote it down for him.

"I'll use the name Jack Smith, if you need to reach me."

"Why Jack Smith?"

"My cop friend, Rick Grant, suggested it."

"Okay. Can I reach you tonight?"

"Let's skip a night. See if anybody follows you to or from work. If the coast seems clear, then we can get together tomorrow, for the weekend."

"Okay, my sweet. Hang onto the key to my house, just in case you need a bolthole."

"I'll do that."

She gave him a big kiss and left.

Stone got up, laid out his clothes for the day, and packed everything else, then shaved and got into a shower. He had just turned off the water and stepped out when he heard the front door of the house open and someone enter. More than one, he thought, and male. He could hear their voices. It was one thing, he thought, to be followed on well-lit city streets, but it was another to be caught alone in this house. He started grabbing at clothes.

20

Stone quickly got some clothes on, rearranged the bed to make it look as though only one person had slept in it, and grabbed his bags. He looked out the window, but he was on the second story, and it was a straight drop. He could hear the voices downstairs better now; they seemed to be coming from Betty's study.

Carrying his bags, he looked out into the upstairs hallway; a dozen feet down the hall was a pair of slatted bifold doors. He tiptoed down the carpet, set down his suitcases, and very slowly opened the doors. He was greeted with the sight of a washer and dryer, which took up almost the whole of the closet. Carefully, taking care to make no noise, he set his cases on top of the washer, then hoisted himself into a sitting position on the dryer and slowly closed the doors. He could hear footsteps coming up the stairs now, and he looked around the closet, dimly lit by light coming through the slatted doors, and found an iron. He held it at shoulder height and waited to be discovered. At least one of them was going to get his forehead ironed, he swore to himself.

"I don't give a shit," one of the intruders was saying as he walked from the stairs toward the bedroom.

"What are we looking for?"

"Barrington."

"But he didn't come here after we lost him; his car was nowhere to be seen around here."

"All right, then look for something that might tell us where the fuck he is. Oney was pretty pissed off when I talked to him this morning."

"Oh, right."

They went into the bedroom, and their voices became less distinguishable. A couple of minutes later they came out and he could understand them again.

"What's down there?"

"I'll see." The voice was coming down the hall.

A shadow passed the linen closet, and Stone cocked the iron.

"Another two bedrooms; real neat, like they haven't been used." The shadow passed again, going the other way. "What now?"

"Let's drive around a little and see if we see his car."

"Aw, come on, he's long gone by now."

"You want to explain that to Oney?"

"All right, all right." They started down the stairs.

Stone put the iron back onto the shelf and carefully opened the bifold doors. He hopped off the dryer and tiptoed to the top of the stairs, anxious to get a good look at both men for future reference. He caught sight of their backs as they walked out the front door. Stone ran down the stairs and, keeping near the wall, peeked out the venetian blinds of the front windows. This time he got a better look at them as they got into the silver Lincoln. They were beefy, tanned, and fairly conservatively dressed, for California. He waited until they drove away, then went back upstairs, glancing at his watch. He'd give them half an hour.

Ten minutes later, impatient, he set his bags down in the front hall, stuck his head out the door, and looked both ways; there was no sign of the Lincoln. He had thought about going out the back way and picking his way through the back yards, but that could get him arrested. Instead, he left the house and walked steadily but not hurriedly up the street, toward Wilshire Boulevard. At the Beverly Wilshire he entered the hotel through the front door, took the elevator down to the garage, paid for his parking, and drove out into the street, still looking for the Lincoln. He drove slowly and watchfully back to Betty's house, parked the car, retrieved his luggage, and drove away.

Shortly he was back at the Beverly Hills car rental company. "Hi," he said to the young man behind the desk, "I'm bringing back the SL500; I'd like another car, please."

"Something wrong with the Mercedes?"

"I'd like something a little less conspicuous."

"In Beverly Hills, there's nothing less conspicuous than an SL500."

"Good point, but what about a nice sedan?"

"Let's take a look," the young man said, leading the way to a row of glittering cars.

127

"That," Stone said, pointing. It was a Mercedes, the E-class sedan, metallic green, a nice neutral color.

"The E430? Great car; it has the V8 engine."

"That will do nicely."

Stone signed the new paperwork and transferred his luggage to the new car, then noticed the name of the rental agency next to his license plate. He dug a hundred-dollar bill from his stash and approached the desk again. "It's just possible that somebody might come around asking about me," he said, pushing the bill across the counter. "If that happens, I'd appreciate it if you'd tell them that I turned in the car this morning and that you drove me to the airport."

"You bet," the young man said, pocketing the hundred. "Which airline?"

"What flies to New York?"

"United; there's a flight leaving about now."

"Tell them I took that, okay?"

"Absolutely. When are you bringing the E430 back?"

"A few days."

"And where are you staying?"

"With friends; I'm not sure which ones yet."

"Anything you say, Mr. Barrington; enjoy the car."

Stone consulted his map and drove to Le Parc, the hotel Betty had recommended. At the front desk he asked for a suite.

"For how long, sir?"

"Two or three days, maybe longer."

"We can do that. Your name?"

"Jack Smith."

"May I have a credit card, Mr. Smith?"

"How about if I leave a cash deposit?"

"That will be fine; we'll need fifteen hundred dollars."

Stone counted out the money, in hundreds.

The desk clerk rang for a bellman, and shortly Stone was in a comfortable suite, complete with kitchenette. It wasn't the Bel-Air, but it was nice. He unpacked, then phoned police headquarters.

"Lieutenant Grant," Rick's voice said.

"It's Jack Smith," Stone replied.

"Hi, Jack; what can I do for you?"

"I need the office and home addresses and phone numbers of Louis Regenstein, David Sturmack, and Onofrio Ippolito."

"Can I call you back?"

"Yeah, I'm at a hotel called Le Parc, in West Hollywood, registered as the unforgettable Jack Smith, and keep it to yourself." He gave him address and number.

"Yeah, I know the place; I'll call you back in a few minutes."

"Thanks." Stone hung up and rummaged in his kitchenette for breakfast. He found some croissants and orange juice, and he made himself some coffee. The phone rang.

"Jack?"

"Yeah, Rick."

"I'm on a pay phone now. Here we go: Regenstein is at Centurion Studios; Ippolito is in an office building over the main branch

129

of Safe Harbor, downtown, and Sturmack has an office in the same building." He gave Stone the addresses, plus the home addresses and numbers. "The home numbers for all three are unlisted, so don't let anybody know where you got them."

"Thanks, Rick; you free for dinner later? I'm buying."

"Sure."

"Someplace not too Hollywood."

Grant gave him the name of a Greek restaurant on Melrose. "It's good, but you won't run into anybody in the movie business."

"Sounds perfect. Eight o'clock?"

"Make it seven."

"See you then." Stone hung up and called his secretary in New York.

"Hi, Alma, how's it going?"

"Not bad." She gave him a few phone messages.

"I've got a new address, or you can reach me on my portable." He gave her the name of the hotel and the number. "You can give that to Dino or Bill Eggers, but not to anybody else. I'm registered as Jack Smith. If I get any calls, especially from Vance Calder, say that you're expecting me back in New York tonight, and I'll return the calls then."

"Got it."

Stone finished his breakfast, then went down to the garage and got his new car. His pocket phone rang.

"Hello?"

"It's Alma; Vance Calder called, asked that

you call him at home as soon as you get home."

"Got it. Anything else?"

"Dino; I told him to try you on the portable. He said he'd call later."

"Okay. I'm going to mail you a cashier's check for fifteen thousand dollars; deposit it and write a check for ten thousand to the IRS and send it to my accountant."

"Where'd you get fifteen thousand dollars in L.A.?"

"You wouldn't believe me if I told you."

"Been selling your body?"

"That's it. Oh, Alma, one other thing; if Arrington should call, give her the portable number; tell her it'll be on day and night."

"Arrington?"

"Don't ask."

21

Stone, weary of finding his way around the city with a rentacar map, stopped at a bookstore and bought a city atlas, then headed for downtown L.A., which was a lot farther than he had imagined. The terrain downtown was different from the lush, low-rise Beverly Hills; here there were skyscrapers and concrete, and it looked like any other large American city. He wasn't sure why, but he wanted to see the building where Ippolito and Sturmack had their offices. The sight was unrewarding; it was a fifty-story tower of black glass and anodized steel, vaguely sinister in appearance, which he thought appropriate. He was wondering what to do next when his phone rang.

"Hello?"

"Stone, it's Rick Grant; I've got another sighting of the girl's car."

"Where?"

"It's at Marina Del Rey, parked along the waterfront outside a chandler's shop." He gave Stone the address.

"I'm on my way."

"This time, I'll have my patrol car sit on it; if it moves, I'll call you back."

"Thanks, Rick."

"Tell the cops when you get there, so they can be on their way."

"I'll do that." Stone consulted his map and headed for the coast.

It took some time to find the chandlery, but Arrington's car was still there, and so was the patrol car. Stone found a parking space a few yards away and walked over to the cop car. "Thanks for waiting, fellas," he said. "Lieutenant Grant says you can be on your way now."

The cops drove off without a word, and Stone had a look around. There were *thousands* of boats—he couldn't believe how many— everything from small sailing yachts to sports fishermen to large motor yachts, lined up in berths that stretched into the distance, and, he thought, she could be aboard any one of them. He went into the chandlery and, keeping an eye on the car through the window, bought a pair of cheap binoculars.

132

Back outside he climbed on top of a large ice-dispensing machine and began sweeping the giant marina, looking for some sign of Arrington. It was Friday afternoon now, the car park was filling up, and hundreds of people were heading down the catwalks to their boats, ready for a weekend on the water. There were too many of them; it was like trying to pick somebody out of a crowd headed into a ballpark. Stone went back to his car and got in. He was facing Arrington's Mercedes, and he'd be able to see anybody approaching it. His phone rang.

"Hello?"

"It's Dino."

"How you doing?"

"I'm okay; I did some checking around about Ippolito. I found a retired cop who remembered him a little from the old days with Luciano. Ippolito was a bachelor, no kids."

"Any other relatives?"

"He didn't know; this was before we starting cataloging these guys' private lives, remember, and there was a thing about not messing with their families. It just wasn't done."

"I see."

"You making any progress?"

"Well, I'm sitting here looking at Arrington's car. Rick Grant got it found for me."

"She's not in it?"

"Nope."

"You got any idea what's going on?"

"I wish I could tell you I did. I'm just looking for a way into this thing, and so far, except for the car, I'm hitting a blank wall. Oh, there were a couple of hoods following me last night, but I hope they think I've gone back to New York."

"Anything I can do from here?"

"I can't think of anything. I'm getting good help from Rick, though."

"Glad to hear it. Call me if anything breaks."

"As long as it's not my neck."

"Yeah. See ya." Dino hung up.

Stone sat for another hour, watching the car. Bored, he got out, looked around, and approached the vehicle. The top was up, and it was locked. There was a pack of matches from Elaine's on the passenger seat. He tried the trunk; that was locked, too. He went back to his car. After another hour had passed, he had to go to the toilet; he squirmed for a while, then went into the chandlery.

"Pardon me, have you got a john I can use?"

"Sure," the girl behind the counter said. "Down the hall, second door on your left."

Stone looked out at the car, then down the hallway. "Would you do me a favor for just a minute?"

"What's that?"

"Could you keep an eye on the white Mercedes convertible, parked right there?" He pointed.

"Sure."

He walked quickly to the men's room, used it and hurried out. The Mercedes was gone.

"It's gone," Stone said to the girl.

"Yeah, a woman just got in it and left."

"Shit," he muttered.

"What? Did you want me to shoot out the tires or something?"

"Sorry, thanks for your help. Oh, what did she look like?"

"Tall, dark hair, wearing a bikini with a guy's shirt over it."

"Thanks." Stone ran for the parking lot and looked up and down. The car was nowhere in sight. He ran to his own car and raced through the car park to the street, looking both ways. Lots of traffic, no white Mercedes. No Arrington.

He pounded on the wheel again and again, swearing.

22

Stone found the Greek restaurant on Melrose, was seated at a good table, and ordered a drink. He had half an hour's wait before Rick Grant showed up.

"Sorry to be late," Grant said as he slid into a chair and ordered a scotch. "Somebody squatted in my office for half an hour just as I was about to leave."

"That's okay; it gave me some thinking time, not that it did much good."

"How'd it go with Arrington's car?"

"Your guys did good; they were still there when I arrived. Marina Del Rey is a big place; lots of people there. I waited and watched for

135

more than two hours, and the second I went to the can she drove away."

"The girl was the driver?"

"Yeah; somebody saw her."

"Were you in plain sight all of this time?"

"Most of it I was sitting in my car; I did walk around a little when I first got there."

"Could somebody have recognized you?"

"Well, I was standing on top of an ice machine with binoculars for a good five minutes. I'd have been hard to miss."

"If somebody had an eye on you, she could have waited for you to disappear into the john before driving off."

"I don't think Arrington is *avoiding* me," Stone replied. "After all, she's tried to telephone me twice."

"Good point. Was anybody with her when she drove off?"

"No, and what's more, she was wearing a bikini under a man's shirt."

"Sounds like she was just sunning herself on somebody's boat and decided to leave."

"Yeah, that's twice she's been seen alone in her car, and I have to think she could have driven anywhere she wanted to, including back to Calder's house."

"Doesn't sound like there's any duress involved."

Stone sighed. "There's all kinds of duress."

Grant handed him a menu. "Let's order."

"You order for me; I don't think I can get my mind around a menu right now."

Grant ordered for both of them, and soon

Stone was enjoying a selection of pâtés and a moussaka, along with a Cypriot wine.

"Feeling better?" Grant asked.

"Yeah, I am; I guess I was a little depressed."

"Not without cause. You've got a real mystery on your hands."

Stone looked around; the restaurant was only half full and was very quiet. "You mind if I make a phone call?" He produced his pocket phone."

"Go ahead."

"Calder called me in New York; he thinks I'm back there." He dialed the number in Bel-Air.

"Good evening, Mr. Calder's residence." It was the Filipino butler.

"Good evening, this is Stone Barrington; I'm returning Mr. Calder's call."

"Oh, yes, Mr. Barrington; please hold."

"Stone?"

"Hello, Vance."

"Did you have a good flight home?"

"Yes, thanks."

"I understand you stayed over for a couple of days."

"Betty is very attractive."

"Of course she is; I don't blame you a bit."

"Is Arrington back home yet?"

"Not yet; she's still out in the Valley, but everything is all right."

"Vance, are you absolutely certain about that? I have to tell you that my impression when I was out there is that things are not entirely all right."

"Well, I can see how you might have gotten that impression, but I assure you, they are."

"How's shooting going on your film?"

"We wrapped today," Calder said, "and I think we've got a winner. Certainly your work helped."

"Thank you. Well, please give Arrington my best when she's home. Ask her to give me a call when she has a moment."

"Of course, yes. Goodbye, Stone."

Stone closed the phone. "It's all very weird," he said to Grant.

"How is it weird?"

"Vance's wife has disappeared; I don't think he has any idea where she is, but he pretends she's staying with a friend in the Valley, and that he's talking to her."

"Why is that weird? Sounds reasonable to me."

"She was seen in Marina Del Rey this afternoon, so I know she's not out in the Valley."

"Maybe that's just what she told Calder."

Stone blinked. "She's with another man, you mean?"

"That's what I mean. If you look at this as purely a domestic matter, it all fits. They have a fight, and she takes off for a few days; not the first time *that* has happened. Calder panics and calls you. You arrive, and Calder is feeling a little stupid for having done so, so he entertains you for a while, then ships you back to New York. In the meantime, the Calders haven't settled their differences, one of which might be another man, so she hasn't come home yet. Maybe she's cranking up for a divorce."

"But why would they stick me in Vance's movie, pay me a lot of money, then replace me with another actor?"

"To keep you out of Calder's face about his wife. He certainly has enough power to ask the producer to do that; maybe he even reimbursed Centurion for their costs. He's rich enough."

"Yes, he is, I suppose. But if the explanation is as simple as that, why were Ippolito's men following me last night?"

"Maybe Ippolito is doing Calder a favor. Look, I think your presence here has been an embarrassment for Calder—it shows him up as something of a schmuck—and movie stars don't like being seen to be schmucks, not to mention cuckolds."

"Why would the two guys who were following me break into Betty's house and search it?"

"To find out if you're still in town?"

"Maybe. I think I shook them by changing cars." He thought for a moment. "Why would Arrington call me from Grimaldi's?"

"Because she wanted to talk to you?"

"What would she be doing there?"

"Maybe she's seeing somebody who frequents the place."

"So you're saying that every move that everybody has made this week can be explained by a domestic quarrel and a boyfriend on the side?"

"Stone, try and look at this business like a cop. Doesn't that scenario answer all the questions? If you had been assigned to investigate possible foul play, would you continue to investigate at this point?"

"No, I wouldn't," Stone admitted.

"So, maybe your personal stake in all this is what's driving you. I mean, I admit that a lot of screwy stuff has happened in a very short time, but I've seen screwier stuff happen without a crime being committed, haven't you?"

"Sure."

"I'm not underrating the value of a good hunch; if you've got a hunch, then that's a good enough reason to pursue this."

"I guess a hunch is all I've got," Stone said. "What would you do, in my place?"

Grant thought about that for a minute. "I guess I'd pursue it until I was convinced one way or the other." He laughed.

Stone laughed with him. "I guess that's what I'm going to do," he said. "I'm going to find out what's going on, one way or the other."

23

Stone was wakened by a ringing telephone at his bedside. He tried to ignore it, but it rang on and on. Finally, he picked up the instrument. "Hello?" he said grumpily.

"Rise and shine," Betty said. "Today, you're mine."

"What time is it?"

"Nearly eight o'clock."

"I haven't slept like that in months," he said. "I could have kept going another four hours."

"Today we play, pal. Now here's what you do; you pack an overnight bag, and don't bring a necktie. A swimsuit and tennis clothes would be nice, but if you didn't bring them we can pick them up later. Got that?"

"Where are we going?"

"To a favorite place of mine, and that's all you need to know. I'll pick you up in half an hour."

"No, don't come here. Take a cab to the Beverly Hills Hotel, make sure nobody's following you, and I'll pick you up at the front door in an hour."

"Whatever you say, sir," she replied, then hung up.

Stone sat up in bed and thought about how he felt. A hell of a lot better than last night, was the verdict. He'd gotten some sound sleep, and he didn't feel the heavy weight of depression that had burdened him the previous evening. He struggled out of bed and into a shower.

Betty was standing at the entrance of the hotel, a suitcase beside her, when he drove up, having made sure that no one was behind him.

"Hullo, sailor," she said, tossing her bag into the back seat and getting in.

"Where to?" he asked, kissing her.

"Just follow my directions."

141

"You had breakfast?"

"Only a cup of coffee."

"There's some stuff in a box in the back seat, from my kitchenette."

She got them both a croissant and a container of orange juice, and started giving Stone directions. Soon they were on the Santa Monica Freeway, heading east.

"So where are we headed?" he asked.

"I told you, no questions," she replied tartly, "and I don't want to talk about anything else, either. I just want to drive and relax. We'll be there in time for lunch."

"Yes, ma'am," he replied obediently. The road became the San Bernardino Freeway, and he thought they must be headed for Palm Springs, but they zipped right through the town.

"Take a left on Sixty-two," she said. It was the first time she'd spoken in an hour.

Stone started seeing signs for Joshua Tree and Twentynine Palms, but they blew through Joshua Tree, and beyond Twentynine Palms was a zillion square miles of desert, if he remembered his geography. The terrain was arid, and mountains rose to their left.

"Take the next right," Betty said.

Stone slowed. "It's a narrow dirt road, and it seems to go up that mountain," he said.

"Take it, and shut up."

Stone turned right onto the dirt road. There were no signs of any kind and no road number. Soon they left the plain and started to climb, and he was beginning to feel nervous. He had been trained to suspect everybody, and

Betty was not exempt. She had been with him when they had been followed from the restaurant, and now he was with her on a dirt road to nowhere, and he wasn't feeling great about it. He checked the fuel gauge; he still had half a tank of gas. His options were narrow; he could continue to follow orders and get himself into God knew what, or he could turn around and head back to L.A.

"Take that little road to the left," she said.

This road was even less promising than the one they were on, and Stone stopped the car. "I have to know where we're going," he said.

She turned and looked at him. "Don't you trust me?"

He made his decision, though he wasn't happy about it; he turned left. This little track was very steep and deeply rutted, and he drove slowly of necessity. They were near the mountaintop when she issued further instructions.

"Turn right," she said.

He turned, went around a sharp bend, and found himself in a small parking lot, along with a dozen other cars, all expensive.

"You get the bags," Betty said and got out. She went to a post that held a box, opened it, and took out a telephone handset. "This is Betty Southard," she said. "We're in the parking lot."

Stone trudged over to her with the bags. "Now what?" he asked.

"They're coming for us."

He set down the bags and noticed, behind Betty, a set of narrow railway tracks. A moment

143

later a small tram came down the mountain-side and stopped. It was something like a rollercoaster car with a canvas top to keep off sun or rain.

"Hop in," she said.

He placed their bags in a luggage rack and got in beside her. She pressed a button, and the car started up the mountain. Stone looked back at the desert behind them; he reckoned they were at least four thousand feet above the desert floor now, and his ears were popping regularly.

The car leveled off and came to a stop beneath an awning; a young man in a polo shirt and Bermuda shorts stepped up and took their bags. "Welcome to Tiptop," he said. "Please follow me."

They walked up a short flight of steps and suddenly they were at the mountaintop. They were in a small lobby with windows that looked out over both sides of the mountain range, and the view was spectacular. Betty signed a registration card, and the young man took them out a rear door, past a large pool, and to a cottage just beyond.

"Lunch begins at noon," he said, "and your program starts at one."

Stone tipped him and he left them alone in the spacious and beautifully decorated cottage. There was a sitting room, a bedroom, a bath, and a wet bar. "Our program?" he asked.

"I told you," she said, putting her arms around his neck and kissing him, "no questions. It's nearly noon; we may as well have some lunch." She took his hand and led him to a table at poolside. Half a dozen other couples were seated around the pool now, and two of them were naked.

"Well, I guess it's warm enough," Stone said, nodding toward them.

"Clothes are optional," she replied. "I'll be shedding mine when our program starts, and I won't be putting them back on until dinnertime, if then. You can do whatever makes you comfortable."

"Thank you," Stone said. "I certainly don't object to nudity where you're concerned."

"Order," she said.

Stone had a delicious lobster salad, and they shared a bottle of very good chardonnay. "Don't I get to ask you any questions about anything?"

"Not until we leave this place," she said. "Until then, you are mine to command. Try to keep that in mind."

"Yes, ma'am," he said, sipping his wine. He was relieved that Ippolito's men were not sharing the table with them.

"Isn't this a beautiful spot?" she asked.

"It certainly is. How do you know about it?"

"I've been here once before. It's very private; the phone number is unlisted, and in order to get your first reservation, a former guest has to recommend you. It's practically a club."

"I like the clubhouse," Stone said, looking around, "and I can't wait to start the program."

"Looks like we're starting now," Betty said, nodding toward an approaching young woman, who was wearing a short cotton robe.

"Good afternoon, Ms. Southard," she said, "and to you, Mr. Smith. Your mud bath is ready."

"Mud bath?" Stone repeated.

"Shut up and do as you're told," Betty said. "I apologize for Mr. Smith," she said to the young woman. "He's a New Yorker, and he's experiencing culture shock."

"That's quite all right," the woman replied. "He's not our first New Yorker. They seem to loosen up after the mud bath."

Stone stood up. "Do with me as you will," he said.

24

The young woman led them down a flagstone path rimmed with dense desert plantings for a hundred yards, then opened a high bamboo gate. They were outdoors, except for the bamboo screen through which they had entered, and a thatched roof that kept off the strong sun. Under the roof were two rectangular tubs, carved from stone and filled with steaming, bubbling mud.

"I'll take your clothes," the young woman said. "By the way, my name is Lisa."

"How do you do, Lisa?" Stone said, stripping off his clothes and handing them to her. Betty did the same, and with Lisa's help, they lowered themselves into the tubs.

"I'll take your clothes to your suite, and I'll return in half an hour," Lisa said. She set two pitchers, one of iced water, the other of lemonade, on a stool between them, along with paper cups. "If you get too warm, drink something, or just get out of the tub." She took their clothes and left.

Stone found that the bottom of the tub was contoured to fit his body, and after the initial shock of the heat, he settled in. The two of them lay in the mud for half an hour, melting, relaxing, not speaking, until Lisa returned.

"I think that's enough," she said. "We wouldn't want you to shrivel up."

They climbed out of the tubs and stood on a slab of stone while Lisa washed them down with cool water to remove the mud.

"Who will be first for a massage?" Lisa asked.

"You go first, Stone," Betty answered. "I want to take a walk." She left the hut, naked.

Lisa took Stone's hand and led him to a padded table behind the mud baths. She directed him to lie on his stomach, with his face in an opening for breathing, then, using heated, scented oils, began massaging his back, shoulders, legs, and buttocks. After half an hour she asked him to turn over.

Stone turned over, expecting her to cover his genitals with a towel, but she did not. Lisa began with his neck, face and scalp, then covered his eyes with a cool cloth and worked her way down his body. Stone found himself becoming tumescent and squirmed a little.

147

"Don't be embarrassed," Lisa said. "I'd be hurt if you weren't feeling just a little excited."

"More than a little," Stone breathed.

She laughed. "Good. I'd take advantage, but I have the feeling that your friend would kill us both."

"I believe you're right," Stone said. He heard the bamboo door open and close, but he could see nothing. Suddenly, Lisa's hands were cooler and much more explorative. "Lisa?" he said.

"Shhhh," came the reply.

Stone felt her climb onto the table with him, and in a moment, she was sitting astride him.

"Lisa, I'm saving myself for Betty," Stone said.

Betty burst out laughing. "That was a politic thing to say. Now be quiet; there are things I want to do with you."

She brought him fully erect, then lifted herself and came down gently upon him.

Stone made little noises. The dry, warm desert air, the soft breeze, and the girl on top of him seemed to be all he had ever wanted in the world. They took each other noisily, then collapsed. After a few minutes, Betty led him to a futon overlooking the valley to the south. She kissed him sweetly, then returned to the table and the waiting Lisa for her own massage.

Stone drifted into a dreamless sleep.

An hour later, Betty crawled onto the futon

with him, and they made love again, less urgently this time, slowly and more sweetly. When they had recovered, Betty tugged at his hand. "I want a swim," she said. "Come with me."

Protesting mildly, Stone allowed himself to be drawn back up the path, naked, toward the pool. It occurred to him that he had not been nude in front of this many people since the showers at the police academy, where the circumstances were less inviting. He dove into the pool and swam a couple of lazy laps, with Betty alongside him.

"Feel like some tennis?" she asked when they stopped.

"Absolutely not," he said. "I wouldn't want to get all tensed up again after all this relaxation. How about tomorrow?"

"Tomorrow is good," she replied.

They lay naked on lounges beside the pool and drank exotic fruit juices and watched the other guests go by.

"Anybody you know?" Stone asked.

"Not a soul, and that's fine with me."

"Me too," he said. The last thing he wanted was to run into somebody either of them knew.

Betty caught him glancing furtively at a very beautiful girl as she walked past, naked. "It's all right to look," she said, "but don't touch."

They dressed for dinner and dined at sunset on some of the best food Stone had ever tasted, and he chose a wonderful cabernet from an outstanding list of California wines. He noticed that other couples were gravitating toward a terrace adjoining the dining room, and when they were done, Stone and Betty joined them. Soon a fireworks display began and went on for a quarter of an hour. The deep desert night was shattered by bright explosions and dazzling trails of light. When it was over, everybody drifted away, and soon the area was deserted. Stone and Betty were the last to leave, walking hand in hand to their suite.

The following morning they played tennis, and Betty turned out to be very good indeed.

"I'll bet you beat most of the men you play with," Stone said when they had finished.

"I beat *all* the men I play with," Betty replied, tossing him a towel.

They had lunch, and Betty said it was time to leave. "They like everybody out by midafternoon, so they can get ready for the new week and give the staff some time off."

"I'll get the bill," Stone said.

"It's on me," she replied.

"It's too expensive; let's at least share it."

"I'll take it out in sex," she said, laughing.

"IOU."

"You bet your ass you do."

When Stone had driven down the mountain and they were back on the road to L.A., he started to ask questions. "I'm sorry, but I have to," he said. "What did Vance say to you on Friday?"

"Not much, which is unusual," she replied.

"He came in at mid-morning and shut himself up in his office, told me to hold all calls."

"Who called?"

"Lou Regenstein, but not the other two," she said. "I know that's what you wanted to know."

"Was Vance there all day?"

"He didn't leave until late afternoon; had lunch at his desk. It was very unlike him. Normally, he'd have lunch with a friend, often Lou, and he's usually in great spirits after finishing shooting, but not on Friday."

"Have you ever seen him like that before?"

"No. He was worried, I think, and I've never seen him worried before. Vance is not, by nature, a worrier."

"Did he give any indication of what he was worried about?"

"None; he hardly spoke to me all day."

"But it must have been Arrington."

"Maybe."

"My cop friend, Rick Grant, thinks she might be having an affair. Do you think that's possible?'

"Sure, I guess. It surprises me when married people *don't* have affairs."

As they entered Interstate 10 for the quick drive back to Los Angeles, Stone thought for a moment that he caught sight of a silver Lincoln Town Car a quarter of a mile behind them, but then he wasn't sure. They drove the rest of the way in silence, and Stone dropped Betty at her house, after having driven around the block a couple of times to be sure no one was watching. Then he headed back to his hotel.

When he walked into his suite, he had the immediate impression that someone had been there, someone besides the maid. He walked through the place cautiously, ready for anything, then he went through his belongings to see if anything had been disturbed. The place was neat, as only a hotel maid could leave it, but there was one anomaly. A glass sat on the bar, one he had not left there. Stone picked it up, holding it by two fingers at the very base, and held it up against the light. Somebody's fingerprints were there, and they couldn't be his.

25

Stone slept late the next morning, and when he was finally up and dressed he went to his kitchenette, found a plastic garbage bag under a counter, slipped the bar glass into it, and left the building. From his car he called Rick Grant.

"Rick, it's Stone. Can we meet somewhere for half a minute? I've got something for you."

"Where are you?"

"In West Hollywood."

"Can you find police headquarters on your map?" He gave Stone the address.

"Got it."

"There's a coffee shop directly across the street; I'll meet you there in twenty minutes."

Stone found the coffee shop, and Grant walked over to his car. "What's up?"

Stone handed him the plastic bag. "There's a glass in here from my hotel suite with some clear prints on it; can you run them for me?"

"Sure."

"Call me on my portable," Stone said, then waved and drove off. He had only one place to go where he might pick up some trace of Arrington, and he drove straight to Marina Del Rey. He parked, went into the chandlery, and bought some boat shoes, a light sailing jacket, a floppy hat, and some sunglasses, then he retrieved his binoculars from the car and started walking. His disguise wasn't much, but he figured it would be less conspicuous than a business suit.

He started at the ramp nearest to where Arrington's car had been parked and began ambling down every pontoon, wishing a good morning to those people who noticed him and looking at every boat, from racing dinghies to floating gin palaces. He didn't know what he was looking for, exactly, but he'd know it when he saw it, he hoped. Maybe he'd even see Arrington. He trudged down the pontoons for two hours, stopping occasionally for a soft drink from a machine, and he still was nowhere near inspecting every boat in the huge marina.

Tired of this, he plotted a course back to the parking lot that would take him past new boats. He was nearly back to the entry ramp when he was stopped in his tracks. She was on the top deck of a motor yacht of about forty feet, sunning herself, and he caught sight only because she raised herself from the deck to turn over, clutching her loose bikini top with one hand. She turned away from him, so he couldn't see her face, but with a toss of her head she threw her long dark hair over a shoulder, and that was a gesture he knew. Now, though, she was flat on the deck again, and invisible from below.

His first impulse was to board the yacht, climb to the top deck, and see her, face to face, but he thought better of that. He looked down at the boat's stern and saw the name, *Paloma*, and her home port, Avalon, which, he remembered, was on Catalina Island. If he hung around here for more than a moment, he would become conspicuous, so he walked back to the ramp and up to the parking lot. He was a few feet higher now, but when he looked back toward the yacht he could see little of the girl, most of her being masked by the toe rail around the upper deck. He got the binoculars from the car, walked back to the ice machine that had been his last crow's nest, and climbed on top of it. Panning around the marina as if looking at the boats, he paused momentarily on *Paloma* and focused on the girl. All he could see was an expanse of bare back that was achingly familiar. He got down from the machine and went back to his car. He had three options, he reckoned: he could wait until she climbed down to get a better look at her; he could wait in the car until she left the boat;

or he could confront her. The first two options weren't particularly inviting; he had never liked stakeouts when he was a cop, and he had paid other people to do them after he had retired. The third option caused him some anxiety. If the girl was not Arrington, he could get arrested, depending on her reaction; on the other hand, if she was Arrington, what would he say to her?

She had left him for another man, and they had not spoken for months; she was pregnant, or said she was, possibly with his child, and she had not seen fit to tell him; she had chosen, it seemed, to leave her husband, perhaps for a lover, and in the circumstances, she might be very unhappy to see him. If he were honest with himself, he wanted her to be *happy* to see him. He couldn't bring himself to just walk right up to her, unannounced.

Then his dilemma was suddenly resolved. He saw her stand up, fasten her bikini bra, and leave the top deck, but all this took place with her back to him. Was she leaving the boat, or was she just going below for some lunch? He waited, and his wait was rewarded. She appeared, far down the pontoon, headed his way.

He snatched up the binoculars and focused, but now a boat was interfering, then a car, then some other object between them. By the time she came up the ramp her back was to him again, and she began walking away. Stone got out of the car and followed.

She walked toward the chandlery, then

around it, and when Stone emerged on the other side of the building he saw her walking into a restaurant. He stepped up his pace, and when he arrived at the front door, saw her taking a seat at the lunch counter, her back still to him. Only one thing to do: he walked into the restaurant, took a stool two down from hers and looked at her, head on in the mirror.

She took off her sunglasses, and their eyes met.

Stone reacted as if poked in the eye. The girl and Arrington shared height, build, and hair, but nothing else.

She noted his reaction. "Am I so hard to look at?"

"Sorry," he said, rubbing his eye, "must be a lash. You're certainly not hard to look at."

She permitted herself a small smile, then devoted herself to the menu.

"Can you recommend something?" he asked. "I'm new around here."

"The bacon cheeseburger is great," she said, "if your cholesterol count can take it."

"Sounds good." He took a deep breath and tried to sound casual. "Why don't we order from a booth?"

She looked at him appraisingly, and apparently he appraised well. "As long as you're buying," she said, then hopped off the stool and led the way to a booth at the window.

"I'm Jack Smithwick," he said, offering a hand.

She took the hand. "Barbara Tierney."

A waitress appeared, and they both ordered the bacon cheeseburger and a beer.

"You said you were new around here?"

"That's right."

"New from where?"

"From New York."

"And what brings you to L.A.?"

"I used to get out here on business occasionally, and I liked it, so I was thinking of getting a place here."

"What kind of business?"

"I'm a lawyer—or rather, I used to be. Now I'm an investor." He thought that should send the right message. "What about you?"

"I'm an actress; I came out here a few months ago from Chicago."

"Storming Hollywood?"

"Sort of. What sort of place are you looking for, Jack?"

"Haven't decided yet. I heard that Marina Del Rey was nice, and I like boats."

"Then why don't you buy a boat and live on that?"

"It's a thought. Do you live on a boat?"

"For the moment. It belongs to a friend."

"I'd love to see it."

"My friend doesn't like me to have guests aboard."

"I understand."

"Do you?"

"Maybe not; help me out."

"You understand."

"Well, yes."

Their cheeseburgers arrived, and they were quiet for a while as they ate.

Stone wasn't sure where to go with this. Was Barbara Tierney the girl who had been driving Arrington's car? Or was she just a girl living on a friend's boat?

Barbara finished her cheeseburger and drank the last of her beer. "My friend's out of town," she said.

26

Stone followed Barbara Tierney down the ramp and out the pontoons to *Paloma*. He found himself aboard a very handsomely furnished motor yacht, quite new, he thought, and judging from the instrument panel on the bridge, very well equipped. "Who owns her?" he asked.

"My friend."

"And who is he?"

"He doesn't like his name bandied about," she replied coolly. "He's married."

"Oh. Then I feel even fewer scruples about him."

"Look," she said, "I'd offer you a drink, but I feel very uncomfortable having you on the boat. My friend comes and goes at odd hours, and you never can tell..."

"Sure, I understand. How about if we had dinner ashore tonight?"

"I'd like that better," she said. "Where are you staying?"

"At the Bel-Air Hotel," he lied.

"I hear it's very nice; why don't we have dinner there?"

"Perfect; I'll book a table. Do you have a car?"

She shook her head. "I use my friend's when he's in town, but..."

"Then I'll pick you up here at seven."

"Fine; I'll meet you up by the chandlery, then."

Stone offered his hand, and she took it, but then she pecked him lightly on the lips. "I'll look forward to it," she said.

"Me too." He hopped back onto the pontoon and walked toward his car. Once behind the wheel he called Rick Grant. "Hear anything on the prints yet?" he asked.

"I was just about to call you," Grant said. "The prints belong to a Vincent Mancuso—three arrests, one in a bookmaking operation and two for loan-sharking, the last one eight years ago, no convictions. Those are typically mob crimes, even though he wasn't in our organized crime index. I've started a file on him, though."

"Have you got a description?"

"He's forty-six years old, six-one, two-twenty-five, dark hair."

"Sounds like a lot of guys."

"I'll bring you his mug shot the next time we meet."

"Got a place of employment?"

"He owns—or did, this is a couple of years old—a delicatessen in Hollywood, call Vinnie's.

It's on the Sunset Strip." He gave Stone the address.

"Got it. I have another request."

"Shoot."

"Can you check on the registration of a boat for me?"

"Yeah, but it'll probably take a day or two. We don't have access to that database from here; I'll have to go through the Coast Guard."

"The boat's name is *Paloma*, out of Avalon; she's a motor vessel of about forty feet. I'd appreciate it if you'd ask them to put a rush on it. Right now, I don't know if I'm chasing a wild goose."

"I'll do the best I can."

"I guess I'll change hotels, too, given that Vincent Mancuso is hanging around my room at Le Parc."

"Where you going?"

"The Bel-Air, if they've got a room. I'll register under Jack Smithwick."

"You're moving up in the world."

"Well, at least I'm doing it with somebody else's money."

"That's the best way. I'll call you on the portable number."

Stone hung up, started the car, and drove up to Sunset Boulevard. He found Vinnie's Delicatessen, parked, went in, and looked around. It was still lunchtime, but the place wasn't very busy, and he could see why. It seemed pretty greasy and not very inviting. He ordered a diet Coke to take away, and as he was paying, two hoodish-looking men walked in and, without slowing down, went behind the counter and through a door marked EMPLOY-EES ONLY. Vinnie was probably running a book back there, Stone thought.

He left, tossed the soda into a wastebasket, got back into his car, and drove to his hotel. On the way, he called the Bel-Air and booked a small suite. Back at Le Parc he went to the front desk and laid a thousand dollars on the desk. "I want to extend for a few nights," he said to the desk clerk.

"Of course, Mr. Smith," the man said, making the money disappear.

"I'm going to be in and out, so tell the maid not to worry if my luggage isn't there."

"No problem. Oh, a Miss Betty Southard called."

Stone went back to his suite and called Betty.

"Dinner tonight?" she asked.

"Can't. How about tomorrow?"

"Okay."

"Anything happen I should know about?"

"No. Vance didn't come into the office. He sometimes stays home if he's not shooting, so it's been very quiet."

"I'll talk to you tomorrow, then." He hung up, packed his bags, and carried them down to the garage. Fifteen minutes later, he was checking into the Bel-Air.

"Welcome back, Mr. Barrington," the woman behind the desk said.

161

"Ah, for personal reasons, I'd like to be known as Jack Smithwick while I'm here."

"Of course, if you like."

"Would you let the telephone operators know about that?"

"Surely."

"And if anyone calls and asks for Barrington, deny all knowledge."

"I understand," she said. "Many of our guests travel incognito at one time or another."

Stone followed the bellman to his suite and sent his clothes out to be pressed. He checked in with his secretary and gave her his new name and address.

"What if Vance Calder calls again?" she asked.

"Tell him I went out to the Hamptons for a few days, but you expect to hear from me. You just love talking to Vance Calder, don't you?"

"Well..." She suppressed a giggle.

He hung up and reflected on why he was playing that game with Vance. If some goombah was searching his hotel suite, then *somebody* knew he was still in L.A., and that somebody might tell Vance. The hotel change was probably a good idea, as long as he kept the suite at Le Parc. He was tired of people he didn't know knowing where he was; it was becoming extremely irritating.

He was at the Marina Del Rey chandlery at seven sharp, and Barbara Tierney was only ten minutes late.

"I'm sorry you had to drive all the way down here to get me," she said. "I'd have been glad to drive, if my friend's car had been here."

"What does your friend drive?"

"A Porsche."

A Porsche? Shit. Was this the wrong girl? "Well, if your friend were here we wouldn't be having dinner, would we?"

"Not necessarily," she said. "I'm pretty much a free woman."

"I'm glad to hear it."

"I try to avoid men who make demands; I get irritable when they do that."

"I'll do my best not to irritate you," Stone said. He turned into Stone Canyon.

"Do you always stay at the Bel-Air?"

"Always; it's my home away from home."

They pulled into the hotel parking lot, gave the attendant the car, and walked over the bridge leading to the hotel. Below them swans dozed in a pretty stream.

"You certainly have good taste in hotels," Barbara said.

Stone took her hand. "I have good taste in dinner companions, too."

"Oooh, you should have been an actor," she said.

"You're not the first to tell me that," Stone replied.

27

They were shown to a banquette in a corner of the large dining room, and their drink order was taken. Stone was hungry, and he began looking at the menu.

"May I take your order, Mr. Smithwick?" a waiter asked.

It took Stone a moment to react. "Give us a minute, will you? And may I have a wine list?"

"The smoked salmon sounds good," Barbara said, then she made a little noise.

Stone turned toward her. "What?"

"My God," she half-whispered, "look who just came in."

Stone followed her gaze to the center of the dining room. Vance Calder and a party of six were being seated at a round table.

"I've never seen him in person, have you?"

Stone raised the wine list to cover his face. "Well, he doesn't turn me on as much as he does you." He lowered the list enough to allow him to see Vance's party, and things got worse. Betty Southard was sitting next to him. "Oh, Jesus," he murmured under his breath.

"What?"

"Nothing; I was just trying to pronounce the name of this wine. I think I've read about it somewhere." He was trapped, within plain view of both Vance and Betty. He did not need this.

"I think I'll go and say hello to him," Barbara said.

"What? Who?"

"Vance Calder."

"I don't think you should do that, Barbara."

"Why not?"

"The hotel has a lot of celebrity customers, and they're very protective of them."

"Oh, it'll be all right," she said, pushing the table away. "We have a mutual friend." She got up and started toward Vance's table before Stone could stop her.

Stone watched as Barbara made her way between the tables and came to rest at Vance's elbow. Vance looked up at her. The headwaiter began to move. Barbara spoke. Then, to Stone's amazement, Vance stood up, shook her hand, and started to introduce her to the rest of his party. All eyes were riveted on the beautiful brunette. It was now or never, Stone thought. He pushed away the table, rose, and walked quickly through the dining room, staying as far away as possible from Vance's table, hoping to God that no one there looked away from Barbara. Once in the entrance hall between the bar and the restaurant, he chanced a look back into the dining room. Barbara still held their attention.

Stone signaled to the headwaiter. "I'm not feeling very well," he said. "Would you please ask my dinner companion, Miss Tierney, to phone me in my suite?"

"Of course, Mr. Smithwick," the man said. "I hope you feel better."

"Thank you," Stone said and got out of

165

the restaurant, taking care not to pass the window on the way to his suite. The phone was ringing as he walked in. "Hello?"

"Jack? Are you all right?"

"Oh, yes, Barbara; I'm so sorry I had to leave. It must have been something I ate at lunch."

"We had the same thing for lunch, and I'm all right," she said.

"I've been this way a couple of days. Look, would you mind if we had dinner in my suite? If you're uncomfortable with that I'd be glad to order a car to take you back to the marina, but I do think I should stick close to home this evening."

"All right," she said. "How do I find it?"

Stone gave her directions, then hung up, took off his jacket, left the door ajar, and went into the bathroom.

"Jack?" she called from the door.

"Come on in; I won't be a minute." He threw some water on his face, then grabbed a towel and walked out, mopping his face dry. "I'm so sorry; I'm all right now, I think." He motioned to the sofa. "Have a seat." He handed her a menu. "Would you like a drink?"

"Scotch on the rocks, please," she replied, and started to look at the menu.

Stone poured her a drink and fixed himself a bourbon.

"Maybe you shouldn't drink," she said.

"It'll be all right," he replied.

"I'll have the smoked salmon and the chicken breast," she said.

Stone phoned in their order and sat down

beside her. "So, did Vance Calder remember you?"

"He remembered my friend," she said. "They do some business together."

"What business is he in?"

"Finance."

"What sort of finance?"

"I'm not sure exactly, but he deals in large sums of money. He's in Mexico right now."

"Ah."

"Have you ever been to Mexico?"

"No, and with the state of my innards, I'm not sure I should."

She laughed and gave him a little kiss. "You know, I think I prefer having dinner here instead of in the restaurant."

Stone kissed her back. "So do I."

Sometime after midnight, Stone crept from the bed and tiptoed into the sitting room, leaving Barbara sound asleep. He found her handbag, opened it, and extracted her wallet. Standing next to the window, he used an outside light to illuminate the contents. Her name was really Barbara Tierney, an Illinois driver's license testified to that, and she really was an actress, according to her Screen Actors Guild card. He replaced the wallet and rummaged around in the bag for a moment longer, but found nothing else of interest, just the usual female detritus. He put the bag back where he'd found it and crept back into bed. Barbara rolled over and reached for him.

"More," she said.

"Absolutely," he replied.

Stone was awakened by the doorbell, and Barbara called out that she'd get it. He fell back into bed. A moment later, she pushed a rolling table into the room.

"I ordered you a big breakfast," she said.

"Thanks," he replied, sitting up and arranging pillows. He tucked into bacon and eggs, a luxury he rarely allowed himself. "First bacon cheeseburgers, now bacon and eggs," he said. "If I hang around you long enough I'll have a coronary."

"Oh, I don't know," she said, eating her own breakfast. "You seem in pretty good shape to me."

"That's because I lead an abstemious life, when I'm not with you."

She threw back her head and hooted. "I love it!" she cried. "You were a virgin before I came along, right?"

"Absolutely. You've taught me everything I know."

She set down her plate and took his away. "Well, I must be one hell of a teacher," she giggled.

"You certainly are."

"Now, let's see, what shall we learn this morning, class?"

"Entirely up to you, ma'am."

"Well, we've already tried positions one, two, and three."

"I don't think I remember position three," he said.

"I can see that you learn only by repetition."

"That's always the best way, isn't it?"

"Well, it's *one* way."

"Not the best way?"

"Sometimes, my dear, you have to improvise."

"Improvise? How does one do that?"

"Like this," she said, "for starters."

"That's a very nice starter. What's the main course?"

"You're not ready for the main course."

"I think I'm getting there."

"I think you are, too!" she cried. "What a good student!"

"I do my best," he said.

"You'd better, or you'll have to repeat the course."

"Oh, God," Stone moaned, "I don't think I could repeat the course."

"We'll see," she said.

28

The hour was near eleven when Stone, drained of any sexual desire and close to exhaustion, drove Barbara Tierney back to Marina Del Rey. As they pulled into the parking lot, she gasped and brought a hand to her mouth. "Oh, shit," she said.

"What?"

"My friend is back; there's his Porsche. What am I going to do? I can't show up on the boat having been out all night."

"Um," Stone said, helpfully. Then he had an idea. "Why don't you run into the chan-

169

dlery and buy some shorts or something. Change, and you can say you've been for a walk." He peeled off a couple of hundreds and handed them to her.

"You have a devious mind," she said. "Thank God. Listen, you'd better beat it out of here before someone sees us together." She leaned over and kissed him, then dug in her handbag, found a slip of paper, and wrote down a number. "You can call me here," she said, handing it to him, "but only daytimes and..."

"If a man answers, hang up."

"Right."

"Before you go," he said, "satisfy my curiosity."

"About what?"

"I was in the chandlery the other day, and I thought I saw you drive away in a Mercedes roadster. Whose car was that?"

"I don't know what you're talking about," she said. "Bye." She hopped out of the car and ran toward the chandlery.

Stone drove away, but not before he had made a note of the Porsche's vanity plate, which read BIGBUKS. He got out his portable phone and called Rick Grant.

"Lieutenant Grant."

"Rick, it's Stone."

"Hi. I was promised something on the boat registration before lunch."

"Something else; can you run a plate and a phone number for me?"

"Sure."

"The plate is a vanity, BIGBUKS." He dictated the phone number.

"These won't take long."

"How about lunch?"

"Sure. See you at the Grange on Melrose in an hour?" He gave Stone directions.

"Good."

"I should have something on the boat by then."

"See you then." Stone hung up and turned in the general direction of Beverly Hills.

They were seated in a garden again. Stone liked L.A.'s alfresco dining, which was a rarity in New York.

"Okay," Rick said, taking out his notebook, "the plate you gave me is registered to a Martin Barone, of a Beverly Drive address in Beverly Hills; he's CEO of something called Barone Financial Services. The phone number you gave me, however, is not in Barone's name; it's just an extension off the Marina Del Rey's number, which means it's on a boat."

"What about *Paloma*?"

"The boat is more interesting; it's registered to Abalone Fisheries, which is a processor of canned seafood."

"Why is that interesting?" Stone asked.

"I pulled up some stuff about Abalone out of our financial database. It's a cannery, all right, but it's also a holding company; it owns, among other businesses, twenty-two percent of the stock of the Safe Harbor Bank. It also owns seventy-five percent of Barone

Financial Services. Martin Barone owns the other twenty-five percent."

"A cannery owns a bank and a finance company?"

"You don't understand. You've heard of Warren Buffet?"

"The richest man in America? Sure."

"His principal holding is Berkshire Hathaway, a textile mill. Years ago he bought the company, and he used it to invest in a lot of other companies, like Coca-Cola, and it's now worth billions."

"Yeah? Who owns Abalone Fisheries?"

"Onofrio Ippolito and David Sturmack. It's their version of Berkshire Hathaway."

"Ahhhhh."

"I thought you'd like that."

"Seems like every time I turn over a rock, Ippolito is under it."

"What's your interest in the boat?"

"When your guys spotted Arrington's car at the marina, a girl drove it away, and the same girl, I think, is living on the boat. She's a thing on the side for this Martin Barone, who's married. Will you see what you can dig up on Barone?"

"I can find out if he has a sheet."

"Thanks." Stone took some prefolded hundreds from his pocket and slipped them into Grant's jacket pocket. "Something on account."

"I thank you."

"By the way, I dropped by Vincent Mancuso's deli on the Strip yesterday; I'd give you odds he's running a book out of there."

"I'll mention it to the relevant squad," Grant said. "Stone, something's been bothering me."

"What's that?"

"This business of Mancuso being in your hotel room."

"Bothers me, too."

"You moved there from the girl's house, right? Calder's secretary?"

"Right."

"Who else knew you moved in there?"

"My secretary, Dino, and a lawyer friend in New York."

"And neither Dino or your lawyer friend would have mentioned it to somebody who knows Mancuso, would they?"

"Unlikely in the extreme."

"That leaves the girl."

Stone shook his head. "I've thought about this. I think I was followed to the hotel by Mancuso and his buddy."

"Oh, I almost forgot," Grant said, reaching into a pocket, "here's Mancuso's mug shot."

Stone looked at the photograph. "He's older and heavier now, but that's the guy who was driving the Lincoln that followed me the other night."

"And you think he followed you to the hotel?"

"Yeah, that's what makes the most sense."

"No, it's not."

"What do you mean?"

"You told me you changed cars at the rental agency and told the guy there to say he'd driven you to the airport if anybody asked."

"Yeah," Stone said. He didn't like where this was leading.

"Assuming he did as you asked, that should have broken the tail, shouldn't it?"

"Unless Mancuso followed me to the rental agency and saw me drive away in the sedan."

"Were you followed?"

Stone shook his head. "If I was, then Mancuso dramatically improved his tailing technique overnight."

"So that leaves the girl."

"I find that hard to believe."

"You think the girl might be screwing Calder?"

"She used to, she told me."

"Okay, so she's Calder's former squeeze, and she works for him; he's her sole means of support?"

"As far as I know."

"How long you known her?"

"A few days."

"So where do you think her loyalties lie?"

"She's made it clear that they lie with Calder, but she knows I'm not doing anything to threaten him; I'm trying to find his wife, for Christ's sake."

"Calder sees that as a threat, doesn't he?"

"How do you mean?"

"I mean, he tried to hustle you out of town, didn't he?"

"Yeah, he did."

"So he must think your presence in L.A. is not in his best interests."

"I guess not."

"So, if he feels that way, why wouldn't Betty feel that way, too?"

"You could have a point," Stone said, but he didn't really want to admit that to himself.

"Let me ask you something else: where were you when Mancuso was in your hotel room?"

"I was at a resort out in the desert."

"Alone?"

"No."

"Who were you with?"

"Betty Southard," Stone said.

"Whose idea was it to go out there?"

"Betty's."

"Stone, I think you're letting your cock do your thinking," he said, "and remember, a cock doesn't have a brain."

29

Stone met Betty Southard at an Italian place called Valentino. He had intended to pick her up at her home, but she had insisted on meeting him at the restaurant. She gave him a big kiss, and they were shown to their table. They ordered drinks.

"How're things going?" she asked.

"Not well," Stone said. "I'm getting nowhere, and I'm thinking of packing it in and going back to New York."

"I would be desolated," she said, sipping her martini.

"I'm grateful for your desolation, but all I'm doing is chasing my tail and not getting any of my own work done."

"Arrington's home," she said.

Stone blinked. "When?"

"Yesterday, apparently. Vance came into the office this morning whistling a merry tune and had me order some flowers for him."

"Funny, I thought I caught a glimpse of Vance last night," he said, "and he was alone."

"Where?"

"I was having dinner with my cop friend, Rick Grant, at a Greek restaurant, and I could have sworn I saw him drive by in the Bentley."

She shook her head. "Nope. Vance and Arrington had dinner last night at the Bel-Air Hotel with some Centurion stockholders; I made the reservation."

The lie wilted Stone inside. "Must have been my imagination."

"Not really; there are two other green Bentleys just like Vance's around town. You saw one of them."

"Oh, well; I'm glad she's back."

"Vance thinks you're in New York," she said. "He dictated a thank you note to you this afternoon."

"I wanted him to think that, after being followed from the restaurant last week. I wanted everybody but you to think I was back in New York."

"I understand," she said. "Shall we order?"

They both ordered a Caesar salad and the

176

osso bucco, and Stone ordered a bottle of the Masi Amerone '91. "It's a big wine," he said. "I think you'll like it."

"You seem a little depressed, baby," she said, rubbing the inside of his thigh with her toe.

"It always depresses me when I've wasted a lot of time," he said.

"I hope it wasn't *all* a waste of time." She pushed her toe into his crotch.

He smiled. "Certainly not. In some ways, this has been an extremely lovely trip."

"Well, if this is going to be our last night together, I'll have to make it a special one," she said.

"They've all been special," he replied. "Especially the weekend at Tiptop."

"I'd give you their unlisted number," she said, "but I wouldn't want you going there with anyone but me."

Their food arrived, and Betty returned her toe to her shoe.

"I left a couple of messages for you at Le Parc," she said. "Why didn't you call me back?"

"I'm sorry; I haven't been by the desk, I guess. I tend to go straight from the garage to my room. Was it something important?"

"I just wanted to tell you about Arrington."

"Why didn't you call my portable number?"

"I always feel as though I'm interrupting something when I do that."

"Oh."

"Stone, something's really wrong, I can tell. Why won't you talk to me?"

Because I might as well whisper it into Vance's or Ippolito's or somebody's ear, he thought. "There's nothing, really."

"It's Arrington; you'd hoped to see her again, hadn't you?"

He shrugged. "Maybe."

They finished their dinner in silence. He paid the check, and she took his hand on the way out.

"I'm going to make you forget her," she said.

"Sounds good."

"I'll meet you at Le Parc in fifteen minutes."

"No," he said, "meet me at the Bel-Air Hotel. I've moved."

"See you in the parking lot there," she said.

He followed her all the way, checking his rearview mirror to see if anyone were following him. As far as he could tell, there was no one behind him.

She walked ahead of him into the suite, shedding clothing as she went. Stone allowed himself to be undressed, then she went into the bathroom and came back with a bottle of body lotion.

"Where does it hurt?" she asked, kneeling over him on the bed.

"All over," he said.

She warmed the lotion between her palms and began rubbing his chest. "I watched you having your massage at Tiptop," she said.

178

"There was a peephole for that very purpose. I saw the effect Lisa had on you."

"And what effect did watching have on you?" he asked.

"It made me want you both," she replied, pouring more oil into her hand.

"Then why didn't you have us both?"

"I didn't think I should tamper with the staff."

"My impression was that Lisa would have enjoyed being tampered with," he said.

"Would you have enjoyed it?"

"What's not to enjoy?"

She laughed. "I like your attitude. Maybe the next time you come out here I can arrange something like that."

"What an exciting idea."

She had his genitals in both hands now, and they were both unbearably excited. She lay down beside him and took him into her, throwing a leg over his body. From that time until morning they did not speak again.

"So, you're leaving today?" Betty asked over breakfast.

"Maybe. Or maybe I'll stick around a little longer."

"What for? Last night you sounded determined to leave."

Tired of cat-and-mouse, he decided to go for broke. "Ippolito interests me," he said.

"The banker? Why?"

"I think he's behind all this."

"Behind what?"

"Arrington's disappearance."

"That doesn't make any sense at all, Stone," she said, sounding worried.

"I'm beginning to think it does. I think the two men who followed us the other night work for Ippolito."

She stopped eating. "Stone, I think it's better that you stay away from Mr. Ippolito."

"Why? It's a free country. I've been a cop and an investigator long enough to know that you can find out anything about anybody, and I'm going to find out more about Ippolito."

"That could be dangerous," she said quietly.

"I thought you didn't know anything about the man," he said, "and here you are telling me he's dangerous."

"It's just an impression."

"And how did you get that impression?"

"Just from things I've heard." She looked at her watch. "God, I've got to get to the office; Vance is coming in early this morning for a meeting about a new film."

Stone walked her to the door. "I want to thank you," he said. "You've been wonderful."

She put her arms around his neck. "If you want to thank me, go back to New York today."

"I don't think so," Stone said.

She looked frightened but said nothing. She kissed him and ran out the door.

Stone watched her go, wondering how long it would take to pass on their conversation.

It took until just before lunch. The phone rang.

"Hello?"

"Mr. Barrington?"

"Yes."

"This is Onofrio Ippolito. How are you?"

"I'm very well, Mr. Ippolito. I'm surprised to hear from you; hardly anyone knows I'm staying at the Bel-Air."

"It's a small town."

"I suppose so."

"I'm sorry we didn't get to talk more at dinner at Vance's house. David Sturmack tells me you're going to be doing some work for him in New York."

"We discussed it."

"I have many interests in New York, too; I wonder if we might talk about your doing some work for me?"

"Of course."

"Tell you what; I'm giving a dinner party on my yacht this evening. Why don't you come to dinner, and we'll find a few minutes to talk privately."

"I'd be delighted."

"The yacht is moored off Catalina Island, so if you'll be at Marina Del Rey at eight o'clock, I'll see that you're ferried out there."

"Fine."

Ippolito gave him a slip number and a boat's name, *Maria*. "I'll look forward to seeing you," he said.

"Thank you; I'll see you this evening."

Stone hung up the phone and sat back. Time to face the man and ask some direct questions. In the meantime, he thought, he'd have a swim. He got up and went to look for a robe.

30

Stone arrived at Marina Del Rey at a little after eight and parked the car. He had dressed in one of his new Purple Label suits, dark blue with a white pinstripe, and had worn one of the new Sea Island cotton shirts and a new tie. He would probably be over-dressed at the dinner party, but better that than underdressed.

He walked down the ramp and along the pontoons, looking for the berth number he had been given. The light was going now, and as he passed the pontoon where *Paloma* was berthed, he noticed no lights were on. Maybe he'd see Barbara and her boyfriend at dinner. He finally found the correct pontoon and worked his way down the berth numbers until he came to *Maria*, a sports fisherman of thirty-odd feet, complete with a tall flying bridge. Standing in the stern of the boat was one of the two men who had followed him in the Lincoln.

Stone experienced an urge to turn around and walk the other way, but before he could, the man smiled and spoke.

"Mr. Barrington? We've been waiting for you; come aboard, please."

Stone walked up the small gangplank.

"I'm Manny," the man said, as another man came up from below. "This is Vinnie. We both work for Mr. Ippolito."

Vincent Mancuso stuck out a hand, and Stone shook it. After all, they had never been formally introduced. "We're all ready," Vinnie said. He turned, switched on the ignition, and started the engines, while Manny dealt with the gangplank and the mooring lines.

"Where's Mr. Ippolito," Stone asked, "and the other guests?"

Vinnie put the throttles ahead, and the boat moved out of the berth. "Most of the guests are already aboard the big boat. Mr. Ippolito and the others are choppering out from a meeting downtown."

"Can I get you something to drink?" Manny asked.

"A beer would be good."

Manny went below and came up with a Heineken and a glass on a silver tray. "There you are; would you like to stay in the cockpit or ride down below?"

"I'll stay up here, I think," Stone replied. "It's a nice evening." He felt more comfortable now, and he took a seat near the stern and sipped his beer.

"Yeah, it is a nice night, isn't it?" Manny said. "When we're clear of the marina we'll see a hell of a sunset."

Stone watched the moored boats go past as the sports fisherman moved down the channel toward the breakwater. Five minutes later they were on a calm Pacific Ocean, and Vinnie put the throttles forward. "How long will it take us to get to Mr. Ippolito's yacht?" Stone asked.

"Oh, forty or forty-five minutes, I guess," Manny shouted over the rumble of the engines. "It's about twenty-five miles, and we're gonna be doing a good forty knots. This baby is fast."

The boat was roaring through a flat sea now, into a giant red ball of a sun, and Stone began to enjoy the ride. They passed other boats coming from and going to Marina Del Rey, then after a while, they were alone on the water, tearing along.

Stone began to think about what he was going to say to Ippolito. Not much, he decided; he'd listen instead. He doubted if he was ever going to get any legal work from either Sturmack or Ippolito—that had just been the bait to get him out here. He was dying to know what they wanted to tell him.

They had been moving fast for more than half an hour when Vinnie began slowing down. Stone stood up and looked ahead. The sun was gone, Catalina was at twelve o'clock, and the mooring lights on a hundred yacht masts lay ahead. People had anchored for the night and were having drinks and dinner aboard their boats. It occurred to Stone that he was getting hungry. They continued on for another few minutes, and Vinnie slowed down further.

"Don't want to rock anybody's boat with our

wake," he said, then made a ninety-degree turn to the left and pulled the throttles back to idle, out of gear. The boat drifted.

"Where's Mr. Ippolito's yacht?" Stone asked. Then, from behind him, he heard the metallic sound of a gun being cocked, and he felt cold steel on the back of his neck. He turned to find Manny holding an automatic pistol to his head.

"You're not going to make it to the yacht," Manny said.

Stone opened his mouth to speak as Vinnie applied a strip of duct tape to his mouth.

"Hold out your hands," Manny said, as Vinnie tore more tape from the roll.

Stone didn't move.

Manny held the pistol against Stone's left eye. "We can do this neat, or we can do it messy," he said. "What's it gonna be?"

Stone held out his hands, and Vinnie taped his wrists together, then bent over and taped his ankles together as well. Vinnie then went to a locker and extracted a fathom of chain and a plow anchor.

Stone's bowels turned to water, and he contracted his stomach muscles to keep something embarrassing from happening. This was bad enough without making it worse. He began, somewhat late, looking for a way out. Why had he gotten aboard this boat? The sun was down and a nearly full moon had risen, bathing the cockpit of the boat in a pale light.

Vinnie and Manny were talking about shackles now, but their voices seemed distant. Stone watched as one of them took a tool kit from a locker, found a shackle, attached it to the chain, and tightened it with pliers.

Now they were coaxing him toward the stern. At first Stone resisted moving, but then he saw the toolbox. At Manny's urging, he took a hop forward, then fell on top of the toolbox, spilling implements over the deck.

Vinnie and Manny were swearing and looking for the pliers, while Stone was feeling for something else. He'd seen a marlin spike in the top tray of the toolbox, he was sure, and he wanted the shiny tool more than he had ever wanted anything in his life. While they rummaged through the tools for the pliers, he got the marlin spike wedged between his taped hands.

He was yanked roughly to his feet, and somebody handed him an anchor. They actually wanted him to hold the anchor! There didn't seem much point in not holding it, so he did.

"Any last words?" somebody said.

Stone shot the man a hot look, and both the hoods burst out laughing. Then they were dragging him toward the stern of the boat.

"You get us moving a little," Manny said, "and I'll handle this end." Vinnie went forward, the engines rumbled, and the boat began to move.

Stone started taking deep breaths through his nose, deeper each time, packing air into his lungs. Then he was standing all alone in the stern of the boat, holding the heavy anchor, trying not to fall overboard.

"Compliments of Onofrio Ippolito!" he heard Manny yell over the engines.

Stone took one more deep breath, and then he felt a solid kick in the small of the back. He hung on to the breath as he fell astern, striking the cold, foaming water, and then everything went quiet except the retreating roar of the engines and the scream in his head.

31

He was sinking rapidly, head first. He had no idea how deep the water was, didn't know when the increasing pressure would force the air from his lungs. He held on to that air with all his strength; he needed the buoyancy as much as the air.

Twisting his wrists back and forth to gain as much slack as possible, which wasn't much, he held the anchor and the marlin spike with one hand as he found the shackle with the other. The spike had a slot at its top, made for this very job, if not this very moment. Frantically, he got the nub of the shackle pin into the slot in the marlin spike, loosened it, then, using his fingers, quickly unscrewed the pin, yanked it out, and let go of the anchor. He stopped sinking, seeming to have achieved neutral buoyancy. Then he made an awful discovery. When he had let go of the anchor he had let go of the marlin spike, too, and there remained one shackle to defeat, the one holding the chain around his waist.

Once, as a boy, he had been sent to a socialist summer camp by his left-wing parents, and some of the camp counselors had amused themselves by binding the boys hand and foot and tossing them into the lake, just to see how long they would last before they had to be rescued. There were no rescuers at hand now, but at least camp had given Stone some experience of swimming with his hands and feet tied. He tried once to loosen the shackle pin with his fingers, then, with his lungs exploding, began to kick and paddle as best he could toward the surface. Looking up, he could see the bright moon lighting his way, but he had no idea of how deep he had gone. The going seemed painfully slow.

To take his mind off the struggle, he thought about how long he had been underwater. He figured he was at about one minute now, and the surface still seemed miles away. Air began to leak from his nostrils, and he fought to hang on to it, since there was nothing to replace it but seawater. He struggled on, wishing his mouth wasn't taped so that he could scream, and still the surface eluded him.

He thought of himself as a porpoise and tried to propel himself faster with the kick he had been taught at camp as part of the butterfly stroke. The seconds flew like hours. And then, suddenly, he could see the moon clearly, and he was expelling air and ripping at the tape over his mouth. It came free and as he broke the surface he gulped in air, shouting as he expelled it, then gulped in more.

A minute passed before his intake of air began to catch up with his need for oxygen. He looked around and saw, in the distance, the running lights of the sports fisherman as it turned toward Catalina, then he looked for other boats. There was a fleet of them, but they were a long, long way from where he struggled to keep his head above water.

He tried floating on his back, but the chain around his waist and the weight of his sodden clothing made that impossible. The best he could do was to continue his porpoise kick and draw his taped hands through the water. He felt for the end of the tape with his tongue, thinking to pull it off his hands with his teeth, but apparently the end was inaccessible. There was nothing to do but swim for it as best he could.

He developed a kind of rhythm, a two-hands-together dog paddle which, combined with his porpoise kick, moved him through the water, though not very fast. His goal was the forest of lighted masts ahead of him—how far? Two hundred, three hundred, a thousand yards away? He thought about the strength he had left and wondered if it would be enough or if, finally, the chain would drag him down, short of the goal ahead. He remembered reading somewhere that drowning was an easy way to die, but he didn't believe it. He thought of himself drifting along the bottom, being fed upon by the crabs and—oh God—sharks. Sharks were nocturnal creatures, weren't they? They were attracted by splashing at the surface, and he was doing a lot of splashing in his effort to reach something he could hang on to. He could not get used to the cold of the water; it seemed to be right at the freezing point. Why were there no chunks of ice floating in it? He could hang on to an ice floe and rest his weary muscles.

Cold water. The great white shark was a cold-water creature, wasn't it? Didn't fishermen catch great whites in these waters? Clips from the film *Jaws* flashed through his mind. A naked girl hanging desperately on to a buoy as the giant fish tore its way through her lower extremities. At least he wasn't naked, though he knew he could swim faster if he were. He thought about kicking off his shoes, but they didn't seem to be slowing him down, and anyway, he had paid six hundred and fifty dollars to have them made. He'd hang on to the shoes.

He thought about making love to Betty the night before, but then he recalled that Betty was responsible for his being where he was, and he thought about Barbara Tierney instead. Where was she now? Drinking champagne aboard Ippolito's yacht, anchored at Catalina? Or was the yacht really there? Or was there really a yacht? Yes, there was; he recalled the bank manager telling him that Ippolito had a veritable flotilla—was that the word he had used? Stone had already been aboard two of Ippolito's boats, albeit briefly.

He tried a sidestroke but began sinking, so he went back to his crippled dog paddle. There was no way to rest—the chain prevented that—so he slogged on, stroke after stroke, kick after kick, gulp after gulp of air, on and on into the night. At this rate he might miss Catalina entirely and continue on toward Hawaii.

The lights were closer now, but not that much closer, and he was fading. His strokes were getting shorter and slower, and nothing his brain could say to his muscles would make them work better or longer. Thank God there isn't a sea running, he thought; I'd be dead by now. He thought about dying and discovered that he wasn't ready to do it. The thought gave him new strength, but not much; you couldn't call it a second wind, hardly that. He thought about Arrington and the child she carried inside her. Was it his? If he died tonight, would there be a son to carry on the Barrington name, such as it was? No, he would carry on the Calder name, no matter to whom he owed his DNA.

He lurched onward, but something was wrong. The mast lights were no longer visible. He turned his head and looked around; had he gotten off course? He was sure he hadn't, so he paddled on. Then something very strange happened; he reached out in front of him with his bound hands, pulled the Pacific Ocean toward him and struck his head very hard on a very hard object.

Dazed, he put out his hands and they met

the object, too; it was smooth and dark, and he couldn't hold on to it. With new, brief strength he turned and swam parallel to it, and he came to its end. It was a small boat with a black hull, and at its stern there was the most wonderful thing: a boarding ladder. He grasped it in both hands and laid his cheek against the hull, panting and whimpering.

After a moment, he felt himself slipping into unconsciousness. He shook his head. "No!" he screamed as loudly as he could, and it wasn't very loud. The ladder unfolded in his hands and the bottom rung fell into the water as it had been designed to do, for swimmers. He got his feet on the rung, which was about a foot underwater, and tried to stand on it, but his hands slipped and he fell sideways into the water.

He had so little strength left now; he began to think that perhaps it would feel better if he just gave himself to the sea and let everything go. But he couldn't; he had one more try in him, he was sure. He lurched toward the ladder again and got his feet on the bottom rung. Holding a higher rung with both hands, he pulled himself upward until he was standing with his knees locked. He stayed that way for a good minute, hearing the water running from his clothes, back into the sea. The next rung would be harder, since he no longer had any buoyancy.

He reached up and grabbed the stainless steel railing above him with his two hands, then, holding on for dear life, he pulled his feet up and felt for the next rung. Miraculously, he found it. The deck of the little yacht was now at the level of his knees, and he could get his arms over the top steel railing. That allowed him to pull his feet on the deck, and with his last strength, he pushed himself over the railing and fell headlong into the cockpit. Almost immediately, he was unconscious.

32

He half awoke with a start, thinking that he had heard a woman scream, then he fell back into a stupor. The boat under him moved, annoying him; he wanted to sleep, and the cradle was rocking.

"Holy shit!" a man's voice said loudly.

Stone tried to tell him to shut up, but his voice wouldn't work. He went back to sleep.

"Give him CPR," a woman's voice said.

"He doesn't need CPR," the man replied, "he's breathing, and he has a pulse."

"Why are his hands like that?" she asked.

"How the fuck should I know, Jennifer?" the man asked, exasperated.

Stone, who had been lying on his right side, tried to turn onto his back.

"He moved!" she said.

"So he can move; big deal. Go below and get my rigging knife; it's on the chart table."

"But he might be dangerous," she said.

"In his present condition, he's not dangerous to anybody," the man replied. "Now go below and get me the knife. Jesus, he's got a length of anchor chain shackled to him; bring me the pliers, too."

Stone drifted off again, then he was moving, but he wasn't doing the moving. He opened his eyes.

"He's conscious," the man said. "Can you talk, sir?"

Stone's mouth wobbled, but nothing came out.

"Get me some water," the man said.

A moment later Stone tasted something fresh and sweet. He swallowed some, then some more. Then he vomited it back up, along with some salt water.

"Take some more," the man said. "You're going to be all right."

"Ah min fuff," Stone said.

"Don't try to talk yet; just drink some more water, and take some deep breaths."

Stone swirled some of the water around in his mouth and spat it out, then drank some more.

"Gd," he said.

"Don't talk; plenty of time for that later. Jennifer, go below and bring me a couple of dry towels."

"Okay," she said. She was back in a moment, dabbing at Stone's face.

Stone began to shiver violently, his teeth chattering loudly.

The man got the shackle loose and removed the chain. "Help me get this suit off him," the man said. "Let's get all his clothes off; he'll never get warm while he's sopping wet."

194

This took some time, and Stone wasn't much help. Finally he was naked, and both people were drying him with the towels.

"Can you stand up?" the man asked.

Stone tried to speak, failed, then nodded.

"Help me with him, Jennifer; we've got to get him below and into a sleeping bag; he's hypothermic."

Stone, with their help, got onto a cockpit seat, still shaking, then got his feet onto the companionway ladder. In another moment he was lying on a saloon berth being zipped into a clammy sleeping bag.

"Boil some water and make some of that instant soup," the man ordered.

Gradually, the shivering went away, and they got Stone into a sitting position and were feeding him hot soup from a cup.

"Thank you," he managed to say.

"Don't worry about it," the man replied. "I think we ought to get you to a hospital, but I don't think there's one on Catalina."

Stone shook his head. "No," he said.

"You don't want to go to a hospital?"

"No. I'm dead."

"You're not dead, but I think you had a pretty close call."

"Stay dead," Stone said.

"You want to stay dead?"

Stone nodded. "Gotta."

"Just finish the soup and get some rest; you'll feel better soon."

Stone fell back onto the berth and let go. Finally, he could let go. There were sounds of an engine starting and the anchor being pulled up, then they seemed to be moving. He went back to sleep.

When he woke, the clock on the bulkhead read just after 1:00 A.M. Stone struggled to sit up.

"Tom, he's awake," the woman said. She was sitting on the opposite berth, watching Stone.

"Will you come and take the helm?" he called back.

The boat heeled, and Stone could hear water rushing past the hull.

"The wind is coming up a little," the man said. "Just aim her at that star there; your course is a little north of east, and the wind's on the beam." He came below.

"Hi," Stone said.

"Feeling better?"

"Better is too strong a word, I think, but I'm feeling vaguely alive, which is an improvement."

The young man laughed. "I'm Tom Helford," he said. "I'm a medical student at UCLA, fourth year, which is why I haven't yet called the Coast Guard to get you to a hospital. My diagnosis was that you'd be all right after some rest and nourishment. You hungry?"

Stone nodded. "I missed dinner. Where are we headed?"

"Long Beach; that's where I keep the boat. Don't get to use it much these days, though."

"I'm sorry if I've cut your cruise short," Stone said. "By the way, my name is Stone Barrington."

"Good to meet you. Surprised to meet you."

"Yeah, I guess so."

"You want to tell me what happened?"

"I was on my way to a dinner party aboard a yacht anchored off Catalina, but I think the invitation wasn't sincere."

Helford laughed. "I guess not, what with the chain around your waist. Must have been hard to swim."

"It was harder when there was an anchor shackled to the chain."

"Holy shit! They didn't intend for you to come up again, did they?"

"No, they didn't."

"I've got a cell phone aboard. Why don't we call the cops and have them meet us at Long Beach?"

"That reminds me," Stone said. "There was a cell phone in my suit."

"Here it is," Helford said, holding it up. "I emptied your pockets onto the chart table."

"Will you take out the battery and soak the phone in some fresh water?"

"Sure, if you think it'll help."

"It can't hurt; I know the salt water won't help."

Helford pumped some water into the galley sink and dropped Stone's cell phone into it, then started making some sandwiches. "I see by your ID that you're a cop."

"Retired."

"Pretty young for retirement, aren't you? The

knee have something to do with it? I saw the surgical scar."

"Yep."

"You've got a New York driver's license."

"Yeah, I'm just a visitor to L.A."

"Speaking as a native Californian, I'd like to apologize for the reception; we usually treat tourists better."

"Apology accepted."

"What yacht were you headed for when you... took the detour?"

"I don't know her name; she's probably big, though."

"We were ashore for dinner, and on the way back to the boat we passed something of about a hundred and fifty feet called *Contessa*. Could that be her?"

"Could be."

"She was the only really big thing in the anchorage; nothing else over eighty, ninety feet."

"*Contessa*," Stone repeated. He wanted to remember that. "What sort of boat am I on?"

"A Catalina Thirty-five, elderly."

"She's nicely kept," Stone said, looking around, "but I think your masthead light is out."

"You're right; I haven't taken the time to go up and replace it."

"I didn't see her coming," Stone said, rubbing his forehead.

"You've got a bump there."

"It'll go away."

Helford handed Stone a sandwich and

another cup of soup. "Something I need to ask you," he said.

"Shoot."

"Am I involved in something illegal here?"

"No. You just thwarted something illegal."

"You're a lawyer, according to your business card; should I be hiring a lawyer?"

Stone shook his head. "No need. The sandwich is wonderful."

"Thanks. You're sure I'm not going to be in any difficulties because of your problem?"

"Positive. You're a Good Samaritan, and that's it."

"You said something about wanting to be dead."

"No, I *am* dead, and I want to stay that way for a while."

"So that whoever did this to you won't try to do it again?"

"They're not going to get a *chance* to do it again. It's just that what I have to do now will be easier if they think they don't have to worry about me."

Helford took a bite of his own sandwich and munched it thoughtfully. "Stone?"

"Yeah?"

"You're not going to kill anybody, are you?"

Stone thought about that for a minute. "No," he lied.

33

They made their berth at Long Beach at a little after 3:00 A.M. Stone, wearing some borrowed jeans and a UCLA sweatshirt, helped them to tie up and set the boat in order, and they walked up to the car park together.

Jennifer handed Stone a plastic shopping bag with a large, wet lump at the bottom. "Your clothes," she said.

"Stone, can I give you a lift somewhere?" Helford asked. "Finding a cab will be tough this time of night."

"My car is at Marina Del Rey; is that too far for you?"

"No problem. Jennifer, honey, you go back to the boat and get some sleep; I'll be back in half an hour."

"I'll give you no argument," she said wearily.

Stone climbed into a Mazda Miata with Tom Helford, and they set out.

"I keep having the feeling that I should be doing something more to help you," Helford said.

"There really is nothing else you can do," Stone replied. "Give me your address, and I'll send you the jeans and sweatshirt."

"Give them to the nearest homeless person."

They pulled into the car park at Marina Del Rey.

"I wish I could tell you more about this,"

Stone said, "but it's a long, long story, and it wouldn't make any sense, anyway."

Helford scribbled something on a piece of paper and handed it to Stone. "Here's my address and number; I'd like to hear that story someday."

"If it turns out to have a happy ending," Stone replied. He reached into a pocket and came out with money.

Helford held a hand up. "Forget it."

Stone peeled off three hundreds. "I'd like to buy you and Jennifer the best dinner you ever had."

Helford grinned and took the money. "Since you put it that way."

They shook hands, and Stone got out of the car and watched it roar away, then found his own car. He looked around and saw a night watchman a hundred yards away, headed in the opposite direction; then he opened the trunk of the car, tossed his sodden clothes inside, removed the tire iron, and closed the trunk.

Keeping a careful lookout for anyone who might be out at that hour of the night, he padded down the pontoons in his bare feet until he spotted the sports fisherman *Maria*. He came up on it carefully and found it dark; he doubted very much if Vinnie or Manny was sleeping aboard, but he wanted to be sure.

He stepped softly aboard and peered through the glass door into the cabin. The light on the pontoon illuminated the interior of the boat, and he could see no one. The cabin door was locked, but it was flimsy, and he made short work of it with the tire iron, making some noise in the process. He half hoped he would wake somebody aboard, so that he could use the tire iron in another way. He walked through the saloon and checked the sleeping cabins; both empty.

Free to work undisturbed, he found the engine room and switched on the lights. There were two large gasoline engines, and he inspected them carefully; they were cooled with raw sea water, as he had hoped. He found a screwdriver and loosened the clips that held the water hoses onto the seacocks, then he pulled the hoses free. He looked around for another opportunity but saw none, so he opened both seacocks and watched the sea water gush onto the engine room floor, then he went forward and did the same for the seacock at the ship's toilet. Satisfied, he went back on deck, looked around for traffic, then padded back to his car. By dawn, he figured, *Maria* would be resting comfortably on the bottom.

He drove back to the Bel-Air Hotel and, avoiding the front parking lot, drove through a rear gate and parked as close as he could to his suite. Once there, he showered, changed clothes, threw away the jeans and sweatshirt, then packed and carried his cases to the car. As he drove away, the sun was rising. He went back to Le Parc, where he was still paying for a suite, drove into the garage, and carried his cases up the rear stairs to his suite.

Then he got into bed and fell immediately asleep.

He woke at eleven, then called Rick Grant and made a lunch date.

Lunch was a hot dog on the Santa Monica Pier.

"How's it going?" Grant asked.

"I'll tell you, but I want it understood that I'm not reporting a crime; this is strictly off the books."

"Agreed," Grant replied.

"Yesterday, Onofrio Ippolito called me at the Bel-Air and invited me to a dinner party aboard his yacht, anchored off Catalina. I went to Marina Del Rey for my ferry ride, which was conducted in a fast sports fisherman by Vincent Mancuso and a friend of his called Manny. When we were almost there, one of them pulled a gun, then they bound me hand and foot, attached a chain and an anchor to me, and kicked me overboard. Just before they did that, one of them said 'Compliments of Onofrio Ippolito.'"

Grant looked at him oddly. "And why are you still here?"

"I got very lucky, shed the anchor, and made it to a moored sailboat. Some very nice people brought me back to the mainland."

"And you're not reporting the crime? You don't want me to arrest Ippolito and his boys for attempted murder?"

"No. Not yet, anyway. You could nail the two hoods, but I don't think you could make

203

the case against Ippolito on the basis of the phone call, and Vinnie and Manny sure aren't going to implicate him."

"Probably not. What do you want to do?"

"Well, I've made a start; I sank their boat, *Maria*, very early this morning. She's right in the middle of Marina Del Rey; they'll have a hell of a time getting her up, and it will be very expensive."

Grant burst out laughing. "You're right, that's a start. What next?"

"I told you I thought there was a bookie operation running out of Vinnie's Deli. Can you have it raided?"

"I'd need probable cause for a warrant."

"How about a tip from a snitch?"

"Who?"

"Me. You can even put my name on it, if you have to."

"I think I can arrange a raid."

"Good; I hope your guys won't be too careful with the fixtures and fittings."

"I'll mention that. What else?"

"This guy, Martin Barone? I'd like to know everything there is to know about him and Barone Financial Services."

"Okay."

"Do you know somebody at the FBI that you can trust?"

Grant thought about that for a minute. "What part of the FBI?"

"Them that deal with financial institutions."

"Yeah, I know a guy."

"I'd like to meet him."

"I'll see what I can do."

"Tell him there might be a kidnapping involved; those guys love a kidnapping."

"Okay. Where can I find you?"

"I'm back at Le Parc. I figure they won't be looking for me there."

"No, but they might send a cleanup crew."

"Jesus, I hadn't thought of that; I'd better get out of there fast."

"You need a place? I live about three blocks from here; my kid's in college, you can have his room."

"Thanks, but I'd rather stick with hotels; I'll let you know where I am." Stone pulled out his cell phone and switched it on; it lit up, as usual. "Son of a bitch, it still works. I'll have to write Motorola a nice letter."

"I can check with you on that number?"

"Yep."

"Anything else?"

"Rick, can you get hold of a handgun for me?"

"Something untraceable, I suppose."

"I'd rather not fill out any federal forms."

"Stone, are you planning to shoot somebody?"

"Not at the moment, but you never know."

34

Stone got himself out of Le Parc as fast as he could, first calling the Beverly Hills Hotel for a reservation. He might as well be comfortable, he thought, and hide in plain sight. He checked into a small suite and rang for the valet.

"Yes, sir?" the man said when Stone opened the door.

Stone held up his sodden suit, which he had hung on a hanger, and his shoes, into which he had inserted trees. "Do you think you can do anything with these?"

The man gingerly lifted a sleeve and sniffed it. "Salt water?" he asked.

"I'm afraid so," Stone said. "A boating accident."

"I'll have to soak it in fresh water first, to get out the salt, and then press it several times as it dries."

"Can I hope for the best?" Stone asked.

"You can always hope, sir, but I won't make any rash promises."

"Do the best you can," Stone said, slipping the man fifty.

"I most certainly will, sir."

The man disappeared, and Stone closed the door. He got some more sleep, and late in the afternoon took a call from Rick Grant.

"I got the meet set up with my FBI guy, but it's going to cost you an expensive dinner."

"Fine; where?"

"Place called Michael's, in Santa Monica, seven o'clock." He gave Stone the address and directions.

Refreshed and rested, Stone was at Michael's on time; Rick and another man were waiting for him at a table in a lovely garden.

"Stone, this is Hank Cable," Grant said.
Stone shook hands with the FBI agent.

"We've met before," the man said.

"Where?" Stone asked, puzzled.

"We had a meeting about the Sasha Nijinsky case, a few years ago, in New York. I was stationed there then."

"Now I remember."

"You were doing everything you could to keep us out of the case, as I recall."

"I believe I was," Stone agreed.

"I didn't particularly hold it against you; it's what we expected from the locals."

"I'm glad. What have they got you doing out here?"

"I run the financial investigations division."

"Just the man I want to talk to," Stone said, smiling.

"Let's order," Grant said.
They ordered drinks, perused the menu and ordered dinner, then got down to business.

"So, what do you want from us?" Cable asked.

"It's more what I'm going to give you," Stone replied.

"How much is it going to cost me?"

"It's a freebie; I don't want any glory, just to see justice done."
Cable hooted with laughter.
Grant stepped in. "Hank, I think it might react to your benefit if you listened."

"Okay, okay, shoot, Stone."

Stone turned to Grant. "Rick, did you get anything on Barone Financial Services?"

"It's registered with all the right state and federal agencies, but it's some kind of bucket shop. Headquarters is a rundown office building on La Cienega; they've got the top floor, the sixth, about two thousand square feet of space."

"Not a big outfit, then? Are there any other offices?"

"Just one, in Tijuana, Mexico."

"Fairly weird."

"What's really weird is that this little outfit has forty telephone lines, including several special lines for fast modem transmissions."

"Sounds like a bookie joint," Cable said.

"You ever hear of a bookie operation that was registered with the state and federal governments as a broad-base financial services organization?" Grant asked.

"Now that you mention it, no," the FBI agent replied.

"Neither have I," Stone said. "What it sounds like to me is money laundering, especially with the Mexico connection."

"Now you're talking," Cable said. "I *love* money laundries."

"Barone's girl told me he was in Mexico a lot," Stone said. "What about Barone himself? Does he have a sheet?"

"Two arrests as a teenager, in New York, for running numbers."

"He's connected, then," Cable said. "Why don't I see what I can do about some wiretaps?"

"Good idea," Stone said, "but I think there's a lot more to this than Barone and his company."

"Like what?" Cable asked.

"Ever hear of Abalone Fisheries?"

"Yeah. Holding company, isn't it?"

"Right, but it's who's doing the holding."

"Who?"

"Two guys named David Sturmack and Onofrio Ippolito."

"Ippolito, the chairman of Safe Harbor Bank?"

"The same. Abalone owns twenty-odd percent of Safe Harbor and nearly all of Barone Financial."

"Now you're getting really interesting," Cable said.

"You ever hear of Sturmack?"

"Can't say as I have."

"He's a lawyer who doesn't practice law, son of a guy who worked closely with Meyer Lansky. He's clean on paper, but he had major connections with the unions, especially the Teamsters."

"And Ippolito is in business with him? I mean, Ippolito has a reputation as upstanding."

"This upstanding citizen," Stone said, "ordered a hit on me last night." He told Cable the story.

"Had you ever met Ippolito before?"

"Once; I had dinner with him."

"And you're sure it was him on the phone?"

"I am."

"Holy shit."

"You look worried, Hank," Grant said.

"It's like this," Cable said. "I can look into Barone Financial on my own—check out the directors and the employees. If enough of them have records, I can probably get a wiretap order. But I can't go straight at Safe Harbor or Abalone without support from a lot higher up, and that's going to take a lot of evidence."

"If Barone Financial is dirty, won't that give you what you need to go after Abalone?"

"Maybe, depends how dirty, but you can be sure that if Ippolito and Sturmack are mob, they're going to have some distance between them and Barone. It'll be hard to nail them for one dirty operation; they could lay it off on Barone himself. I'll bet he doesn't report to either of the two big guys; there's got to be a layer in between."

"What about the raid on Vinnie's Deli?" Stone asked Grant.

"It's set for two P.M. tomorrow. We thought it best to go in when the tracks are open."

"Good. Did you get a personal warrant on Vinnie?"

"Yeah; it's too much to hope we'll catch him on the premises."

"If I were you, I'd have a tail on him before the raid. If he gets a call, he could run."

"I agree."

"Hang on," Cable said, "what's this about a raid on a bookie joint? How does that tie in?"

"Vincent Mancuso, the owner of the deli

210

where the bookie joint is running, works for Ippolito," Grant said.

"Directly?"

"Yeah."

"Well, if you get a good bust on the book-making charge, maybe you can use it to turn Mancuso."

"I doubt it," Grant said. "He'll plead it down and do some time, and Ippolito will take care of him."

Stone spoke up. "How about if you add attempted murder to the mix? Mancuso and his pal tried to kill me."

"I thought you wanted to stay dead."

"Tell him you've got a witness to the attempt, and you traced the boat to him. That's not an outright lie."

"It might work; who knows? I'd like to have something really heavy to hit him with, though. Pity the murder didn't take; then we could use the threat of the death penalty to get him talking."

Stone laughed. "That's more than I'm willing to give for the cause." Then he thought of something. "Wait a minute; Mancuso doesn't know the murder didn't take; charge him with murder."

"I can't do that, Stone; I know you're alive."

"Okay, then don't charge him, but tell him you're going to in interrogation."

"It's worth a try, but he's going to lawyer up the minute we get him to a station."

"Then ride him around a little; talk to him

in the car. Tell him that if he hands you Manny and Ippolito for the murder and tells you what he knows about Ippolito's operations, he'll walk on both charges."

"Come on, Stone, that's not going to work. We can't charge Ippolito for a murder that didn't work out, and I doubt if somebody like Mancuso knows anything of importance about Ippolito."

Cable spoke up. "You're better off getting what you can from Mancuso using the bookie charge as a weapon, without implicating Ippolito. That would only tip him off; he'd pull up the drawbridge, and I don't want that. I want to get a *lot* of stuff on him before we move."

"I guess you're right," Stone said.

"Look, Stone," Cable said, "I get the impression that you want all this to happen *now,* but it's not going to. It takes time to get enough evidence to prosecute financial crimes."

"I understand."

"Of course, if you could come up with a witness who knows at least some of the inside workings of Abalone, that would move things right along."

"Let me think about that," Stone said.

"Oh," Cable said, "there was mention of a kidnapping."

"I'm not sure about that yet," Stone replied. "I'll have to get back to you."

"Stone," the FBI agent said, "try not to get anybody killed, okay? Kidnappings are dicey."

"I'll try," Stone replied.

After dinner, Grant and Stone said good night

to Hank Cable, then walked into the parking lot.

"I've got two things for you," Grant said, taking a package from his car and handing it to Stone. "This is a little Walther 7.65 millimeter that conceals easily, along with a shoulder holster."

"Thanks, Rick," Stone said. "It's perfect."

Grant handed him an envelope. "This is a carry permit," he said. "I walked it through myself. It's the kind of thing retired cops get, and it doesn't specify a particular weapon. I don't want you to get caught carrying, even accidentally, without a license."

"I really appreciate that, Rick."

"I also don't want you to shoot anybody with that pistol, although it's as clean as a weapon can be. It would be a great embarrassment to me if you popped anybody."

"Rick, I understand your position, really I do. I can't promise you I won't use the piece, but I do promise you that if I do, it will be a good shooting."

Grant sighed. "I guess that's the most I can hope for," he said.

Stone drove slowly back to the Beverly Hills Hotel. He had registered there under his own name, and he hadn't changed cars. He was hoping against hope that somebody would mess with him again, particularly since he was now armed.

35

Stone had a mid-morning breakfast on his terrace overlooking the hotel's gardens, thinking about what Hank Cable had said at dinner the night before. He needed a witness to get enough on Ippolito to persuade his superiors to go after somebody so prominent. Stone could think of only two candidates. He telephoned the first.

"Hello?" Her voice was careful, neutral.

"Barbara, it's St... Jack Smithwick."

"What number are you calling, please?"

"Is he there?"

"I'm sorry, you've dialed the wrong number," she said. Then, just before she hung up, she whispered, "Call in an hour."

At loose ends, Stone went down to the pool for a swim, read the papers at poolside, then asked for a phone and called again.

"Hello?"

"I believe the appropriate question is, 'Is the coast clear?'"

She laughed. "Yes, it's clear."

"You free for lunch?"

"Sure, and I've got a car this time."

"Meet me at the pool at the Beverly Hills Hotel, and bring a bikini—a very small one."

"I'll be there in an hour." She hung up.

Stone swam a few laps, then hailed a pool-boy and arranged for a cabana.

She saw him from a distance, then walked

toward him, along the poolside, unbuttoning her cotton dress as she came.

For a moment he thought she was stripping in public, but when she stepped out of the dress she was wearing a very, very small bikini. She turned heads, and they didn't stop looking when she sat down at the table next to him and gave him a big wet kiss.

"I was hoping you'd call," she said. "I wasn't sure you would."

"I'm glad I did. I ordered us both a bacon cheeseburger; I hope it's as good as the last one."

"I'm sure it will be," she said.

They ordered piña coladas, and then lunch came. When they were finished, Stone got serious.

"Barbara, I want to ask you some questions, and I hope you'll give me straight answers."

"Okay."

"First of all, was everything you told me about yourself the other night the truth?"

"Yes, but that's more than I can say for you."

"What?"

"Your name isn't Jack Smithwick, is it?"

Stone reddened. "How did you know?"

"You think I'm so dumb that I can't tell when a man gives me a false name? Anyway, nobody is named Smithwick."

"I apologize," he said.

"Let's start over." She held our her hand. "I'm Barbara Tierney."

Stone took the hand. "My name is Stone Barrington."

"Stone," she said. "I like that."

"It was my mother's maiden name."

"It's nice. Now, why didn't you tell me your real name from the beginning? I would have liked you a lot better."

It escaped Stone how she could possibly have liked him better than the first time they met. "If you'll forgive me, I'll answer that later, but I will tell you the truth."

"All right. What do you want to know from me?"

"What do you know about Martin Barone?"

She blinked. "How do you know his name?"

"I got lucky."

"Stone, you said you'd tell me the truth."

"I had him investigated, but I didn't find out much; I need to know more."

"Why on earth did you have him investigated?"

"I promise, I'll fill you in, but later."

"What, exactly, do you want to know?"

"How did you meet him?"

"A girl I know, another actress, introduced us at a party."

"What sort of party?"

"It was at a bank downtown. We were hired to... just be decorative, I guess, and she had met him at a previous party. He was charming, one thing led to another, and he offered to let me live on the boat. I had been living at a friend's place, and we were crowding each other."

"Did you form any impressions about the kind of business he does?"

"Not at first, but over a period of a couple of weeks I heard his end of some telephone conversations."

"What did you learn?"

"He talked about moving stuff—he didn't say exactly what, but I think he was talking about money. At first I thought it was drugs, but now I think money."

"Did he talk about how he moves it?"

"He talked about pickups and deliveries."

"So he moves *cash* around?"

She nodded. "I think so; between here and Mexico."

"Does he keep any sort of schedule?"

"He goes away two or three times a week, but I'm not sure if it's always to Mexico."

"Do you think he's moving money personally, as in his car?"

"The Porsche doesn't have a lot of room in it," she said.

"I know; was there ever any talk of anything larger?"

"He mentioned a truck once."

"Do you know who his boss is?"

"He's his own boss; it's his company."

"But you met him at the Safe Harbor Bank?"

"How did you know which bank? I didn't tell you."

"It was more than a lucky guess. Did you meet a man named Ippolito there?"

"Yes, he's the head of the bank, I think; somebody pointed him out to me at the party. I got him a drink at one point."

"What was your impression of him?"

"I think his impression of me was that he thought I was a hooker, which annoyed me."

"Did you notice what kind of relationship Barone had with Ippolito?"

"Marty was doing a lot of major sucking up," she said.

"I can imagine. Did Marty say anything to you about his relationship with Ippolito?"

"He refers to him as the boss sometimes. Not to me, but on the phone. I'm sure that's who he's talking about. My turn for some questions."

"All right."

"Are you a cop?"

"No, but I used to be; now I'm a lawyer."

"What's your interest in Marty and Ippolito?"

"I think that both of them are mixed up in organized crime."

She rubbed her forehead. "I was afraid of something like that," she said. "I was beginning to get this feeling."

"Where is Marty now?"

"He left this morning for Mexico, or that's what he said, anyway."

"Barbara, I think you ought to get off the boat as soon as possible."

"I don't have anywhere to go," she said, "and I'm about out of money."

"What about the friend you stayed with before?"

"We didn't part on such good terms."

"Have you got a lot of stuff on the boat?"

"Two suitcases and a hanging bag."

"Tell you what: you go back to the marina,

218

pack up, and I'll meet you at the restaurant where we met in an hour, okay?"

"But where will I go?"

"You can stay with me, until we figure something out. Don't worry about money."

"Okay, let's do it."

"One other thing: remember I asked you if you had ever driven a white Mercedes convertible?"

"Yes."

"You didn't really answer me. Do you know the car?"

"I drove it here today," she said. "It's in the parking lot."

36

Stone arrived at the Marina Del Rey restaurant on time, but there was no sign of Barbara. Arrington's car was parked near the chandlery, though. When she was fifteen minutes late, Stone began to worry. Then she came up the ramp from the pontoon, struggling with her bags, one of which was on wheels. Stone ran to help her.

When they were in the car, she looked into her handbag. "Damn," she said, "I've still got the keys to the Mercedes; I'll have to take them back to the boat."

"Wait," Stone said, thinking. "Don't take the keys back; drive the car to the hotel."

"I can't just steal the guy's car," she said.

"It's not his car, and don't worry, he won't report it stolen."

"Stone, I don't want to get into trouble."

"Believe me, I'm getting you *out* of trouble."

"Oh, all right." She went to the Mercedes, and Stone led the way back to the hotel.

He called the parking valet aside. "Bury the SL500 somewhere," he said, handing the man a twenty. "We won't need it for a while." He gave his room key to Barbara, along with tip money for the bellman. "You go on upstairs; there's something I have to do."

"What am I supposed to do in a hotel room?"

"I've arranged for you to sign, so do some shopping downstairs, or go out to the pool again, if you like."

She brightened. "Okay; see you later."

It wasn't very far down Sunset to Vinnie's Deli. Stone parked on a side street facing the boulevard and looked at his watch: just in time, he thought. Ten minutes passed, then an unmarked car pulled up to the deli, and Rick Grant and another man got out and went into the place. Stone raised his binoculars and watched as they stood at the counter, ordering something and watching the counterman buzz two hoods through the door to the back room. Rick and his companion sat at a table and began eating their sandwich. From down the block, a large white van slowly approached the deli.

It was beautifully coordinated. Rick and the other cop got up from their table, walked

220

behind the counter, and pinned the counterman to the wall. The van opened, and a dozen SWAT team members spilled out and into the deli. Rick hit the buzzer under the counter, and the door to the back room opened as SWAT cops poured into the room. A moment later, two paddy wagons arrived on the scene, and a moment after that, the cops started loading arrestees into the wagons; among them was Vinnie Mancuso, Stone's swimming instructor. The whole thing took less than ten minutes.

When Rick Grant left the restaurant, Stone turned onto Sunset and pulled up in front of the deli, rolling down the opposite window. Grant walked over to the car.

"That seemed to go well," Stone said.

"Couldn't have gone better," Grant replied. "You want to come down and watch while I interrogate Mancuso?"

"Love to. Come on, I'll give you a lift."

"I'm going to stage a lineup for Vinnie's benefit," Grant said. "Just to get him worried."

Stone sat behind a one-way mirror and watched Vinnie Mancuso twitch. He was alone in the interrogation room, and he was nervous. A moment later, Rick Grant and another officer walked into the room and sat down at a table opposite Mancuso. Stone could hear the scraping of their chairs through the speaker in his room. One of the cops offered Mancuso a cigarette.

"No thanks," the hood said, "I gave them up."

221

"I'm glad to see you're concerned about your health, Vinnie," Grant said. "I guess you want to live a long life."

"You bet," Mancuso replied.

Grant shook his head. "It's not looking very good for a long life," he said. "Not for you."

Mancuso frowned. "What are you talking about?"

"Still, it's not as bad as it used to be," Grant said. "You don't have to sit in the gas chamber and hold your breath the way you used to; now you just get the needle. I'm told it's not unpleasant."

"Are you insane?" Vinnie asked incredulously. "For a bookmaking rap?"

"Not for that, Vinnie; we've got you cold for murder one."

"You're nuts. Where's my lawyer?"

"You called him; I assume he'll be here soon. I thought you might like a moment before he arrives to consider your position. My witness made you in the lineup, but good."

"Witness to what?"

"To the murder of Stone Barrington."

Mancuso looked across the table for a long moment. "Who?"

"The man you dumped in the Catalina channel the other night; a witness on a small boat made both you and your friend, Manny. We're picking him up now."

"I don't know what you're talking about," Mancuso said.

"I'm talking about the corpse we pulled

off the bottom of the channel this morning, with an anchor shackled to it. My witness watched you and Manny kick Barrington off the sports fisherman *Maria* at around nine in the evening. He was watching through night binoculars; he saw *everything*."

Mancuso's face began, very slowly, to fall.

"The only question now is, who gets the needle?" Grant said. "You or Manny? Or both?"

Mancuso said nothing, but it was obvious he was thinking hard.

"We got you first, so you get dibs on the deal," Grant said. "Once we bring Manny in, he'll get the same offer, if you haven't taken it."

"So you want me to nail Manny for you? Is that it?"

"Not just Manny," Grant said.

Mancuso's eyes narrowed. "What are you getting at?"

"We want the guy who gave the order."

Mancuso was shaking his head now. "Forget about it," he said.

"We want Ippolito."

The name startled Mancuso. "Where did you..." Then he stopped. "I don't know anybody by that name," he said.

"Vinnie, your lawyer is going to be here soon, and when he arrives it's going to be a lot harder to make a deal. After all, who's *he* working for? You're not paying his bill."

Mancuso was sweating now. "Look, I..." He took a deep breath. "I don't want to take the fall for this."

"Then don't take the fall," Grant said soothingly. "Talk to me."

Mancuso sweated some more but said nothing.

"You know Manny well," Grant said. "You think *he's* going to take the fall for you and Ippolito?"

"Manny's a standup guy," Mancuso muttered. "He don't give nobody up."

"You really believe that, Vinnie? You really believe that Manny will take the needle for you and Ippolito?" He shook his head sadly. "I don't think so."

Mancuso thought about that for a moment, then he looked at Grant and started to speak. Then, at that moment, a man carrying a briefcase walked into the room.

"My name is Larry Klein," he said. "I represent Vincent Mancuso; what's going on here?"

"We were just having a chat," Grant said.

"My client has nothing to say at the moment," Klein said. "Have you been attempting to interrogate him?"

"Mr. Mancuso knows his rights," Grant said. "He's signed a statement to that effect."

"Well, he's not saying anything further," the lawyer said, "and I want him removed to a secure room where I can talk with him without having somebody on the other side of a mirror."

"Whatever you say, counselor," Grant said. He turned to the other cop. "Take Mr. Klein and Mr. Mancuso down to Room Three, and leave them alone," he said.

The cop left with Mancuso and his lawyer. Grant turned toward the mirror and gave a big shrug. A moment later he arrived in Stone's room.

"Shit," Stone said. "Another three minutes and he would have caved."

"Win some, lose some," Grant said.

"What about Manny? Did you pick him up?"

Grant shook his head. "I've got somebody on it, but unless we pick him up before Mancuso's lawyer can make a phone call, our chances of getting him anytime soon are poor."

"How long can you hold Mancuso?"

"He'll have dinner at home tonight. I can't charge him with your murder."

"I guess not."

"His lawyer is going to wonder why, after Mancuso tells him about our conversation."

"And Ippolito will know within the hour."

"Probably," Grant said. "I wonder how the information will affect him. I expect it will confuse and annoy him."

"I hope so," Stone said.

37

When Stone arrived back at the Beverly Hills Hotel, he was approached by the parking valet.

"Oh, Mr. Barrington, I thought you said you wouldn't be needing the SL500 for a while," the man said.

"That's right."

"Well, your friend Miss Tierney left in it about ten minutes ago."

"She *left*?" Stone asked incredulously.

"That's right."

Stone went into the hotel, baffled, and went to his suite. Barbara's things were still there, and there was a note on the bedside table.

Dear Stone,
I left my makeup kit on Marty's boat, so I've gone to pick it up. I might do some window shopping, too, but I'll be back later this afternoon.

Barbara

"Oh, Jesus," Stone groaned. He ran down the stairs and ordered his car.

The parking valet looked baffled when he brought it. "Mr. Barrington, if you're only going to be a couple of minutes, we can keep your car here up front," the man said.

"Sorry about that," Stone said, slamming the door and yanking the car into gear. He drove to Marina Del Rey as quickly as he could, worried that Martin Barone might have turned up and caught Barbara in the act of moving out. He wasn't sure of what story she'd tell under pressure, and the last thing he wanted was to put this girl in any danger. When he arrived, Arrington's car was parked outside the chandlery.

He parked and walked quickly down the pontoons toward where *Paloma* was berthed. She seemed deserted. He looked around for unwelcome visitors, then jumped aboard. The cabin door was locked, and he couldn't see Barbara inside. He got off the boat in a hurry and started back toward his car; then, a couple of pontoons away, he saw something that gave him pleasure. A large crane on a barge was being maneuvered between the pontoons. He walked down the main pontoon and found a spot where he could watch the salvage operation from a distance. It took the divers a few minutes to get lifting straps under *Maria*'s hull, and then the crane went to work. Slowly, the sports fisherman broke the water and was raised to pontoon level. The divers stripped off their wetsuits and got pumps going to empty her of water. It would take quite a while, Stone reflected with satisfaction. He hoped her interior was thoroughly ruined.

He walked back toward the parking lot, and as he came back up the ramp he stopped in his tracks. Arrington's car was gone. He climbed back on his old perch on the ice machine and looked up and down the street, but he could not see the car. He hopped down in time to see a Porsche turn into the parking lot and take the space that Arrington's Mercedes had vacated.

A slickly handsome man in a pinstriped suit got out, locked the car, and walked down the ramp to the pontoon. Stone watched as he made his way toward where *Paloma* was berthed. This, he decided, was Martin Barone, and he was definitely not in Mexico. Barone disappeared among the boats, then, as Stone was about to leave, he suddenly reappeared, running.

Stone got into his car and pulled down the sun visor. Barone, in a great hurry, ran to the intersection and looked up and down the street, obviously looking for Barbara. He came back talking to himself, looking very unhappy indeed. He stood in the parking lot, deep in thought, for a minute, then got into the Porsche and drove out of the car park.

What the hell, Stone thought, *let's see where he goes.* Staying at least a block back, he followed the sports car into the canyons of downtown Los Angeles. *I know where he's going,* Stone thought, and he was right. Barone turned into the garage at the headquarters building for the Safe Harbor Bank. Stone wished he could follow him up to Ippolito's offices and listen to him explain that his girlfriend had run off with Arrington Calder's Mercedes. He would enjoy that conversation.

Stone sat in his car, waiting, for some forty minutes, then, suddenly, the Porsche emerged from the garage and turned east. Stone followed the car to Beverly Hills and watched as it turned into the gates of a house on Beverly Drive. He made a note of the address, then drove back to his hotel.

"Any sign of Miss Tierney?" he asked the parking valet as he surrendered his car.

"No, sir, not yet."

"Thanks," Stone said, then went to his suite.

228

He had been there for two hours, idly changing channels on the television, when Barbara walked in.

"Hi," she said brightly.

"Hi," he replied. "I'm glad to see you're still alive."

"Why shouldn't I be?" she asked, flopping down beside him on the sofa.

"Because the people Martin Barone deals with are bad people, and if they thought for a minute that you could be a bother to them, they would hurt you."

She frowned. "Why would they do that?"

"Barbara, I'm going to tell you as much of it as I can," Stone said. "The car you were driving belongs to Arrington Calder, Vance Calder's wife. She's a friend of mine."

"How good a friend?" Barbara asked.

"We used to be close, but she married Vance."

"You know Vance Calder?"

"Yes."

"Then why didn't you say hello to him in the restaurant the other night?"

"Because I didn't want Vance to see me."

"Why not?"

"Let me explain, and please don't ask any questions until I've finished."

"All right."

"Vance's wife disappeared a couple of weeks ago; nobody knows where she is."

"Not even Vance?"

"Especially not Vance. You promised not to ask any questions until I'm finished."

229

"Sorry, go ahead."

"Something is terribly wrong. Vance called me in New York and asked me to come out here and find Arrington, but when I got here, he was no longer anxious for me to find her. I thought that was very suspicious, so I started looking into her disappearance on my own. Apparently this became a concern to Mr. Ippolito, Martin Barone's boss."

"You know Mr. Ippolito?"

"I met him at a dinner party at Vance's."

"You've been to Vance's *house*? What's it like?"

"Barbara..."

"I'm sorry, I won't ask any more questions until you're finished."

"Good. Now, where was I?"

"You made Mr. Ippolito mad."

"Yes, I did. He invited me to a dinner party on his boat, then he had two goons tie an anchor to me and throw me into the Pacific Ocean."

She opened her mouth in horror, but Stone put a hand over it.

"I didn't drown; I got loose, and some people on a boat picked me up. Now I'm trying again to learn what happened to Arrington Calder, and I don't want Ippolito to know that I'm still alive. I asked you to take Arrington's car and bring it here because I want to worry Ippolito and his people. Apparently, that worked because Martin showed up at Marina Del Ray this afternoon, found you and the car gone, and then he went directly to Ippolito's office to report the missing car. That means

230

that they will want to know what happened to the car, and they will want to know what happened to you, so I think you should be very careful and stick close to the hotel. If you really have to go somewhere, I'll rent a car for you, but don't drive the Mercedes again, because it could be dangerous. Understand?"

She nodded, opened her mouth, then closed it again.

"Now you can ask questions."

She smiled brightly. "What's Vance Calder's house like?"

38

They ordered dinner sent to the suite and ate well. Barbara had only one glass of wine, but it seemed to have an amorous effect, since she was playing footsie under the table. Stone, though, was preoccupied. He felt that having Arrington's car at the Beverly Hills Hotel was a liability, no matter where it was parked; in fact, he was beginning to wonder if he'd chosen the best possible hotel for his purposes. The traffic of movie people through the lobby and the Polo Lounge was phenomenal, he knew, and he didn't want to run into Louis Regenstein or David Sturmack, or anybody he had met at Vance's house. He'd deal with that in the morning, but in the meantime, he wanted to get rid of Arrington's car. He thought it might be time, too, to explain some facts to Vance Calder.

"Let's go for a drive," he said.

"I thought maybe we'd..."

"Love to, but later."

"Where are we going?"

"To Vance Calder's house."

"Great!"

"We're not going inside."

"Oh." Her face fell.

"But you can get a good look at it."

"If we're not going inside, why bother?"

"I'm going inside, but I don't want Vance to see you; it might be dangerous."

"How?"

"Trust me on this, Barbara."

"Oh, all right."

While Barbara followed in the E430, Stone drove Arrington's car, and it made him nervous; the vanity plate was just too conspicuous. Still, he made it to Bel-Air unmolested. A block from Vance's house he stopped the car, got out, and went back to the sedan. "I want you to wait here," he said.

"But I haven't seen his house yet," she complained.

"I promise I'll show it to you when I'm finished, all right?"

"All right. Suppose the police come and want to know what I'm doing here?"

"The police are not going to bother a beautiful woman in a Mercedes," he said. "But if anybody asks, just tell them you're waiting for a friend." He wrote his portable number on a card and gave it to her. "If you have any problems, just use the car phone and call me; my cell phone is in my pocket."

"Okay."

Stone got back into the convertible and drove around the corner to Vance's house. He could see lights on inside, but the gates were locked. He was about to press the buzzer outside the gates when he had a thought. He opened the compartment under the center armrest, rummaged around, and came up with what he had been looking for. He pressed the remote, and the gates swung silently open.

Farther up the drive, it forked and he turned toward the garages. Using the remote control again, he opened the garage door, drove the car inside, and parked it next to Vance's identical, except black, convertible. He didn't want to enter the house this way, so he left the garage, pressing a button inside the door to close it, and started up the walk toward the front door. As he did, a car's lights flooded the driveway, and he stopped behind a bush. The car was at the front gate, and a moment later, the gates swung open, and the visitor drove up the driveway.

The visitor parked his car and entered the house, but Stone's view of the house was not good enough to reveal the identity of the driver. He had wanted to see Vance alone; a visitor was not in his plans, so he started back down the driveway. *Another time,* he thought.

He reached the gates and found them closed.

How would he open them now? From the inside, he reflected, they probably opened on a magnetic sensor as a car approached them; what he needed was some object of ferrous metal large enough to make the sensor react. He looked to his left and right and saw a rake on the edge of a flower bed; that might do it. He walked toward it, and as he did, another car suddenly arrived at the gate. Stone jumped into the shrubbery and waited while the car was admitted and made its way up the drive. The gates closed before he could get to them.

He was about to try the rake when he became curious about who was visiting Vance at this hour of the evening. It was after ten, too late for a social occasion. He dropped the rake and walked up the driveway again, remembering the layout of Vance's house. Lights were on at the front, so he couldn't go peeking in windows; then he remembered Vance's study, which was at the rear of the house, off the living room.

He walked past the garage and around toward the rear of the house. He saw a light in a window ahead and made for that. Keeping low, parting the shrubbery as silently as he could, he made his way to the window and, at a corner, raised his head above the sill. Three men were in the room—Vance, Louis Regenstein, and a man Stone didn't recognize. He was around forty, casually dressed in a tweed jacket, red-haired, probably of Irish extraction.

Regenstein was saying something, but Stone couldn't hear what it was. Whatever he was saying, it was making Vance angry. "No!" Vance said loudly, then lowered his voice and continued in a strident manner.

Regenstein and the other man were obviously trying to placate him, but Vance was very angry indeed. Stone looked across the room and saw that Vance was standing near a window on the far wall. Maybe Stone could hear from there. He was about to move to that side of the house when the telephone in his pocket rang, loudly. He flattened himself against the house and scrambled for the phone, finally getting to it after the second ring.

"Hello," he whispered.

"Vance, it's Barbara; how much longer are you going to be? I'm getting tired of sitting here."

"A few minutes; listen to the radio or something, and don't call me again unless it's an emergency."

"What kind of emergency?"

"Just don't call again." He snapped the phone shut and peeked into the room again. The three men were looking around, trying to discover the source of the noise. Stone pushed slowly back through the shrubbery, and as he did he was hit from all sides by water. Half blinded, Stone blundered through the flowerbed to the grass, but got no relief from the continuous spray. It must be on a timer, he thought, and the sprinkler heads were placed to give full coverage. He ran to the corner of the house, and as he turned it, lights came on—bright lights, floodlights, activated by a motion sensor, most likely. There was probably a silent alarm, too. There was nothing for it but to run.

The floodlights revealed a tall wrought-iron fence at the rear of the house, and he thought it might be electrified, so the front gate seemed his only chance. He sprinted past the garage and across the lawn, not bothering with the driveway, and as he did, the front lawn sprinklers came on, too. He charged across the grass, grabbed the rake, and started waving it at the gates. Nothing.

Stone looked desperately around for a sensor and saw a small box on a foot-high steel pole. He waved the rake at it and, finally, the front gates started to open; he threw away the rake and ran into the street, legs pumping. The police were going to arrive any second, he reckoned, so it was no time for a stroll. He made the corner, turned it and ran up the block, looking for the car. It was gone. Through some trees to his right he saw a car wearing flashing lights turning a corner. He crossed the road and dived through a hedge, hitting the ground on all fours, then flattened himself on the grass as the car sped past. He caught sight of a car door that proclaimed the vehicle to be from the Bel-Air Security Patrol. The car turned the corner toward Vance's house, and Stone broke back through the hedge. Somewhere behind him a dog–a *very* large dog, from the sound of him—had begun to bark. He stood in the street, soaking wet, grass-stained, and completely exposed, and tried to think what to do next.

As he thought, another car turned the corner to his right, and Stone was about to plunge through the hedge again when he realized the approaching headlights were a familiar oval shape. He ran at the car, hoping to God it was not somebody else's E-class Mercedes, and waved it down. Shielding his eyes from the headlights, he could see Barbara behind the wheel. He flung himself into the passenger side.

"Get out of here!" he said. "Take a left at the corner!"

"Stone, what happened?" she asked. "You're dripping wet."

The car had not moved.

"Barbara," Stone said as quietly and as slowly as he could, "please drive away and make a left. Do it *right now*."

"Oh, all right," she said, and she drove slowly away.

"Faster," he said.

"How fast?"

"Faster than this!" he hissed.

"Maybe you'd better drive," she said.

"Stop the car." He got out, ran around the car, and, when she had settled herself in the passenger seat, smoothed her skirt, fastened her seatbelt, and closed the door, roared off into the Bel-Air night.

"Stone," she said.

"What?"

"I didn't get to see Vance's house."

39

Stone paced up and down the living room of his suite, trying to think. It was mid-morning, and the California sun streamed through the sliding glass doors to the terrace. Barbara was sitting up in bed, picking at her breakfast and watching Regis and Kathie Lee. The doorbell rang; Stone opened it and found the valet standing there, holding his cleaned clothes.

"Morning, Mr. Barrington," the man said. "I think we did pretty good with these things."

"Thanks very much," Stone said, tipping the man and taking the clothing.

"You sure are hard on your clothes," the man said. "But at least the second one was fresh water instead of salt."

Stone hung up the clothes, closed the doors to the bedroom, picked up the phone, and dialed Rick Grant's number.

"Lieutenant Grant."

"Rick, it's Stone."

"You all right?"

"Yes."

"I was worried when I didn't hear from you yesterday."

"Anything new?"

"Nothing; Mancuso is out on bail, and we haven't found Manny yet. Oh, somebody spotted Mrs. Calder's car on Sunset in Beverly Hills last night about ten, but I didn't hear about it until this morning."

"That was me; I was returning the car to Calder."

"What did he have to say?"

"I didn't get to talk to him," Stone said. "I just left the car in the garage."

"It must be driving him nuts, wondering how it got there."

"I hope so. Anyway, you can take the car off the patrol list."

"Okay. What else can I do for you?"

"Listen, Rick, I've got a big favor to ask."

"What's that?"

"I've got to get rid of a girl."

Rick was instantly wary. "What do you mean, 'get rid of'?"

"I mean find her a safe place to stay. She's Martin Barone's girlfriend; I got her packed up and off his boat, and she stayed the night with me at the Beverly Hills, but I've got to get her out of here; she's driving me nuts. Do you maybe know some nice policewoman who could take her off my hands for a few days?"

"What does she look like?"

"Tall, brunette, gorgeous."

"I know a nice police*man* who could, maybe, take her off your hands for a few days. My boy's away at college, so there's a room at my place."

"What about your wife?"

"Divorced eight years ago."

"Where can we meet?"

They met at Rick's house in Santa Monica.

"But I don't understand," Barbara said as they pulled up. "Why can't I stay at the Beverly Hills with you?"

239

"Because it's too dangerous," Stone said, getting her luggage from the trunk. "I'm moving out, too, remember."

"Where are you moving to?"

"I don't know yet," he lied. "I've got to find a place."

"Why don't we just move to another hotel, then?"

"I have too much to do, Barbara; I can't take care of you."

"So how's your friend going to take care of me?"

"You'll be safe with him; he's a cop."

"A *cop*?" she said, as if she were being asked to move in with a criminal.

"A very important detective, high up in the LAPD. Nobody will touch you if you're staying at his house."

"Oh," she said.

Stone rang the bell, and Rick appeared at the door.

"Come on in, both of you."

"Barbara, this is Lieutenant Richard Grant."

"Call me Rick," he said, shaking her hand and looking her up and down in a distinctly approving manner.

"Hi, Rick," she said, smiling brilliantly. "I'm Barbara Tierney."

"What a lovely name," he said.

"Look, I've got to get moving, so I'll leave you two alone," Stone said.

Rick followed him out the door. "She's amazing," he said.

"You don't know the half of it."

"Where will you be?"

"I'm moving back to the Bel-Air. They've got a suite for me that's at the top end of the hotel, so I can park outside and stay away from the bar and restaurant, where I might run into somebody I don't want to see."

"Mancuso's lawyer called me, wondering about this murder charge I threatened his client with. I told him I intended to charge him, but in my own good time."

"Good."

"I wouldn't be surprised if he ran."

"Neither would I; Ippolito will want to get him out of town."

"Sorry this hasn't been more productive."

"You get any more on Martin Barone?"

"Not yet."

"Barbara knows him well," Stone said. "You might want to question her closely."

"My pleasure," Rick grinned.

"I'll talk to you later; you two have a good time."

"We'll try."

Stone moved back into the Bel-Air Hotel, into a small suite at the north end of the property, with a car park nearby. He ordered some lunch from room service, then called his secretary in New York.

"Hi," she said. "Vance Calder called."

"What did he have to say?"

"Just wanted you to call him back, said he'd be at home all day. Say, I never got that cashier's check you said you were mailing."

"I've still got it, but it's a little worse for the

241

wear. I'd better hang onto it; I'm getting low on money."

"Whatever. I've paid all the bills, and everything seems to be in pretty good shape here."

"Glad to hear it; I'm not ready to leave L.A. yet. I'll call you tomorrow."

He hung up and dialed Vance's home number.

"Hello?"

"Vance, it's Stone Barrington."

"Oh, Stone, thank you for calling."

"What can I do for you?"

"I hardly know how to answer that, Stone; I wish I could talk to you face to face and try and explain what's been going on."

"We can arrange that, if you like."

"You mean you'll come back out here?"

"I never left."

"What? You're still in L.A.?"

"Yes, but you can't tell anyone that—not a soul, do you understand?"

"Of course, whatever you say."

"I mean it, Vance; if you tell *anyone* I'm in L.A., it could be very dangerous for me."

"I promise, I'll say nothing to anyone."

"Not even Betty."

"If you say so."

"Are you alone?"

"Yes, it's the servants' day off; I'm at home, reading scripts."

"All right, I'll be there in ten minutes; open the front gate."

"Thank you, Stone; I appreciate this."

"Don't appreciate it until we've talked.

You have a lot to tell me, and this time I'm going to have to have the truth."

"I understand."

"See you in an hour."

Stone had lunch on his tiny garden terrace, changed clothes, and started out for Vance's house.

40

Stone was sitting at a stop sign, waiting to turn into Vance Calder's street, when a Rolls-Royce convertible drove past. The driver was David Sturmack. Stone turned right, then turned right again, into Vance's drive. The gates were closed. Stone rang the buzzer.

"Yes?" Vance's voice said over the intercom.

"It's Stone, Vance."

"Oh, Stone; something's come up; can I call you later?"

"No, I want to see you now."

"Stone, I'm sorry, I just can't."

"Vance, open the gate and talk to me, or I'll go straight to the tabloids and the police with what I have."

After a moment's silence the gates swung open. By the time he had parked and walked to the front door, Vance was waiting, and he looked grim.

"Stone, I'm sorry you came; I just can't tell you anything," he said, standing in the doorway.

Stone brushed past him. "Let's go into your study, shall we?"

Vance followed him through the living room. "I really can't talk; I just wish you'd take my word for it."

Stone went into the study and settled into a comfortable chair, pointing at one for Vance.

Vance sat down on the edge of the chair and looked at the floor.

"You've got to let me help you, Vance."

The actor shook his head. "I can't; I'm sorry."

"Are they threatening to harm Arrington?"

Vance looked up. "I'm talking to her every day; she's fine."

"And what does she say, Vance? 'Get me out of here? Take me home? Protect me?'"

Vance winced. "It's just awful," he said. "I've agreed to what they want, but it's going to take a few days to set it up, before Arrington can come home."

"What do they want?"

"I can't tell you."

"Who are 'they'?"

He shook his head. "I can't."

"David Sturmack was just here; he must be deeply involved."

"I didn't say that, you did," Vance said, looking alarmed.

"And Lou Regenstein."

"I didn't say that."

He wanted to ask who the red-haired man was who had been in his study the night before. "And Ippolito."

"Stone, please stop it; I can't tell you any more. You just can't imagine what's at stake."

"I think I can; Arrington's life and that of her baby are at stake."

"Is that what this is about? The baby?"

"Certainly, that's part of it; that's what you used as bait to get me out here."

"Stone, I'm terribly sorry I asked you to come. When... the situation changed, I tried to make it profitable for you to have made the trip."

"I cannot describe the trip as profitable," Stone said.

"What is it you want, personally?"

"I want Arrington to be free to... come home or do whatever she wants to do."

"Like go back to you?"

"Do you think that's what she wants?"

"I don't know what she wants; we can't talk about that in our phone conversations."

"Vance, I am not going to walk away from this, and you'd better get used to the idea." There had been no mention of Arrington's car; perhaps Vance hadn't been in the garage yet.

"Stone, if they find out that you're not back in New York, they'll... there's no telling what they'll do."

"They know I'm not in New York."

"What?" Vance asked, alarmed.

"They think I'm dead."

"Dead?" he asked weakly.

"Did you go to a dinner party on Ippolito's yacht at Catalina a few nights ago?"

"I was invited, but I didn't go."

"I was invited and didn't go, either. On the way to the party, I got dumped into the

Pacific with my hands and feet bound and an anchor shackled to me."

Vance's mouth dropped open. "I don't believe it," he said. "They wouldn't do something like that to..."

"They've been threatening to do it to Arrington, haven't they? Why wouldn't they do it to me?"

Vance buried his face in his hands. "Oh, shit, shit, shit. I'm so sorry, Stone; I never meant for something like that to happen to you, and it's my fault."

"How so?"

"I told them you were at the Bel-Air."

"And how did you know?" Stone asked, knowing the answer.

"Betty told me."

"She told you but not them?"

"Yes. She doesn't know who's involved; she doesn't know anything about this, except what she might imagine. She told me because she would never hide anything from me."

"I'm glad to hear she didn't tell Ippolito," Stone said, and he was. He felt better about Betty now.

"Betty would never do anything to harm you," Vance said. "I think she's half in love with you."

"You're very lucky to have her," Stone said, reflecting that Vance seemed to have the women he wanted.

"I certainly am."

"Vance, if you will trust me enough to tell me what's going on, I can help, I'm sure I can."

Vance looked at him, his jaw set. "Stone, if

I could, I would; but I can't do *anything* that might have even the slightest chance of harming Arrington."

Stone nodded. "Then I guess I'd better be going."

Vance walked him to the door. "I hope I can tell you all about this someday, when it's over."

"Vance, are you going to tell Ippolito I was here, that I'm alive?"

"No. I swear to God I won't."

Stone shook his hand and left. He hoped the actor wasn't lying.

41

Stone walked into the Beverly Hills branch of the Safe Harbor Bank and asked to see the branch manager. Shortly he was seated at the man's desk.

"Welcome back, Mr. Barrington," Marshall said. "I hope you've come to open an account with us."

"I'm afraid not, Mr. Marshall; I've just come to cash the cashier's check you arranged for me on my last visit."

"Of course."

Stone took the check from his inside pocket and handed it over. "I'm afraid it's a little worse for the wear; I had a boating accident."

Marshall inspected the check closely. "Yes, it is a bit worn, isn't it? Still, I can make out the check number and what's left of my signature. Of course we'll cash it; how would you like the money?"

"In hundreds, please."

Marshall was no longer looking at Stone, but over his shoulder.

"Good afternoon, Mr. Ippolito," he said, rising. "Would you excuse me for just a moment?" he said to Stone. Marshall walked past his desk toward the door of his office.

Stone froze in his seat; he could hear the voices of both men from behind him.

"What brings you to see us?" Marshall asked.

"I was in the neighborhood, and I just thought I'd drop in," Ippolito said.

"I'm just cashing a check for a customer," Marshall said. "If you'll wait just a moment my office will be free, and we can talk, if you like."

"No, no," Ippolito said. "I really was just in the neighborhood. I do want to compliment you, though, on the very nice increase in new accounts."

"We've been working hard on that," Marshall said.

"Well, I'll be off, then; you get back to your customer."

"Good to see you again, Mr. Ippolito." Marshall returned to his desk. "That was our chairman," he said to Stone. "I'm sorry, I should have introduced you."

"That's quite all right," Stone said, dabbing at his damp forehead with a handkerchief. "If you don't mind, I'm in a bit of a hurry."

"Of course; I'll be right back with your money."

Stone allowed himself to look over his shoulder. Ippolito was still in the bank, shaking hands with a man just inside the front door.

Marshall returned with Stone's fifteen thousand dollars and handed him an envelope. "Be sure and count it."

"Thank you," Stone said, standing up. "That won't be necessary." He shook hands with Marshall and looked over his shoulder again before he turned around. Ippolito had left the bank.

Stone walked quickly to the window and peered into the street. A familiar gray Lincoln Town Car was pulling away from the curb. He ran for his own car, got it started, and followed, staying well back. He had nothing pressing to do; he might as well see where Ippolito was going.

He followed the Lincoln to Santa Monica Boulevard, then nearly all the way to the beach. To Stone's surprise, the car stopped at Grimaldi's. He looked at his watch: half past three, a little late for lunch. He parked half a block away and watched Ippolito get out of the car and go into the restaurant.

He had a thought; he called the FBI and asked for Hank Cable.

"Agent Cable."

"Hank, it's Stone Barrington."

"Hi, there, how's it going?"

"You ever heard of an Italian restaurant in Santa Monica called Grimaldi's?"

"Nope."

"It's a wiseguy joint; I had dinner there last week and saw Ippolito and a couple of goombahs having a meet. I'm sitting outside the place right now, and Ippolito just went in."

"A little late for lunch, isn't it?"

"That's what I was thinking. Maybe something besides pasta is being made there. You think you could get it on your wiretap list?"

"I'll see what I can do. We're scheduled to wire Barone Financial tonight; I'll let you know what we get."

"Great." Stone gave him the address of the restaurant and hung up.

Ippolito was in the restaurant for the better part of an hour. Stone thought about going to the back door and snooping, but it was too risky in broad daylight. Finally, Ippolito came out and got back into the Lincoln. As it turned onto Santa Monica Boulevard, Stone got a look at the front seat. Vinnie Mancuso and his buddy, Manny, had been replaced by two others right out of the same mold. Stone followed as the car drove toward the beach, then turned north along the coast. Soon they were on the Pacific Coast Highway, heading toward Malibu.

They were well into the beach community when the Lincoln turned into a garage attached to an elaborate house behind a high fence, close to the road like all the other houses. Stone looked the house over carefully; it was of a style that might be called contemporary traditional. A fence obscured the ground floor, but there was a palladian window in the peak of the second floor, and a cupola perched atop the roof. He made a U-turn, parked, and waited. A moment later, the Lincoln backed out of the garage and drove back toward L.A. The rear seat was empty. It was after five now; maybe it was Ippolito's own house.

He made another U-turn and stopped at a restaurant a few doors away, went inside, and found a stool at the bar. Happy hour was just starting, and people were stopping for a drink on the way home from work. Stone had a gin and tonic and kept to himself. After an hour had passed he got a table, ordered another drink, and asked for a menu. The sun was sinking loudly into the Pacific, a giant red ball given a hard edge by the smog.

It was dark outside by the time he had finished his dinner. He ordered another drink, and when it came he paid his check and walked out onto a deck, where people were dining. There was a stairway down to the beach, and Stone took it. He set his drink down on the bottom step and walked along the sand for fifty yards, watching for the house; the cupola on top made it easy to pick out, even in the dark. There were lights on, and perhaps ten feet above his head he could see that a sliding glass door to the deck was open.

Stone looked around; the beach was deserted now. He walked under the house's deck and listened. Soft music wafted out into the night air. Above his head he could see the outline of a folding stairway to the beach, in its retracted position. He looked around in the dark until he found a rusty coat hanger, then, after listening for a while, he climbed up on a supporting beam between two of the pilings that supported the house, unbent the hanger, hooked the end of the stairway, and pulled it slowly down until it reached the sand.

Carefully, he climbed the stairs until his head was at deck level, then stopped and listened again. To the right of the sliding glass doors a window was open, and human noises were emanating from it, grunts and groans, sighs and little shrieks. Ippolito was getting laid. Stone continued softly up the stairs.

Finally at deck level, he looked around. There was an assortment of deck furniture and a charcoal grill; a folded beach umbrella leaned against the house; he saw nothing and no one else. Stone carefully peeked through the open sliding door and saw a handsomely furnished living room. A fire was crackling in the fireplace, and the romantic music was louder now. He had hoped that Ippolito was meeting with somebody and that he might overhear something useful, but all he heard was the continuing sounds from the bedroom.

The least he could do, he thought, was to disturb the fun. On the deck beside the charcoal grill was a can of firestarter and a box of matches. Stone picked up the can, which was nearly full, and unscrewed the top. Still standing on the deck, he squirted a stream of the fluid onto the living room carpet, making a trail back out to the deck. He made a little puddle on the deck, then carefully tossed the can into the living room; it landed on the trail of fluid. He looked up and down the beach but could see no one. After checking his escape route again, he struck two matches, let them burn for a moment, then stuck them into the box, and closed it. A minute or two would pass before the box and then the matches in the box ignited. He turned and hurried quietly down the stairs, then gave them a push, sending them back into their retracted position with little noise.

He walked quickly back to the restaurant, picked up his drink from the steps, and climbed to the deck. He walked to the opposite end and took up a position there, sipping his drink. A moment later he heard a soft *whoomp* as the can of lighter fluid exploded, followed a moment later by a female shriek and male cursing. The diners looked toward the house with the cupola, some of them standing up and pointing.

"Call the fire department," somebody told a waiter, who ran inside to the phone.

Stone leaned against the railing and watched the glow of the fire against the glass of the sliding doors. Another three minutes passed before he heard the sirens. The sound made him smile to himself.

It wasn't much of a fire, but it had surely ruined Ippolito's evening. Pretty soon, after Ippolito thought about the sinking of his sports fisherman and the fire at his beach house, he was going to start thinking that somebody was out to get him.

He would be right, Stone reflected, sipping his drink. Then his hand began to shake. He had committed arson. Ippolito and the woman in the house might have died, and then he would have been a murderer. He hadn't carried the pistol today, and that was good, because in his present frame of mind he might have just walked into the house and shot Ippolito.

He had better start carrying the weapon now, he thought.

42

Stone had finished breakfast and was getting out of a shower when the phone rang. He grabbed a robe, got into it, and made the bedside table on the fourth ring.

"Hello?"

"It's Rick; did I wake you?"

"Nope; I was just getting out of a shower."

"Get dressed and meet me at the back gate of the hotel in ten minutes; I want you to take a look at something with me."

"Okay, I'll be there." Stone hung up, toweled his hair mostly dry, got into some slacks, a shirt, and a blazer, and started out the door. Then he remembered; he went back, took off the blazer, slipped into the shoulder holster, fitted the pistol into it, slipped an extra clip into his pocket, got back into the blazer, grabbed a tie, and left the suite.

Rick was waiting at the rear gate. "Morning," he said.

Stone got into the car. "Morning. What's up?" He began knotting the tie.

"I'm not sure, exactly, but I have a hunch; we'll see if it's a good one." He handed Stone the late edition of the *Los Angeles Times* and pointed to a story in the stop press column on the front page, then drove away.

Stone read the short piece.

Last night, late, the Malibu Fire Department answered a call from the Pacific Coast Highway home of Onofrio Ippolito, chairman of the Safe Harbor Bank and a well-known Los Angeles philanthropist.

A spokesman for the department said that Ippolito, whose wife was out of town, was at home alone and had an accident with a charcoal grill while fixing himself some dinner.

The fire was put out in less than fifteen minutes. There was little structural damage to the house, but a deck and the contents of the living room were destroyed. Mr. Ippolito was not injured.

"Sounds like an exciting evening," Stone said, smiling.

"And where did you spend *your* evening?" Rick asked.

"I went out, had a few drinks and some dinner."

"Where?"

"I don't remember exactly; I'm a stranger

in town, remember? The geography of this city confuses me."

"Yeah, it can be confusing," Rick said, sticking a flashing light on the roof of the car. They were on the freeway now, driving fast, weaving in and out of the mid-morning traffic. Occasionally he used the siren.

"Where we going?"

"Long Beach."

"For what?"

"I'm superstitious about predictions; indulge me."

Half an hour later they parked next to an ambulance, got out of the car, and walked down a long dock between fishing boats. At the end of the dock a clutch of uniformed and plain-clothes cops loitered around a trawler that was moored stern to.

"Hey, Rick," a detective said, shaking his hand. "I didn't know you left headquarters any-more."

"I like a little sea air," Rick replied. "What have you got?"

The detective pointed into the boat, where a tarpaulin covered something.

Rick beckoned Stone to follow him, then jumped down into the boat and pulled back the canvas. "Confirm my guess," he said. "The other one is Manny."

Stone looked at the two bodies. Vincent Mancuso and Manny were wet, dead, and chained together with a hefty anchor. "Good guess," he said.

"When the call came in I had a feeling." Rick

turned to a man in a suit, who was writing in a notebook. "Did they drown?"

The man shook his head. "They each took two rounds behind the right ear. Small caliber, very neat job. It was the wildest kind of luck that they ever turned up; the trawler brought them up with the catch between here and Catalina."

"Thanks," Rick said. He turned to Stone. "I think we've seen enough."

Stone followed him up the ladder and back to the car.

"Who says there's no justice?" Rick said.

"Poetic, isn't it?" Stone agreed.

"Now there's nothing to tie *your* little swim to Ippolito."

"Except me."

"Yeah. You carrying that piece I got you?"

"I started this morning."

"Good idea. If things keep happening to Ippolito, like his boat sinking and his house catching fire..."

"Yeah, I might need it."

"You think he has any idea you're alive?"

"Not unless Vance Calder told him, and I honestly don't think he would."

"You spoke to Calder, then?"

"Yeah; I called him yesterday and then saw him at his house. I think he was ready to talk to me, but when I got there, David Sturmack was just leaving."

"Did Sturmack see you?"

Stone shook his head. "He was driving away, looking preoccupied."

257

"What did Calder have to say?"

"Zip. I had to practically force my way into the house. They've got his wife, and he's terrified they'll hurt her."

"And terrified of the tabloids?"

"Still. He thinks that if he does what they want him to he'll get Arrington back and everything will be all right again."

"He's a fool."

"You and I know that, but he doesn't."

"What do they want from him? It can't be money."

"I don't know; what could America's biggest movie star do for Ippolito and Sturmack that they couldn't do for themselves?"

"You think Regenstein's involved?"

"He was at Vance's house the night before last, arguing with him."

"The night before last? How would you know that?"

"I returned Arrington's car to the house; I was there when they arrived. I got a look through a window."

"You said 'they' arrived?"

"Regenstein and another man, around forty, red-haired, Irish-looking."

"Sounds like Billy O'Hara—ex-cop, head of security for Centurion Studios." Rick frowned.

"Maybe Regenstein isn't involved, and they're using O'Hara to get Arrington back."

"Sounds like what a studio would do."

"What kind of guy is O'Hara?"

"He was a decent cop, very ambitious, had

a flair for publicity. He got pissed off when some other guys made lieutenant and he didn't; I guess that's when he went to work for Centurion. Must be five, six years ago. If he'd stuck with the department he might have gone places."

"Is he the sort of guy who would abet a kidnapping?"

Rick shook his head. "My guess is no, but it's only a guess; I didn't know him all that well. He came along after me."

"We're not getting anywhere much, are we?"

"Oh, I don't know. We keep plugging away, something might pop. Calder's the way in. You know him; what would it take to get him on our side?"

"I'm worried that it might take Arrington's death. Jesus, I *think* that would do it. His secretary explained movie stars to me once, and from what she says, they think only about the career; there's nothing else they love as much."

"You don't think he loves his wife?"

"According to Betty's theory, sure, but she isn't as important as his remaining a movie star. Of course, that's just her theory."

"Then again," Rick said, "she knows Vance Calder better than you or me."

"Yeah. All we can do is hope she's wrong," Stone replied. "Say, how are you and Barbara getting along?"

Rick smiled a little. "Very well, thank you."

"I thought you'd like her."

"You're very perceptive. You should have been a detective."

43

Stone parked on the quiet Beverly Hills street and switched off the engine. He had driven around the block twice, and there was no sign of unwanted company. He got out his pocket cell phone and dialed the number.

"Hello," she said.

"Hi, it's Stone." He waited tensely for the reaction.

"Well, hello, stranger," she said, and there was delight in her voice. "I was beginning to think I was never going to hear from you again."

What did she mean by that? "You don't get off that easily," he replied.

"How are things in New York?"

"Lonely."

"Me, too. I might be able to get away for a few days while Vance is between pictures; all I need is an invitation."

"Let me work on that. You home alone?"

"Yes. Sad, isn't it?"

"You going to be there for a while?"

"Nothing else to do. Vance hasn't been in for days; I'm underworked."

"A friend of mine is going to drop by with a present for you."

"Who's the friend?"

"An ex-cop."

"What's the present?"

"Wait and see."

"I'll be waiting."

"Talk to you soon." Stone broke the connection, got out of the car, walked to the front door, and rang the bell.

"Coming!" she called, her voice muffled. There were footsteps, and she opened the door.

"Good evening, Ms. Southard," Stone said.

Her mouth dropped open, and just for a moment he knew she wasn't glad to see him.

"May I come in?"

"Of course." She stood back and let him in. "What are you doing back in L.A. so soon?"

"Fix me a gin and tonic, and I'll tell you anything."

She waved at the living room sofa. "Sit." Then she went into the kitchen, came back with two drinks, and sat down beside him.

"I don't think you're really glad to see me," he said.

She didn't deny it. "You surprised me."

"Not entirely a pleasant surprise, I take it."

"I wish I could say it was. You're back here to make trouble for Vance, aren't you?"

"I never left town," he said.

She looked at him, astonished. "You don't know how dangerous that was."

"And I couldn't possibly make more trouble for Vance than he already has on his hands."

"It was very dangerous, Stone."

"More dangerous than you know. Ippolito had two of his goons drop me in the Pacific with an anchor attached."

Her eyes grew wide.

He held up a hand. "Don't worry, I survived."

She sank half her drink and set it down. "Oh, God," she said. "It was my fault."

"How so?"

"I told Vance you were still here, and he must have told Ippolito."

"That's accurate, I think."

"What are you going to do about it?" she asked apprehensively.

"Well, I don't have to find the two goons. They were dredged up by a trawler this morning in a similar condition to what they intended me to be."

She shook her head. "Swell. What have I gotten myself involved in?"

"Kidnapping, murder, probably a number of other major crimes."

"You don't think I had anything to do with... what they did to you?"

"No; not intentionally, anyway."

"Well, thank God for that much, at least. Please tell me what is going on, Stone."

"I think you're in a better position to tell me."

"I've already explained myself on that point."

"You've got to help Vance."

"That's right."

"Well, right now, Vance is well on his way to getting his wife killed and destroying himself. Are you going to help him do that?"

"I don't really know all that much," she said, picking up her drink and finishing it off.

"You know more than I do," Stone said. "If you'll tell me what you know, maybe it will be enough to help me get Vance out of this."

She stared off into the middle distance.

"Start at the beginning," he said.

"I've always done what Vance wanted," she said. "How do I know that what you want me to do is the right thing?"

"You'll have to take my word for it."

"I don't know if I can do that."

"The alternative is for me to involve the police and the FBI and for the gossip mills to get hold of it."

"You wouldn't do that," she said.

"Wouldn't I? Unless you help me, I won't have a choice. My nose is pressed against a brick wall, and I have nowhere to go. If I don't do something, Vance is going to get Arrington killed, and I can't allow that to happen. I hope you understand my position."

"If I tell you what I know, will you promise not to go to the police, the FBI, or the press?"

"No. I'll do whatever I think is the best thing for Arrington. You might consider that that might be the best thing for Vance, too."

"If there's a way to help her without making this public, will you do that?"

"Yes. But I'll be the judge of how to proceed."

"Vance is a very brave man, you know. You might not know him well enough to know that."

"He may well be a brave man," Stone said, "but he's also a very foolish one."

"All that stuff I spouted about movie stars and how they behave—it's true, of course, but not of Vance."

"Isn't it? Isn't he jeopardizing Arrington's life in order to protect his career?"

"I honestly don't think he is."

"Then what is he trying to do?"

"I think he thinks he can beat them at their own game."

"Oh, Jesus," Stone moaned. "Not that."

She nodded. "He figures this is between him and them, and he doesn't really want any outside help."

"Then why did he ask me to come out here?"

"He panicked, for just a moment. By the time you got here he had gotten hold of himself again."

"Exactly what is he trying to do?"

"Save Arrington, save Lou Regenstein, save Centurion Studios. For a start."

"What else?"

"I think he would very much like to kill Onofrio Ippolito."

"That makes two of us," Stone muttered.

"You're too smart to do something like that, Stone, but Vance isn't. Vance would kill him in a minute, if he could figure out how to do it without harming Arrington."

"That's about all that's kept me from killing him," Stone said.

"I hope you can help Vance. He's a fine man,

and I'd hate to see him pulled down by his own anger."

"Betty, if I'm going to help him, you're going to have to help me."

A long pause. "All right," she said at last.

"Start at the beginning," he said.

And she did.

44

Betty started slowly, reluctantly. "I guess it was a couple of weeks ago, maybe a little more. Vance came into work, and he was nervous. Vance is never nervous. He has this glacial calm about him; I think it's one of the things that makes him come over so well on screen. The only other actor I've ever seen with that kind of calm was Alan Ladd."

Stone didn't interrupt.

"But he was nervous that day—anxious, angry, nearly shaking with it. I'd never seen anything like it from him. I didn't ask what was wrong; I knew he'd never tell me. Instead, I just watched and waited, to see if I could figure it out. He made a lot of phone calls that morning, and he dialed them himself, instead of asking me to get somebody on the line, as he usually did. Some of the calls were in-studio; I could tell that because the studio lines are separate from the outside lines. And then he did something odd: he asked me to get his Centurion stock certificates from the big safe.

"We have two safes in the office—a small fire safe that's mostly for important documents and computer disks, and then the big safe that's half as tall as I am. He keeps cash in there, along with some gold bars and some treasury bills. I think there's a part of Vance that's deeply insecure, that's always ready to bolt. I think he has this fantasy of packing a briefcase, getting on a plane, and disappearing. Maybe it's something in his past, I don't know.

"Anyway, he asked me to get the Centurion certificates. Vance owns about twelve percent of the studio, and Lou Regenstein owns around thirty percent, so between them they can pretty much control the business."

"How much of the studio do David Sturmack and Ippolito own?" Stone asked. It was the first time he had spoken since she began.

"They each own ten or eleven percent."

"Not enough to take control, then?"

"I'm not so sure about that. I think somebody has been quietly buying shares. The stock isn't all that widely held, and I think some of the smaller shareholders have been selling."

"Why do you think that?"

"I think that's why Vance wanted to see his certificates. He's like that; he likes to touch and feel the things he owns. I'm not sure they're real to him otherwise. I had the feeling he was thinking of selling them."

"Why would he do that?"

"He wouldn't. Not ever."

"Go on."

"Then Lou Regenstein came into the office,

and he was looking very grim. He and Vance were in Vance's office with the door closed for more than an hour. Vance hardly ever closes his office door, not the one that opens into my office. Then they left the office and went somewhere together, and Vance didn't come back until late in the afternoon. When he did come back, he did something very strange: he told me to take the Centurion shares to the bank—not Safe Harbor, where he does all his banking, but to the bank that's right outside the studio gates—and he told me to rent a large safe deposit box in my name and to put the shares in it and not to bring the key back to the office."

"How much room did the share certificates take up in a large box?"

"Hardly any; I found that odd."

"Did you ever give the key to Vance?"

"No, I still have it; it's in my own deposit box at Safe Harbor."

"Did he ever ask you to put anything else in the box?"

"No, but I had the feeling he was going to, otherwise he'd never have had me get a large box."

"What else happened?"

"Nothing else that day. Oh, he asked me to get Arrington a plane reservation for Virginia—to Washington National, actually–and to deliver the ticket to the house that evening. And I did that.

"The next morning, Billy O'Hara came to Vance's office, stayed nearly an hour, then Lou

Regenstein joined them and they were there most of the morning. Billy is head of security for the studio."

"Is it unusual for Vance to see O'Hara?"

"Very. The only other time I ever saw him in the office was right after he took the security job. Lou brought him around and introduced him to us."

"What does studio security consist of?"

"Well, the usual—guards at the gates, studio passes, guard patrols, that sort of thing. In the old days—this isn't quite so true nowadays—the security people were in charge of protecting stars and contract players from trouble—drunk driving charges, rape, wife beating, that sort of thing. These days, stars are independents and there aren't any contract players to speak of."

"Did you get the impression that O'Hara was there to get Vance out of some kind of trouble?"

"It was the first thing I thought of. Vance obviously had a problem."

"Did he ever confide in you?"

"In bits and pieces. He told me that he wanted to get you out of town—I had to arrange that." She smiled. "Of course, I wasn't as anxious for you to leave as Vance was."

"What other bits and pieces did he tell you?"

"He told me he was having problems with Ippolito and Sturmack, and that I was to be very solicitous of them on the phone and if they came to the studio. He was anxious that they not think he was being rude to them."

"What else?"

"He told me that Arrington wouldn't be back for a while, but to go on telling anyone who asked that she was visiting family in Virginia. He told me that he wanted to be a little more accessible to the press, which was unusual. Normally he doesn't speak to anyone from the press. He doesn't do interviews, he doesn't do the *Tonight Show*, he's never even done Barbara Walters. It's part of the Calder mystique, that he's so inaccessible. I think he changed the policy, however slightly, so that he wouldn't seem to be covering up anything. That's why he had me invite that woman to the dinner party."

"So Vance was setting things up to protect himself."

"And Arrington. He was very worried that something would appear in the press that would jeopardize her."

"When did you learn that Arrington wasn't in Virginia?"

"Right before you got here. Vance told me that she hadn't gone home, that they had had an argument and that she had just run off somewhere. That made his attitude about the press more understandable. If someone called to ask if they were apart he could deny it instead of just stonewalling and, by doing so, exciting more interest."

"Makes sense. When did you learn that Arrington had been kidnapped?"

"I think I learned that from you."

"But I didn't know."

"But you knew something was wrong, and I didn't, at first. Part of it was your coming out here. I didn't think Vance would want you here just to settle a domestic dispute."

"Good guess."

"So finally I went to Vance and said that it was obvious to me that something was very wrong and that I wanted to help. He actually broke down and cried, something I'd never thought I'd see him do. He said that Arrington was in danger and that I had to be very careful not to do or say anything that might make it worse. He was handling it, he said. He actually used the word 'negotiating,' so I thought she was being held for ransom. It occurred to me that the price of her release might be the Centurion shares, but that didn't make a lot of sense."

"No, it doesn't, not in a kidnapping. If Ippolito and Sturmack have Arrington, then they obviously want a lot from Vance, probably more than the shares."

"That makes sense to me," Betty said. "I think that if Arrington's safety depended on his surrendering the stock, he'd do it and try to get the stock back later."

"Exactly. Now, what else does Vance have that Ippolito and Sturmack could want?"

"I don't know," she said. "I just can't imagine what it could be."

Stone thought about that. "Does Vance

have a contract with Centurion, a long-term contract?"

"Not in the sense that the old studios had stars under exclusive contract. Vance's deal with Centurion is as an independent producer; he brings projects to the studio—films that he doesn't always star in—and they have the right of first refusal. If they don't buy the project, he can take it elsewhere, as he has done in the past."

"Maybe that's not enough for Ippolito and Sturmack."

"What?"

"Maybe they want more than the studio; maybe they want Vance."

"They could never own Vance; he's too big for that."

"Maybe. Tell me, do you know where Ippolito keeps his yacht?"

"He has several yachts, I think."

"I mean the big one, *Contessa*."

"Oh, yes, I've been aboard her, as recently as last week, in fact."

"To a dinner party that Vance was invited to but didn't go?"

"Yes."

"I was invited, too, but I didn't make it."

"That was when they tried to..."

"Yes, but back to the boat; where is it kept?"

"I know he has a berth at Marina Del Rey, but I think she spends most of the time on a mooring at Catalina. That's where she was for the dinner party."

271

"Who was at the party?"

"A lot of the same people who were at Vance's party, the one you came to. And a lot of others, too."

"How many in all?"

"Nearly a hundred, I should think. It's a big yacht."

"I wonder if Arrington's aboard that yacht?" he asked.

"I wouldn't think he would hide Arrington on the yacht, then invite a hundred people aboard, would you?"

"No, I guess not."

"Why are you so interested in the yacht, then?"

"It doesn't matter," Stone said.

45

Stone didn't make it back to his hotel suite until the following morning, the reunion with Betty having kept him at her place all night. When he arrived the message light was blinking on his telephone, and he called for his voice mail.

"Stone, it's Hank Cable; you might want to call me."

Stone returned the call immediately. "Sorry I wasn't in when you called. What's up?"

"We got the tap into Barone Financial, and it's paying off already."

"What did you hear?"

"A lot of the phone conversations are conducted in a kind of code, which, of course, makes us even more suspicious. Our people say a lot of the conversations are to do with deliveries, maybe drugs."

"You don't need forty telephone lines to arrange drug deliveries," Stone said.

"Good point."

"I think it's money."

"There is some wire transferring going on, but not at such a heavy rate to be suspicious."

"Then maybe they're not transferring it by wire. Maybe they're shipping cash."

"Money laundries, when they ship cash, ship it out of the country. Our people think the shipments are coming this way. Why would they ship money into the States?"

"To buy things," Stone ventured.

"Well, of course, but what could they do with raw, unlaundered cash?"

"Launder it."

"Obviously, but we're talking about major quantities, is my guess."

"So they're buying big things, like businesses; big businesses."

"You don't understand, Stone; you can't go buy a business with, say, a hundred million dollars and bring cash to the closing. The money has to be laundered, to appear legitimate, to appear to be after-taxes. It has to be in a bank and then wire transferred to another bank, or be put into a negotiable instrument, like a cashier's check."

"Ippolito has a bank at his disposal, doesn't he?"

"He does, but I've checked with Treasury and the state examiners, and Safe Harbor has always been squeaky clean."

"Then he must be using it in some way we don't know about. I think people like Ippolito are too greedy to be happy with the income from a legitimate business; they want more. They want it all, too; they don't want to share it with stockholders or the IRS."

"Well, it's early days; I expect we'll come up with more as time passes."

"I don't have a lot of time," Stone said.

"Are we talking about the kidnapping again? I can have fifty agents on that in an hour."

"Not yet."

"Not until what? Until the abductee is dead? It gets a lot harder after that."

"Hank, if I knew where she was I'd welcome fifty agents on it, but I don't know."

"So it's a she."

"Yes, and that's all I'm going to tell you."

"Suit yourself, buddy; I just hope it doesn't blow up in your face. We take a dim view of people trying to deal with kidnappers. It's like this with ransom: you can pay the ransom and get the abductee back, or you can not pay the ransom and get the abductee back. Or—and this is the tough part—you can pay the ransom and lose the abductee, or you can not pay the ransom and lose the abductee. It's a crapshoot."

"You really think that? You really think that even if these people get what they want, they could still kill her?"

"Stone, it's likely that the decision, one

274

way or another, was made before they grabbed her. She could already be dead."

"I don't think so; a family member talks to her every day."

"That's good news, but it doesn't mean it will last."

"You're depressing to talk to, you know that?"

"It's part of my job to bring a ray of darkness into other people's lives."

Stone laughed ruefully. "Well, you're good at your work."

"I'll call you if anything worth reporting comes up, and I'll tell my people to listen for any talk on Barone's lines about your abductee."

"Thanks, Hank." Stone said goodbye and hung up.

Stone found a little printing shop with a sign in the window: 100 BUSINESS CARDS PRINTED WHILE YOU WAIT—$19.95. He drew a little sketch for the printer, and, while he waited, bought a cheap plastic briefcase, some file folders, and paper. When the cards were finished, he left the shop and dumped all but a dozen into the nearest trash bin, then drove to Marina Del Rey and found the marina office.

He asked for the dockmaster and handed him a card that read REED HAWTHORNE, ADJUSTOR, CHUBB MARINE INSURANCE. He didn't know if Chubb even wrote marine insurance, but at least it was a recognizable name. "I'm here about the sinking of a sports fisherman called *Maria*," he said.

"Yeah, I know about that," the dockmaster replied. "We raised her a couple of days ago. She was a mess."

"Can you show me where she's berthed?"

"Sure, come with me."

Stone followed the man down to *Maria*'s berth, unconcerned that he might be recognized, since both the people associated with the boat who knew him were dead.

"You want to go aboard?" the dockmaster asked. "I've got a key."

"No, I'm primarily concerned with security for the future, since she was obviously maliciously sunk. What kind of security do you provide here?"

"We've got a night watchman who has a walkie-talkie for contacting the night man at the office. We don't have a lot of trouble here."

Stone nodded sagely, opened his briefcase, and consulted several blank sheets of paper in a file. "We're insuring two other vessels here as well—one called *Paloma* and one called *Contessa*. Can you show me those two?"

"Sure. *Paloma* is this way."

Stone followed him to the deserted motor yacht. "How many passes a night does the watchman make past this berth?"

"He's by here about once an hour."

"Okay, where's *Contessa* berthed?"

"Down near the breakwater, with the other big yachts," the dockmaster said. "This way."

Stone followed the man down a series of pontoons until larger boats began to appear.

"You're lucky she's in here today," he said. "She spends a lot of time over at Catalina."

"At a marina there?"

"No, on a mooring. They put down a special heavy one for her."

They approached the big yacht from the rear; she was lying alongside, rather than being moored stern to. The dockmaster waved at a man on deck. "Hey, Dino! How you doing?" He turned to Stone. "I'll introduce you to the skipper."

"Thanks," Stone replied.

Dino came down the gangplank, smartly dressed in whites with shoulder boards and a peaked cap.

"Dino," the dockmaster said, "this is Reed Hawthorne, from your insurance company."

"Hello," the skipper said, looking at the card Stone handed him. "You're with Chubb? Marine Associates are our insurers, and we've only got liability, not hull insurance."

"I know," Stone lied, "but after the sinking of *Maria* they're apparently getting nervous. I was asked to take a look at your yacht to assess her general condition."

"Okay," the skipper said, "come aboard."

Stone smiled inside. Now he had a free pass to check out from stem to stern.

46

Stone followed the captain up to the yacht's bridge, where a technician had pulled out some of the electronic gear to work on it.

"We've got everything," Dino said, waving a hand. "The latest color, chart-display GPS, satphone, the works. That's why we're at Marina Del Rey now instead of Catalina, where the owner likes to keep the boat. We came over here for some adjustments."

"Do you have a lot of electronic problems?"

"Not really; this is new gear, and we're still getting the bugs out."

Stone took a file folder and some blank paper and started scribbling fake notes. A cell phone mounted on the instrument panel rang, and the captain picked it up.

"Hey," he purred into the phone.

A woman, Stone thought. He waved at the skipper, who covered the phone with his hand. "Look, I don't really need a guided tour; I'll look around on my own, if that's all right."

"Sure, help yourself," the skipper said.

Stone thanked the dockmaster for his help and went below. *Might as well make it stem to stern,* he thought. He quickly toured the large saloon, the dining room, and the galley, then headed below to where he figured the crew's quarters must be, up forward. He saw half a dozen small cabins and a larger one for the skipper, then he moved aft.

The size and quality of the cabins increased

as he walked toward the yacht's stern. Each was individually decorated, with expensive hardwoods and fabrics, and the owner's cabin was huge, rivaling Stone's hotel suite in style and comfort.

He went down another deck and looked into the cabins on either side of the hallway. These were smaller than the ones on the deck above, but still beautifully furnished. Something caught his eye in the aftermost of the small cabins. A U-bolt mounted in a plate had been welded to a bulkhead under a porthole. It seemed odd, out of place, but he had more yacht to cover, so he moved on. He checked every door and hatch on the yacht, no matter how small.

Finally, he came to the engine room, three decks below the bridge, and it was very impressive. Two huge diesel engines occupied half the space, and a large generator was bolted to the deck on either side of the engines. Stone began looking for seacocks.

"How you doing?" a voice said.

Stone jumped, then turned to find the captain standing in the doorway. "Sorry, you startled me," Stone said. "I'm doing fine; just about finished. Tell me, how are the engines cooled?"

"There's a heat exchanger mounted to each engine," the skipper replied, pointing to the equipment, "with a mixture of fresh water and coolant; that cools the top end. Then there's a raw-water flow to the bottom end of each engine."

"Where does the raw water come from?" Stone asked. It was what he most wanted to know.

"A seacock on each side of the engine room," the skipper replied, indicating a large valve operated by a wheel.

Stone had been looking for the sort of lever found on smaller boats; he was glad to have the big valve pointed out to him. This time there was no rubber hose, but a steel pipe running to the engine. "Got it," Stone said. Then he saw something he didn't recognize. "What's that?" he asked, pointing at a six-inch pipe that rose from the bilges to about two feet above the deck plating. Attached to it were half a dozen smaller pipes, each with its own seacock. There were two of them, a few feet apart, and he had never seen anything like them.

"Those are called seaboxes," the skipper said. "They bring in raw water for all sorts of uses—air conditioning, toilets, everything."

Stone nodded. "Well, I guess that just about does it for me."

"I'll show you the way up," Dino said.

Stone continued to pump the man as they climbed toward the upper decks. "How often does the owner use the yacht?"

"Practically every weekend, and sometimes he'll spend a night aboard during the week."

Stone continued making notes. "How many guests at a time?"

"We've got a dozen guest staterooms, sleeping twenty-four, plus the owner's cabin."

"How many crew?"

"We go light on crew; there's a cook, a steward, two maids, a mate, and me. When there are dinner parties, the caterers furnish the help."

"So that's six living aboard?"

"At the weekends, yes, and whenever the owner is aboard. During the week we usually manage a lot of time off. I can run the boat with the help of one crew between here and Catalina, and when we're on our mooring out there, there will often be just one man aboard."

"Any worries about security problems?"

"Nah. Some big boats have armed guards, but our owner doesn't believe in intrusive security—makes the guests wonder what they're being protected from. Anonymity is the best security, we reckon."

"Makes sense," Stone said. They had reached the main deck now. "Well, thanks for the tour; I've got all I need to make my report."

"We're changing insurance companies, then?"

"It's by no means certain; we'll make our proposal and see what happens."

"Who are you dealing with at our end?"

"Not your owner; one of his people, I think. I don't have any direct contact with clients; I'm just the technical guy." Stone shook the man's hand, then went ashore. One thing he was sure of: He had checked every part of the yacht, and Arrington was not aboard *Contessa*.

He gave some thought to going back to *Maria* and sinking the sports fisherman again.

It was a quiet day at the marina, and he could probably get away with it. Maybe he could sink *Paloma* as well. It would be fun to drive Ippolito even crazier.

Finally he decided against it. The police investigation would turn up the fact that somebody from an insurance company had visited the boats, and the simplest sort of check would reveal that he was bogus. The police would have a description of him, and he didn't want that.

Eventually, the skipper of *Contessa* would mention to somebody that an insurance man had been aboard, and give a description of Stone. That didn't trouble him greatly, since Ippolito himself would be unlikely to be involved, and he was the only man in his organization who could recognize Stone by sight.

He made his way back to his car and telephoned Betty Southard at her office. " Hi, it's Stone; can you talk?"

"Sure, go ahead."

"I want to take a closer look at David Sturmack; what can you tell me about him?"

"What do you want to know?"

"Let's start with his address and all the telephone numbers you've got for him."

She read the information out to him.

"Does he have a second home?"

She gave him an address in Malibu that sounded as though it might be next door to Ippolito's slightly scorched beach house.

"What can you tell me about him personally?"

"He's always been very cordial to me; he's one of those people who can make you feel, when you're talking to him, that you're the only person in the room. He likes beautiful women, and from remarks that Vance has made, I think he always has something on the side. His wife seems cowed by him, so I don't think she'd object, even if she knew."

"Got any names?"

"There was an actress on Vance's last picture, Veronica Hart, that he seemed to be very interested in. Want her address?"

"Sure." He wrote it down, along with the phone number. "How big an actress is she?"

"Struggling, but pretty good. She reminds me of me a few years ago."

"Any idea how Sturmack spends his time when he's not conspiring with Ippolito or getting laid?"

She laughed. "He and Vance play golf at the Bel-Air Country Club once in a while. He seems to have lunch there most days."

"You got any private numbers from Ippolito?"

"Let's see." She flipped some pages and gave him home, office, and car numbers, plus the number aboard *Contessa*.

"I think that'll do me for a while," he said. "Thanks."

"Dinner tonight?" she asked.

"You mind doing it in my suite at the Bel-Air?"

"I don't mind doing anything in your suite."

"Seven o'clock?"

"Make it eight."

"You're on." He hung up and headed for Sturmack's address. Maybe he hadn't devoted enough attention to the man thus far, but he was going to remedy that now.

47

David Sturmack lived in a Georgian mansion less than a five-minute drive from Vance Calder's house, in Bel-Air. It seemed to be on at least ten acres of land, which Stone thought must have cost a very large fortune. He had been struck by how little land most expensive L.A. houses occupied, especially in Beverly Hills, but also in the even ritzier Bel-Air. A platoon of men were working on the front lawn, employing tractor mowers, string trimmers, rakes, and hoes. One operated what appeared to be a large vacuum cleaner. God forbid a stray blade of cut grass should mar the perfect greenery.

The Rolls convertible was parked outside the front door, and as Stone drove past the house, Sturmack came out, got into the car, and started down the driveway. Stone made a U-turn and followed at a very discreet distance, wondering how best to shake up Sturmack's world. He had already shaken up Ippolito, and now it was Sturmack's turn. He had an idea. He dialed a New York number.

"Lieutenant Bacchetti."

"Dino, it's Stone."

"How you doing, Stone? I was beginning to wonder if you'd got lost."

"Not yet, but people are working on it. Do me a favor?"

"Sure."

Stone gave him Sturmack's car phone number. "Call this number; a man will answer. Say to him, 'Stone Barrington has a message for you from the other side; he's not through with you and Ippolito yet.'"

"I got the number," Dino said, "now what the fuck are you talking about?"

"Just do it, Dino; it's important."

"You want me to tell him who I am?"

"For Christ's sake, no! Just say the words and then hang up and call me back on my cell phone."

"Whatever," Dino said, and hung up.

Sturmack turned left on Sunset, and Stone followed. Perhaps a minute later, Stone saw the man pick up his car phone and speak into it. Suddenly the brake lights on the Rolls came on, and Sturmack pulled over. As Stone drove past him, he could see Sturmack shouting into the car phone. Stone turned right, made a U-turn, and waited for the Rolls to pass on Sunset, then he fell in behind it again, perhaps a hundred yards back. His cell phone rang.

"Yep?"

"It's Dino, I did it."

"What did he have to say?"

"First there was a stunned silence, then he

started calling me names, said he would have me castrated. I don't know why—I've never even met the guy. Who was he?"

"Fellow by the initials of D.S. We talked about him before?"

"I remember. What's this about?"

"I'm just rattling his cage. He and a friend of his tried to off me a few days back."

"Sounds like you make the man nervous," Dino said.

"I'm just getting started."

"Oh, by the way, you remember the other name you asked me about? About his family connections?"

"Sure."

"I told you the old mob guy didn't have any sons, but he had a nephew. Apparently he had a brother who was an honest man, relatively speaking, worked in the garment district. The brother had a son. I believe the French say 'Voilà!'"

"Indeed. It's not all that useful at the moment, but it's nice to know about."

"Stone, are you working on getting yourself killed?"

"Far from it," Stone replied. He missed Dino, and he had a thought. "I could use somebody to watch my back. Have you got any off-time coming?"

"To come out there?"

"I'll spring for a first-class ticket and a room at the Bel-Air Hotel."

"That's a very tempting proposition," Dino

said. "Okay, but if you ever tell Mary Ann that it wasn't department business, I'll have you offed myself."

"No loose lips here. Catch the next plane you can, rent a car at the airport, and they'll give you directions to the Bel-Air. I'll have a room waiting for you, and we'll have breakfast in the morning."

"You want me to come heavy?"

"Good idea. Rick helped me out in that regard."

"Am I out of my fucking mind?"

"You'll like it here, I promise."

"Am I gonna get laid out there?"

"I won't stand in your way," Stone laughed.

"Bye-bye." Dino hung up.

Sturmack was passing the Beverly Hills Hotel now, still headed up Sunset. When he reached the Sunset Strip, Sturmack parked the Rolls and entered a small business.

Stone was surprised. He called Rick Grant.

"Lieutenant Grant."

"It's Stone."

"Hi."

"Are you aware that Vinnie's Deli is back in business?"

"What?"

"I just saw the lawyer who doesn't practice law go in, and he's not the only customer."

"They're operating illegally," Rick said. "When we raided the joint I had their business license canceled."

"Is that grounds for busting them again?"

"You bet it is! I'll have a couple of cars over there in a few minutes. We'll see if they're taking bets again, too."

"Can you bust the customers, too?"

"I can bring 'em in; I can't hold 'em."

"I'd love to see the guy ride in the back seat of a black and white."

"I'll probably feel the mayor's hot breath on my neck, but what the hell, it sounds like fun."

"I'll wait and watch from a distance," Stone said. He pulled into a side street and parked facing the deli. Nineteen minutes later, by his watch, two police cars and two vans pulled up in front of the deli, and the raid went down exactly as before.

Minutes later, people were being led out in handcuffs, and Stone was delighted to see David Sturmack shackled to two men in dirty aprons, protesting loudly to whoever would listen. Nobody did. There was a bonus, too: Martin Barone was among the arrested. Sturmack must have been meeting him there. Stone's phone rang.

"Yeah?"

"It's Rick; did it happen, yet?"

"You bet, and they bagged Barone, too."

"If they were just having a sandwich, I'll have to let them go, but if they were in the back room, I can charge them."

"Great! By the way, our man arrived in a Rolls convertible. Can you impound that?"

"Why not? I'll send a tow truck."

"I hope they won't be too gentle with it."

"They usually aren't," Rick said, laughing.

"Let me know how it comes out, okay?"

"Sure, I will."

"By the way, Dino is on his way out here; you want to have lunch tomorrow and catch up?"

"Love to."

"Meet us in the outdoor cafe at the Bel-Air at twelve-thirty."

"See you then."

Stone hung up and drove back to the hotel, whistling a merry tune all the way. Things were looking up: he was unsettling his enemies, his best friend was coming to help him, and he had a wonderful evening planned in his suite.

48

Stone and Dino had breakfast on the terrace of Stone's suite and caught up. "You staying busy?" Stone asked.

"If I was busy, could I come out here and screw around with you? The crime rate in New York is dropping like a stone, you should excuse the expression—murders down, robberies down, even burglaries down. It's terrible!"

Stone laughed.

"It's not funny; pretty soon they'll be laying off cops. Already we're getting 'nice' lessons from the mayor's office, so we don't annoy the tourists."

"It's a better city for us all, Dino."

"I liked it the way it was before—people getting popped at all hours of the day and night, hookers on 42nd Street, three locks on every door—it was a cop's city, you know?" He waved a hand. "Not like this miserable excuse for a metropolis. You call this a hotel? There's not a fire escape in the place, there are no hookers in the lobby, and it's located in a jungle!"

"A garden."

"A garden is, like, in the back yard of a brownstone; this is a fucking jungle! There are plants here that only belong in the rain forest; there are swans in a creek, for Christ's sake! In New York I wouldn't give 'em twenty-four hours before somebody'd be barbecuing 'em!"

"I like it here—the hotel, I mean."

"You would. How the fuck can you afford it?"

"I told you about my part in the movie. I made twenty-five grand in a couple of days. I'm spending it."

"All of it?"

"Maybe, we'll see."

"How's Rick Grant?"

"He made lieutenant, and he's got a big job at headquarters; he's really being a big help, too. We're having lunch with him today."

"What's this about somebody trying to off you?"

"They made a first-class stab at it, let me tell you."

"Tell me."

"I'll try to bring you up to date." Stone started with the phone call at Elaine's and told Dino some of the things that had happened to him since arriving in Los Angeles.

Dino listened, rapt, his chin in his hand, his omelet getting cold; he didn't speak until Stone had finished. "That's fucking outrageous," he said, "them tossing you in the ocean like that."

"You bet it is."

"And what have you done about it? Have you killed the fuckers?"

"I didn't have to; Ippolito did it for me, the same way they did it to me."

"Nothing like mob justice," Dino said with satisfaction. "Have you killed this Ippolito yet?"

"I've gotten a couple of licks in." Stone told him about sinking the boat and setting Ippolito's living room on fire.

Dino's mouth dropped open. "Stone, have you gone out of your fucking mind? You're committing crimes! That's not the sort of thing you would do. It's the sort of thing I would do. Congratulations, it's nice to see you pissed off."

"So, Lieutenant Bacchetti, you approve of my illegal actions?"

"Heartily. Let's do some more."

"Maybe; I've got something in mind."

"What?"

"If I get pissed off again, I'll let you know."

"So what are you doing about Arrington?"

"Everything I can, which isn't much. There's no way to know where they've put her, and they could be moving her around."

291

"I hope you didn't tell the fucking FBI about her; they'd get her killed, for sure."

"No. Rick and I have talked to a guy there who's wired Barone Financial for sound; he knows somebody was snatched, but he doesn't know who, and he's keeping it unofficial."

"Don't tell the fuckers anything."

"There may come a time when we'll need the feds, you know."

"I doubt it. You and I can figure this out; we've figured out worse."

"I hope you're right."

"Who was the broad who was leaving as I arrived?" Dino asked.

"Vance Calder's secretary. We've become... close."

"Don't blame you a bit. She got a friend?"

"Dino, it's one thing for your wife to cut your balls off; it's quite another for her to cut mine off, and we both know she would do it if she found out I had anything to do with your getting laid out here."

"You said you wouldn't stand in my way."

"I didn't say I'd pimp for you."

Dino sighed.

"Look, go have a swim, have a massage, get over your jet lag. Lunch with Rick is at twelve-thirty in the outdoor cafe."

"Yeah, yeah, okay," Dino said.

Stone and Rick had been seated at a shady table for fifteen minutes before Dino showed up with a small blonde on his arm, his hair still wet from his swim. He gave her a kiss, patted her on her backside, and sent her on her way before sitting down.

"How you doing, Rick?" Dino asked, shaking his hand.

"Good, Dino, you?"

"Since the last hour, great! I met her at the pool; you should see her in a bikini!"

"Down, Dino, down," Stone said.

"You see the eleven o'clock news last night?" Rick asked Stone.

"He was busy," Dino said.

"Too bad. You'd have seen David Sturmack leaving the lockup with a coat over his head. His lawyer told the cameras he went into Vinnie's for a corned beef sandwich, that the whole thing was a terrible misunderstanding."

"I love it," Stone said, smiling broadly.

"Same with Barone. Can you believe the bookie joint was already back in business at the same location?"

"I'd believe it if they were back in business this morning," Stone said. " They've got to have somebody at LAPD on the pad."

"Now, now," Rick said. "You can't go applying NYPD methods to us."

"Was Sturmack in the back room?"

"Unfortunately, no, but the embarrassment factor is not any less because of that."

"I wonder what he's telling his pals at the Bel-Air Country Club today," Stone said.

"Wish I could be there," Rick replied.

"Rick," Dino said, "can't we just kill these guys, so I can go back to New York? It's too sunny and clean out here."

"No, Dino, you can't kill anybody. It's frowned on."

"Oh," Dino said. "But we can keep on driving them crazy?"

"Be my guest."

"Good. What's our next move, Stone?"

"I want to sink Ippolito's big boat."

"I didn't hear that," Rick said, holding up his hands.

"How we going to do that?" Dino asked.

"I had a real good look around her yesterday; told the skipper I was from an insurance company. I figured out how to do it, but we've got to pick a night when nobody's aboard but a couple of crew. I don't want to drown anybody, unless it's Ippolito."

"I'm not hearing any of this," Rick groaned.

"Hear no evil," Dino said. "That's my policy. Do evil, if it works for you."

"I'm sorry, Rick," Stone said. "Dino is a depraved individual. He can't help himself."

"You're not doing so bad with the depravity yourself," Rick replied. "How can I help?"

"We're going to need a fast boat, something that'll get us to Catalina and back in a flash."

"I think I know where I can borrow one. When?"

"I'm not sure yet, but could you line it up on short notice?"

"Consider it done."

49

Stone and Dino drove down to Santa Monica Airport, a small general aviation field with a single 5,000-foot runway, near the beach and just next door to Los Angeles International.

"What are we doing here?" Dino asked as they pulled into a parking lot behind a large hangar.

Stone found the sign he was looking for: AIRCRAFT FOR RENT. "We're going to do some aerial sightseeing," Stone said. "I want to show you the layout of where we're going, and it's the fastest way."

"What's the hurry?" Dino asked.

"This weekend that yacht will be full of people. I want to get to her first. Wait here."

Stone went into the office, passing a large sign offering various airplanes for rent, and inquired about rates from a young man at the desk. He produced his pilot's license, his medical certificate, and his logbook on request.

"What sort of airplane do you want?" the man asked.

"Something slow for sightseeing."

"Where do you want to go?"

"Just out to Catalina and back. A couple of hours."

"I've got a Cessna 172, a nice one—good radios, GPS. It's IFR certified, and it's a hundred and fifty bucks an hour, wet."

"I won't be doing any instrument flying, but

it sounds fine." Stone gave him a credit card to imprint, then followed him out to the hangar.

"Let's see you preflight her," the man said.

Stone walked slowly around the airplane, doing the checks he'd done a hundred and fifty times, including the fuel.

"That's pretty good without a checklist," the man said.

"I did my initial and a lot of my instrument training in a 172," Stone explained. "It's all in my logbook." He helped push the airplane out onto the tarmac, then the man handed him the keys.

"Go safely," he said. "I'll look for you back before the fuel runs out."

"Thanks," Stone said. He went back to the car and got Dino. "This way," he said, and led the way back to the airplane.

Dino looked at the little Cessna with concern. "It's kind of little, isn't it?"

"A very sturdy aircraft," Stone said. "More of them produced than any other; think of it as a kind of Volkswagen Beetle of the air."

"I always hated those little cars," Dino said.

"Hop in the passenger seat."

Dino climbed in, and Stone got the seatbelt on him and fitted him with a headset, then walked around the airplane and got into the left seat.

"Where's the pilot?" Dino asked.

"You're looking at him."

"Now, wait a minute, Stone," he said. "I

know you screwed around out at Teterboro for a year, but that doesn't mean I'm going anywhere with you in the pilot's seat." His protests were drowned out when the engine roared to life.

"Don't worry about it, Dino; I'll get you home safely." He ran through the pre-taxi checklist, then called the ground frequency for a taxi clearance. He was told to taxi to Runway 21.

"You're sure you can do this, Stone? I mean *really* confident?"

"Don't worry about it," he said. "I've got something like two hundred hours in this airplane."

"This same one?"

"Several just like it." He pulled onto the runup pad at the end of the runway, revved up to 3,000 rpms, checked the magnetos, the oil pressure, and the temperatures, then called the tower. "Ready for takeoff on Twenty-one, VFR departure to the west."

"Cleared for takeoff," the tower controller replied.

Stone taxied onto the runway, eased the throttle all the way forward, and released the brakes. They were off the ground in less than a thousand feet.

"Where are we?" Dino asked.

"Open your eyes, and you'll see," Stone replied.

They were crossing the beach now, and they could see the dim outline of Santa Catalina Island in the smoggy distance.

"That's where we're going," Stone said.

He leveled off at a thousand feet. "Watch for other airplanes; we don't want a collision."

"A *collision*?" Dino cried.

"Help me avoid one, okay?" He consulted the chart to stay well out of the Class B airspace surrounding LAX. "Down there is Marina Del Rey, where I've been spending a lot of time lately." He dipped a wing so that Dino could see out the left side of the airplane.

"Don't *do* that," Dino said through gritted teeth.

Stone pointed out another light airplane off the coast and made a course adjustment to avoid it. "That's what I was talking about," he said. "Watch for more."

"Yeah, yeah," Dino replied.

They flew along for ten minutes without speaking while Catalina grew larger in the windshield. Stone pointed again and put the nose of the airplane down. "Look at that," he said.

"The big boat?"

"Let's get a closer look." He descended to five hundred feet and flew past the yacht on a parallel course.

"Her name is *Contessa*," Dino said.

"That's the one we're looking for; she's on her way back from Marina Del Rey to her mooring off Catalina." The yacht was slowing now as she approached the anchorage, and Stone circled. "See all those little things floating in the water? Those are empty moorings. They'll be full this weekend, so tonight is a better time for us to go." The yacht slowed, and a man in a small boat drove up to her mooring and tossed a rope onto her decks, where it was received by another crew member.

"Two aboard," Stone said. "One at the helm." As they watched, the man in the small boat turned toward the harbor and went away. "The skipper told me he could run her with a mate when the owner isn't aboard."

"Well, it's a very nice boat," Dino said. "Can we go back to land now?"

"Look at the anchorage; I want you to have a good idea of where we're going when we come back here."

"Yeah, yeah, I see it, now let's get back to land, okay?"

"There's a life jacket in the back seat, in case we have to put down in the water."

"Just shut up and get me back to land," Dino said.

"All right, we're done. Aren't you enjoying the flight?" They hit a patch of bumpy air, and Dino clung to his seat.

"Not much," he said. "Get me out of here."

Stone turned back toward Santa Monica and tuned in the recorded weather information. When they were ten miles out, he called the tower. "I'm a 172 approaching from Catalina for landing; I have information bravo."

The tower came back. "Enter a left downwind for Twenty-one; you're number three for landing after a 182 and a Citation."

Stone entered the traffic pattern as the other Cessna landed. "I have the Citation," he said to the tower.

"Keep the Citation in sight, cleared for landing."

"Jesus, will you look at this city," Dino said, at last seeming to appreciate the view.

"Yeah. There's LAX, where you landed, right over there; the tall buildings are downtown L.A., and over there on that hill you can see oil wells."

"They have oil wells in a city?"

"I think the oil wells were there first," Stone said, "and nobody's going to shut them down until they're dry." He turned at right angles to the runway, then turned onto final approach.

Dino was finally taking an interest in the flight. "You found the airport," he said.

"It's easy, when you've got all these instruments."

"And there's the runway right in front of us."

"Where it's supposed to be."

"Look at all the cars; they look like hamsters."

They flew across the road at the edge of the airport, and Stone set the airplane down lightly and taxied off the runway. A moment later they were stopped in front of the hangar, and he shut down the engine.

"Hey, that was fun!" Dino said. "Let's do it again sometime."

Stone burst out laughing. "Come on, let's call Rick and see about that boat."

50

Late in the afternoon, Stone took Dino shopping. They went to the chandlery at Marina Del Rey and bought two sets of sailing waterproofs in dark blue, a large roll of duct tape, two heavy, rubber-encased flashlights, and a set of socket wrenches. Stone also bought a large-scale chart of the area, laminated in plastic.

"What's all this stuff for?" Dino asked.

"It will be easier to show you than to tell you," Stone said.

They arrived at Rick Grant's house at eight. Rick got them a drink, then led them into the back yard, where Barbara Tierney was grilling steaks.

"She can *cook*?" Stone asked.

"Isn't it amazing?" Rick said. "I'm gaining weight since she got here."

Dino went over and introduced himself to the beautiful woman, then they all sat down at the table.

Rick handed Stone a set of keys and gave him a berth number at the Long Beach marina. "It belongs to my ex-brother-in-law," he said. "It's a big Boston Whaler with two one-hundred-horsepower outboard engines and a lot of gear."

"Sounds ideal," Stone said.

"He wants five hundred for the night."

Fair enough. Stone peeled off the money.

"I don't want to know the details, either before or after," Rick said.

"We will preserve you in your ignorance," Stone laughed. "Before and after."

"What, exactly, have you got in mind, Stone?" Dino asked.

"Didn't you just hear Rick say he doesn't want to know?"

"Yeah, but..."

"I'll tell you later."

Barbara set plates of spinach salad on the table, and the three men began to eat.

"Let's talk about general strategy," Rick said. "What's your plan?"

"Beyond tonight, I don't have much of a plan," Stone said. "I'm just trying to shake them up, to let them know that they're not *entirely* in charge, cost them some money. If I can do that, then maybe they'll start to make mistakes that we can capitalize on."

"Won't they think Calder is behind this?"

"He knows nothing, and he's a very fine actor, remember? He'll convince them of his ignorance."

"What if they hurt the girl?"

"They don't have any way to relate what I'm doing to Arrington. They're just having a run of very bad luck, and the only thing they can assign to it is what Dino said to Sturmack on the phone."

"What did you say, Dino?"

"I said that Stone was getting them from the grave," Dino grinned.

Rick laughed a lot. "Well, you're right,

302

they're certainly having a run of bad luck. They've had an expensive motorboat sunk, two of them have been arrested—what next? They must be wondering."

"I'm not going to keep them in suspense," Stone said.

Stone and Dino arrived at the Long Beach marina after midnight and found their rented boat. It was painted black, for which Stone was grateful, and it looked very fast indeed. They tossed their gear on board, then Stone handed Dino the duct tape. "Tape over the name of the boat wherever it's painted on and also the Coast Guard numbers. We don't want any trouble for Rick's ex-brother-in-law later."

Dino went to work while Stone got familiar with the boat and its equipment. He was delighted to find a Garmin GPS unit, which had a color screen that displayed all the land masses and buoys in the area. That would make navigating at night a lot easier. He switched on the VHF radio and tuned it to Channel 16; if the Coast Guard were patrolling the area, he wanted to hear them before they saw him.

He dug out a pair of life jackets from a locker and handed one to Dino. "Better put this on."

"I spent a lot of time on Sheepshead Bay with my old man in his boat," Dino said. "I'm a lot more comfortable in boats than in airplanes; I don't need that."

"Dino, we're going to be traveling fast at night; if we hit something and capsize, we need the jackets. Put it on."

Dino reluctantly got into the life jacket and adjusted it. "Happy now?"

"Not yet, but I'm planning to get a lot happier." Stone double-checked everything, then started the engines. Dino let go their lines and, keeping the big engines at idle, Stone maneuvered out of the marina. A few minutes later they were on their way at thirty knots. "Keep a sharp lookout," Stone said. "There are fishing boats out here this time of night towing nets and trawls. We want to give them a wide berth."

"Right," Dino said.

It was a lovely night, with many stars, clear of the usual smog. They were making a lot of wind with their speed, and Stone was glad to have the warmth of his weatherproof suit. Catalina loomed ahead.

Contessa turned out to be easy to find. She was the biggest thing in the anchorage by far, and she was wearing a bright anchor light; her bow and stern lights were on, too. Stone throttled back while they were still three hundred yards out and made his way among the moored yachts and empty moorings. Not many people would be sleeping aboard the small boats during the week, and Stone was glad for that. As they approached *Contessa*, she seemed to get bigger and bigger.

"Jesus," Dino said, "that's some piece of work, that boat. "How much you think it cost to build it?"

"I don't know—eight, ten million dollars, I would guess. Depends on when she was built. These days, she'd cost a lot more."

"Okay, you think you can tell me what your plan is now?"

"First I'm going to have to get the crew off."

"How many?"

"Two, I think."

"And what the fuck are we going to do with them?"

They were at the stern boarding ladder of the big yacht now, and Stone pointed up to the deck. "There's a rubber dinghy up there; I saw it from the air. I'll toss it down to you. We'll put them in that and set them adrift; somebody will pick them up after daylight."

"Okay, whatever you say."

They cut the engines and tied the Whaler to a teak swimming platform on the stern. Stone stuffed the duct tape and the socket wrench kit into his jacket's large pockets, climbed up the boarding ladder, and stuck his head above deck; there was no one in sight, but operatic music wafted from somewhere. The rubber dinghy was gone. Stone looked around for another tender, but all he saw were two large speedboats, slung in davits. Maybe somebody had gone ashore; he hoped so.

With his flashlight in one hand and his pistol in the other, Stone started forward toward the bridge. Along the way he looked into every port and window, watching for anyone stirring on the yacht, but he saw no one.

He climbed the stairs to the bridge and peeked in. There was one deckhead light on, and a radio was playing, but no one was in sight. Very slowly, he opened the door and stepped onto the bridge, the pistol out in front of him. There was no sound but the radio.

He carefully opened two doors on the bridge; one led to a stairway below, the other was, apparently, the captain's cabin. A lamp was on, and the bed was mussed, but not unmade. He poked into the captain's toilet, and that was empty as well. Surely the crew wouldn't leave the big yacht entirely untended?

It seemed preposterous, but perhaps there really was no one aboard. He opened the door to the stairway and started slowly down, listening at every step.

51

One flight down, Stone looked into the large saloon and dining room, then into the galley. A light was on in there, and an open jar of mayonnaise with a knife stuck in it sat on a countertop. Looked as though someone had made a sandwich earlier.

Stone went back to the stairs and descended another flight. He could no longer hear the music now; there was only an unearthly silence. Surely the ship's generators would be running. He bent down and placed a hand on the deck, feeling for vibration. Nothing. The ship must be on battery power. He walked down a hallway, still keeping quiet, and looked into every cabin, switching on a light in each. No one. Good.

Having searched the deck, he walked down another flight of stairs, where he found a door on either side of him. A sign on the one to his right read CREW QUARTERS. A sign on the other door read GUEST QUARTERS. The crew must be asleep instead of on watch, he thought.

He put the flashlight in his jacket pocket, set down the bag he was carrying, removed the roll of duct tape, opened the door to the crew's quarters, and listened. Silence. Leaving the bag in the hallway, he checked every cabin and found no one. Bad crew, he thought, ashore drinking when there was an intruder on the yacht in their charge. He went through the other door and checked the guest cabins on that deck, finding them all empty.

Finally, he descended to the lowest deck and went into the engine room, switching on the lights. There were no ports in here, so no one could see the light from shore.

Now he had his work to do. He set down the bag, took out the socket wrench kit, and went to the nearest seacock. The valve was joined to the cooling water pipe by two flanges—one on the seacock and one on the pipe. He closed the seacock, selected the proper socket, and went to work on the six bolts holding the two flanges together. When he was done the two flanges remained stuck together with some sort of sealant, and he couldn't pull them apart by hand. He'd come back to that.

He went to the seacock for the other engine and repeated the process, then turned to the big ones—the seaboxes. The two six-inch pipes rose vertically from the steel-plated deck, each capped by a steel plate that sealed the top of the pipe. Smaller pipes branched off the sides of the larger one, each with its own seacock. He closed all the valves, found the right socket, and removed the eight bolts securing the sealing plate to the top of the pipe. Water began to leak through the seal, but the plate remained in place. He left it there while he performed the same operation on the other seabox.

"Now," he said aloud, "I've got to find something that will dislodge the sealant on each pipe, and I'm in business." He looked around and saw a workbench nearby; he walked over to it, opened a closet adjacent to the bench, and found a selection of large tools. He chose a small sledgehammer with a three-foot handle.

He went to the first engine cooling pipe and fetched it several blows with the hammer. Gradually the sealant let go; then he repeated the action with the other engine's pipe. He dropped the sledgehammer on the deck near the door, then went back to the workbench, found a chisel and a hammer, and went to work on the sealing plate of the starboard seabox. After his first blow, water began to squirt under high pressure; he hit it twice more. The plate flew off, and a six-inch column of water rose from the pipe, striking the deckhead. The noise, echoing off the steel plates, was deafening.

Working quickly now, he chiseled off the plate on the port seabox and another column of water exploded from the pipe. Finally, he opened the seacocks for the port and starboard engines, and he had two more three-inch blasts of water pouring into the engine room.

He stepped back to the door and admired his handiwork. All told, he had the equivalent of a sixteen-inch column of water flowing, under great pressure, from the Pacific Ocean into the big yacht.

Pleased with himself, he went back to the stairs and started up. Then he stopped and remembered. On the other side of the engine room was yet another corridor of guest cabins. Shit. He'd have to check them.

He ran back down the stairs and was greeted by a good two feet of water at the bottom. He waded through the engine room to its other door and into the corridor, checking cabins on both sides. The last cabin on the port side was locked. He'd have to hurry now, because soon access to the forward stairs would be under water, and unless there was an aft way up, he'd be trapped. Already the angle of the deck told him the yacht was increasingly down by her bows. He was about to turn back when he thought he heard a noise over the roar of incoming water, a kind of thumping. He listened, then walked aft and listened again. It had stopped. He turned to leave, and it started again. He put his ear to the last port cabin, the one that was locked, and was rewarded with a thump. Someone was inside the cabin, and he had no idea where the key was.

He rammed his shoulder and all his weight against the door, but it didn't budge. He put his back against the opposite side of the corridor, grabbed a handhold above his head, lifted his feet, and kicked with all his might at the lock. Again and again, he kicked, and suddenly the door burst open and water flooded from the corridor into the cabin. The lights were still working, and he hit the switch in the cabin. The lights flashed on, and Stone looked inside, stunned. A woman was lying on a berth, her hands bound with duct tape and her mouth taped as well. Her frightened eyes stared at him. She had been kicking the bulkhead at her feet.

"Arrington!" he shouted. He ran to her and yanked the tape from her mouth.

She made a noise of pain. "Stone! Dear God, how did you get here?"

"Never mind that," he said, yanking at the tape that bound her wrists, "we've got to get out of here; the yacht is sinking!"

The tape came free; he grabbed her wrist and pulled her toward the cabin door. Then she stopped with a jerk.

"Wait," she yelled over the roar of water, "my ankle!"

Stone looked down. He had seen such shackles a thousand times when moving prisoners, but this one was longer. One end closed around her right ankle; the other was attached to a U-bolt in a plate welded to the hull of the yacht. He remembered seeing it on his inspection, and now he knew what it was for. "Who has the key?" he shouted.

"The captain!"

"Oh, shit," Stone said.

"What?"

"Let me think!" He thought. Dino would have a handcuff key on his key ring, he was sure of that. Almost. But he wouldn't have time to run up three decks, get the key, then get back down before the lower deck was completely swamped and Arrington had drowned. He'd never make it. He had one other chance, though.

"Wait here," he shouted, "I'll be right back!"

"Don't leave me here!" she screamed, clutching at him.

With difficulty, he pulled her hands away. "I've got to get something," he said, then left her. He waded up the corridor to the engine room door, which stood open. The water here was waist deep now, and it was pouring through the doorway. Stone struggled against the current, using the yacht's handholds. When he got through the engine room door and across the space, he took a deep breath and went under the water.

The engine room deckhead light was still on, but he could see nothing under the water. He felt along the deck, hoping against hope.

311

Nothing. He came up, grabbed another few deep breaths, packing oxygen into his lungs, then submerged again.

He wanted the hammer and chisel, but he couldn't remember where he had dropped them. Probably the rushing water had moved them around anyway. But his hand touched something else, and he grabbed at it, breaking the surface with the sledgehammer in his hands.

He waded quickly back down the corridor with the water above his waist and got back into the cabin with Arrington. "Get back on the bed," he yelled, "and give me room!" Seeing the hammer in his hands, she obeyed him.

"Hurry!" she screamed.

Stone grabbed the chain to her ankle and followed it in the other direction, to the U-bolt. Pulling on the chain with his left hand, he swung the hammer at the U-bolt with all his strength, but he was working under water, and the weight of the hammer had less effect than it would on the surface. He banged away at the bolt and its plate, hoping to God that it was spot-welded and not welded for the whole circumference of the plate.

"For Christ's sake, Stone, hurry!" Arrington screamed. The water was up to her waist, since she was standing on the bed, but it was up to Stone's neck.

He didn't have the breath to answer her, he just kept on banging away at the U-bolt. Finally he dropped the chain, grabbed the hammer with both hands and swung it with all his might. He thought he felt something give. He felt underwater for the chain, grabbed it, and held it above the surface with the U-bolt and its plate dangling from the end. "I got it!" he screamed, and sea water came into his mouth.

Then the lights went out.

52

Stone grabbed Arrington and helped her down off the bed. They had to duck underwater to get through the door, which was now submerged, then surfaced in the corridor, and, half walking and half swimming, they made their way aft. The yacht was sinking much faster than Stone would have believed possible.

Gradually, as they moved toward the stern, the depth of the water decreased, since the yacht was down by the bows. Stone remembered that he had a flashlight in his pocket, and he stopped feeling his way and turned it on. Protected by its rubber covering, it still worked. "Do you remember a stairway back here anywhere?" he asked. The noise of the water coming in was less in the after part of the ship.

"No," she said. "I was blindfolded when we came aboard."

"There's got to be a way up," Stone said, half to himself. "It would be crazy to have only one set of stairs to all the decks." He kept wading aft; the water was only waist-deep now.

"Where did you come from?" she asked. "How did you find me?"

"There's a long answer to your first question," he said. "I'll tell you later. As to finding you, I had no idea whatever you were aboard. If you hadn't been kicking the bulkhead, you'd still be in that cabin."

"Thanks for telling me," she said.

The light finally shone on what Stone had been looking for; a spiral staircase was only a few feet ahead. "There!" he shouted.

"Hurry!" she shouted back.

They started up the stairs, but then there was a rumble, and the yacht seemed to stand nearly on her head.

"What was that?" she asked.

"The door to the crew quarters must have given way," Stone said, "and the water all rushed forward."

They were now moving almost horizontally up the spiral staircase. They made the next deck and continued to move along, walking carefully on the curved banister risers.

"What do we do when we get out?" Arrington asked.

"Dino is waiting in a boat."

"*Dino?* What the hell is he doing here?"

"We've all been very concerned about you."

They finally emerged into the main saloon, which, like the rest of the yacht, was standing nearly on end.

"We've got to make that door," Stone said, pointing above them. A round table was a few feet away, apparently bolted to the floor. "I think I can grab the pedestal," he said. He stood on the banister of the nearly horizontal staircase, got an arm around the pedestal, and hoisted himself onto it.

From somewhere deep in the bowels of the big yacht there came a menacing rumble, and the ship began her final journey to the bottom. Water rushed at them from below as Stone got hold of Arrington's wrist and pulled her up with him.

"It's too far to the door," he said. "We'll never make that."

"Look!" she cried. "The window."

Stone followed her finger and saw a latch on the window a few feet above her head. "Take my hand and steady me," he said. "I think I can reach it if I stand on the edge of the tabletop." He got one foot there and, holding on to Arrington, the other. He flipped the latch and tugged at the window. It slid open about two feet and stopped. The water level was rising fast now; it was up to their necks again, and climbing.

"We're going to have to rise with the water," Stone said. "Grab for the window and get yourself out. I'll be right behind you."

Then the yacht gave up the ghost and began sliding under the waves. The water engulfed them, but Stone kept the flashlight trained on the open window. Arrington slipped away from him, but he couldn't see where. Then his shoulders were stuck in the open window. He pushed himself back inside the sinking yacht, stuck one arm through the window, then got his head, shoulder, and the other arm through. As he broke free, he pushed hard off the window sill and made for the air above.

He broke the surface with a shout, expelling all the air he had been saving, and began looking for Arrington.

"Stone, over here!" she called from behind him.

Stone turned and saw her being hauled into a rubber dinghy by two men; one of them was the captain of *Contessa*. Stone looked around for Dino and the black boat, but saw nothing. He made for the dinghy and grabbed the side.

The yacht's skipper leaned over and looked at him. "You!" he shouted angrily.

Stone swung the flashlight at him and caught him full on the side of the head. The man fell backward and out the other side of the dinghy. Stone hoisted himself half into the rubber boat and saw the other crew member coming at him with an oar. He pushed himself back into the water, narrowly avoiding the swinging blade. When he broke the surface again, a few feet away, he heard the dinghy's outboard start up. Arrington was struggling with the man now, as the rubber boat started to move away from Stone.

Then, like the cavalry, Dino showed up. He was drifting toward the dinghy in the black Whaler, and he had his flashlight in his hand. He swung it mightily and made contact with the back of the man's head. The man fell overboard.

"Help me get them!" Stone yelled. "We can't just let them drown!" He was already swimming around the dinghy. With Arrington's and Dino's help, he got both the unconscious men back into the dinghy. They stank of alcohol.

"Are they hurt badly, do you think?" Arrington asked.

"They'll live," Dino said. "What do you want to do with them, Stone?" He was holding the dinghy next to the Whaler.

Stone hoisted himself into the dinghy. "Arrington, get into the boat with Dino," he said. He began unscrewing the outboard from the dinghy's plywood transom. "Hurry up!" He got the outboard loose and dropped it overboard, where it joined *Contessa*, then he flung the oars as far away as he could, hopped into the Whaler, and got the engines started.

From the direction of the shore a large motorboat was headed toward them. "I hope that isn't a Coast Guard cutter," Stone said. He switched off the Whaler's running lights, put the throttles forward a little, and motored slowly for fifty yards as a spotlight played on the water behind them. For another few hundred yards he increased speed slightly, hoping to keep the sound of his engines quieter than those aboard the approaching boat, then he pushed the throttles wide open and roared away toward the mainland. A few seconds later they were doing forty knots through the black night. "Everybody keep a lookout for other boats!" he shouted over the engines.

Dino took off his jacket and helped Arrington into it. "How are you?"

"Don't ask!" she shouted back.

53

An hour later they had secured the boat, hosed it down with fresh water, and removed the tape from its identifying marks. In the car, Stone sat up front, while Dino drove and Arrington occupied the rear seat.

"You think we got out of there without being seen well enough to identify us?" Dino asked.

"The captain of *Contessa* recognized me."

"That's not good."

"Somehow, I don't think he'll mention it to the police; he knows he's involved in a kidnapping."

"He'll mention it to Ippolito."

"Good. I don't think Ippolito will mention it to the cops, either."

"What about his insurance company? Those guys don't give up easily."

"The yacht wasn't insured."

"You're kidding."

"Nope, the skipper told me they had liability only. I guess Ippolito believes in self-insurance. I hope so." Stone directed Dino onto the freeway, then used his phone to call the Bel-

Air's night manager. "Is the room next to my suite free?" he asked.

"I'll check," the woman said. "Yes, it's available."

"Will you please have the adjoining door to my suite unlocked? I'll be needing the extra space."

"Of course, Mr. Barrington."

"Thanks; I'll be there in a few minutes." He hung up and turned to Arrington. "How are you doing?"

"I'm pretty wet, but apart from that, I'm okay. Aren't you taking me home?"

"No, not yet; we'll sort that out later. You look awfully tired."

"I am," she said, and she stretched out on the back seat. "Let me know when we're there."

Back at the hotel, they parked and got Arrington to Stone's suite.

"Thanks, Dino; I'd better put her to bed. I'll see you in the morning."

"Not too early," Dino said, and left.

Arrington was out on her feet. Stone got her wet clothes off and put her into a hot shower long enough to wash away the salt, then he put her into a terry robe and took her to the room next door. He turned down the bed and tucked her into it.

She put her arms around his neck and pulled him close. "Sleep here with me," she said.

"I can't," he said. "You sleep; don't think about anything, we'll fix it tomorrow."

But she was already out. He tucked the covers under her chin and went back to his own room. He took a shower and got into bed with a brandy, somehow unable to sleep. He dozed a little, and then it was dawn.

At six o'clock he called Vance Calder.

"Hello?" He seemed wide awake.

"Vance, I think you know who this is; don't talk, listen. Do you remember where I'm staying?"

A pause. "Yes."

"Get over here now; come through the back gate. I'll be waiting."

"Is it..."

"Shut up. Just get over here." He hung up, and got into some clothes. When Vance drove up to the back gate, Stone was there to meet him. They walked up to Stone's suite together.

"What's going on, Stone? Why were you so careful on the phone?"

"For all I know, your lines are tapped; I wouldn't put it past them."

"What's wrong? Has something happened to Arrington?"

"No. Arrington is asleep in the next room."

Vance headed for the door, but Stone stopped him. "Don't wake her; she's had a rough night. Let's have some breakfast."

Vance finished his coffee and put down the cup. He had said little for the past hour; Stone had done all the talking. "Thank you, Stone," he said finally. "What has Arrington had to say about... her experience?"

"Nothing; she was too exhausted."

"It's important that I talk to her before you do."

"She's your wife," Stone said.

"I have some things to explain to her before you start asking her questions, as I know you will. Then you can ask your questions, and I'll take her home."

"I don't think you should do that, Vance."

"Why not?"

"Because this isn't over by a long shot, and she may not be safe. I think it would be better if you arrange a suite here, move in, and not talk to anybody."

Vance thought about that. "All right. I'd better go and get some clothes for us both."

"Good idea; I'll talk to the manager. Come back here when you're done, and don't tell your staff where you're going."

Vance nodded, got up, and left.

Stone called the manager. "Thank you for the adjoining room," he said. "Is there a suite on the other side of it?"

"Yes, there is." He checked for a moment. "And it's empty."

"Please open it up and slide the key under my door."

"Certainly, Mr. Barrington."

"And please be sure to deny any knowledge of me. If any phone calls come in, say that I checked out this morning."

"As you wish."

Stone hung up. Arrington was standing in the doorway, naked.

She came to him and put her arms around him.

"Aren't you cold?" he asked lamely.

She shook her head. "I was hot, so I took off the robe."

"Did you sleep well?"

"I had some bad dreams."

"I'm not surprised. Do you want some breakfast?"

"I want to make love to you."

Stone wanted that, too, more than he had wanted anything for a long time. "Vance was just here," he said. "He's gone to get some clothes for the both of you, and he's moving into the hotel until we get this figured out."

She didn't respond.

"I think you'd better be back in your room when he gets here."

"All right." She kissed him for a long time, then she turned and started for the door.

"Are you sure you don't want some breakfast?"

"Maybe later."

"I'll send Vance in when he gets here."

"All right." She closed the door.

Stone wanted very badly to follow her, but he didn't. He sat down weakly and put his face in his hands.

Vance arrived a few minutes later, loaded down with suitcases; he hadn't bothered with a bellman.

"I think she's awake," Stone said.

Vance knocked, then he went into the bedroom, carrying suitcases, and closed the door behind him.

Stone took the coffee pot out onto the terrace and sipped it until it was cold. Vance was in the bedroom with Arrington for more than an hour, and he could hear nothing.

Finally Vance emerged from the bedroom, looking tired and drawn. "Arrington wants to talk to you," he said.

Stone went into the bedroom and closed the door. Arrington was taking things out of suitcases and putting them into another.

"Please sit down," she said.

Stone sat on a sofa and waited for her to begin.

She came and sat next to him. "First, you need to ask me some questions about the last couple of weeks; let's get that out of the way, then I have some things to say to you."

Stone nodded. "All right." Then he began to ask the questions.

54

She was terribly calm, he thought, considering what she had been through. She sat looking at him, waiting for his questions. "How were you taken?" he asked, finally.

"I was shopping on Rodeo Drive; I went back to the parking lot to get my car, and two men pushed me into a van. They taped my eyes and mouth and hands, and I heard them going through my handbag, talking about my car keys. I think one of them drove my car."

"Where did they take you?"

"I don't know. They moved me every day; sometimes they took off the blindfold when I got there; sometimes they untaped my hands. I got to a phone in some back room somewhere and tried to call you. Twice."

"I figured that out," Stone said. "You were in the storeroom of a restaurant. I found the matchbook."

She smiled. "Good detective."

"Did anyone ever tell you why you were taken?"

"A couple of times, one of them said, 'Don't worry; we're not going to hurt you. When your husband comes through, we'll take you home.' I asked what they meant by 'comes through,' but they wouldn't say. I assumed they meant ransom."

"But you talked to Vance every day."

"Yes, but they would only allow me to say that I was all right. They wanted me to beg him to get me back, too. I tried not to do that."

"Did anyone ever tell you who had ordered your kidnapping?"

"No. I asked, but they wouldn't tell me. I heard an occasional reference to 'the boss.'"

"When did they take you to the yacht?"

"I was on two boats, at different times; I was on the big yacht twice."

"Did they take you there by boat?"

"The first time they did; the second time the boat was at a dock. That was yesterday."

"Did they ever hurt you? Rough you up?"

"Once one of them slapped me, after I used the phone. His name was Vinnie, I remember that. I'd like to kick him in the balls, if I ever have the chance."

"You won't; he's dead. Was there another one named Manny?"

"Yes, but they kept changing. There was a Tommy and one they called Zip too."

"Any other names?"

"No, just the four of them."

"Did you ever hear the names of Sturmack or Ippolito mentioned?"

"No; I know them both, so I would have remembered."

"It was Ippolito's yacht."

"I got that impression from your conversation with Dino last night."

"Did you ever hear the name of Martin Barone?"

There was a flash of recognition. "I heard one of them mention 'Marty' once."

"In what connection?"

"It was something like, 'Better check with Marty.'"

"About what?"

"I don't remember."

"Do you have any idea at all what they wanted from Vance? He's been very close-mouthed."

"No, I don't. As I said, I thought they wanted ransom, and you can't blame Vance for not talking about it; I heard them say over and over to him on the phone that if he said anything to anyone, I wouldn't be coming back."

"How did you know that I was in L.A., at the Bel-Air?"

"The trade paper. It said you were at a party at Vance's house, so I figured he had turned to you for help." She put her hand on his. "I'm glad he did."

"Would you recognize the other two men—Tommy and Zip—if you saw them again?"

"Oh, yes."

"Do you know their last names?"

"No."

"Can you describe them?"

"Tommy was about six-four, well over two hundred pounds, a weightlifter, I'm sure; coal-black hair, about thirty. Zip was shorter, a little under six feet, but heavily built; he had black hair going gray, and I guess he was in his early forties."

"Good. Can you think of anything else about your captivity that might help us find out who was responsible?"

"It must be Ippolito, since I was on his yacht. Do you really think David Sturmack is involved? He was always very kind to me; I liked him."

"I think the two of them are in it together. What was your relationship to Ippolito like?"

"There was none. I only met him twice, once at a dinner party at David Sturmack's house, and once at a cocktail party at the Beverly Hills Hotel, a charity thing."

"I guess that's all I have to ask."

"My turn, then."

"All right."

"First of all, I want to tell you about the beginning, when I was supposed to come sailing with you. I had begun to believe that you were never going to make any kind of real commitment..."

"I was going to ask you to marry me when you got to St. Marks."

A tear spilled down her cheek. "Boy, my timing was great, wasn't it? I guess I was kind of hurting, more fragile than I thought, and Vance made me feel better. The more time we spent together the better it got, and after I came back to L.A. with him, well, I guess I became infatuated. I thought I was in love with him."

"Aren't you still?"

"I haven't entirely figured that out yet, but I intend to. I'm certainly very fond of him, and I have great respect for him as a man."

"Even after you were kidnapped, and he didn't get you back right away?"

"I knew he was doing everything he could, and he's explained his actions to my satisfaction. I don't hold anything against him for what happened—I believe it was completely beyond his control."

"He told you he'd be moving here with you while we sort everything out?"

"Yes, but I'm not staying."

"Arrington, this isn't over; we have to protect you."

"I'm going back to Virginia; Betty Southard is arranging a chartered jet right now, and there'll be some security people to meet me at the other end."

"Why are you going back?"

"Vance told you I was pregnant, didn't he? I figure that's the only way he could have gotten you out here."

"Yes, he did."

"Don't you have any questions about that?" she asked.

"I think I'll just let you tell me what you want to."

She smiled. "That's like you, Stone; you were always a good listener."

"Thank you."

"You didn't give away much, but you did listen."

Stone said nothing.

"I am pregnant. I've spent the last two weeks trying to figure out who the father is, but my periods have been irregular for months, and I honestly don't know; it could be either of you."

"I see," Stone said, because he couldn't think of anything else to say.

"So here's what I'm going to do about it," she said. "I'm going back to Virginia to be with my family and to have my baby. Vance has agreed to submit to a blood test, and I want one from you, too."

"All right," Stone said. "I want to know as much as you do."

"If the baby is Vance's, I'll come back to California and be the best wife and mother I can. I know I don't love Vance as deeply as I've loved you, but I think we can still make a good marriage of it, and a home for the child."

"And if the baby isn't Vance's?"

She placed a hand on his cheek and kissed him lightly. "I love you, Stone, I really do. But I don't know what you're feeling, and..."

"I'll tell you..."

"Don't," she said. "It wouldn't do me much good to know right now. If the baby is yours, I'll tell you, and we'll talk about it. Certainly, you can be a part of his life. Or hers. But you and I have some things to work out, and we have to face the fact that we may not be able to work them out. I can't let myself think too much about that until the baby is born; I have to protect myself emotionally. It's no good for me to make a commitment to you and then find out the baby is Vance's. Surely you can see how hard that would be for me."

Stone nodded.

There was a knock on the door.

Arrington kissed him again, and then got up and opened the door. Betty Southard was waiting there.

"Good morning, Arrington," she said. "I'm glad to see you back. They're flying the Centurion jet from Van Nuys into Santa Monica; they should already have landed and refueled by the time we get there."

"I'm ready," Arrington said. She closed

329

her suitcase and handed it to Betty. "Bye," she said to Stone. "I'll call you, but it may not be for a while."

"I'll look forward to it," Stone said, past the lump in his throat.

55

Vance came back to the suite after Arrington had gone. He called room service for more coffee, and after it had come, he sat down on the terrace with Stone. "First of all, I'd like you to represent me as my attorney in this matter. Will you do that?"

"I'm not licensed to practice in California," Stone said, "and if you should somehow become involved in a trial, you'll have to get a California attorney. But for the moment, at least, I will advise you, and you may consider anything you say to me to be privileged, as communication between a lawyer and his client."

"All right," Vance said, "what do you want to know?"

"Everything," Stone said. "And don't leave anything out."

"It started with stock," Vance said. "Centurion stock. The company isn't publicly owned, it's very closely held, only a dozen or so shareholders of any size, and a couple of dozen smaller ones, mostly valued studio employees. Somebody began contacting shareholders, offering to buy their stock, obviously trying to find a way to gain control of the company."

"Who?"

"No one knew at first; it was being done through a third party. Lou Regenstein got wind of it, but it was his strong impression that people were being intimidated into selling or, at least, keeping their mouths shut about having been approached. It was very bizarre, very ominous."

"When did they approach you?"

"Wait, there are other things I have to tell you that will make this make more sense."

"All right, go ahead."

"David Sturmack and I have been good friends for a long time; I guess he and Lou have been my closest friends. It was David who introduced me to Oney Ippolito. I was involved in a real estate development project—a shopping mall—and our financing fell through. I was faced with either coming up with a very large amount of cash—thirty million dollars—or losing the five million I had already invested. I called David for advice, and he arranged a lunch with Ippolito. A week later, we had the financing from Safe Harbor."

"Was the project a questionable one?"

"I never thought so. The managing partner had had some problems in the past with repaying debt on a project, and that made our lender shy away. The mall is open now, and doing excellent business. It was a good deal for Safe Harbor."

"What happened next?"

"It was all very gradual. I began shifting my banking business to Safe Harbor, until finally they had everything—checking accounts, CDs, T-bills, and all the trusts I had set up over the years, including one for Arrington. Whenever I had a business investment that required financing, they were always willing and eager. When Oney asked me to join their board, I accepted."

"How long have you been on the board?"

"Seven or eight months, I guess. I haven't been happy."

"Why not?"

"It became apparent to me early on that Oney expected me to rubber-stamp any decision he made, particularly the ones concerned with his personal compensation—stock options, bonuses, et cetera. The other directors, David Sturmack among them, were obviously in his pocket. I'm on three other boards, and I take an active part; I take my responsibilities to the shareholders seriously. I was ready to quit early on, but Oney persuaded me that I owed him something, and that I shouldn't make him look bad by resigning. I agreed to stay on for a few months more. Then he came to me and said he wanted me to be the television spokesman for the bank. I flatly refused."

"How did he take that?"

"Not well. I explained that I had never done a television commercial and that I never would. I've carefully built a persona as an actor, and I didn't want to squander that. He said that persona was the very reason he wanted me. After all, I was connected to the bank as a customer, I had done business with it, I was on its board; it made sense for me to be a public spokesman. I refused again, and I told him I was giving him thirty days' notice, and then I would resign from the board. He had that time to put the best face on it, and I promised him I would not make my reasons public."

"Did he put further pressure on you?"

"Not immediately. But the following week, David Sturmack came to me and said that someone was willing to pay handsomely for my Centurion stock—double what it's worth, I reckon. I told David that I couldn't even consider that until I'd talked to Lou Regenstein about it."

"What did he say to that?"

"He urged me not to reveal to Lou that I'd been approached, and especially not that he was the one who'd done the approaching. There was something very hard about it, almost threatening."

"What did you do?"

"As soon as he left my office I called Lou and told him what had transpired. Lou was very angry about it, and I promised him I wouldn't sell the stock. I had Betty put my shares in a new safe deposit box the same day."

"You felt that threatened?"

"It's hard to explain, but yes."

"Is Centurion a very profitable studio?"

"Not wildly so, but year in and year out, it does well. The studio has always operated without much debt, but the last year or two there had been a couple of expensive failures, and Lou started to borrow from Safe Harbor, with the board's approval. I'm on the board."

"Why were they so anxious to get the studio, if it's not all that profitable?"

"The real estate."

"What real estate?"

"The land the studio sits on. That was Lou's theory, anyway. All the stockholders and everyone on the board knew that the land was as valuable as the business itself. The back lot had been sold off years ago, for a few million dollars, which was stupid. It would be worth twenty times as much now. The studio sits on the biggest piece of land remaining in Los Angeles that is still held by a single owner—more than four hundred acres. If you tried to put together that much well-located, contiguous land in L.A. by assembling it from different owners, it could cost hundreds of millions of dollars, maybe as much as a billion."

"Why doesn't the studio sell it, move to the sticks, and build a new studio?"

"The costs of doing that, of building from scratch, would be nearly as much as would be gained by selling the land. Anyway, all the stockholders are deeply involved in the movie business; all of them—producers, directors, studio executives—know that what we have is unique and can never be re-created. They're all wealthy people, so they don't need a lot of money from the sale. There's a traditional practice, but not a hard rule, that if someone wants to sell his stock, the studio will buy it back, with the price determined by a previously agreed formula. The same if someone dies—the studio will buy back the stock from the heirs. There's no real market for small parcels of stock outside the studio family, so it worked for everyone. Whoever was behind this wanted to gain control by assembling a block of shareholders, ignoring the buy-back tradition, then buying out everyone else."

"I see. But then the new owners would be in the same position as the old owners, wouldn't they? They'd have a big asset that makes money and that would cost as much to move as to stay. They wouldn't just close down the studio, raze it, and sell the land, would they?"

"Lou thinks there's more to it. He thinks they're using Century City as their example."

"The big group of office buildings?"

"Yes. Century City was built on what used to be the back lot of Twentieth Century—Fox; they sold out to developers. Lou thinks the prospective owners—let's call them Sturmack and Ippolito, since they already own a substantial minority of the shares—don't want to sell the land; he thinks they want to do the development themselves, and with Safe Harbor and other money behind them they could do it. It would be worth billions in the end."

"One bank could finance all that?"

"No. But there's something else I haven't told you."

"Go ahead."

"A couple of years ago, Oney sent me to a man named Barone, who runs some sort of financial services company. Barone asked me if I'd like to make a substantial investment for an absolutely amazing return, tax-free."

"Uh-oh."

"Yes, but I didn't see it at the time. I gave him half a million dollars, and every month a man delivered a cash payment to me. I'd give the money to Barone, and he would send it abroad, for a fee, where it would be invested in a company name."

"He'd launder the money?"

"Yes, I suppose that's what you'd call it."

"Sounds like loan-sharking or drugs. Nothing else could bring that kind of return on an investment."

"It was working out to about ten percent a month," Vance said.

"Sounds like a lot, Vance, but if Barone was loan-sharking, he'd be bringing in ten percent a *week*."

"I was stupid, I know. After a few months, I put in another million dollars."

"They were digging you in deep, then."

"Yes, very deep. So when I told Oney I wouldn't be his television spokesman and that I was resigning from the Safe Harbor board and moving all my accounts, Barone came to see me."

"I can guess what's coming next, I think."

"Probably. I told him I was pulling out of his investment scheme, too. He told me that I couldn't—that if I tried, I'd be in deep trouble with the IRS, that the publicity would destroy me. I got pretty angry. I—I believe the expression is cleaned Mr. Barone's clock—and I threw him out of my office into the street. I was about to call my lawyer when I got a call from David Sturmack. He asked me to wait twenty-four hours while he tried to sort things out to everyone's advantage. I agreed. That was around one o'clock. Late that afternoon, Arrington was kidnapped. I got the first phone call around six."

"Let me guess," Stone said. "In all this, Ippolito and Sturmack can't be directly implicated; they could deny everything, and it would be your word against theirs."

"I realized that when I got that phone call; that's when I decided to take matters into my own hands."

56

Stone listened to this with a sinking heart, having the strong feeling that a bad situation was about to get worse. "What did you do?" he asked Vance Calder.

"First, I talked with Lou Regenstein, and told him I planned to fight these people. He didn't disagree with that, because he and his studio were under attack, and he was not inclined to just fold. He suggested we confide in Billy O'Hara, who is the head of security for Centurion."

"I've heard of him," Stone said.

"Billy was very sympathetic, and I was surprised, since he is a former police officer, that he didn't insist that I go immediately to the police and the FBI."

"So am I," Stone said.

"It was the first thing *you* said to me," Vance said. "I expected the same from Billy, but he didn't even mention doing that."

"What did he suggest?"

"He suggested that I turn the whole thing over to him, that I let him deal with both the kidnappers and the business of the stock."

"Is O'Hara a stockholder?"

"In a small way; he's one of the valued employees who own small parcels."

"Go on."

"So the next time the kidnappers called, I told them that Billy would be dealing for me, and then negotiations began. Billy met with them, and brought me back a series of proposals. They included paying a ransom of a million dollars, which he knew I could well afford, selling my stock, keeping my money in Barone's hands and giving him more, and..."

"Becoming a television spokesman for Safe Harbor and remaining on the board," Stone said. "Now we've got them. That implicates Ippolito, though not necessarily Sturmack."

"Yes, I suppose it does, under certain conditions."

"What conditions?"

"That I become Ippolito's chief accuser and testify against him in court. I should tell you right now that I will *never* do that. The only real leverage they had against me was Arrington's safety, and now that she is safe, that is gone."

"But Vance..."

"No buts about it; I am not going to become publicly involved in this; there is simply too much at stake for me."

"You're forgetting something, Vance; they still have a great deal of leverage against you."

"What are you talking about?"

"Your investment with Barone."

"I will deny that. They have no contract, nothing with my signature on it. All I have to do is take the loss of the million and a half dollars I invested, and then wash my hands of them."

"It's not going to be as easy as that, Vance."

"What are they going to do? Report me to the IRS? They can't do that without implicating themselves. If the IRS began to investigate me, I would just deny everything. The only way they could tie me to Barone is on Barone's testimony and, in the unlikely event that he gave it, it would be his word against mine."

"Vance, let me tell you, nobody ever achieved happiness by lying to the IRS. If they believed Barone's story—or more likely, an anonymous tip—they could make life very difficult for you."

"How?"

"Have you ever heard of a tax audit?"

"I've been audited three times; on each occasion they had to accept my return as filed, and on one occasion they actually had to refund nearly fifty thousand dollars. Let them try again, if they like."

"It's not going to end there, Vance; first of all, the reasons for the audit would somehow find their way into the press, and then your coveted privacy would be gone. At least half the people who read about it are going to believe you've done something illegal, which, of course, you have."

Vance furrowed his beautiful brow, but said nothing.

"Moreover, if Ippolito and Barone want to sink you, they'll do more than just make an anonymous phone call; they'll give the IRS chapter and verse on your foreign investments. They'll fax them copies of the offshore bank statements; they'll do whatever is necessary, and you may be sure that none of the documents will make any reference to Barone or Ippolito. It will be your word against theirs, all right, but the evidence will all point to you, not them."

Vance was looking really worried now.

"You have to understand that the day you gave them that money, you kissed it goodbye."

"But they did actually produce a return on my investment," Vance protested.

"Which you gave back to them to reinvest, right?"

"Well, yes."

"So, in fact, you gave them a million and a half dollars, and you've never actually collected a dime in earnings from it."

"Well, not yet, I suppose."

"Not ever, Vance. Somewhere along the line, Barone would have come to you, very apologetically, of course, and told you that the market in whatever your investment is had crashed, and you'd lost everything. He would sob that you're not alone, *he* lost everything, too. He didn't, of course, but that's what he'd say. You couldn't even take a tax loss, the way you could have if your investment had been legitimate."

Vance looked slightly nauseous now. "I don't believe this," he said. "It was an investment, not a gift."

"It was a scam, pure and simple, Vance."

Now anger flicked across the gorgeous suntanned face. "The sons of bitches," he said quietly.

"Makes you want to get back at them, doesn't it? They've kidnapped your wife, robbed you, humiliated you, and tried to extort your investment in Centurion right out of your hands. And that would be only the beginning, if they're allowed to get away with it. Eventually you would end up as their creature, a puppet controlled by Ippolito, with Sturmack on the sidelines stroking you and telling you everything was really all right. Centurion would be gone, all those talented people would be out of work, and some of them would never work again. Lou Regenstein would be ruined, your career

341

would be fatally damaged. In the end you'd be lucky to get a TV movie of the week. And Ippolito would own you—lock, stock, and the barrel you'd end up wearing."

"Jesus fucking Christ," Vance said wonderingly.

"Exactly." *Vance,* Stone thought, *is beginning to get the big picture.* "Now, what are you going to do about it?"

Vance shone the full force of his persona at Stone. *"Whatever it takes!"* he said slowly.

"Will you bare your soul to the IRS?"

"Yes!"

"Will you tell everything about Barone's and Ippolito's financial dealings to the FBI?"

"Yes!" Vance was into his scene, now.

"Will you help me pull Ippolito's and Sturmack's little empire down around their ears?"

"Goddammit, yes!"

"Will you testify against them in court?"

Vance's handsome face dissolved into consternation. "Absolutely not!" he said, outraged.

Stone sighed deeply. "Vance," he said.

"Yes, Stone?"

"There's a chance—just a sliver of a chance—that I can get you out of this without it becoming public."

Vance beamed, revealing startling dental work. "I knew you could do it, Stone."

"I haven't said I *could* do it. I've said there's a *tiny* chance I could do it. And it means you're going to have to tell the IRS and the FBI everything."

"All right, as long as it doesn't get into the papers."

"And it means that you're never going to see *any* of your million and a half dollars again."

"Really?" Vance asked plaintively.

"Really. And there's always the possibility that the feds will simply subpoena you, and you'd *have* to testify."

"I'd take the Fifth!" Vance said indignantly.

"Vance, that would completely destroy your reputation."

"Oh," Vance said.

Stone had hoped to bring Vance to the full realization of what faced him, but he was not sure he had succeeded. After all, the man *was* a movie star.

57

While Vance took a nap in his suite, Stone tried to assess his position. He had a witness, an accuser, now, one who knew some of what was going on in Ippolito's empire, but one who, in the end, would not testify in court. What was more, now that he had declared himself Vance's attorney, he had lost some of his powers of persuasion, such as threatening to go to the tabloids with what he knew of the movie star's dealings. He was going to have to sell part of Vance to the feds, and it was time to see what they would give Vance for what he knew. He called Hank Cable at the FBI.

"Hello, Hank, it's Stone Barrington."

"Hi, Stone."

"Anything new?"

"I've got some codebusters working on what we're hearing from the taps on Barone Financial, but our warrant is about to expire, and we're not there yet, and I don't know if we have enough to get an extension."

"Maybe I can help."

"I hope so. We're pretty much at a dead end, unless the code boys come up with something startling."

"Do you know the chief investigator for the IRS in L.A.?"

"Sure; we talk from time to time."

"I'd like to meet with both of you, today, at the earliest possible moment."

"If you'll hang on a minute, Stone, I'll see if I can get him on another line."

"Sure." Stone waited for a couple of minutes.

"You still there?"

"Yep."

"How about lunch? You're buying."

Stone gave him his suite number at the Bel-Air. "In an hour?"

"See you then."

Stone hung up and called Rick Grant. "Rick, I'm having lunch with Hank Cable and the IRS; will you join us in my suite?"

"Sure. What's up?"

"I think there may be something good for you in all this, but I warn you, the feds are going to take the biggest helpings."

"So what else is new?"

"Can you be here in an hour?"

"Sure, but can you fill me in a little before we meet the feds?"

"It wouldn't do any good right now. What I hope you'll do is just listen and back me up when I ask for it."

"I'll listen, and I'll back you up if I can, but if we're getting official here, I have my department's interests to protect."

"If it's any consolation, your department is going to get more than the feds would ever give you if I weren't in the middle of this. At least I have something they want; I just have to see how bad they want it."

"Okay, I'll trust you."

"See you in an hour." Stone hung up, walked down to the manager's office, and borrowed a computer. They were happy to help.

"By the way, Mr. Barrington, there have been a couple of calls for you, but I denied all knowledge, as you requested," the desk woman said.

"Anybody leave a name?"

"No, sir."

"I didn't think so." Stone sat down at the computer, quickly wrote a document and printed out several copies, then went back to his suite. Vance was up now.

"What's going on?" he asked.

"I've got some people coming here for lunch, and I'd like you to stay out of sight until I need you. Why don't you order some lunch and have it in your suite?"

"Okay."

"And don't go out. Somebody has been calling the hotel looking for me, and I think we can both guess who it might be."

"Don't worry, I'll stay put."

"Vance, if I call you into this meeting, that will mean that it's time for you to tell everything to these people, do you understand?"

"Yes, I suppose so; I'll depend on you to protect me."

"I'll explain the circumstances before I ask you to say anything."

"All right, but remember, no testifying, and no public knowledge of my involvement."

"I'll aim for that," Stone said.

Hank Cable showed up with his IRS friend on time; the man didn't look at all they way he had imagined. He was tall, fiftyish, gray at the temples, and looked more like the stereotype of a judge.

"Stone, this is John Rubens," Cable said. "He heads the investigations division of the IRS in Southern California."

The two men shook hands, then Rick Grant arrived and was introduced. Shortly a waiter showed up with the lobster salad lunch Stone had ordered for them all, and with two bottles of a very good California chardonnay. Lunch was served on Stone's private terrace. They ate, they drank the wine, then coffee was served.

"Well, gentlemen, it's time to tell you why I'm buying you such a good lunch," Stone said.

"Please do," Rubens replied. "And thank you for the lunch."

"I have as a client a person who may be a very important witness in a very big prosecution," Stone said.

"For what crime?" Rubens asked.

"Tax evasion, for a start, to the tune of maybe hundreds of millions of dollars."

"I like the sound of that," the IRS man said.

Cable spoke up. "I can only assume we're talking about the people we've been talking about all along."

Rubens broke in. "You've been talking all along? How long?"

"Only a few days," Cable replied.

"And tax evasion came into it only this morning."

"All right, proceed," Rubens said.

"My client can't conclusively make your cases for you, but I believe he can be invaluable."

"And what does your client want in all this?" Rubens asked.

"A number of things, of course, and all in the gift of you gentlemen."

"Go on."

"Immunity, for a start; complete and total."

"Immunity for what?"

"My client has been naive; he has been sucked into an investment scheme by prominent businessmen which has turned out to be, shall we say, extra-legal?"

"And how much has your client lost?" Rubens asked.

"Nothing, as of the moment; in fact, he has made large profits, which he allowed

347

these businessmen to reinvest for him."

"Would this involve offshore bank accounts, tax evasion, and the like?" Rubens asked.

"On a monumental scale."

"And is your client's involvement monumental?"

"His total investment is one and a half million dollars."

"Well, from my point of view, this doesn't sound insurmountable," Rubens said. "Hank, how about you?"

"We haven't heard what else Stone's client wants," Cable said.

"Well, immunity, as I said, from all federal prosecution—and Rick, I'll expect the same for local and state officials. But just as important, my client's identity must never be revealed to anyone outside your offices."

"I take that to mean your client doesn't want to testify," Cable said.

"His greatest value will be not in his testimony, but in his ability to steer your investigations in the right direction."

"Does your client have a criminal record?" Cable asked.

"He does not. He is an upstanding citizen, a taxpayer on a grand scale, and of unimpeachable reputation."

"Except for this little indiscretion you mentioned," Rubens said.

"His only lapse, and believe me, he was snookered into it." Stone knew that was a half-truth, but he had to win this negotiation now, if he was going to protect Vance.

"Well, let's hear what he has to say, and I'll discuss this with my superiors," Cable said.

Stone shook his head. "He says nothing until we are in complete agreement, and I must tell you that this offer will be short-lived. My client is aware that if he says nothing, he will probably escape your attentions."

"That's blackmail," Rubens said.

"Actually, it's extortion," Stone replied, "a technique not unknown to the IRS."

Rubens, to his credit, laughed.

"Suppose we just pursue this on our own and arrest your client later? I'm sure he'd be willing to testify then," Cable said.

"Hank," Stone said, "you've already told me that you're coming up dry so far, and without my help and that of my client, your whole investigation is likely to just grind to a halt."

The two men looked at each other, and Stone knew what they were thinking.

"Gentlemen, I'm sure you'd feel more comfortable if you ran this by your superiors and the U.S. Attorney. There's a phone in the living room and one in the bedroom, and I promise you privacy." He handed them each a copy of the document he had prepared. "You might read this to them."

They each read the document.

"You don't want a hell of a lot, do you?" Cable asked sarcastically.

"My client is asking for a lot less than he is willing to give," Stone replied.

The two men, without another word, got up and went to find the phones.

"You're some piece of work," Rick said. "Do you really think they're going to buy this, sight unseen?"

"I think they very well might," Stone said, handing a copy of the document to him. "Aren't you?"

"Well..."

"You had better start convincing the DA, if you want your department to participate."

Rick went to look for a phone.

58

They were all gathered around the dining table in Stone's suite now, and he was anxiously awaiting their decision. John Rubens, without a word, signed Stone's document and passed it to him. After a moment's hesitation, so did Hank Cable.

"How about you, Rick?" Stone asked.

Rick Grant signed the document, and Stone gave them each a copy for their records.

"When do we meet your witness?" Rubens asked.

Stone got up, went into the adjoining suite, and came back with Vance Calder. The IRS man and the FBI agent suddenly became movie fans. They were both on their feet, almost to attention, shaking hands with the famous man, and Rick Grant's reception was almost as welcoming. They all sat down.

"Vance," Stone said, handing him a copy of the agreement, "the IRS, the FBI, and the

LAPD have all agreed to offer you immunity from prosecution and complete confidentiality in return for your account of recent events; in addition, you will not have to testify in court, and the kidnapping will be kept out of it. In return, you are expected to be completely frank with them and to answer their questions truthfully. I have to warn you that should you not tell the truth, you can be charged with lying to a federal agent. Do you understand the terms of the agreement?"

"Yes," Vance said.

"I think it would be best, gentlemen, if you let Mr. Calder start at the beginning and tell his whole story without interruption. When he is finished, you can ask all the questions you like. I'd like to remind you that I consider Mr. Calder still to be in danger, and I expect you to keep his location confidential. Vance?"

Vance Calder proceeded to give a performance that, had Stone seen it in a theater, he would have stood up and applauded. The federal agents and the L.A. policeman listened, rapt, as the story unfolded. When he was finished, the questioning began, and Vance's answers were as impressive as his monologue had been. Stone began to believe that the actor should write his own scripts.

When it was over, Vance retired to his suite, and Stone faced the feds again.

"That was very impressive, but it wasn't enough," Hank Cable said.

"I told you that it wouldn't be," Stone replied, "but now you have a direction. I suggest that you begin by arresting Martin Barone on charges of tax evasion, money laundering, and whatever else you can come up with from the wiretap of his offices. You can at least threaten him with Vance's testimony. Even though that won't happen, Barone doesn't know. You could throw in the kidnapping charge, too; I can give you a witness who'll testify that Barone was in possession of Mrs. Calder's car for several days."

The meeting broke up, and Stone asked Rick Grant to stay behind.

"You were right," Rick said. "There's not going to be much left for the LAPD."

"Oh, there might be," Stone said. "How about murder?"

"You're still alive."

"Vinnie Mancuso and his partner, Manny, aren't."

"You'll never tie that to Ippolito."

"There's a new way in," Stone said. "Let me make a couple of phone calls." He called Betty Southard and made a request and had a longer conversation with Lou Regenstein; then he invited Rick to join him in the car.

"Where are we going?" Rick asked.

"To Centurion Studios," Stone replied.

"For what?"

"To see Billy O'Hara. He's up to his ass in this." As they drove, Stone explained what he had in mind.

"The guy was a cop," Rick said. "You really think he'll go for it?"

"One way to find out. If he doesn't, you and I have a lot more work ahead of us."

At Centurion they picked up the visitor's passes that Betty had left for them and asked directions to the security director's office. They hadn't made an appointment. O'Hara's secretary disappeared into his office, then came out. "He'll see you," she said.

"Please call Mr. Regenstein's office and tell him we're with Mr. O'Hara," Stone said. He and Rick went into the private office and closed the door behind him.

"Rick!" O'Hara said, rising to greet him with a handshake. "How are you?"

"Very well, Billy," Grant said. "I'd like you to meet someone; this is Stone Barrington."

O'Hara's handshake stopped before it got started; he was clearly nonplussed. That was enough to convince Stone.

Stone and Rick sat down.

"What can I do for you?" O'Hara asked. He was making an effort to regain his poise.

"You'd better deal with the phone call first," Rick said. Immediately, the phone rang.

The secretary's voice came over the intercom. "Mr. Regenstein for you," she said.

"Tell your secretary to go to lunch," Rick said.

"She's already been to lunch," O'Hara replied, his hand on the phone.

"Tell her to go again."

"Robin," O'Hara said into the intercom, "go over to Office Supplies and stock up on everything. Give me an hour here." He picked up the phone. "Lou? How are you?"

Stone and Rick could hear Regenstein's voice blaring over the instrument; he was clearly very angry.

"Wait a minute, Lou," O'Hara was saying, "let's talk about this."

Regenstein went on at some length, and O'Hara wasn't getting a word in edgewise. "All right," he said finally, then hung up.

"Billy," Rick said, "even though you no longer work for Centurion Studios, we have Mr. Regenstein's permission to use this office for as long as it takes."

"As long as what takes?" O'Hara said shakily. Most of the color had drained from his face.

"Billy, you were a good cop, maybe even an outstanding one, but that's not going to help you now, unless I have your complete cooperation."

"About what?" O'Hara asked.

"Here's how it is: you're under arrest for kidnapping and murder one; there'll be other charges later. You know your rights, but consider that I just read them to you."

"Kidnapping? Murder? What are you talking about, Rick?"

"Shut up and listen to me. I'm going to give you an opportunity you'll never have again after this meeting. I'm going to go out on a limb and offer you complete immunity from prosecution, if you tell me *everything* right now. You'll have to testify against Ippolito, Sturmack, and Barone, and anybody else involved, but after they're convicted, you're off the hook.

"You certainly have the right to remain silent, but if you do, I promise you, from the bottom of my heart, that you will have spent your last day on this earth as a free man. You know there won't be any bail. In addition to that, I promise you the roughest ride in the joint that I can muster, and that's pretty rough. I'll personally see to it that you do the hardest possible time in the worst prison this state has to offer, and that's pretty bad; I'll see that you're put on the same cell block with some of the people you sent up when you were a cop." He paused for effect. "That's my offer, and time is running out. What's it going to be?"

Stone tensed as O'Hara's hand went inside his jacket, but he came back with a handkerchief and mopped his face. "You said *complete* immunity?"

"I did."

"From *everything*? I'll walk?"

"That's right. I don't give a shit what you did."

"Can I have it in writing?"

"I'm the only friend you've got, Billy; don't abuse my friendship."

O'Hara opened his desk drawer, causing Stone concern again, but he came up with a bottle of pills. He poured himself a glass of water and took one, then he sat back in his chair, a beaten man. "Okay, Rick: I'll play it your way. Ippolito can go fuck himself."

59

Rick placed a handheld tape recorder on the desk between himself and Billy O'Hara and switched it on. He counted to ten aloud, played back the sound to be sure he had a level, then rewound it and pressed the record button.

"My name is Richard Grant," he said. "I am a lieutenant of detectives of the Los Angeles Police Department attached to the chief of detectives. I am interviewing William O'Hara, a former police officer and, until recently, chief of security at Centurion Studios. Mr. O'Hara has agreed to give me a full statement of his activities without counsel present and to testify against others, in return for guaranteed immunity from all prosecution. Also present, as a witness, is Mr. Stone Barrington, a retired New York City police officer." He stated the date and time, then looked up at his interviewee. "Are you William O'Hara?"

"Yes, I am," O'Hara replied.

"Have you been informed of your constitutional rights?"

"I have."

"Do you understand them?"

"Yes, I do."

"Do you wish to have legal counsel present during this interview?"

"No, I do not."

"Are the statements which you are about to make given freely and without duress?"

"Yes, they are."

"Have you been promised anything by me or any other law enforcement official, except immunity from prosecution, in return for making these statements?"

"No, I have not been."

"Tell me, as fully as possible, how you became involved in the crimes presently under investigation by the LAPD and the federal authorities."

O'Hara took a deep breath and began. His presentation was that of a police officer testifying in court, as he had been trained to do. "I retired from the Los Angeles Police Department five years ago, on the offer of a job from Mr. Louis Regenstein, chairman of the board, as director of security for Centurion Studios. After I had been employed by Centurion for a year I was offered the opportunity to purchase stock in the company. I bought one hundred shares at a price of five hundred dollars a share. The studio loaned me the money to make the purchase.

"Approximately three months prior to the present date I was approached by Mr. David Sturmack, a member of the board of Centurion Studios, with an offer to trade my shares in Centurion for an equal number of shares of Albacore Fisheries, which is a company controlled by Mr. Sturmack and Mr. Onofrio Ippolito, who is also chairman of the board of the Safe Harbor Bank."

"Was this an advantageous offer?"

"It represented an increase in the value of my investment by a factor of ten."

"What did Mr. Sturmack tell you he wanted in return for this windfall?"

"He asked me to assist him in doing intelligence work at the studio directed at causing other stockholders to sell Albacore their shares."

"Did you agree to help him?"

"Yes."

"Did he ask you to do anything else?"

"Not at that time."

"Later?"

"A few weeks later, Mr. Sturmack came back to see me. He said that he had learned that Louis Regenstein was planning to fire me as head of security. He said that he would use his influence in the company to prevent such an action, if he could count on me for other work."

"What other work?"

"He made an appointment for me to see Mr. Onofrio Ippolito the following day. At Mr. Ippolito's office at Safe Harbor Bank I was searched for weapons and recording devices, then I met with Mr. Ippolito alone."

"What was the substance of that meeting?"

"He first told me that he had evidence, in the form of witnesses, that I had participated in illegal actions when I was a police officer."

"What actions?"

"He said he had witnesses who could testify that I had accepted bribes from members of organized crime."

"Had you accepted such bribes?"

"Yes."

"Then what transpired?"

"Mr. Ippolito said that he had a use for me, and that if I did as he asked I would become rich beyond my wildest dreams. He said he had business plans that would increase the value of my Albacore stock by a factor of fifty, perhaps a hundred, and that if I served him well, I would be allowed to buy more stock at favorable prices. He also offered me a salary of two hundred thousand dollars a year in cash, tax free, and said that I could continue to collect my salary at Centurion."

"Did you accept his proposal?"

"Yes, I did."

"What work did you do for Mr. Ippolito?"

"I searched the employee files at Centurion and made a list of all stockholders and gave it to Mr. Sturmack. I transported large sums of cash from a Mr. Martin Barone to the offices of Albacore, which are on the floor below Mr. Ippolito's office in the Safe Harbor building. I did many other routine jobs for Mr. Ippolito, including the disciplining of a loan shark who reported to Mr. Barone."

"What was his name?"

"Ralph DiOrio."

"How did you discipline him?"

"I beat him into unconsciousness with a blackjack."

"Did Mr. Ippolito ask you to commit any other violent crimes?"

"Yes, he ordered me to arrange three murders."

"Did you do so?"

"Yes."

"Who were the victims?"

"The first was Mr. Stone Barrington, who I now realize escaped death."

"And who carried out the attempt on Mr. Barrington's life?"

"Vincent Mancuso and Manolo Lobianco."

"Did Mr. Ippolito subsequently learn that Mr. Barrington had escaped death?"

"Not to my knowledge."

"Who were the other two murder victims?"

"Vincent Mancuso and Manolo Lobianco."

"Why were they murdered?"

"They had been arrested on other charges, and Mr. Ippolito was concerned that they might connect him to Mr. Barrington's death."

"Who carried out these two murders?"

"Thomas Cosenza and Joseph Zito."

"How were they murdered?"

"On Mr. Ippolito's specific instructions, they were shot in the head and dumped into the Pacific Ocean with weights attached."

Rick wrote something on a piece of paper and showed it to O'Hara. "I show you a name; is this a name you recognize?"

"Yes."

"For the purposes of this interview, you will refer to this person as Mr. X."

"All right."

"Did anyone ask you to do anything with regard to Mr. X?"

"Yes. Mr. Ippolito instructed me to have the wife of Mr. X kidnapped and held until I received further instructions from him."

"Did you do so?"

"Yes."

"Who conducted the kidnapping?"

"Vincent Mancuso and Manolo Lobianco."

"Where was she taken?"

"She was moved daily from one location to another."

"Did Mr. Ippolito ask you to contact Mr. X to arrange the return of his wife?"

"No, I believe others did that."

"Do you know who?"

"Other employees of Mr. Ippolito. I don't know their names."

"Did Mr. Ippolito ask you to do anything else with regard to the kidnapping of Mrs. X?"

"When Mr. Regenstein asked me to help in the recovery of Mrs. X, I told Mr. Ippolito. He instructed me to pretend to help Mr. X, but to report all communications to him or Mr. Sturmack."

"Was Mr. Sturmack involved in the kidnapping?"

"He was aware of it."

"What was the purpose of the kidnapping?"

"To persuade Mr. X to sell to Albacore his stock in Centurion Studios. Mr. X is a large stockholder."

"Was there any other purpose?"

"I believe Mr. Ippolito wanted Mr. X to participate in other of his business activities, but I am not familiar with those."

"I ask you again, Mr. O'Hara, have you given this interview without duress, and with only the seeking of immunity from prosecution as your motive?"

"Yes."

Rick switched off the recorder. "All right, that's enough for now. I'm going to get you a promise of immunity from the feds, then allow them to question you in a lot more detail about Ippolito's, Sturmack's, and Barone's business affairs."

"I'll have a lot more to say," O'Hara said.

"Good." Rick picked up the phone on the man's desk and dialed a number. "This is Rick Grant; I'm arresting a man who has given me a statement implicating a number of other people in serious crimes. I want a secure hotel room arranged for him *now*, where he can be interviewed in greater depth. Yes, I'll hold." He covered the phone. "I'm going to move Billy now, then we can talk again to Cable and Rubens." He went back to the phone. "Good. Send an unmarked car and two detectives to the Centurion Studios security department now to pick up my man. His name is William O'Hara. Yes, the same. Got all that? Good." He hung up.

Less than ten minutes passed before the two detectives arrived.

"Put him in the back of the car, no cuffs, no fuss, and take him to the hotel," Rick said. "Then get his house keys, go there, and get him some clothes. I don't want him touched."

The men departed with O'Hara.

Rick picked up the phone again and called

Hank Cable at the FBI. "Hank," he said, "we've got a witness against Ippolito, Sturmack, and Barone." He gave him the name of the hotel. "Can you and Rubens meet us there in an hour? Ask for me at the front desk." He hung up and turned to Stone. "Let's get over there; I want Cable and Rubens to interrogate Billy. Once that's done we'll know our next move."

60

Stone was shaken awake by Rick Grant. He was laying fully dressed on a bed in one of the two bedrooms of Rick's secure hotel suite.

"Come on into the living room," Rick said.

Stone looked at his watch; it was seven-thirty in the morning. He followed Rick into the living room, where two video cameras, two tape recorders, and some lights had been set up. "Where's O'Hara?" Stone asked.

"We let him get some sleep," Rick said. "Hank and John have pretty much bled him dry, and it's all on video and audio. They want to talk to you."

Stone sat down and poured himself some coffee from a thermos. "How'd it go, gentlemen?"

"It went very well," Hank Cable said, "but he may not be all we need."

Stone didn't like the sound of that. "Why not?"

"He'll be a good witness, but a defense

363

lawyer of the quality that Ippolito and Sturmack will hire will give him a very hard time on the stand."

"So?"

"Sturmack and Ippolito will take the stand and say that sure, they hired him to help in acquiring the Centurion stock, but that was all. They'll blame any of his confessed illegal activity on O'Hara himself, and their lawyer will make much of O'Hara's accepting bribes from organized crime and his involvement in murder."

"So what are you saying?" Stone asked.

"I'm saying that as good as O'Hara is, he may not be enough. If we could persuade Vance Calder to testify, that would help, of course, but... "

"But Vance is not going to do it," Stone said. "You can't count on that for a minute."

"If we want to button this thing up, we're going to need more," Cable said.

"What about your wiretaps? Surely O'Hara's testimony will get you extensions on your search warrants and some new warrants too."

"That will take time," Rick Grant said. "Sturmack will hear that Regenstein has fired O'Hara, and Ippolito's people are going to notice that O'Hara has vanished off the face of the earth. When they do, they could shut down Barone's operation, leaving us high and dry. They could even cut and run, if they're nervous enough. I just don't think we have weeks or months to sit and listen to wiretaps and try to decipher them."

"Have you arrested Barone yet? He knows where the bodies are buried, and I'll bet he could be broken."

"Maybe, but he'll more than likely lawyer up, get out on bail, and disappear. We don't want to take him until our case is solid."

"Anybody got any ideas?" Stone asked.

There followed a long silence on the part of everybody.

Finally Hank Cable said, "We were hoping that you might have an idea. You've been pretty good so far."

It was Stone's turn to be silent. "Ippolito doesn't know that I'm alive," he said at last.

"We're not absolutely certain of that," Rick said. "Remember, Ippolito's yacht captain knows you by sight."

"But not by name. O'Hara doesn't think Ippolito knows I'm alive."

"Okay, maybe he doesn't know," Rick agreed.

"Why don't I pay him a visit? Have a talk with him? You could wire me."

Rick was shaking his head. "You heard O'Hara say yesterday that when he went to Ippolito's office he was searched for weapons and a wire."

"Good point," Stone said.

Cable spoke up. "What size shoe do you wear, Stone?"

"A 10 D," Stone replied. "Why?"

"Maybe there's a way. Tell you what: you go back to your hotel, get some breakfast, a shower, and a change of clothes, and I'll meet you there in a couple of hours."

Stone arrived back at the Bel-Air to find Dino still sound asleep. He got undressed, shaved, and got into the shower. When he came out, Dino was up.

"Where the hell have you been all night?" Dino asked. "I was worried."

"Sorry I didn't call home, Mom; I was at an all-night interrogation."

"Of who?"

Stone brought him up to date while he got dressed.

"What's this about shoes?" Dino asked.

"Beats me," Stone said. "Let's get some breakfast."

They had just finished eating when Hank Cable and Rick Grant arrived. Cable had a shoebox under his arm.

"Take off your shoes and pants," Cable said. "Your underwear too."

Stone followed his instructions. "No pictures," he said.

Cable opened the shoebox and took out a pair of wingtips. "They're 9½ C's," he said. "It was the best I could do."

"I take it these are some sort of federal high-tech wingtips," Stone said.

"Good guess. Put them on."

Stone put on the shoes. "They're tight," he said.

"You'll live," Cable replied. He took some wires and a roll of tape out of the shoebox. "Here's how it works," he said. "In the heel of one shoe is a tape recorder; in the heel of the other shoe is a transmitter." He plugged a very slim wire into a tiny receptacle at the top rear of each shoe. "Turn around."

Stone turned around.

Cable began running a wire up the back of Stone's right leg, taping it in place, then he followed with the left leg. "Okay, now put your shorts and your pants on."

Stone got dressed.

"Now we tape the wires running around your waist to the front," Cable said, "and we attach these two little microphones to the two wires." He did so, then he taped the tiny microphones to Stone's belly. They were nestled in his navel.

"Now you can stick your shirttail in and buckle your belt."

Stone did as he was told.

"Now," Cable said, "if they frisk you for a wire they'll be looking for a small transmitter taped to your chest or in the small of your back, or maybe even in your crotch. They won't be looking at the heels of your shoes. Even if they pat you down very thoroughly, the wires are too thin to feel through the fabric of your suit."

"I see," Stone said. "That's pretty good; I might just get away with it."

"I'd be willing to bet that you will," Cable said.

"How do I turn on the transmitter and the tape recorder?" Stone asked.

"All you do is stamp each heel firmly on a hard surface, like concrete. It might now work on carpet. The transmitter we can pick up from as much as ten miles away; the tape in the recorder will last for two hours."

"I don't understand about the recorder," Stone said. "Why don't you just record it at the receiving end?"

"Oh, we will, but we need a backup, in case there's any interference that screws up some part of the transmission."

"Here's what we do," Rick said. "You go down to the headquarters building of the Safe Harbor Bank and take the elevator up to the top floor, where Ippolito's office is. Tell the receptionist or secretary who you are and ask to see Ippolito."

"Suppose he won't see me?"

"Don't take no for an answer. I'm betting that his curiosity will be too much for him, especially if he still thinks you're dead. He'll see you, I'll give you odds."

"Then what?"

"Engage him in conversation; get him to incriminate himself."

"How the hell am I supposed to do that?"

"You're a good talker, Stone; you'll figure a way. Just get him talking and keep him talking for as long as possible."

"And where will you guys be all this time?"

"We'll be all over that building, just an elevator ride from you. If he cuts and runs, there's no way he can get past us and out of the building."

"Suppose he just takes a gun out of his desk drawer and shoots me?" Stone asked.

"Come on, he's not going to commit murder in his own office, for Christ's sake."

Cable spoke up again; he held up a Mont Blanc fountain pen, the fat model. "More goodies; this little beauty fires one twenty-two-caliber hollowpoint cartridge. You'll be able to hit somebody at arm's length—any farther away than that, no guarantees. I'd go for the head, if I were you." He held up another pen. "Here's a second one; put them in your inside coat pocket, where a man would normally carry a pen." He unscrewed the cap and revealed a pen point. "It will actually write," he said; then he screwed the cap back on. "To fire it, you point it and press down hard on the tip of the gold clip, see?" He demonstrated without actually firing the weapon.

"I don't see a barrel."

"That's concealed under the plastic tip. The bullet will blow the end off the pen when it's fired."

Stone took the pens and put them in his inside coat pocket.

"Now," Rick said, "after you've gotten him to incriminate himself, or if anything should go wrong, just say the word 'police' in any sentence. If you say 'cops' or 'FBI' or 'IRS' or anything except 'police,' we won't move. But the minute we hear that word from you, we're on our way with SWAT teams. We'll have the elevator keys, and we can be with you in no more than a minute, a minute and a half at the outside."

"And if I'm in trouble, what am I supposed to do for those ninety seconds?"

"That's what the pens are for," Cable said.

"Okay," Stone said, "I'll do it."

61

Stone sat with Rick Grant and Dino in the parking garage of the Safe Harbor building. Stone took off his shoulder holster and handed it, with the pistol, to Rick. "I don't think I'd get into Ippolito's office wearing that, do you?" he asked, slipping back into his jacket.

"Probably not," Rick said.

Dino, who had been uncharacteristically quiet during the planning of this event, spoke up. "Stone, I got a lot of problems with this," he said.

"What problems?"

"You're walking into this place, and you don't know anything about it. On top of that, all you know about this Ippolito is that he's a very, very bad guy who has already tried to kill you once. This is not a recipe for a nice day."

"I take your point, Dino, but I have a personal interest in this; I don't want to sit around and wait for the feds to take forever to make a case against this guy. I want to hurt him myself."

"You already did that—twice," Dino pointed out.

"I cost him money, that's all. I want to put the son of a bitch in prison forever."

"All right," Dino said, "if you have to do it, then do it."

"Stone," Rick said, "you don't have to do this; I can call it off right now."

"I *want* to do it," Stone said. "Now both of you shut up and let's get on with it."

"Let me tell you the setup," Rick said. "We've got a van parked across the street with a power company logo on it and a manhole open. The van is where all the radio equipment is. They'll receive your signal, then amplify it and broadcast it to our handheld radios, so everybody can hear you all the time. We've got two FBI SWAT teams in vans here in the garage; they've taken an elevator out of service, and it's just sitting there, waiting to go straight to the top. We've got plainclothes people loitering near every security station in the bank, so that there's no early warning to Ippolito's suite that we're on the way. We've got people sitting on David Sturmack and Martin Barone; we'll bust them the minute you're safe. Also, the feds have got search warrants for Safe Harbor and all its branches; also for Barone Financial and Albacore Fisheries, and we've got the bank examiners ready to roll the minute you're out of the building."

"Sounds good," Stone said, then he pointed at something. "Look at that," he said.

A Rolls-Royce convertible drove past and parked in a bay across from them; David Sturmack got out and went to the elevators.

"Maybe he's going up to Ippolito's office," Rick said.

"Maybe he's gonna cash a check," Dino said.

"Wouldn't it be sweet if you could get both of them talking?" Rick asked.

"I'll do the best I can," Stone said. He got out of the car and stamped both heels on the concrete floor. "Testing, testing," he said.

Rick held up his radio. "Loud and clear. Good luck."

"Yeah," Dino said. "Good luck. I wish I was going with you."

Stone started for the elevators. He had to wait a while, since one was out of service, but eventually he got into the car and pressed the top button, the twenty-fifth floor. The elevator stopped several times, taking on and discharging passengers, but by the time he reached the twenty-fifth, he was alone. "I'm here," he said to the wire. He got off the elevator and walked into a large, plushly furnished reception room. David Sturmack was sitting in an armchair, flipping through an issue of *Fortune* magazine. He didn't look up.

"May I help you?" the receptionist asked cordially.

"Yes, would you please tell Mr. Ippolito that..."

A buzzer rang. "Excuse me," the receptionist said, picking up the phone. "Yes, sir, I'll send him right in." She turned to Sturmack. "Mr. Sturmack, Mr. Ippolito will see you now."

Stone turned his back and coughed into his fist as Sturmack walked past, taking no notice of him. The receptionist pressed a button under her desktop, and Ippolito's office door opened for Sturmack.

"Oh, there's David," Stone said to the receptionist with a smile, and started for the door. "I'm here for this meeting."

The receptionist nodded and smiled.

Stone caught the door before it closed and stepped in behind Sturmack. Ippolito was sitting at his desk, his back to the door, talking on the phone. Sturmack still had not noticed that he had been followed into the office.

It was a large and handsomely designed room, with spectacular views over the city, all the way to the Pacific. It was an unusually clear day, free of smog. Sturmack walked to the desk and settled himself in a chair, his back to Stone. Stone walked over and took the chair beside him.

Sturmack glanced idly at Stone, then blanched and stood up, alarmed. Simultaneously, Ippolito hung up the phone and turned around. Stone made himself comfortable in the chair.

"Good morning, gentlemen," he said.

Sturmack looked as though he were about to have a coronary, but Ippolito, though momentarily surprised, maintained his composure. "Sit down, David," he said. He reached under the desktop and fiddled with something.

"Where did *you* come from?" Sturmack asked shakily.

"From the depths of the Pacific," Stone said. "I'm sorry to disappoint you."

Two men burst into the room from a side door, each with a gun in his hand.

"Search him," Ippolito said, pointing to Stone.

Stone stood up and allowed himself to be patted down.

"He's clean, except for a telephone," one of the men said, holding up Stone's cell phone.

"Thank you, Tommy; you can give it back to him."

The man handed back the telephone, and Stone slipped it into his pocket. The two men, at a nod from Ippolito, left the room.

"So it was you," Ippolito said. "My yacht captain described you, but I didn't believe it."

Stone shrugged. He didn't want to admit to sinking the yacht while wearing a wire.

"I don't understand," Sturmack said, looking distinctly ill.

"It was Mr. Barrington here, who sank my boat. Both my boats, in fact."

Stone smiled, but said nothing.

"So what brings you to see us, Mr. Barrington?" Ippolito asked.

"I thought perhaps you and I might do some business," Stone replied.

"After the money you've cost me?" Ippolito asked, outraged. "I should do business with *you*?"

"And what about you, Mr. Ippolito? You're a very bad dinner host indeed, inviting me aboard your yacht, then trying to have me murdered on the way. Why did you do that?"

"You were getting in my way," Ippolito said, shrugging. "I kill people who get in my way."

Stone smiled. He hoped to God the wire picked up *that* little tidbit.

"Well, I figure we're about even," Stone said. "You gave me a bad fright, I gave you one. I don't think we should let that stand in the way of business, do you?"

"What kind of business did you have in mind?" Ippolito asked.

"I'd like to invest in Albacore Fisheries," Stone said. "I think the stock is going to go way, way up. With my help."

"And how could you help our stock to go up?" Ippolito asked.

"By helping you gain control of Centurion Studios," Stone replied. He was improvising, but he had their attention.

"And how could you possibly do that?"

Sturmack seemed to have regained control of himself. "This is ridiculous," he said to Ippolito. "Kill him now; have Tommy and Zip take him somewhere and shoot him. We don't need this."

Ippolito held up a hand and silenced him. "Easy, David; let's hear what Mr. Barrington has to say." He turned his attention to Stone. "You were about to tell us how you could be helpful in acquiring Centurion."

"Well, for a start, I can deliver Vance Calder's shares to you, for a price, of course.

375

I can also deliver his services to Safe Harbor as a television spokesman."

"And how will you accomplish those things?" Ippolito asked.

"Let's just say that Mr. Calder and I have reached an understanding; he values my advice."

"You're an interesting man, Mr. Barrington," Ippolito said. "I know something about you, of course; in fact, just about everything there is to know. I know, for instance, that you have something over a million dollars in marketable securities in your brokerage account, so you can afford to invest in Albacore. And if you could arrange the exchange of Mr. Calder's Centurion stock for Albacore stock, I might let you buy in."

"Oh, I can do better than that, Mr. Ippolito," Stone said. "I can arrange for you to buy Mr. Calder's stock for cash, and at a reasonable price. No need to give him Albacore stock when that stock is going to go through the roof."

"Now that *is* interesting," Ippolito said.

"In fact, I can help you buy nearly all, perhaps all of Centurion's stock, including Louis Regenstein's shares."

"You amaze me, Mr. Barrington. How did you suddenly acquire all this influence?"

"I have replaced Billy O'Hara in Mr. Regenstein's affections," Stone said.

"That's what I came to tell you, Oney," Sturmack interjected. "Regenstein fired O'Hara yesterday, and I haven't been able to find him."

Stone had an idea. "You won't find him," he said.

"Why not?" Ippolito asked.

"Because Mr. O'Hara expired last night, during a conversation I was having with him. He's where you believed me to be."

"He's dead?"

"Regrettably, yes."

"And you killed him?"

"Not until he had told me everything he knew about you and your plans for Centurion—also about the murders of Vincent Mancuso and Manolo Lobianco."

Ippolito thought about that for a moment, then he stood up, walked to the window, and beckoned for Stone to join him.

Stone walked over, stood next to Ippolito, and looked out at the view.

Ippolito put a hand on Stone's shoulder and pointed. "There's Centurion Studios," he said, indicating a large mass of land and buildings a few miles away. "And over there is Century City, one of the most successful real estate developments in the history of Los Angeles. What I'm going to do is to build something twice as large and twice as valuable. It's going to make billions of dollars over the next ten years or so, and a very select group of people are going to be allowed to participate in that. Is that what interests you, Mr. Barrington?"

"Yes," Stone replied, "it is." And as he spoke he saw something besides the view outside Ippolito's window. He had changed his

377

focus, because something much closer had caught his eye. He leaned slightly toward the window and concentrated. What he saw was, imbedded in the tinted glass, a screen of tiny wires, smaller than human hairs. He suddenly understood that the radio signal from the transmitter he wore was not going to be heard outside this office.

Ippolito returned to his seat and motioned for Stone to return to his.

"And I think I can tell you how you're going to finance all this," Stone said, mindful that the tape recorder in the heel of his other shoe was still operational.

"Please do," Ippolito said.

"You're somehow laundering—I haven't quite figured out how—millions, perhaps billions of dollars in income from loan sharking, drugs, and probably casino skimming, considering Mr. Sturmack's connections in Las Vegas, and you're pumping it into Albacore, then using the laundered money for acquisitions like Centurion. How much more land have you bought up around the studio?"

"Oh, parcels amounting to around two hundred and fifty acres."

"My God," Sturmack said. "Don't tell him things like that!"

"David, shut up, I'm talking," Ippolito said. "Mr. Barrington is not going to reveal a word of this to anybody; it would not be in his best interests, would it, Mr. Barrington?"

"Not if you and I can come to an arrangement," Stone said.

"Tell you what," Ippolito said, standing. "David and I are going to a meeting that bears on our conversation. Why don't you join us? You'll learn a lot more about what we're doing."

For a moment Stone was alarmed, but he knew that Rick's men and the feds, when they began receiving transmissions from his wire, would move with them. "I'd like that," he said. "Where are we going?"

"You'll see," Ippolito said. He pressed the buzzer under his desk again, and Tommy and Zip appeared. "Escort Mr. Barrington to transportation," he said. "We're all going together."

"This way, Mr. Barrington," Tommy said, indicating the side door.

Stone stood up and walked toward the door, followed by Ippolito and Sturmack. He was expecting a private elevator, but instead, the door led to a hallway, which led to a staircase going up. They were already on the top floor, and this did not seem like a good idea to Stone.

"Tell me," he said to Ippolito as they walked up the stairs, "have the *police* ever gotten wind of what you're up to?"

"Certainly not," Ippolito said. They emerged onto the rooftop, where a helicopter was waiting, its blades beginning to turn.

"Great," Stone said. "If the *police* aren't on to you, then I think you can pull off this deal. Where are we going in this *helicopter*?"

"You'll see," Ippolito said, but his words were

drowned out by the helicopter's rotors as they started to spin.

62

In the garage, Rick Grant and Dino listened to their radio as the elevator doors opened and closed, as people got on and off. Then they heard Stone say, "I'm here."

"Jesus," Dino said, "that's some wire. I want some of those for my people."

"Shhh," Rick said. "He's in the reception room."

They could hear Stone begin to announce himself to the receptionist, then stop. They heard the receptionist tell Sturmack to go into Ippolito's office, then heard Stone speak again to the receptionist. There were some soft footsteps, then nothing but low-level static.

"They found the wire," Dino said, opening the car door. "Let's go."

"No, wait. Nobody has searched him; we'd have heard that. He's just in a place that's blocking the transmission. Wait and listen."

They began to hear snatches of words, nothing intelligible, just a word or two at a time.

"At least he's got them talking," Rick said. "We've still got the tape to fall back on."

They continued to listen to the static, with an occasional word coming through. "Maybe the problem is between us and the van," Rick said. "Let's get out there." He got out of the car and started out of the garage, with Dino right behind him.

Rick crossed the street, walked around the van, and rapped sharply on its sliding door. The door opened a crack. "It's Grant and Bacchetti," Rick said. "Let us in."

The door slid back, Rick and Dino crowded in and the door closed behind them.

"Are you getting anything from Barrington?" Rick asked.

"No, just a word now and then. Something's screwing up the transmission."

"I don't like this," Dino said. "I think we ought to go in."

"Not yet," Rick replied. "At least we know they're talking. If we hear anything that sounds like trouble, I'll give the word, but not until then."

The static continued for a couple of more minutes, then suddenly stopped.

"I can hear them now," the radio operator said.

"Turn that thing up," Rick commanded.

They could hear footsteps on a hard floor, then the sound of people climbing steps, then Stone's voice, loud and clear. "Have the *police* ever gotten wind of what you're up to?"

Rick grabbed his handheld radio. "This is Grant," he said, "it's a go! Everybody move!"

Dino grabbed his arm. "Wait, listen."

Stone's voice came again. "Where are we going in this *helicopter*?" Then the sound of the rotor, spinning faster and faster.

"Oh, shit!" Grant hissed. He threw open the door of the van, stepped out, and looked up. A large black helicopter was lifting off the roof of the Safe Harbor Bank building. He stepped back into the van. "Put me on the command channel," he ordered the operator. The man turned a knob and nodded.

"This is Lieutenant Richard Grant," Rick said. "Patch me through to aviation."

A moment later a woman's voice came on. "LAPD aviation."

"This is Lieutenant Richard Grant. Let me speak to your watch commander *now*."

"Yessir, putting you through to the watch commander."

"Aviation watch commander," a man's voice said.

"This is Lieutenant Richard Grant; I'm speaking for the chief of detectives. A large black helicopter has just taken off from the Safe Harbor Bank building in downtown L.A., heading in a south-southwesterly direction. I want you to put everything you've got in the air and intercept that helicopter. Do not, repeat do *not* fire on it; one of our people is aboard. I want it forced down, and if it's heading toward Mexico, under *no* circumstances is it to be allowed to cross the border."

"Roger, I read you, Lieutenant," the watch commander said.

"How many aircraft can you muster on this?"

"I've got two choppers on the pad, fueled and ready to go, and four others in the air in

382

various places. I've also got two fixed-wing aircraft flying traffic."

"Put them all on it. I want a maximum effort."

"Roger, sir."

"Remember, don't let them cross the border; alert air traffic control not to issue any clearances to a chopper headed south, you read me?"

"Loud and clear, sir; we're on it."

"Hey, while you're at it, have me picked up downtown. Where can your man land?"

"How many people, sir?"

"As many as it will hold."

"I've got one in the air near MacArthur Park right now; it can take two besides the pilots."

"We're on the way." Rick turned to a cop. "Crank this thing up and get me to MacArthur Park! And keep monitoring Barrington's wire!"

Somebody slammed the door, and the van made a U-turn. Somebody put a flashing light on top and turned on a siren.

"I knew he shouldn't have gone up there alone," Dino said.

63

Stone sat on one of two leather-upholstered bench seats, between Tommy and Zip, while Ippolito and Sturmack occupied the opposite bench. It was remarkable how quiet it was inside the machine, he thought. The rotors were a distant thump.

"Where to, Mr. Ippolito?" the pilot asked over his shoulder.

"Ensenada," Ippolito answered. "Maximum speed."

"I'll have to call ATC for a clearance," the pilot said.

"Fuck the clearance; you get down low over the water and you get us to Ensenada fast. What's our ETA?"

"That will take just a minute, sir."

Sturmack spoke up. "Oney, what are you doing? Why do you want to go to Ensenada?"

"Because Tijuana is too obvious." He picked up a cell phone fixed to a bulkhead and punched in a number. "This is Mr. Ippolito," he said. "I want the G–5 off the ground immediately; file for Ensenada, full fuel, you got that?"

There was some sort of reply from the other end.

"Thirty minutes is too long, make it fifteen. I'll meet the airplane there." He hung up.

"Oney," Sturmack said, "I don't get it; why are we headed for Mexico?"

"Come on, David, you're not that stupid. Do you think Barrington is dumb enough just to walk into my office with no backup? He didn't kill Billy O'Hara, he's not the type. O'Hara has spilled everything, and I'd give you odds my office is swarming with cops right this minute."

Stone smiled. "Good guess," he said.

"What about my wife?" Sturmack asked. "I can't just leave her."

Ippolito handed him the phone. "Call her and tell her to get the next plane to Panama; we'll only be in Ensenada long enough to change aircraft."

Sturmack began dialing.

Stone looked out the window. They were crossing the coast now, at about a thousand feet, he reckoned.

"Charlie," Ippolito yelled, "get this thing down on the water, do you hear me? The cops have choppers too, you know."

The helicopter began a rapid descent. Stone watched the masts at Marina Del Rey flash by.

Sturmack handed the phone back to Ippolito. "I can't believe we're just running," he said. "I'm seventy years old; I don't want to live in Panama."

"We'll be headed south from there," Ippolito said. "You can pick your country; I'll send you wherever you want to go in the G–5. Besides, it may not be over; we may be able to come back when the lawyers get a grip on this."

Stone spoke up. "No, it's over, Oney; within twenty-four hours they'll have it all. There'll be nothing left but a shell."

"I'll get to you in a minute," Ippolito said. He dialed another number. "Hello, this is Onofrio Ippolito; let me speak to Martin Barone." He listened for a minute, then disconnected. "Was Marty at his office?" he asked Sturmack.

"Yes, I was with him before I came to your office."

"Then the cops have got him; they're answering the phone there."

"That'll be the FBI," Stone said, "along with the IRS. They've not only got Barone, they've got all his computers. Oh, and don't bother to call Albacore; it's the same there and at the bank. There is no longer any safe harbor for you, Oney."

Ippolito glared at Stone for a moment, then turned to the pilot. "Charlie, you got that ETA for Ensenada?"

"One hour and forty-one minutes, sir," the pilot said.

"How far offshore are we?"

"About five miles."

"How fast you going?"

"A hundred and thirty-five knots."

"At what speed is it safe to open the door back here?"

"I'd have to hover for that, sir."

Ippolito looked at Stone again. "Hover, Charlie," he said.

Rick and Dino piled into the police helicopter, and the machine rose into the air. The noise was deafening. Rick put on a headset and handed one to Dino.

"Where to, Lieutenant?" the pilot asked.

"South by southwest; we're looking for a large executive helicopter, black in color."

"That sounds like the Safe Harbor Bank chopper," the pilot said, picking up speed. "I know a lot of the local choppers by sight, and that's the only black one I can think of."

"That's the one," Rick said. "Can I hear your radios on this thing?"

"Yessir."

"You listen for reports of that chopper; we've got everything we can muster in the air, looking for it."

"Yessir."

"Pilot, if you were running for the border now, how would you do it?"

"I'd get out over the water and stay low, under the radar, sir."

"Do it."

It was clear to Stone that he was not going to make it to Ensenada, let alone to Panama. The helicopter was slowing rapidly. Stone reached into an inside pocket for his hand-kerchief and mopped his brow. When he replaced the handkerchief his hand came out holding both Mont Blanc pens.

Ippolito looked at Tommy and Zip. "When this thing is hovering, open the door, shoot Bar-rington and throw him out. And don't make a mess in the helicopter, you got me?"

Both men nodded.

Stone had two shots to fire, and there were four men in the helicopter with him. Sturmack was still looking ill and didn't seem much of a threat; Ippolito probably wasn't armed. Tommy and Zip certainly were. He could go for the pilot, but that would just take every-body with him; he didn't want to go at all.

They were hovering now. Zip reached out and slid back the door of the helicopter, and when he sat back, there was a gun in his hand.

Go for the weapons, Stone thought. He quickly raised both hands under the chins of the two goons and squeezed both pens. There was a very loud noise and blood and brains were suddenly everywhere. Stone reached over and took the gun from Zip's dead hand.

David Sturmack's face changed from ill to horrified. He began clawing at his chest as if he wanted to dig out his heart.

Ippolito looked at him with disgust. "I should have known you weren't up to this, David," he said, then he grabbed Sturmack by the shoulder and pushed him out of the helicopter.

Stone watched him fall the fifty feet into the water, and that was a mistake. Suddenly Ippolito was all over him. The man was solidly built, and he was motivated. Stone was taking punches to the head from Ippolito's right, while his left had hold of the barrel of the automatic in Stone's right hand.

Stone fought back with his left, landed a couple of punches, but was taking more than he was giving. He took a hard fist to the temple, and his vision went blurry, then he was on the floor of the helicopter, on top of the corpses of Tommy and Zip, and Ippolito was on top of him, flailing away. Stone managed to turn on his left side, bringing Ippolito down to his level and limiting the power of his punches.

Then Ippolito gave up throwing punches and

used his right to help his left hand deal with the gun. He grabbed hold of it with both hands and yanked, and it went off with a roar.

Stone saw the back of the pilot's head explode.

The helicopter began to rotate, at first slowly, then faster and faster.

Stone couldn't tell whether it was going up or down, until it hit the water with a crash. With the rear door open, the machine had no chance to float. Stone forgot about Ippolito and started trying to get out. The gun left his hand; he didn't know if Ippolito had it or if it was going to the bottom.

Stone broke the surface. He seemed always to be doing that, he thought. How many good suits had he ruined? The black helicopter was gone now, but somehow it was still making noise; the air was filled with the sound of the rotor.

Then, as Stone watched, Ippolito broke the surface some six feet in front of him. He looked very angry, and he was holding Zip's automatic, which, Stone reckoned, still had another twelve or fourteen rounds in the clip. Stone ducked under the water.

His eyes were open, and he saw something good: the water just next to Ippolito exploded, and the pistol that had been in the banker's hand was sinking fast.

Stone surfaced. Above and in front of him was an LAPD helicopter; Rick Grant was sitting in its open door, his feet on the strut below him and a shotgun in his hands. The shotgun was pointed at Ippolito, who was angrily treading water.

Then Stone saw Dino, holding a bunch of life jackets, jump out of the police helicopter. He came up sputtering. "You owe me one Armani suit!" he yelled, handing Stone a life jacket and tossing one to Ippolito.

Stone grabbed him and kissed him on the forehead.

"Get off me!" Dino screamed. "The suit will be enough!"

Other helicopters arrived, and other people were in the water, dealing with Ippolito. Rick's helicopter had its struts in the water now.

Stone and Dino started swimming for the chopper.

EPILOGUE

Stone sat at the window of his study in Turtle Bay and watched the season's first snow fall on the gardens behind his house. The phone rang, and he picked it up.

"Hello?"

"It's Arrington."

His voice warmed. "How are you?" He had not talked with her in months, because she didn't want him to.

"I'm okay. How did the business in L.A. turn out?"

"Ippolito goes on trial shortly after the first of the year; I'll be going back out there to testify."

"There was certainly enough in the papers about it. I think the *Wall Street Journal* was more upset than anybody."

There was something in her voice that bothered him; she seemed to be straining for small talk.

"I still find it hard to believe that David Sturmack was involved; he and his wife were always so sweet to me."

"They haven't found her yet," Stone said. "She apparently got to Panama after cleaning out the safe at their house, and she hasn't been seen since."

"Imagine, a woman like her on the run."

"She's very rich, so don't worry about her; I'm sure she's making some gigolo very happy."

"Vance told me he sent you a tape of *Out of Court;* he had it cut especially, so you could see yourself in the movie."

"Yes, he did. It was very embarrassing to look at." He couldn't take the chat anymore. "What's happening, Arrington?"

Her voice changed. "Stone, there's news."

Stone flinched. He had an awful feeling he knew what was coming.

"Vance's child was born last night."

Stone let out the breath he had been holding. "Congratulations to both of you," he managed to say.

"The blood tests left no doubt," she said. "I want you to understand that; there was no need to go to DNA tests."

"I understand," he replied. A memory flooded over him: he was walking through F.A.O. Schwarz, the big toy store, looking for a first gift for a new baby. He snapped himself out of it. "I understand what you have to do."

"I'm glad you do," she said, then she started to cry.

"It's all right, Arrington," he said. "You're doing the right thing."

"I have to," she said.

"I know."

"Vance did pay your bill, didn't he?" she said, incongruously.

"He reimbursed all my expenses," Stone said. "I didn't send him a bill; I didn't do it for him."

"Stone, I will never be able to thank you enough for what you did."

"Don't worry about that..."

"Really, Vance and the baby and I owe you so much."

Stone was extremely uncomfortable with this. "Was it a boy or a girl?"

"A girl. Seven pounds, one ounce."

"She'll be beautiful, like you."

"Let's hope she looks like her father."

"I have to go," Stone said. "I have an appointment." If he talked to her any more he'd make an idiot of himself.

"I do love you, Stone," she said, then hung up.

Stone hung up the phone and, to his astonishment, he began to cry. A moment later, he had control of himself. He dialed Dino's direct extension.

"Lieutenant Bacchetti," Dino said.

"Dinner tonight?"

"Sure." Dino listened to the silence for a moment. "You've had some news?"

"Yeah. Elaine's, at eight-thirty?"

"Sure."

"You're going to have to drive me home."

"What are cops for?" Dino asked, then hung up.

Stone sat and looked out the window at the snow. He sat there most of the day.

Washington, Connecticut
July 23, 1997

393